D0588980

Get **more** out of libraries

Please return or renew this item by the last date shown.
You can renew online at www.hants.gov.uk/library
Or by phoning 0845 603 5631

 Hampshire
County Council

C014323496

TO THE READER:

On page 145 of *The Book With No Name*, the Mystic Lady issued this warning about the Eye of the Moon:

> It has a powerful presence, and it will draw evil towards it wherever it goes. You're not safe as long as you have it with you. In fact, you're not really safe if you've ever had contact with it.

Dear Reader,
In your hands you now hold *The Eye of the Moon*.
Enjoy it while it lasts . . .

ANONYMOUS

The Eye of the Moon

A novel (probably)

Anonymous

Michael O'Mara Books Limited

First published in Great Britain in 2008 by
Michael O'Mara Books Limited
9 Lion Yard, Tremadoc Road
London SW4 7NQ

A CIP catalogue record for this book is available from the British Library.

ISBN: 978-1-84317-303-8

1 3 5 7 9 10 8 6 4 2

Designed and typeset by www.glensaville.com

Printed and bound in Great Britain by Cox & Wyman, Reading, Berks

www.mombooks.com

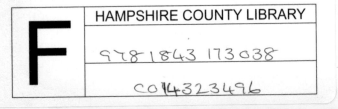

One

Joel Rockwell couldn't remember ever being this nervous before. His career as a nighttime security guard in the Santa Mondega Museum of Art and History had been uneventful, to say the least. He had wanted to follow his father, Jessie, into the police force, but he hadn't measured up at the Academy. In some respects he was relieved that he had failed. Police work was far more dangerous. As had been proved just three days earlier, when his father had been gunned down by the Bourbon Kid in the aftermath of the eclipse during the Lunar Festival. So a soft job as a security guard had seemed like a safer option. Or at least it had done, until about five minutes ago.

The most burdensome part of his nightly duties was having to sit in the security office watching a bank of monitors, which generally showed that absolutely nothing was happening within the museum walls. The grey uniform suit that Joel was obliged to wear in the job was itchy as hell, too. It had probably been worn by countless other employees long before it had been handed to him on his first day, and it just wasn't designed with sitting around in mind. Staying comfortable in it was usually the biggest task of the night. Except that what he'd just seen on monitor number three had changed all that.

Joel Rockwell was not an imaginative man. He was not an especially intelligent one, either, and it was the lack of these two qualities that had eventually led to him flunking the Police Academy course. As one of his instructors – a grizzled thirty-year lieutenant – had noted on his confidential report, 'This guy is so dumb even his fellow cadets noticed.' None the less, he had a certain doggedness and honesty that made him a good witness and a reliable guard, if only because he lacked the imagination and intelligence to be anything else.

If his eyes weren't playing tricks on him, he'd just witnessed a murder on the screen. His colleague Carlton Buckley appeared to have been attacked and killed while wandering around on the floor below ground level. Rockwell would have called the police, but describing what he thought he'd just seen would only have made them laugh, and maybe arrest him for wasting their time. So he did the next best thing, and called Professor Bertram Cromwell, one of the museum's directors.

He had the Professor's number saved in his cell phone, and despite feeling a little uneasy about calling him at such an ungodly hour he went ahead and did it anyway. Cromwell was one of those exquisitely polite gentlemen who would never make him feel bad for calling, no matter how trivial the issue.

With his heart pounding in his chest and his phone held to his ear waiting for Cromwell to pick up the call, he headed out of the security office and down to the lower level to check out for himself what he thought he'd just seen in the Egyptian display.

He reached the foot of a flight of stairs and had just taken a right turn into a long hallway when Cromwell finally answered. Unsurprisingly, the Professor sounded like a man who'd been woken from a deep sleep.

'Hello? Bertram Cromwell speaking. Who is this, please?'

'Hi Bernard, it's Joel Rockwell at the museum.'

'Hi Joel. It's Bertram, by the way, not Bernard.'

'Whatever. Look, I think we've got an intruder here at the museum, but I'm not totally sure, so I thought I'd call you before I, you know, got the police an' everything.'

Cromwell seemed to wake up a little. 'Really? What's happening?'

'Well, this is gonna sound kinda nuts, but I think someone just broke out of the Egyptian Mummy display.'

'Say again?'

'The Mummy display. I think someone just came out of the goddam tomb thing.'

'*What*? That's impossible! What on earth are you talking about?'

'Yeah, I know it sounds nuts. That's why I called you first. See, I think whoever it was has just attacked the other security guard.'

'Who's the other guy on with you tonight?'

'Carter Bradley.'

'You mean Carlton Buckley?'

'Yeah, whatever. I'm not sure if it's him, like, playing a prank or not. But if it's *not* a joke, then he's gotta be in serious trouble. Like real serious trouble.'

'Why? What's happened?' The Professor, now wide awake, paused for a second to gather his thoughts, then said quietly, 'What have you actually *seen*, Joel? Facts, my boy – I need facts. If you'll forgive me saying so, you're not making a great deal of sense at the moment, and I'm rather tired.'

During his conversation with Cromwell Joel had continued walking along the broad, dimly lit hallway until, sooner than he would have liked, he arrived at the end of it. He took a deep breath, then turned right into the vast open gallery known as Lincoln Hall. *That was when he heard the music.* A light piano tune was being played. A gentle sad tune, not unlike the 'Lonely Man' theme tune played at the end of *The Incredible Hulk* TV show that he had loved as a kid in the late seventies. He knew there was a piano down here somewhere, but who the fuck was playing it? Yeah, and playing it so fucking badly, as well . . .

'Hold on a minute, Professor Crumpler. You're not gonna believe this, but I can hear a piano playing. I'm just gonna put my phone in my pocket for a second. Hold tight and I'll let you know what I see.'

Rockwell slipped his small phone into the breast pocket of his grey shirt and pulled his nightstick from its loop on his belt. Then he stepped into the huge hall to investigate further. The piano was tucked away behind a sand-coloured wall on his left that ran halfway down the hall. Paintings of famous musicians were hung along its entire length. Ignoring the music for a second, he focused his attention on the Egyptian display to his right, an imposing permanent exhibit billed as 'The Mummy's Tomb'. It had been trashed. There was glass all over the floor where the protective shield around the display had been shattered. And, mixed in with the glass, there was blood. Lots of blood.

Most notably, the golden sarcophagus that stood upright in the centre of the display was open. The front of it was lying on the floor, and the mummified remains of its late occupant were gone. Rockwell knew that Professor Cromwell loved this particular exhibit. He would be mighty upset if his prized possession had been stolen, or even tampered with. It was the museum's centrepiece, the rarest and most valuable object in the entire, vast collection. And now the best part of it was missing.

Rockwell thought back to what he believed he'd seen on the monitor in the security office, and shook his head in confusion. Only a few minutes had passed since then, but he was already beginning to think he'd imagined the attack on Buckley. This had to be a prank, yeah? Not a well-timed one, what with all the recent killings in Santa Mondega and thereabouts – kinda tasteless, really, you wanted his opinion – but a prank even so. And what was the deal with the fucking piano? *Learn to carry a tune, whoever you are!* he thought, with, even for him, breathtaking inconsequentiality.

To reach the piano – which, if rumours were true, had once been owned by a famous composer – he was going to have to manoeuvre himself around the mess of glass and blood and past a giant statue of the classical Greek hero Achilles to a small alcove on the other side of the long, sand-coloured wall. If he remembered correctly, a life-size wooden mannequin sat at the piano, styled and dressed to resemble the noted composer who had owned it. *Who was it?* he pondered. *Beethoven? Mozart? Manilow?* It wasn't important enough to dwell on, and in any case he soon had his answer. As he headed past the statue of the great, if sulky, Greek warrior and rounded the end of the sand-coloured wall, he saw the mannequin lying on its back on the floor some distance from the piano, as though thrown there with considerable force. It was wearing a purple-coloured jacket over a white shirt, the ensemble finished off with dark flared trousers above shiny black shoes. There was a name tag pinned to the left breast of the jacket. 'Beethoven', it read, but Rockwell didn't notice it as he stepped over the wooden figure, so he was still none the wiser as to which composer this was meant to be.

Clearly it wasn't the mannequin that was playing the piano. It was something else. He took a few steps closer to the instrument in the corner of the alcove in order to get a look at the musician responsible for the badly played tune. When he was finally close enough, he saw a figure sitting on the small stool in front of the grand piano, tinkling the ivories with rather more verve than skill. The sight sent a cold shiver down his spine.

This figure was wearing a long, hooded robe of rich scarlet cloth. With the hood pulled up over its owner's head, it looked like the kind of thing a boxer heading into ring might wear. The cloaked individual with the hooded face was passionately moving from side to side, swaying its head like Stevie Wonder as it played its terribly-out-of-tune piece of music. There was no sign of Rockwell's colleague, Buckley, although, rather worryingly, a trail of blood spatters led across the floor to the hooded figure at the piano.

Keeping his distance, Rockwell decided to call out and hope to get a look at the face of the mysterious pianist. If he didn't like what he saw, he had at least a twenty-yard head start if he had to take the 'run-like-fuck' option.

'Hey, you!' he called out. 'Do you know we're closed? You shouldn't be here! Time to go, buddy.'

The figure stopped playing, its bony fingers quivering almost imperceptibly above the gleaming black and white keys. Then it spoke.

'You hum it, and I'll pick it up!' a rusty-sounding voice

crackled from beneath the scarlet cowl. A loud guffaw followed; then the hands dropped as the figure took up the tune again.

'What? Hey, where's Carterton?' Rockwell called out taking a step closer, his hand sweating on the nightstick he was gripping so very tightly.

Again the figure stopped playing , and turned its head to look directly at him. Since Rockwell was not exactly walking briskly towards it, stopping dead in his tracks was not a problem. There followed an awkward moment during which he seriously considered pissing his pants.

Within the hood, the figure had only half a face. In the shadow beneath the cowl, the terrified security guard could make out what looked mostly like a yellow skull. Foul remnants of flesh still clung in places to the cheeks, jaw and brow, and there was one rather odd-looking green eye, but the other eye socket was empty, and the face appeared to have no lips or nose. Revolted, Rockwell looked away, only to realize that the bony fingers that had been tapping away at the piano keys were exactly that. *Bones*. Fingers with no fucking skin on them. *Oh Christ*.

Before he had time to turn and run, the cloaked figure rose from its stool. It stood well over six feet tall, seeming to dominate the vast gallery, its bony fingers reaching out in his direction. Then it did something strange. It waved one of its hands through the air as if it were manipulating the strings of an invisible puppet. All the while its expressionless face somehow managed to look as though it was smirking at him.

To Joel Rockwell, even though he was twenty or so yards away, those bony hands looked like they were gonna start coming his way pretty goddam soon. As he turned on his heel with the intention of running like fuck out of the hall – hell, something that dead couldn't be much of a sprinter – he received the second massive shock of the past few moments.

The mannequin of Ludwig van Beethoven had climbed to its feet, somehow animated by the waving hands of the – *the thing* – at the piano. Now it was right in front of Rockwell, its glass eyes staring vacantly at him from beneath a great mane of hair, its arms extended and wooden hands thrust out to grab him by the throat. The stunned security guard swiped at it with his nightstick, but the effect was only a loud thudding noise as the dummy's wooden head absorbed the blow, although part of one ear splintered. Fingers stinging, Joel dropped the useless weapon, pulled the cell phone from his breast pocket and held it to his ear, even as the mannequin took a grip on his neck. As he fell to the ground with the wooden assassin on top of him, squeezing his neck tightly and driving the breath from his lungs, he managed one brief cry for help into the phone, hoping above hope that Cromwell might hear it and, somehow, come to his rescue, or at least send a rescue party.

'Bernard, fer Chrissakes! You gotta help me!' he gasped. 'I'm bein' attacked by fuckin' Barry Manilow!'

Whether the Professor replied, or even heard, Rockwell was never to know. Dropping the cell phone, he battled with every ounce of his fading strength to escape his attacker, but to no avail. The mannequin was too strong, as well as impervious to his weakening attempts to fight it off. It simply kept him pinned to the floor, its hands around his throat.

Rockwell struggled on despairingly until eventually a figure loomed over him and he found himself staring up into the hideous face of the mummy. The undead Egyptian needed to gorge on yet more human flesh to help replenish his decayed body, and Rockwell's would serve that purpose admirably.

During the next ten minutes the terrified security guard was ripped apart and devoured by the barbarous creature. It took some minutes for Joel Rockwell to die in unbearable agony. It had taken only three days for him to follow his father into the afterlife.

Having feasted on the flesh of the two dead security guards, the mummy – the immortal, formerly embalmed remains of the pharaoh once better known as Rameses Gaius – felt just about ready to re-enter the world of the living. He would seek – indeed, demand – two things. Revenge on the descendants of those who had incarcerated him for so long, and the return of his most prized possession during his days as ruler of Egypt: *the Eye of the Moon.*

Two

31 October - eighteen years earlier

Santa Mondega High School's annual Halloween fancy-dress ball was, to the students, the highlight of the year's social calendar. Fifteen-year-old Beth Lansbury had waited patiently since the beginning of term for this night. This was her great chance – probably her only chance, she thought – to catch the eye of a certain boy in the year above her. She didn't know his name, and she would have been way too embarrassed to ask anyone else, in case they realized that she had this big crush on him and teased her for it. Which they would certainly have done.

Beth had no friends at the school. She was still fairly new there, and being extremely pretty didn't exactly help matters. This was one of the principal reasons why all the other girls seemed to resent her. More to the point, Ulrika Price didn't like her, and had made it clear to all the other girls that Beth was not to be spoken to, unless it was to say something spiteful to her.

As was the vogue in these parts, the school's gym hall was the venue for the ball. Earlier in the day Beth had helped Miss Hinds, her English teacher, to decorate the place. It hadn't looked all that great when they had finished, but now, on the night, with the flashing lights and the music, it took on a whole new vibe. Beth was pleased to see that despite the spasmodic flashing of the disco lights, the hall was for the most part very dark – perfect cover for outsiders and loners like her.

There was another cause of Beth's anguish. Her overly controlling stepmother had insisted on choosing her costume, and, typically, had picked a hideously unsuitable outfit. While everyone else was dressed appropriately in Halloween attire (such as ghosts, zombies, witches, vampires, skeletons – even a rather unconvincing bat and at least four Freddy Kruegers), Beth was dressed as Dorothy from *The Wizard of Oz*, right down to the shitty red shoes. She had convinced herself she would have a good time in spite of it, but she was still upset that her stepmother had picked such an inappropriate and stupid outfit.

To say that Olivia Jane Lansbury was extremely domineering was akin to saying that Hitler could sometimes be a bit naughty. Worse, she seemed to be hell bent on preventing her stepdaughter from ever meeting any boys. This may have stemmed from a certain degree of bitterness she felt at having been widowed shortly after she had married Beth's father. Beth's real mother had died giving birth to her, so Olivia Jane had been her only parent for most of her life. Growing up had been pretty tough for Beth so far. *And tonight wasn't going to be a bed of roses either*, she reflected.

So there she was on the evening of Halloween, dressed like the Dweeb That Time Forgot and without a friend in the world, a prime candidate for a stream of bitchy comments from Ulrika Price and her circle of cronies. Ulrika and her three closest followers had come to the ball dressed as cats. The latter were all in black panther costumes, whereas Ulrika was wearing a Bengal tiger outfit, complete with sharp claws attached to the ends of her fingers.

The cats had spotted Beth where she sat in a plastic chair at the edge of the dance floor along with a few other rejects, each desperately hoping a boy would ask her to join him on the floor for a dance. That the butt of their scorn was dressed as Dorothy meant that a situation like this didn't require any bitchy comments – Ulrika and her friends merely pointed at Beth and laughed loudly and ostentatiously. This drew sufficient attention to the wretched girl for everyone else who, until then, had been ignoring her, to join in the laughter and sniggering too. If Ulrika and her friends were laughing, then everyone else wanted to be seen to be appreciating the joke. Social acceptance was important at Santa Mondega High, and if Ulrika Price the bottle-blonde cheerleader thought you weren't laughing along with her, then you might as well pack up and head home. Beth's only crumb of comfort was that she hadn't been forced by her stepmother to dye her hair ginger for added authenticity. At least she was lucky enough to have kept her beautiful long brown mane.

It was small consolation, as it turned out, for her humiliation was just about completed shortly after eleven o'clock when one of the black panthers convinced the guy in charge of the lighting to train a spotlight on Beth. As the harsh beam illuminated the forlorn figure the deejay (another of Ulrika's friends) announced that, yep, ol' Dorothy over there in the spotlight was the 'yoo-NANNY-muss' winner of the award for lamest costume. The horribly amplified announcement brought yet more howls of laughter from what was rapidly turning into a baying mob of teenagers high on drink and drugs.

Beth sat in dignified silence, waiting desperately for the spotlight to move away as she struggled to hold back the ocean of tears she could feel building up. But the spotlight stayed. Not wanting to miss out on a photo opportunity, Ulrika sauntered over and patted her on the head.

'You know what, honey?' she smirked. 'If there was a contest to find the world's biggest loser, you'd come second.'

That was the end for Beth. Tears began to stream down her face, and a great pent-up sob caught at her throat. The only thing left to do was get up and run out of the hall. As she fled he could hear the laughter behind her from everyone there. Even the other outsiders would join in – to be seen not laughing might make one of them the next victim. And nobody wanted to be lumped into the same loser category as the girl who had come dressed as Dorothy from *The Wizard of Oz*.

As Beth burst through the double doors at the end of the hall and out into the corridor she felt she had reached an all-time low. She had pleaded with her stepmother not to pick a shitty costume for her. But her pleas had fallen on deaf ears, as she had known they would. Even so, the bitch had cackled in pleasure when Beth begged to be allowed to change the costume. Everything – her public humiliation, her tear-stained flight from the hall – was her stepmother's fault. Yet she knew that when she got home and told her about her humiliation, the bitch would smile with satisfaction and gloat over how she had warned her stepdaughter that it was a mistake to expect others to accept her. Since her father's death, Beth's stepmother had delighted in telling her she was worthless. Now she was really feeling it. She was actually beginning to understand why people took their own lives. Sometimes living was just too hard.

As she staggered down the corridor to the front entrance of the gym, desperate to be free of the place and far enough away to rid herself of the echoes of laughter from the hall, she heard someone call out behind her. It was the voice she had longed to hear all night. The boy from the year above. She had only heard him speak once before, when he had asked her if she was all right that time she had been tripped up in the schoolyard by one of Ulrika's cronies. He had helped her to her feet, asked her if she was okay, and when she didn't respond – because she was too dumbstruck – had merely smiled and gone on his way. Ever since, she had regretted not having thanked him at the time, and had vowed to find a way to speak to him and show her gratitude for helping her up. And now it was his voice that had asked, 'Your mother too, huh?'

She looked back. He was there, halfway down the corridor behind her. Bizarrely, he was dressed as a scarecrow, with a pointy brown hat perched on his head, his face covered in brown makeup meant to look like mud, and with an orange cardboard carrot secured over his nose with string tied at the back of his head. His clothes were essentially nothing more than brown rags, although he did have a pretty cool pair of brown ankle boots.

'Wha–?' was the best response Beth could muster, as she tried to wipe away a few tears to make herself look a little less of a spectacle.

'My mother's a *Wizard of Oz* nut, too,' he said, waving a hand up and down at his outfit. Beth finally managed to force a smile, something that had seemed impossible only a minute earlier. She looked down ruefully at her blue gingham pinafore dress and short-sleeved white blouse. 'I'm guessing you didn't pick the outfit yourself?' the scarecrow suggested.

Beth suddenly found herself dumbstruck again. This was the moment she had planned for. She had waited for it all night, and had been bitterly humiliated in the process. But now it was here, and it wasn't going according to plan. She wasn't meant to be crying and generally looking a mess, even though there was not much she could do about it now. *Oh God*, she thought. *He's gonna think I'm a total loser.*

'Smoke?' the boy asked, holding out a pack of cigarettes as he approached her.

Beth shook her head. 'I'm not allowed.'

The boy shook the pack, raised it to his mouth, pulled a cigarette from it with his teeth and let it hang out of one side of his mouth. Then, still walking towards her, he lifted the cardboard-carrot nose away from his face, drew it down over his cigarette and let it fall to hang around his neck on its securing string.

'Aw, c'mon,' he said, smiling. 'Live a little, why doncha?'

Beth was desperate that he shouldn't think she was totally uncool, and to be honest the only reason for not smoking was that her stepmother wouldn't allow it. Well, right now her stepmother could go fuck herself.

'Okay,' she said, reaching out to take a cigarette from the pack. 'You gotta light?' she asked.

'Nah,' said the boy, straight-faced. 'Can't have a naked flame anywhere near me. I'd be gone in a puff.'

'Huh?'

'The straw, y'know?' He smiled, seeing her confusion. 'Scarecrow outfit?'

Beth gaped, then tried to recover herself. 'Oh yeah – yeah, of course,' she laughed nervously. *You idiot!* she thought to herself. *He makes a joke and you don't get it. Concentrate, fer Chrissakes: don't let him think you're stupid.*

There was an awkward pause as she put the cigarette to her lips and found herself wondering what she was supposed to do without a lighter. 'So how should I light it?' she asked. The boy smiled again, then sucked hard on the unlit cigarette that hung in the corner of his mouth. It lit up like a firework and he took a drag on it.

'Wow, that's so *cool*!' Beth blurted out, finally finding the voice to speak without first thinking too hard. 'How do you do that?'

'It's a secret. I only show my friends.'

'Oh.'

There was another uncomfortable pause as Beth wondered whether to ask if he would show her. Thing was, if he said no then it would mean he was saying they weren't friends. But eventually, after what seemed like a horrendously long and awkward pause, he took another drag on the cigarette and took it out of his mouth with his left hand.

'That Ulrika Price is a real bitch, huh?' he said, blowing out some smoke through his nostrils.

Beth couldn't help nodding frantically in agreement.

'I hate her,' she said, taking the cigarette out of her mouth.

They smiled at each other for a few moments, and then the boy spoke again.

'So, you want me to show you how to light that cigarette or what?'

Still nodding like a lunatic, Beth let a huge smile break out across her whole face. It succeeded in camouflaging the tears that had been streaming down her cheeks only a minute before, such was the beauty of it.

'Yeah, please,' she cooed.

'Come on then, let's get the hell outta here before we set off a smoke alarm.'

The next moment was the greatest feeling of Beth's life. This boy, this guy she had so desperately sought attention from, reached over and put his arm around her shoulder. Nervously she slid her arm around his waist and squeezed him ever so subtly. He obviously picked up on it because he pulled her in a little closer. Then he set off down the hallway to the school entrance with her in tow. Dorothy and the scarecrow walking together, well this was the cue for a song, Beth thought.

'We're off to see the wizard . . . ' she began to sing.

'Don't sing.' Her new beau shook his head.

'Really?' Beth asked, a cold flush coming over her. She feared she had made a fatal error of judgement.

'It's no wonder you've got no friends!' the boy joked. Beth looked up at him and was relieved to see a big smile break out on his face. He then squeezed her in tightly towards him. *Phew, he was just teasing.*

On their way out through the front doors of the school a young man dressed as a giant rodent bounded in past them. His costume was an all-in-one auburn-coloured suit made of fake fur, with a long tail at the back. Part of his face was visible under the headpiece but it was painted a similar colour to the costume, and had whiskers drawn on the cheeks. Beth didn't know him, but her new friend spotted a face he recognized beneath the makeup.

'You're a bit late,' the scarecrow pointed out as the fur ball brushed past him.

'Yeah, left my pills at home. Had to go back and get them,' muttered the rodent. 'By the way, either of you two seen that Ulrika Price broad anywhere?'

'She's in the main hall,' said Beth, nodding back down the corridor.

'Cool, thanks,' said the rodent boy. 'I'm gonna buy that girl a drink.' Then, scratching himself in an area of his rodent costume that implied he was pleasuring himself, he headed off towards the hall.

'Who was that creepy guy?' Beth asked.

Her handsome scarecrow friend knew the other boy well.

'That's Marcus the Weasel,' he said. 'Total perv. Lord only knows what he's got in store for your friend Ulrika.'

Unbeknown to the two youngsters, the unpleasantness that Marcus the Weasel was about to inflict upon Ulrika Price was nothing compared to the horror and suffering they were both about to endure on this most evil of nights.

Three

Beth and the scarecrow strolled along the promenade with the waves lapping up against the harbour wall to their left. A blue moon shone brightly above them in the night sky. It was surrounded by dark rain clouds that looked ready to burst, yet as if out of respect, they stayed clear of the moon, as though not wishing to block it from the view of those below.

In all her life Beth had never felt this alive, this excited. Her stepmother had succeeded in scaring off any boys that had ever come near her, so she had never been able even to hold a decent conversation with a young man before. After being tutored at home since her early childhood she had acquired a decent education, but virtually no life experience until recently, when she had joined the school. And now for the first time in her life she had a boy with his arm around her shoulder, walking her along the promenade. If the dark clouds above them had had numbers on them then it's fair to say she was heading for number nine. Chatting with the scarecrow hadn't been anywhere near as difficult and nerve-racking as she had feared it might be. Her heart was still pounding in her chest, barely able to control itself due to the almighty adrenalin rush she was feeling. It was a warm fuzzy sensation that felt like it would never end, and she dearly hoped that it wouldn't.

'So come on, Mr Scarecrow, are you going to tell me your name, or what?' she asked, squeezing his waist playfully.

'*You don't know my name?*' he asked, surprised.

'No. I only know you as the guy who helped me up from the ground when someone tripped me over once.'

'Wow. You know, I made a point of finding out your

name the day you joined the school. And yet, you've been there now for – what? Two months? And you still don't know my name?'

'No. But don't feel bad. I don't know hardly anybody's name. No one talks to me.'

'No one?' he sounded surprised again.

'Yeah. All the other girls ignore me, because of that Ulrika Price. She's had it in for me since the day I started, so no one else will talk to me.'

The scarecrow stopped walking and removed his arm from where it had been resting around her shoulders. He stepped in front of her to stop her from moving on ahead, and then, when they were close enough to each other that they were almost touching and she could feel his breath on her face, he ran his left hand through her long brown hair.

'JD,' he said.

Beth raised an eyebrow. 'Pardon me?'

'JD. That's what my friends call me.'

'Oh, right. What's it stand for?'

'You'll have to guess.'

'Okay,' said Beth smiling. She took a look up at the moon and tried to think of an interesting name that used the initials J and D.

'Got it yet?' he asked her.

'Joey Deacon?'

JD stopped stroking her hair and gave her a playful shove. 'This is why no one talks to you!'

Beth smiled back at him. Chatting with JD was actually good fun and surprisingly easy. It didn't seem to matter what she said, she knew he would 'get it'. Maybe guys weren't so complicated after all. At least, this one seemed to be right on her wavelength. She'd never had a connection like this with anyone before, let alone a boy. He seemed to understand her, and for the first time ever she wasn't in the least bit terrified of saying something stupid. In fact, she was beginning to feel a sense of confidence flowing through her. This was new.

'I'll tell you what, Beth,' said JD taking a few steps back

as he spoke. 'If you can find out what JD stands for, I'll take you out on a date.'

Beth tilted her head to one side. 'What makes you think I *want* to go on a date with you?' she said with a shrug.

JD rolled his tongue around in his mouth for a moment, pondering his response. It didn't take him long to work it out.

'You *wanna* go out with me,' he said with a wink.

Beth started walking again and brushed her shoulder against his as she passed him.

'Maybe,' she said.

JD watched her walk on down the promenade towards the abandoned pier just a hundred yards ahead. When she was about ten yards in front of him he started walking slowly after her, admiring her gently swivelling hips as she walked. For her part, Beth knew he was checking her out and she exaggerated the hip movement just a little to ensure he kept his eyes fixed on her ass.

'You gonna stay back there all night?' she called back eventually.

'*Shit!*' she heard JD shout. She stopped walking and turned back. His voice betrayed a note of genuine annoyance.

'What is it?' she asked.

'It's nearly twelve!' JD seemed panicked and was looking around him.

'What's so bad about that? Have you got to be home?'

'No, no, it's nothing like that. Look, I've gotta rush. I have to pick my little brother up from church. He'll get panicky and upset if I'm late.'

Beth took a step towards him. 'I'll come with you, if you like.'

'Nah. Thanks for the offer, but my brother will get all excitable if he sees you and we'll never get him home. Then my mom will go nuts if he's late.'

'Well, I can wait here for you, if you can come back.' Beth couldn't hide the fact that she didn't want the evening to end, and she definitely didn't want to head back home to her stepmother just yet.

'You sure?' asked JD

'Sure I'm sure. And I'll tell you what. If you can make it back here by one o'clock, the end of the witching hour, I'll let you take me out.'

JD grinned at her. 'See you at one then. Wait for me on the pier. Be careful though, there's some weirdos around tonight.' With that remark still floating in the air he turned and dashed off in the direction of town.

The promenade was still deserted and the waves were breaking softly against the harbour wall just a few feet from where Beth was walking. The ocean air was refreshing as it filled her lungs and she took several deep breaths of it. At last she was finding out what it was like to be truly happy.

After less than a minute she reached the pier and stepped on to the creaky wooden boards that led out over the water. The pier was no more than fifty yards long and was a little rickety, but it yet hadn't been deemed unsafe by the Mayor. Beth walked along it until she reached the end where she stood leaning over the wooden railing, looking out over the ocean.

The moon was still shining brightly and she lost herself in it, gazing at its reflection across the rippling waves and smiling both inwardly and outwardly. The gentle raindrops that had been splashing on her face intermittently for the last few minutes began to drop a little more frequently. Not that she minded. Nor did she care, either, that she had promised her stepmother that she would be home by midnight.

Unfortunately, there are many unwritten rules in Santa Mondega. One of them clearly states that no one is allowed to be happy for long. There's always something bad on the horizon. In Beth's case it was a lot closer than the horizon she was gazing at across the sea.

Just a few yards away from her was one of the most unpleasant members of the undead world. If she had glanced down she would have seen the fingertips of two bony hands clinging on to the end of the boardwalk. The hands belonged to a vampire. His clawed feet were dangling in the water beneath him. The waves were washing around his ankles because the tide had risen significantly while he had waited patiently for a gullible innocent to come and stare out at the ocean. Beth was that gullible innocent.

Feeding time.

Four

Sanchez hated going to church, so he made a point of not doing so too often. This, though, was a special occasion, by all accounts. With that in mind he'd picked out his best clothes: a pair of blue jeans with no rips in them, and a white polo neck sweater with no visible stains on it. He'd even put some mousse in his thick black hair to give himself that slicked-back, hey-man-you-are-*way*-too-cool, look.

They owed tonight's special event to the new preacher who had recently taken over at the local church, and had a passion for trying new things. The latest fad involved inviting all comers to a midnight mass on Halloween, which was to feature a special guest appearance from what the Reverend claimed was 'the greatest rock 'n' roll act in Santa Mondega'. He hadn't revealed the name of the act, so on the off chance that the act turned out to be some cheesy Osmonds-type group Sanchez had come prepared, bringing along a brown paper sack containing some rotten fruit to throw at anyone whose musical talents didn't meet his exacting standards.

There was no doubt about it: the Church of the Blessed Saint Ursula and the Eleven Thousand Virgins (la Iglesia de la Bendita Santa Úrsula y las Once Mil Vírgenes) was a magnificent spectacle, both inside and out. On a fine night the ancient building showed prominently against the dark sky, its white-stuccoed walls shining in the glow of the moon, its spire reaching towards the stars. This particular Halloween night, however, was as dark outside as it had ever been. Just as the sermon began, the heavy clouds that had been hovering over the church for much of the night released their load, the rain pouring down upon the House of the Lord in torrents.

From where he was sitting ten rows back, Sanchez could hear the rain hammering against the stained-glass windows behind the altar at which the Reverend was standing. The rows of pews in the church were packed with people of all ages and from all walks of life. Sitting next to Sanchez was the local simpleton, a twelve-year-old kid named Casper who, it was said, wasn't quite right in the head. No one knew exactly what was wrong with him, but Sanchez had seen the poor lad bullied mercilessly by other kids all through his childhood. It wasn't just because he was a bit 'country', either. This kid looked funny. His hair was always pointing in eight different directions, and his eyes did much the same, kind of. He was one of those kids who when you saw him you half expected there to be a flash of lightning, followed by a clap of thunder and maybe a church bell chiming sonorously in the background. Of course, just to freak Sanchez out that was exactly what was happening on this particular night.

The church wasn't well lit. On this special evening, it relied for light entirely on candles set in huge sconces around the walls, and on the pair of massive church candles at each end of the altar, the light from which flickered on the tall gold crucifix set in the centre of the altar. (It wasn't gold, in fact, but brass. Anything even resembling a precious metal did not stay long in Santa Mondega, unless bolted down and guarded day and night by semi-wild pit bulls.) The reason for the poor lighting, Sanchez guessed from the incongruous sight of of a mass of state-of-the-art sound equipment and other gear, with the accompanying mess of cables, littering the space before the altar, was that the rock concert that was to follow must be going to involve a flashing strobe-light show.

To Sanchez, the lack of light only made things worse, because every time there was a clap of thunder the candles would flicker a little, while in the sudden flashes of lightning all he would see was the crazy kid beside him staring manically back at him with his mad eyes. Then, as expected, the church bell would chime and the kid would smile at him

with his frightening crazy grin. Sanchez would have moved,
but the church was damn near full. There were no free spaces
in the pews behind him, and he didn't fancy sitting too near
the front and getting called up to participate in any of the
Reverend's over-zealous storytelling. There were rumours
that the recently inducted man of the cloth was a tad 'New
Age', which was why he preferred to be called 'Reverend'
instead of 'Father'. Whatever the truth of that, because he was
young and energetic, he had a habit of hauling members of
the congregation up to take part in impromptu 'David-and-
Goliath'-type role-playing.

After listening to the Reverend talk passionately about
God and Jesus and all that stuff for over an hour, Sanchez
began to get restless. He was only really here to check out the
band. If they were any good he was going to see if he could
get them to play at his new drinking hole, the Tapioca bar in
downtown Santa Mondega. If they were shit he was getting up
and going home. First, though, he'd offload his rotten fruit.

Finally, at five past midnight, the Reverend ended his
sermon and people began to stir themselves in readiness for
the band. From behind a four-foot high wooden pulpit set on
a raised platform in front of the altar, the Reverend (who was
a big fucker for a priest, the bar owner thought) addressed his
audience. Although he was only in his very early twenties he
did have a certain presence about him, and Sanchez sensed
that beneath the long sombre black robe lay a fairly broad,
muscular fella. That would be why the first six or seven rows
were filled with good young Christian women, and hookers
disguised as good young Christian women. They all hung
on his every word. *It's a goddam disgrace*, Sanchez thought
to himself. *Only comin' to see the Reverend. Have they no
shame? And when in the hell is the band gonna start?*

'Well, folks, I'm sure you've heard enough from me for one
night,' said the Reverend, smiling down at the congregation.
He had one of those smiles that melts the hearts of women, and
for a man of the cloth, Sanchez thought, a highly inappropriate
glint in his eye. 'I have just one or two minor announcements

to make before the evening's musical extravaganza gets under way. First up, I would ask that you all give generously, by making a donation in the collection boxes by the main doors as you leave.' There was an unmistakably steely note in his voice, and his listeners shifted uncomfortably in their pews. (Charity began at home in Santa Mondega. Charity stayed there, too.) He paused, clearly reflecting on what he had to say next. 'And secondly,' he boomed, 'and, it must be said, somewhat disappointingly, I've been informed that traces of urine have been discovered in the holy water. Would everyone therefore please avoid the water in the stoups by the west door. For sacred purposes, we have some bottled holy water; otherwise, tap water is available should anyone be thirsty.' He looked sternly around his audience, then added, 'And if I find out who is responsible for this loathsome act, then God help them.'

This was greeted by his audience with a mixture of tutting and disapproving shakes of the head. Sanchez suddenly became very conscious of the loony kid next to him giving him an evil look, as though he suspected that the bartender had been responsible for the contamination.

'*What?*' Sanchez hissed at him, unnerved by the boy's squinting and inscrutable gaze.

The kid shook his head, then pulled the hood of his parka up over his head and turned away to face the front again. Sanchez brought his attention back to the preacher. No sense in being spotted eyeballing a mentally challenged kid. Looked kinda flaky. Not a good rep to get.

Up by the pulpit, the Reverend was flicking a few switches on a control console in front of him. First, lights on the sound equipment began to glow and flicker, and then the music kicked in. The main title theme from the movie *2001: A Space Odyssey* began to blare out from a number of huge speakers. Sanchez liked the tune,* and it created quite an atmosphere,

---

* Which is actually the introduction to Richard Strauss's tone poem *Also Sprach Zarathustra*. Sanchez didn't know that, though. He wouldn't have given a shit, either.

especially in the dark draughty nave of the church, with the rain still beating the roof and windows.

The music had played for less than twenty seconds when from behind him a blast of cold, damp air entered the dimly lit building. A musty, unpleasantly dank smell accompanied it. Someone had opened the large double doors at the back, behind the rows of pews.

Everyone looked round, and from his place by the altar the Reverend peered over his congregation's heads to see who could possibly be arriving so late for the service. What they all saw was a man enter. He was wearing a long black cloak with the hood pulled up over his head. A moment later a number of other men, all dressed identically, appeared through the door, following in his footsteps. They filed in singly, then stopped and spread out in a row behind the pews. There were seven of them in all, and the last one to enter closed the great double doors behind him, making the cloaked figures all but impossible to see amid the looming black shadows at the back. An unnerving sense of evil accompanied them, wafting over the congregation like the smell that had drifted in when the doors opened. They didn't belong here – it didn't take a genius to work that out. Tonight was Halloween, and these seven hooded creatures looked like boogeymen, in church to cause havoc and mayhem.

The Reverend recognized the menace straight away and flicked a switch on his control panel. Immediately the lights at the far end of the church came on. The seven men were now lit up for all to see, the harsh electric lighting eliminating any element of surprise they might have had in mind if they had intended to sneak up on anyone in the shadowy church. Oddly enough, that was exactly what they'd had in mind.

As the music grew louder and more intense the two hundred or so churchgoers in the rows of pews stared back at the seven men, all in mortal fear of what was about to happen. Then the Reverend spoke for everyone, directing his words at the unwelcome visitors.

'Your sort are not welcome here. Leave at once.' He spoke

calmly into his microphone, but loudly enough to be heard over the music. There was an undeniable authority to him now, and even in his own dread, Sanchez noted again, *Yeah, he's a big fucker, all right.*

For a few seconds there was no movement from the seven shadowy figures at the back. Then the one in the middle, who had entered first, stepped forward and lowered his hood. He had a narrow, ghost-white face framed by long dark hair that hung over his shoulders. When he opened his mouth to speak he revealed a huge set of bright yellow fangs.

'It is Halloween, and it is the witching hour,' he hissed. 'We are the vampires from the Hoods clan, and we are claiming this church and all those in it as our own. *No one in here gets out alive!*'

To say that this caused an outbreak of panic would be an understatement. Every single woman and at least half of the men in attendance screamed and got up from their seats. Problem was, no one was quite sure where to run. The entire church was in half darkness except for where the seven vampires were standing, and the Reverend didn't appear to be making much effort to turn on any more lights. At least, not at first. But then, as the theme from *2001* came to an end, another song started up and he flicked more of the switches on his console. A spotlight suddenly illuminated the stage directly in front of the aisle that ran down the centre of the church between the rows of pews. There was no one visible in the bright beam of light, just a microphone stand surrounded by a thick swirling of dust.

The sight distracted everyone for little more than a second. Then the seven vampires let out loud screeches, like wild animals preparing to spring on their prey. One by one, they lowered their hoods and leapt up from the stone-flagged floor, to soar high into the arched vaults of the roof of the nave. Each had only one thing in mind: to pick out a victim below and dive down on the poor soul, to feast upon their blood.

The panicked congregation still had no idea where to run.

The pews were packed with struggling figures, as some tried to climb over them, others barged their neighbours, and others still sought to hide beneath the substantial wooden benches. Like everyone else, Sanchez was petrified. His first thought was to reach into the brown paper sack he had brought with him for some of the rotten fruit to throw the way of the vampires, but he quickly realized that such a course would not be wise. Instead, he decided to crouch down under the pew and hope that some of the taller folk got snatched first. So, with the courage that defined him as both man and bartender, he dropped down on the stone floor and ducked under the seat. For good measure, he pulled Casper, the funny-looking kid in the parka, down on top of him as extra protection. As the vampires swirled around in the cold church air above them, circling their prey and revelling in the fear they were inflicting upon the screaming churchgoers, the sound of trumpets suddenly blared out of the stereo speakers, all adding to the confusion and disorientation everyone was feeling.

Then something unexpected happened. Still standing tall by his pulpit, the Reverend bellowed into his microphone.

'I warned you muthafucking vampires never to set foot in this church!' he yelled, jabbing a clenched fist up at the cloaked undead circling menacingly above the crowd of terror-stricken townsfolk. 'Now get ready to feel the pain. Ladies, gentlemen and muthafuckers! – I give you . . . the King of Rock and Roll!'

A rugged and imposing figure stepped into the previously unoccupied space where the spotlight fell on the stage. There, wearing a white jumpsuit with a thick gold belt around his waist and sporting a dense quiff of black hair and some meaty sideburns, stood Elvis, Santa Mondega's greatest living hitman. He had a blues guitar in his hands. A smart, sleek, black beast of a guitar, shiny enough to suggest that it was his pride and joy. With his hand steady and his nerve unflinching he set about playing it as the backing music kicked in from the stereo speakers. He strummed a few blues chords real hard and began to tap his right foot in readiness for singing the first verse of 'Steamroller Blues'.

Elvis was so wrapped up in his music and in making sure it sounded perfect for his audience that he seemed oblivious to all that was going on around him. And such was his presence on stage that everyone stopped and stared, including the shady vampires hovering just below the roof. Each one of them was eyeing him up as their first kill.

And then he began to sing.

I'm a steamroller baby
I'm 'bout to roll all over you . . .

As the first notes boomed out of the amps, one of the vampires could contain its bloodlust no longer. With a piercing shriek, it swooped down towards the gyrating Elvis impersonator, fangs wide, ready to kill. In response, the King, without missing a beat, simply swivelled his hips one way and swung his guitar the other, aiming the neck upward at the incoming bloodsucker.

A silver dart burst from a concealed hole at the neck end of the supercool black guitar. It zipped through the air faster than the lightning outside and, with a disturbingly audible thud, embedded itself in the heart of the approaching vampire. The shocked member of the undead felt it rip through its chest and stopped dead in mid air, eyes bulging in pain and disbelief. Its last thought was: *Shit! I don't wanna die to no fuckin' James Taylor song . . .* A second later it burst spontaneously into flames and dropped to the floor of the stage at Elvis's feet, where it was swiftly reduced to a small mound of still-smoking ashes.

Inside Saint Ursula's, the mood of panic and dread among the churchgoers changed in an instant to one of hope and optimism. The same could not be said for the circling vampires. Momentarily stunned by the destruction of one of their number, they now refocused their attentions on the singer on stage.

And the King carried on playing the blues.

From his hiding place on the cold stone floor under the
– surprisingly heavy – young kid he had dragged down with
him, Sanchez looked up in awe.

This was gonna be one helluva show.

Five

Kione loved 31 October. There was something distinctive about the kill on Halloween. It just had that oh-so-sweet taste to it.

Santa Mondega was home to vampires from all over the world, but the city centre was reserved for the undead from Europe and the Americas. The early vampire settlers had originated in Paris, and had been joined by many of their European cousins long before Columbus discovered America. In the eighteenth century the city had experienced a vast influx of Latin American refugees. Once settled, a number of them had soon become members of the undead and formed clans of their own. Before long, the vampire population had grown far too big for the city, so that by the time the African vampires, like Kione, had begun to arrive, an unwritten immigration policy had been introduced. As a result, the African and Asian vampires settled in the hills that ringed Santa Mondega. The Orientals and the North Africans, in particular, loved the freedom and fresh air of the hills and valleys, preferring to hunt their prey in the wild on the very edges of the city. All, that is, except Kione. He had long since been banished from the hills for breaking not just some, but all, of the tenets of the vampire code of honour. A creature without scruples, class or pride, he lived under the pier, scavenging nightly for anything he could lay his foul hands upon.

During his time in the hills he had been a member of the Black Plague, a clan that had always kept to themselves. They were vast in number and as vicious as any other vampire clan, and it was well known that if they ever decided they wanted a piece of the action in the city an all-out undead war would ensue. One of the main reasons why they stayed out was because of an old wives' tale that had originated many centuries earlier. Santa Mondega folklore held that for one hour each night scarecrows came to life and hunted down and killed any strangers that had ventured into the city. There had never been any evidence to prove it was true, but since there were scarecrows in the front gardens of many of the houses on the outskirts, it served its purpose in keeping the vampires from the hills on the fringes.

The members of the Black Plague almost always travelled in large numbers on the rare occasions when they ventured into Santa Mondega, and the city clans did likewise whenever they chose to roam in the hills and valleys. Since Kione had no friends of his own kind – or any other, for that matter – he kept himself hidden away at the harbour, sometimes snatching mere fish and crustaceans for food. On other nights, however – like tonight – he would strike gold. Young innocents were his favourites, and tonight's innocent was a mouth-watering proposition.

He had watched the girl's scarecrow companion depart, and had then eyed her up feverishly as she made her way along the promenade to the pier. He had prayed to the Goddess Yemaya to send the young girl his way on this special night. And Yemaya was listening. She had willingly guided the young girl along the promenade and on to the wooden pier to meet Kione. He was not about to turn down such a fine offering.

Clinging by his long fingernails to the final wooden slat at the end of the boardwalk, he waited patiently for the perfect moment to strike. The girl looked so happy and carefree, which was just how Kione liked them best. For a while he allowed her to stand and gaze out at the ocean, as he in turn stared and marvelled at her shiny red shoes. Soon the blue-and-white dress that covered almost all of the flesh on her torso would turn a similar colour, stained with her blood. He couldn't help licking his lips at the thought of it. Eventually, after teasing himself almost to the point of orgasm, he made his move.

With eye-deceiving speed he sprang from his position hanging under the pier beneath her feet and allowed himself the pleasure of floating at eye level no more than a foot in front of her, his clawed feet hovering six feet above the waves. It was a moment of the most exquisite pleasure. He relished watching the expression change on the face of his prey as she realized she was about to be eaten alive by a filthy nightstalker wearing ragged brown clothes and stinking of fish. Despite the terror evident in her pupils, dilating with every passing moment, he took even greater pleasure in the knowledge that she had no idea just how much passion and lust he was about to unleash at the same time as the unbearable pain he would inflict upon her.

As he watched her jaw drop, preparing to scream, he began undressing her with his eyes. Oh, to rip that dress off and feast his eyes, tongue and hands on her silky white flesh.

'Hello, my lovely,' he sneered, in what he fondly considered to be a seductive voice.

To Beth it was nothing of the sort. It was a seedy voice, and one accompanied by a stench of foul breath that might have come from the depths of Satan's rectum. As the initial shock passed she instinctively took a step backwards and considered her predicament. Should she make a run for it? Or stay and try to talk her way out of the situation? Survival instinct kicked in and she turned to run, but no sooner had she whirled round than Kione was in front of her once more. With sinuous agility he had flipped over her in the air and landed on the pier between her and the sanctuary of the promenade.

'Oh please,' she begged. 'Don't hurt me. I have to get home.'

Kione grinned broadly, showing off the yellowed fangs in his mouth, fangs that matched the colour of the whites of his narrow, evil eyes. There were small chunks of day-old flesh still rotting away in the gaps between his crooked teeth. This vampire was a dirty bastard, in every sense of the word. Unclean, unpleasant, untrustworthy, and without doubt a colossal sexual deviant of the highest order.

'Take off your dress,' he said, leering.

'What?'

'Your dress. Lose it.'

'But, but . . . *what?*'

'You heard me. Strip for me. Get going quick, girl, because I can assure you if you don't do it then *I* will, and people say I don't have the most gentle touch in the world.'

Beth looked at his hands. He held them in front of his stomach, the long, bony fingers making groping motions, as if playing with an imaginary pair of breasts. Unsure what to do, but desperate to buy herself some time while she came up with a plan of how to get away from him, she began to slide the blue straps of her dress over her shoulders. Kione couldn't resist licking his lips in readiness for what was to come next.

What actually followed very shortly after the first shoulder strap was loosened was the sound of a pair of hard-heeled boots pounding on the wooden slats of the pier behind him. At first it resonated only in his subconscious, for his lust was taking over his thoughts. The sound of the thudding footsteps grew louder and louder, faster and faster, as their owner drew ever closer at high speed. Kione's lust had control for just a second too long before his instincts took over again. His reaction, when it came, was too late. He turned around just in time to see a scarecrow's fist, which hit him flush on the nose. He fell backwards on to Beth, who shrieked and reeled away, sending the vampire crashing to the planks. As she readjusted her dress she saw the wide-eyed figure of JD staring at his own fist, looking somewhat startled at what he had just seen himself do.

Of the three of them, Kione was the quickest to react. He leapt back on to his feet within a second of hitting the deck. Beth took this as her cue to start running back down the pier towards the promenade. She raced past the vampire and JD, who were too busy squaring up to each other to pay her any heed. Her stupid red shoes weren't best designed for running along wooden boards with gaps in between them, and she knew that she was only ever one stride away from tripping over.

She had only made it halfway down the pier before she stopped. *What about JD? Was he following? Or was he staying to continue his fight with the vampire?*

'OW!' Her answer came when she heard Kione yell out in pain and an equal amount of anger and frustration. She turned back to see the vampire on his knees having received another fierce blow to some sensitive part of his anatomy. He climbed back up again, this time slower than before, and Beth watched JD swing his clenched right fist down on to the vampire's head. Then he began to rain blows upon the now cowering deviant.

Within a minute Kione was on his back, holding up one hand and whining for mercy.

'Please, I'm sorry. I wasn't going to hurt her! We were just playing. Honestly!'

JD stepped back warily and allowed the sheepish vampire to stagger back on to his feet.

'Get the fuck out of here, you rotten piece of shit,' he ordered.

Kione lowered his head, as if he were a naughty schoolboy being lectured about misbehaving in class. JD gave him a look of contempt and turned to check on Beth.

'You okay?' he called.

'LOOK OUT!' Beth screamed in response. Kione had been bluffing, hoping that JD would lower his guard for a moment. The boy had done exactly that. The vampire seized his opportunity, lunging, fangs bared, at his enemy's throat. The young man in the scarecrow outfit was blessed with spectacular reactions, and Beth had barely finished screaming before he whirled round and smashed his onrushing attacker's face to one side. For a few moments the two of them wrestled, holding each other in a tight embrace, each struggling to gain the upper hand. Beth looked on in horror as they tussled. One moment JD would seem to be overpowering Kione, only for the vampire somehow to squirm into a position of ascendancy. Eventually, when Kione had used up all his cunning moves without managing a single bite of JD's flesh, the young man threw him up against the rickety wooden railing that ran along one side of the pier and took a firm grip around the weakening vampire's throat, choking the air from his lungs.

Kione gasped for air, looking with pleading eyes into his assailant's snarling face.

'Please,' he squeaked. 'Don't . . .'

His voice was faint and his face was slowly turning darker. JD looked into his desperate eyes and loosened his grip just enough to allow Kione to suck in a breath of air.

'Please – don't – kill – me,' the vampire gasped. 'I already died – once – years ago. Don't put me – through it again. Please. Let me be. I'll be gone. I promise.'

Grim-faced, JD squeezed hard again, watching his pathetic enemy's undead life draining from him. But taking a life isn't easy, even one that technically doesn't exist. For a start, he'd have to go to confession. So, in a moment of compassion that Kione didn't deserve, JD released his fearsome grip on the creature's neck.

'Get outta here. And don't ever come back,' he snapped, unable to contain the disgust in his voice.

The vampire needed no further invitation. In a moment he had leapt into the air and vanished into the darkness.

Beth rushed over to JD, who was a panting little after his struggle with the creature of the night.

'You okay?' she asked, stopping two yards short of where he was to give him room to stretch and breathe in some air.

'Yeah, I'm all right,' he said, one hand gingerly feeling his neck for any signs of teeth marks. 'Aside from the fact that I've just been in a fight with a vampire, which by all accounts is a fictional being, everything's just fine. How 'bout you? Did he do anything to you before I got here?'

'No, but I think I'd be dead about now if it wasn't for you. How did you know to come back?'

'I didn't. I came back 'cos I forgot something.'

JD stepped closer to Beth and reached out an arm towards her. She felt no wish to recoil, as she might have done just an hour earlier if a boy had reached out to touch her. Instead, she allowed him to brush her hair away from her shoulders and check her neck for any signs of blood or bite marks.

'What did you forget?' she asked.

JD stroked her neck as he felt for grazes, but he looked her right in the eye.

'This,' he said. Then he leaned in and kissed her on the mouth. Beth had never been kissed before, and although she was surprised and caught a little off guard, it was a warm feeling that set every nerve in her body tingling. She kissed him right back, quelling her inexperience by letting her natural instincts take over. As first kisses went, it was everything she had dreamt it would be.

After a good ten-second embrace that made Beth forget the terrifying ordeal she had undergone only moments earlier, JD stepped back. He smiled at her with that cheeky, confident, crooked smile she was rapidly growing to love.

'Come on, let's get you outta here,' he said.

He took her by the hand and they walked back towards the landward end of the pier. The air was growing colder and the night sky darker as the storm clouds from the other side of the city began looming towards them across the promenade. Out in the harbour, the waves were now slowly rising as the inevitable storm steadily began to brew.

Beth and JD were so wrapped up in each other that neither particularly noticed the worsening weather. The first thing that grabbed their attention was a solitary figure which appeared to be waiting for them at the end of the pier. The figure was that of a middle-aged woman, dressed all in black. She had white hair, and from a distance she looked very ugly. As they neared her the ugliness only got worse.

'Was it that goddam vampire again?' she called out in a croaky voice as ugly as her face.

'Yeah, think so,' said JD.

'Rotten fucker,' the woman snarled. 'He's been loitering down there for months now, eatin' shit and all sorts. You're a good boy, chasin' him off like that.' She turned her attention to Beth. 'You all right, missy?' Despite her strangeness and hideous face, there was something curiously reassuring about her. *Odd*, Beth thought. *Probably mad, a bit. But not bad.*

The young couple stopped a yard in front of her, still just on the pier.

'Yeah, I'm fine now, thanks,' Beth beamed, looking up at JD and squeezing his hand, barely able to conceal the inner joy and warmth she felt at being by his side.

'You two should come inside,' the woman said, pointing to a rickety old trailer parked just off the promenade. 'I'll make you a warm drink. The heavens are about to open, an' there's an evil storm comin'. You won't want to be out in it.'

Lightning suddenly lit the sky and the last few words were almost lost in the early rumbling that was followed by a huge clap of thunder and a swirling wind that came out of nowhere. It startled them all, and as the three of them looked up they were greeted by another flash of lightning, then another thunderclap. A second later, with equal suddenness, a chaotic, seemingly endless downpour of rain came streaming out of the dark clouds above.

'Shit, I gotta go,' said JD looking at Beth. 'Seriously, I'm gonna be in big shit if I don't pick up my brother. I'll come back when I've dropped him off. You okay staying here with . . .' He looked at the strange woman. 'What's your name, ma'am?'

'Annabel de Frugyn.'

Amid the roar of the rain and the rumbling thunder it was difficult to hear her clearly, so he just nodded at her. The woman turned and began fighting against the wind and rain to get back to her trailer, a good twenty yards away. She had a terrible limp, suggesting that she had a broken hip or at the very least one leg longer than the other.

JD watched her curiously for a moment, transfixed by her ridiculous walk. When he snapped out of the momentary trance he leaned over and kissed Beth on the lips again, then wiped the wet hair out of her eyes as the wind began to blow it around.

'Look, you go off with this pissed-up lady and I'll be back by one o'clock just like I promised earlier. Okay?'

Beth smiled and kissed him back. 'Okay.'

'Okay. See you soon, I promise.'

JD ran off into the night once more, the sheet of rain hiding him in seconds. He was heading for the church, unaware that his evening was about to take a morbid turn for the worse.

Beth followed after Annabel and caught up with her just before she reached the trailer. The strange woman smiled a hideous gappy smile at her. 'What did your boyfriend just call me?' she asked Beth.

The first thing that struck Beth was the joy of hearing Annabel refer to JD as her boyfriend. The second was the realization that he had called her a 'pissed-up lady'. Clearly, diplomacy was required.

'I think he called you the Mystic Lady,' said Beth, shielding herself from the rain as Annabel unlocked the pink door on the trailer.

'The Mystic Lady, huh?' the woman repeated. 'I kinda like the sound of that.'

As Beth was following Annabel into the trailer, Kione the vampire was half a mile away, flying through the torrential rain and gale-force winds that the storm had blown up. If he had had any pride, it would have been severely dented by the humiliating beating he had taken at the hands of the teenager on the pier. But Kione had no pride. What he did have, however, was the wallet he had siphoned from JD's pocket during their fight. A wallet containing its owner's home address. As he flew through the seedy back alleys of Santa Mondega, Kione the vampire was plotting revenge.

Six

Earlier That Night

Olivia Jane Lansbury, widow of this parish, was a proud woman. She was also one of Santa Mondega's wealthiest residents. The home she had inherited from her late husband twenty years earlier was one of the city's most prominent features. It sat atop a steep hill on the edge of a smart suburb, and overlooked all else. Boasting no fewer than twenty bedrooms it would have qualified as a guesthouse, except that Olivia Jane didn't need the business. She was wealthy enough without having to rent out the many rooms at her disposal. Usually only two of the bedrooms in her home were ever occupied: hers, and that of the stepdaughter she had adopted, Beth.

Her husband, Dexter, had been shot dead in the bath on their wedding night. Initial investigation by a local detective, Archibald Somers, had indicated that the only possible killer was Olivia Jane herself. Shortly after she had offered a reward of $50,000 for any information leading to the identity of the killer, however, Somers had received word from one of his contacts that the killer was in fact a local fisherman. The clever detective had taken the case on personally and tracked the fisherman down. After beating a confession out of the suspect he had been forced to gun him down for resisting arrest, attempting to evade capture and obstructing a police officer in the commission of his duty. Case closed. Nice work.

No one in the city really understood why Olivia Jane

had adopted Beth. She seemed to have absolutely no time for the girl. Nannies had come and gone in the early years, but from the time Beth had been old enough to attend school, her stepmother had brought her up alone and tutored her from home. She had rarely let the girl out of the house, and had taken great care to ensure that she never mixed with other children of her own age. Until recently.

Just two months earlier she had apparently undergone a change of heart and enrolled her stepdaughter in one of the local schools, even encouraging her to attend the Halloween Ball. This had seemed so out of character that Beth had been both extremely surprised and more than a little suspicious. Even so, she had seized the opportunity to be among people her own age with alacrity.

Beth was right to have been suspicious. Olivia Jane's reason for sending her stepdaughter out into the world concerned a plan she had put into action fifteen years earlier. That plan was now to be finally realized. It was party time.

Her dinner guests all arrived together under the cover of night, and when Olivia Jane heard the doorbell chime she felt a huge surge of excitement race through her. Checking her appearance in the full-length mirror by the front door one last time, she readied herself for the evening ahead. She had spent over an hour curling her thick blonde hair into a style that she felt made her look like Marilyn Monroe. The look was completed with a figure-hugging strapless pink dress. *Not bad for forty something*, she thought to herself.

She opened the door, to be greeted by the sight of a tall man in a long white robe, wearing a gold ram's-head mask, its horns curling around just above his ears. Twelve others stood behind. Six men all dressed identically to him, and six women in scarlet robes and plain white masks.

'Greetings, Mrs Lansbury,' said the tall man, sonorously.

'Do come in.' Olivia Jane smiled, gesturing for the visitors to step into the warmth of the entrance hall.

The thirteen guests filed in one at a time, each nodding to Olivia Jane as they passed her, and all marvelling at the sight before them. There was one decorative touch which Olivia Jane insisted upon inside her house: all the walls, ceilings and carpets were bright red, the same scarlet as the robes of her female guest. A walk round the entire building would have confirmed what a magnificent yet creepy sight this was. The evening's agenda didn't actually allow time for a guided tour, however, and none of the guests was about to request one. Each and every one of them was eager for the night's festivities to begin.

Olivia Jane led them through to the living room, a huge, imposing space with a ceiling fully thirty feet above the red-carpeted floor. It was filled with comfortable red furniture, and a pair of dining tables loaded with bottles of wine and dishes of rich foods. Within ten minutes, all of her visitors had removed their robes and were cavorting orgiastically, naked apart from their masks. Soft classical music played as they indulged in all manner of sexual activity, pausing occasionally only to eat and drink.

Their hostess need not have bothered spending so much time on her hair and selecting her outfit. The dress was ripped off her in a moment of frantic lust by one burly man as another tugged at her hair and pulled her maskless head down to his groin. The start of Olivia Jane's initiation into their satanic cult was just beginning. A two-hour orgy would be followed by the evening's main event just after midnight. Her acceptance into the cult was dependent on her offering up a young virgin for sacrifice during the witching hour.

Beth was due home at midnight.

Seven

Sanchez knew he shouldn't have grabbed the mentally challenged boy and dragged him to the floor with him. Now the kid was hugging him tightly like a randy dog humping some poor bastard's leg. He had both arms wrapped around the bartender's neck and was gazing at him adoringly.

'You saved me,' Casper said, smiling inanely.

'Yeah. Yeah, that's right,' said Sanchez. If the kid wanted to believe he had pulled him to the ground for his safety, then why shatter his illusions by telling him the truth? In reality, he had simply used the boy as a shield to keep away any swooping vampires. As it happened he need not have bothered, because the vampires were now all focused on attacking Elvis while avoiding his deadly aim. Two feelings washed over Sanchez. One was a sense of relief at having survived so far. The other, if he was honest, was one of acute embarrassment at being seen cuddling a young boy in church.

'You're my hero,' beamed Casper.

'Yeah yeah yeah. That's enough, okay? Get the fuck off me, will ya? I don't want nobody to see us like this. Fuckin' embarrassin'.'

Casper seemed only further encouraged by Sanchez's show of embarrassment and hugged him even harder. The two of them were lying between two rows of pews practically spooning, legs entwined, looking like a couple of young lovers.

'I don't want no more of this goddam shit,' Sanchez snapped, prising the boy off him. 'Go on, fuckin' move!'

With a single strong shove he pushed the boy off him and

underneath the pew behind them. No sooner had he done so than a vampire swooped down on them from above, grabbed Sanchez by the neck with one hand and pulled him to his feet.

'FUCK!'

Pale-faced and red-eyed, the bloodsucker leaned in, his mouth wide open and his fangs arcing out, ready to tear into the sweet meat of Sanchez's neck. Terrified, the young bartender closed his eyes, wincing. A sharp snapping sound followed, yet he felt no pain. No teeth in the neck either. Then, to his great relief, he felt the vampire relinquish his grip on him. He opened his eyes again and was amazed by what he saw. The vampire had the business end of a rawhide bullwhip wrapped around his neck and was being pulled, hissing in fury, backwards at a rapid pace towards the man holding the whip handle. No ordinary man, either. It was only the Reverend, fer Chrissakes! Now, Sanchez liked this new preacher. He'd been a breath of fresh air in town since he'd arrived, but no one would have expected to see him take on a vampire with nothing but a bullwhip. *That does it,* thought Sanchez. *I gotta stop pissin' in the Reverend's holy water.*

Both Sanchez and the boy cowering beneath the pew watched in awe as the unshaven holy man pulled the struggling vampire right up close to him, the whip still wrapped tightly around the creature's neck. When its face was close enough to feel the stubble on the preacher's jaw something even more unlikely happened. The Reverend pulled a sawn-off shotgun from somewhere within his dark robes and thrust the muzzle into the tight skin beneath the bloodsucker's chin.

BOOM!

Blood and brain matter and pieces of shattered skull sprayed high into the air. Then the remains of the vampire's body exploded into flames and crumpled to the floor. Unfazed, the priest looked around for his next victim.

For the next two minutes the stunned members of the congregation watched as Elvis and the Reverend destroyed the remaining hooded vampires. All the while Elvis was still singing 'Steamroller Blues' and strumming away on his guitar, which he would occasionally point the way of a vampire and fire off a dart or two. Sanchez, in particular, watched on in open-mouthed wonder.

Awesome.

Eventually the one-sided fight ended and a hush descended upon the shocked congregation. The graveyard stink had gone, to be replaced by a smell of scorching and a blue haze of gunsmoke. The Reverend set about checking that the members of his flock were all okay and that none of them had been bitten. When he got to Sanchez – to whom Casper was once more clinging – he looked the young bartender up and down.

'I'm proud of you, Sanchez. That was a brave thing you did.'

Huh?'

'I saw you drag the kid down to the floor with you, and then push him under the pews when the vampire went for him. Takes real guts to do that. You should be proud of yourself.'

Sanchez saw no need to tarnish the holy man's view of him.

'Aaah, it was nothin', Reverend, anyone woulda done the same.' He shrugged, hoping that the movement would shake off the clingy kid. It didn't. The Reverend smiled at them.

'No need to call me "Reverend". My friends call me Rex,' he said.

'Reverend Rex? That's a catchy name for a preacher, ain't it?' Sanchez remarked.

'Well, truth is, I ain't really a preacher. I just kill bad folks on God's behalf, y'know?'

'Oh. Yeah. Right.'

'So, you two want a room out back or what?'

That was the cue for Sanchez to try to shake off the kid in the parka once again.

'Sanchez saved me,' Casper beamed at Rex.

'Yep, he did. You owe him one, I reckon.'

Casper grinned at Sanchez, his new hero. Although the grin was a little freaky, and once again accompanied by a flash of lightning and a thunderclap from outside, it was also faintly endearing. Coupled with the look of helplessness and enormous gratitude in the boy's eyes it was actually starting to melt Sanchez's heart a little. The poor kid was really quite sweet . . . *For a nutcase.*

'Awright, now. That's enough,' Sanchez snapped. 'Shouldn't you be home in bed?'

'He's got a point,' said Rex, turning to address the crowd of bewildered churchgoers, many of whom were resurfacing from between the rows of pews. 'Everyone. Listen up. I suggest you either head home now, or bed down here for the night. There's a heck of a big storm goin' on and it's only gonna get worse.'

In spite of the bad weather, no one actually liked the idea of bedding down in the church after the horrific events they had just witnessed, so most of the congregation headed for the door at the end of the church. As they began filtering out of the building, whispering among themselves about what they had just seen, Elvis jumped down from the stage.

'Thank y'all. Thankya very much,' he called after the departing crowd. Then, after laying his guitar aside, he headed down the main aisle towards Sanchez, Rex and the kid, Casper.

'Yo, Rex, guess I'm done here for tonight. You okay cleanin' up on your own?'

'Shit, man,' groaned Rex. 'You splittin' on me already?'

'I got some other fuckers to take down tonight, buddy,' Elvis protested.

Rex shrugged and smiled at his killing partner. 'Sure thing, man. Do what you gotta do.'

'I'm kinda looking forward to this one,' said the King. 'I gotta go kill some boy band in town.'

This guy Elvis was cool and Sanchez couldn't hide how impressed he was by the guy's self-confidence and all-round swagger. 'Wow,' he gasped. 'This band, are they vampires too?'

Elvis pulled a pair of his trademark sunglasses from his breast pocket and put them on.

'Nope. They're a just a boy band,' he said, deadpan, his eyes now hidden.

'Right. Yeah. O' course,' the barman stammered.

Elvis nodded at him, then began walking towards the door. Just then a young man burst in, fighting his way through the crowd. He was dressed as a scarecrow – if a rather wet and bedraggled one – and he was looking around the church as though frantically searching for someone or something.

'Casper!' he called out.

It was instantly evident that he was someone who meant a lot to Casper. Suddenly the kid who had been so enamoured of Sanchez forgot all about his saviour and ran down the aisle towards the scarecrow, overtaking Elvis as he went. Sanchez watched as the young boy jumped up at the young man, who caught him, nearly falling backwards with the force of the jump.

'What the hell has happened here, Casper? People are going nuts outside. They're saying that a bunch of vampires broke in here. Are you okay?'

'Yeah, I'm okay, bruv.'

Casper was clinging tightly to his older brother, and now that he knew he was safe he began to sob as the enormity of the danger he had escaped began to sink in.

'It's okay, Casper. I'm here now. D'you wanna go home?' There was no verbal response from the boy, just a tighter squeeze. 'Come on, I'll take you home. We'd better hurry, though, it's startin' to rain pretty heavily, and I haven't got a coat.'

'You can wear mine,' said Casper, smiling and pulling down the hood of his parka, ready to offer it to his brother.

'Don't be dumb,' JD said kindly, ruffling Casper's hair. 'You need your coat more than I do. I reckon Mom would probably kill me if I turned up wearing it and you were soaked through.'

Elvis caught up with the pair of them on his way down the aisle. Stopping, he looked the scarecrow up and down.

'You know, you should be thankin' those two guys

back there for savin' your brother from the vampires,' he remarked.

'Yeah,' said Casper. 'Sanchez saved me.'

'Sanchez, huh?' said JD, eyeing the bartender, who was now deep in conversation with the Reverend. 'I guess we owe him a favour.'

'Yeah,' said Elvis. 'You should drop by his bar some time. The Tapioca. He needs the custom. Take a weapon with you, though. It's kinda a rough place.'

'Wh–? Well, yeah. Okay, man.' JD was thoroughly bewildered.

Casper let go of his brother and pointed back at Rex. 'You should meet the Reverend, he's really cool,' he said excitedly, tugging at his elder brother's arm.

'Yeah, sure, maybe another time, bruv. We've gotta get goin'.'

Even though the rain outside was showing no sign of letting up, JD was not overly happy at having Casper hang around in a church where the floors and walls were in places splattered with blood. The sooner he could get his little brother out of there the better. There was already a strong chance of sleepless nights on the horizon if Casper started having nightmares about what he had seen. As JD tried edging his brother in the direction of the main doors Elvis threw a comment his way.

'Ain't you gonna at least shake hands with the new preacher?' he asked.

'I'm sure I'll get a chance to shake hands with him another time,' said JD, offering a polite smile as he pulled Casper down the aisle with him towards the exit.

'Yo, scarecrow man,' Elvis called after him. 'You'll get fuckin' soaked through in that outfit. Wear this.'

The King had picked up a dark cloth from the floor and tossed it at the young man. It was a hooded robe, recently worn by one of the now dead vampires. JD caught it and took a long look at it.

'Thanks, Elvis,' he called back.

'Ain't nothin', man. Just take good care of your brother.'

As JD tugged at the robe so that he could put it on without getting into a tangle, Elvis headed past them and out into the night. He had other business to attend to, taking down the local manufactured pop acts.

JD struggled for a moment to get his arms into the sleeves of the long dark robe. When he eventually managed to do so, he found that it fitted snugly around his shoulders and hung nicely just above his ankles. After securing it around his waist with its narrow leather belt he followed his excited younger brother out into the rain, pulling the hood up over his head as he went.

Eight

Beth sat in one of the two comfortable, but distinctly grubby, dark green armchairs that Annabel de Frugyn had in her trailer. The older woman had sensed that the cold wind and rain had left Beth chilled, so had boiled the kettle to make them both a cup of her finest tea.

The kettle stood on a sideboard behind her at the far end of the trailer in what passed for the kitchen area. With her back to Beth, Annabel poured the steaming hot water into her two best mugs and stirred the contents for a short while, then returned and sat down opposite the young girl and handed her a mug. It contained extremely weak tea; more disturbingly, it had a picture of John Denver on it. The reason for the tea's weakness lay in the fact that she refused ever to use more than one teabag a day. On this particular day she had already had about four cups, so the dried-out prune masquerading as a teabag really hadn't imparted much flavour to the hot water in the mug.

Annabel made herself comfortable in the chair opposite Beth and placed her own mug (decorated with a picture of Val Doonican) on the small table in between them.

'He'll come back, you know,' she said reassuringly.

'Am I that obvious?' Beth asked.

'It's practically stamped on your forehead, my dear. He's the one for you, though. I can tell. I have a nose for these things. I'm a fortune teller by trade.'

'Is that right?' Beth perked up. 'Could you read my fortune?' Then a thought struck her. 'I don't have any money, though,' she said sheepishly.

The darkly dressed woman smiled. 'Of course. Hold out your hands. I'll give you a palm reading.'

'Okay.'

Beth placed the John Denver mug on the table in such a position that it was in a staring contest with Val Doonican. Then she held her hands out to Annabel's examination.

Outside, the rain was falling harder, and making an almighty racket as it pounded on the tin roof. There seemed to be no electric light in the trailer and the only illumination was provided by candles spaced intermittently on a ledge along the walls, each flickering with an eerie green flame. The only window was just behind Beth's head, and every so often a flash of lightning outside would light up Annabel's pale, warty face. One such flash occurred just as she took hold of the girl's hands with both hers and smiled her gap-toothed smile at her.

'Oh, I sense great things for you, Beth, my dear,' she said, after a long pause.

'Really? Like what?'

Annabel looked her up and down and began to nod. 'Yes, yes, you've come a long way to be here. You're not originally from Santa Mondega, are you?'

'No, that's right. My father moved us here a few weeks after I was born.'

'From Kansas, I'm thinking.'

'Delaware actually.'

'Shush. Don't interrupt, unless it's to agree with me. You'll break my concentration.'

'Sorry.'

'Now,' Annabel went on. 'You miss home, don't you? And you want to get back there, but you're not sure how.'

Beth frowned. *Was this woman for real?* Just because she was dressed as Dorothy from *The Wizard of Oz* didn't mean that she was from Kansas and believed that there was no place like home. She couldn't help a feeling of relief that that this would all be over soon and JD would return. This fortune-telling old biddy was, frankly, a joke. Not only that, it seemed she was stupid enough to think that Beth hadn't seen *The Wizard of Oz*. Even so, the girl let her continue anyway.

'And your friend, he searches for something too. His road will come to an end when he finds his soul.'

Beth raised an eyebrow. 'Don't you mean brain?'

'What?'

'In *The Wizard of Oz*, the scarecrow wanted a brain.'

'What's *The Wizard of Oz*?'

'Are you kidding?' Beth was astonished, her surprise overtaking her normal good manners.

Annabel sat back, looking slightly offended. 'Do you want me to tell you your fortune, or not?'

'I'm sorry. Please do go on.'

'Thank you.' There was a hint of suspicion in the fortune teller's voice. She was not used to being challenged in such a direct fashion. 'The path you choose will matter not, for you, my dear, will always arrive at the same destination. All roads lead back to what feels like home for you. Under the light of a sleepless moon, that boy will be with you always.'

Beth raised an eyebrow. *She's lost it,* she thought. *This old fruitbat is absolutely cuckoo.* 'What does that mean, exactly?' she asked, anxious now to get the whole stupid business over with.

Instead of replying, the darkly dressed woman suddenly jumped slightly, as if someone had jabbed a pin in her ass.

'There's somebody at the door,' she hissed.

'What?'

Before the other could reply, there came a loud knock at the door of the trailer.

'That's for you, Beth,' Annabel said quietly.

'Excuse me?'

'By all accounts, I think the wicked witch has found you. You should answer the door.'

Beth felt a cloak of fear fall over her. 'My stepmother is here?'

Annabel nodded. 'She has come to take you home.'

'Oh no. I promised JD I'd wait for him. Can't we pretend I'm not here?'

Three more booming knocks were heard over the roar of the rain as a fist pounded on the door. Then Beth heard the voice that had always chilled every nerve in her body.

'Beth! *By God, I know you're in there!* I saw you through the window. You're coming home with me *right now.* You just wait 'til I get my fuckin' hands on you, you little bitch . . .'

Beth stood up and walked over to the door, readying herself for the mental and physical assault she was about to receive from her irate stepmother.

As she reached out for the doorknob, an action that would undoubtedly initiate the torrent of abuse that was to follow, Annabel quietly made one last comment.

'Beth, you have blood on your hands.'

It was strange thing to say, even by the fortune teller's standards, but it brought the desired reaction. Beth looked down at her palms. *There was no blood.* So she turned her hands over. *Still no sign of a single drop.* She turned back to look quizzically at the strange, ugly woman.

'I can't see any,' she said.

'But you will, my dear. *You will.*'

Nine

JD and Casper fought their way through the torrential rain for twenty minutes before they finally made it home. The rented accommodation in which they lived with their mother, Maria, a small house in a rackety row of two-storeys, was in Santa Mondega's red-light district. There were two reasons for this. Firstly, it was all they could afford. And secondly, their mother was a whore. By reputation and by trade. JD knew it, although Casper had really no idea. One day it might sink in and leave him with some bad mental scars, but that day seemed quite a way off for now.

JD had never expressed any disapproval at his mother's trade. From the moment he had realized what she did for a living he had also understood the reasons why. This wasn't a career she had chosen for herself. She was a single mother trying to provide for two growing sons. JD's own father had run off when he was a small child, without offering up even a half-decent explanation. Things had picked up briefly when his mother had lived with another man, named Russo, who had fathered Casper, but all too soon he too had run off. Russo had returned to his ex-wife by whom he had another child, a son named Bull, who was of a similar age to JD. They still lived near by.

Their front door was hidden away down a dark alleyway, and to get to it they would normally have had to walk past a number of hookers, pimps and drug dealers. It wasn't scary for them because everyone knew who they were. They were Maria's kids, and pretty much everyone who hung in the alleyway either worked with, behind, underneath or on top of their mother at some time or another. Nice folks, though, really. Tonight, with the wind and rain as hard as they were, no one was around, so they made it to their front door without the usual meet-and-greet session.

JD turned his key in the lock and pushed the door open to let Casper run on in. He pulled down the hood of his new robe and allowed it to rest around his shoulders, and then followed his younger brother inside. They stepped into the small entrance hall, its dirty red carpet already muddied, no doubt by a few clients who had dropped by earlier. The mud was barely noticed by either boy though, for what greeted them inside was carnage. Casper became instantly distressed and confused. One look round was all it needed for JD to make a snap decision for his younger brother's benefit.

'Casper, get outside,' he snapped, with uncharacteristic sharpness.

Their house wasn't big, and it would not take long to find more signs of whatever unpleasantness had recently taken place, so JD wanted Casper out of the way before his innocent eyes lit on anything that might give him nightmares. Even as he was speaking JD's own eyes were taking in more and more disturbing signs. And Casper looked utterly bewildered. 'What's happening?' he asked.

JD grabbed his little brother's head and turned it to face him. 'Listen carefully,' he said. 'I want you to run down the road to your father's house. When you get there, tell him something has happened and he needs to come down here right away. But you stay there with Bull, okay? Don't you come back, just send your dad over here. I think we've been burgled.'

'What about you?' There was a catch in the younger boy's voice as fears threatened to overwhelm him.

'Don't worry about me, y'hear. I'm goin' to help Mom clean up here.'

'Where is Mom?'

'She's probably gone to police headquarters. *Casper! Look at me!*'

The kid had momentarily fixed his gaze on the wall behind

JD. At his brother's sharp call he looked back into his eyes. 'Is that . . . ? Is that blood on the wall?' he asked.

'No. It's probably red paint. Burglars often paint houses red when they rob them so they know not to come back.'

'I wanna stay here with you.' Caspar's lower lip was trembling now, and he swallowed hard.

'I know you do, kid, but you gotta go. I'll be along to pick you up again later. I always come and get you, don't I? I know I'm always late, but I always turn up in the end, don't I?'

Casper looked sad. 'Not always.'

'Well, I will from now on. Now hurry up. Quickly. I want you to run as fast as you can, and don't look back until you get to your dad's house. Okay?'

'Okay.' Casper reached out and hugged JD tightly. JD knew his brother was scared so he hugged him back for a few seconds and stroked his thick brown hair, before ushering him out of the door.

In the blood-drenched hall, despite his terror and alarm, JD felt thankful that Casper had only seen the blood on the wall. He had not noticed the vampire standing in the kitchen over to their left, grinning evilly at them with his bloodied fangs on display.

Ten

'I swear you're gonna be sorry for making me come out here and get you,' Olivia Jane hissed at Beth as she tugged her by her long brown hair up the winding path that led up to their home atop the hill. Beth noticed that her stepmother looked a terrible mess, which was extremely unusual, to say the least. She put it down to the wind and the rain, and no doubt to the fact that she was extremely agitated.

'But, Mother, I met a boy,' she pleaded. 'I promised I'd meet him at the pier at one o'clock. Can't I just go back till then and then come straight home?'

'Don't you *dare* talk back to me, missy. You're coming home and that's the end of it. I didn't spend fifteen years raising you just for you to go and mess things up for me at the last minute.'

The storm saw to it that both women were drenched and exhausted by the time they made it to the front door. Beth's blue-and-white dress was stuck to her after its soaking in the rain. She was glad that no one was around, because it had become almost transparent, leaving little to the imagination. Her stepmother was wearing a long red robe that Beth had never seen her in before. It too was stuck to her like a second skin.

When they reached the front door of their enormous home, Olivia Jane pulled a large key from a pocket on her robe and turned it in the lock, before pushing the door open. She pulled her desperate, stumbling daughter inside with her and pushed her roughly on to the floor. Beth skidded face first on the red carpet and felt it burn the skin of her nose and chin.

Rolling over on to her side she was alarmed to see that they had visitors. Through the doorway to her left that led into the sitting room she saw a group of men and women wearing masks and long robes, white for the men, red for the women. One of the men, wearing an ornate ram's-head mask, stepped through the doorway and into the hall to stand next to Olivia Jane.

'So this is our sacrificial virgin?' a deep voice asked from behind the mask. 'Isn't she *pretty*!'

'Not for much longer.' Beth saw her stepmother's lips move, and heard her voice, but could not quite believe what she was hearing. She watched as the masked man handed a small golden dagger to her stepmother. Olivia Jane accepted it willingly, and looked down at her terrified stepdaughter with a face of pure evil.

'Fifteen years I've put up with your whining,' she hissed. 'Fifteen years I've fed you, clothed you, taught you, listened to your stupidities. Now it's time for you to repay me, to prove your value – and for me to take my place as High Priestess.' She glanced up at the masked man by her side and allowed herself a smile. In response, he squeezed her thigh playfully.

'Go on. Do it,' he urged. 'The witching hour is almost over.'

As if to confirm what he had said, the bells of a clock on a church in the city below began to chime. From her place on the floor Beth saw the smile disappear from her mother's face and the look of evil return. Then the man spoke out again from beneath his mask.

'Quickly, Olivia Jane. She must be sacrificed before the bells stop ringing.'

Beth watched in horror as the bedraggled, almost unrecognizable woman lunged down at her, thrusting out the sharp golden dagger, ready to end her stepdaughter's life.

Eleven

'What the fuck have you done?' JD demanded.

Kione grinned back at him so broadly that his bloodied gums were exposed, revealing pieces of gristle stuck in the gaps between his teeth. His raggy brown clothes were spattered with blood and clumps of matted hair, more of which was visible beneath his long fingernails. He was leaning back against the kitchen worktop looking insufferably smug and contented, a complete reversal of how he had felt after his recent encounter with JD.

'You should have killed me when you had the chance,' he sniggered. 'Now look at what you've lost.' He gestured at something to his left, inside the kitchen. Although JD knew he was about to see something horrific he stepped into the kitchen and looked around the doorway at what the vampire was indicating.

Then he vomited. He doubled over as the hot liquid flew up through his body and out of his mouth, spattering the white tiles on the kitchen floor.

And Kione laughed. Kione *cackled*.

JD's mother Maria was lying in a pool of blood on the tiled floor, a gaping hole visible in her neck, blood pumping out of it at an alarming rate. She wasn't dead, but she was staring up at the ceiling in a clear state of shock, her mouth working feebly as she struggled to take in air. Her white blouse was soaked in claret, and her short skirt had been forced up above her waist. It was all too obvious that she had been violated in every way possible by the perverted creature in her kitchen. Although JD had no wish to know the exact details, it was obvious that she had suffered indescribable physical, sexual and mental tortures at the hands of this beast. The physical signs certainly indicated as much, and the look on her face was one that would haunt him for ever, etched into his memory like words carved in stone. His instinctive reaction was to rush to her side. Kione expected as much and in the blink of an eye slammed him backwards into the cupboards that lined the wall behind him, pinning him up against them, preventing him from reaching her.

'See what you get?' the vampire hissed. 'You fuck with me, and I *fuck your mother*. And when I'm done with you and your whore of a mother, I'll have your fuckin' brother for afters. What do you think about that – Scarecrow?'

The long bony fingers on the vampire's left hand were wrapped around JD's neck, keeping the air from his lungs. With his other hand he had the boy's left arm pinned down on the kitchen worktop to prevent him from pushing him back. Frantically, JD reached out behind him with his right hand, hoping to find a weapon of sorts on the sideboard which was pressing hard into his back. His hand scoured blindly along the surface, searching for the kitchen knives that Maria used so often when preparing meals. They were never easily accessible, for the boys' mother was careful not to let Casper get his hands on them in case he injured himself.

Kione squeezed harder, then harder still, watching in glee as his young opponent's face began to drain of colour. Then he leaned in, hungry for a bite of the white flesh of JD's neck.

As the vampire's jaws opened to their widest and he prepared to gorge on one of the bulging veins, he was suddenly struck by an agonizing pain. Kione had felt terrible pain before, but this was about as bad as he had ever known. He screamed in shock and pain and confusion. JD's right hand had caught hold of a sharp chopping knife that had lain concealed behind a rusty old chrome-plated toaster. With one violent stab he had succeeded in thrusting it deep into Kione's left eye. *Right through the pupil.* Blood in all directions, followed by a disgusting popping sound. The vampire's left eye was plucked from its socket as JD heaved back on the knife. It was now stuck firmly to the end of the blade, a short length of severed optic nerve still attached.

In his agony, the vampire released his grip on JD's throat and staggered back. He was visibly distressed, his face a tormented mask of utter shock. His legs seemed to have become like those of a baby giraffe trying to take its first steps, wobbling under the strain of holding itself up. Again Kione screamed aloud, like a small child suddenly denied its favourite toy. One of his hands was pressed over the gaping hole where his eye had once been, trying in vain to stem the flow of blood seeping through his fingers.

JD was unable to take immediate advantage of the bloodsucker's predicament, for he was bent double trying desperately to get his breath back. It took three or four huge, sucking attempts before his windpipe opened sufficiently for a great gulp of oxygen to storm in and fill his lungs. Hauling himself back upright he took one look at Kione and then at the knife in his hand. He had no time to formulate much of a sophisticated plan, but instinct took over. He grabbed the eyeball on the end of the knife, ripped it off and tossed it on to the floor. Before it could bounce or roll away he stamped on it, squelching it into the tiles. Then, holding the knife low in front of him, he readied himself for any fresh lunge from the vampire, who was screaming hysterically and making a godawful racket as he swung wildly around, smashing or knocking down anything in the kitchen that wasn't nailed down.

This was not a situation the sixteen-year-old was familiar with. He'd never held a knife aggressively before. He'd never stabbed anyone before. He'd never plucked anyone's eyeball out and stamped it into the floor before. But then, nor had he ever been confronted in his own home by a vampire that had just raped his mother and bitten large chunks of flesh out of her.

Kione turned towards him, preparing to make another attack, although he now had a good deal less stomach for the fight. This fuckin' kid had bested him twice now, and his confidence was waning fast. In response, JD threw the knife at him in the manner of a knife thrower in a circus. Holding the blade by its tip, he raised the knife above his shoulder and threw it handle first. It spun over once in the air before embedding itself in the vampire's remaining eye. Once again blood spurted out and Kione let out a high-pitched scream of fury, terror and despair, as his world turned to total darkness in an instant. The next thing he felt was his head hitting the kitchen floor as he fell backwards. This was followed by JD's knee pushing down into his chest to prevent him from climbing to his feet. Last of all, he suffered the unpleasant agitation that came with the vile popping sound, indicating that his right eye, too, had been pulled from its socket.

The next fleeting sensation he experienced was a savage blow to the head that rendered him unconscious. A feeling he would get used to.

Twelve

From her position of subjugation on the red carpet in the entrance hall, Beth threw her hands up to defend herself, turning her head away and closing her eyes as she did so. The bell on the church clock was still chiming in the city below, the sound climbing above the roar of the wind and rain. The young girl who had already endured such a rollercoaster of an evening was now on the downward track again. She screamed aloud as she felt the blade of the golden dagger slice through the soft skin of her right cheek, cutting right through until she felt the tip of it scrape against the teeth inside. The blade ripped through three inches of her face before it was withdrawn, just before it reached the corner of her mouth. She opened her eyes, but they were now filling up with tears of pain, so that it was almost impossible to make out where the dagger was. With her hands flailing desperately, she hoped she might grab hold of her stepmother's arm before she was stabbed again.

She saw the flash of bright gold as the dagger swung at her face a second time and instinctively used her right arm to try to bat it away. At the same time, and quite by chance, she managed to seize a handful of the red robe her stepmother was wearing. She pulled on it as hard as she could, and felt the older woman lose her footing as a result. Olivia Jane fell forward on to her terrified stepdaughter, and the struggle between them came to an end.

The chiming of the church bell stopped, and for a moment all that could be heard was the pattering of the rain outside. Then the leader of the cult, the tall man in the ram's-head mask, spoke on behalf of his clan members who had gathered in the hall behind him to watch the sacrifice.

'Olivia Jane?' he intoned solemnly into the sudden silence. 'You okay?'

Slowly, Olivia Jane Lansbury rolled soggily off the body of her stepdaughter, to lie on her back on the red carpet. She did not move again. The golden dagger was lodged in the side of her neck, blood seeping out over her shoulder into her hair. From beside her, Beth's panic-stricken, blood-soaked face stared up at the masked devil worshippers in her home. One further glance sideways at her stepmother's bloodied, dying form was enough for her. With a speed born of sheer terror, she leapt to her feet and rushed out through the front door, which had remained partly open throughout the ordeal. Back out in to the rain she went, covered in her stepmother's blood and also her own, from the horrific face wound inflicted upon her. Her only thought was to head for the pier, hoping to find comfort in the arms of JD, the only person in the world she felt she could trust.

The man in the white robe who had handed the golden dagger to Olivia Jane stepped forward and peered around the door, watching the distraught young girl run down the hill and back towards the sea front. He took off his mask and crushed it in his hands. His craggy, middle-aged features were awash with frustration as he turned back to the twelve other members of the clan.

'Right, you people had better clean up this mess,' he said in a commanding voice. 'I'm gonna have to go and arrest the girl.'

Thirteen

In the bloody, vomit-splattered kitchen, JD leant down to check on his mother, lying crumpled and broken on the floor. The copious amount of blood covering her was extremely unsettling, but he put it to the back of his mind. Crouching beside her, he propped her up into a seated position with her back against one of the lower cupboards. Then he brushed some of her long, dark, bloodstained hair out of her eyes, gently pulling away some strands that the drying blood had stuck to her face. She looked back at him, her eyes betraying the shock and pain she was feeling. He knew it was bad – the blood and the gaping hole in her neck made that plain enough – but confirmation was there in her dilated pupils and shallow, panting breaths. His mother would never normally show her pain, either physical or emotional, but this was a pain she couldn't hide. The woman was dying and she knew it, and JD was slowly realizing it, and attempting to come to terms with it. Finding something meaningful or even comforting to say was all but impossibe. There wasn't enough time to think of the right thing to say – this was a time for the stunned brain to disengage and the autopilot to take over.

'Don't die, Mom. Please don't die. What should I do? What will Casper do?' JD's voice was cracking. This was the last time he would ever speak with his mother, the one and only consistent person in his life. Yet he knew he had to try not to think of himself. She was dying and needed comfort in these last moments.

She looked up at him, still gasping for breath. It was clear that she could barely see or recognize him. It was his voice that was providing her with comfort in her final minutes.

'Son,' she panted. '*Kill me.*'

'You're in shock,' JD mumbled, stroking her hair. 'I'll call an ambulance.'

'It's too late. *Kill me.*'

'Mom, I'm not going to . . .'

'*KILL ME!*' Her voice suddenly took on a different tone. This wasn't a request, this was an order. And it was the voice of a vampire. One of the undead. For that was what she was becoming. Her pupils shrank and she lurched forward at her trembling son, revealing a new set of bright white fangs protruding beyond her lips.

Startled, JD jumped back and fell on to his ass. '*What the fuck?*'

'*KILL ME!*' his mother hissed again. Her body and soul now belonged to the undead, but her heart still belonged to her son, for a short time at least.

'I can't kill you. Don't be stupid.'

'If – you – don't – kill – me – now,' she gasped, 'I'll become one of *them*.' She pointed at the unconscious figure of Kione slumped at the other end of the kitchen. Her voice grew stronger. 'A creature of evil. I'll kill you – and your brother. Don't make me do that. I can feel the bloodlust coming over me already. Please kill me. Quickly, before it's too late.'

JD climbed back to his feet and shook his head. 'I can't. It's crazy. I can't kill you. You're my mother, for Chrissa–'

With shocking speed, Maria suddenly sprang up from the floor and leapt on him, fangs searching for the soft flesh of his neck. His sharp reactions enabled him to fend her off without even realizing what he was doing. Then, using all his strength, he threw her against the cupboards above the sink behind him. Her head hit one of the doors and she slumped to the floor in a heap at his feet.

'Oh God, Mom, I'm sorry. I didn't mean to.' He crouched down and lifted her head from the floor. 'Are you . . . ? Oh fuck. No. NO!'

The realization that his mother was now dead hit him

like a sledgehammer in the back. Her face was almost unrecognizable. Her skin was pale and clammy, blue veins had crept to the surface, her eyes blackened, her teeth pointed and razor sharp. He released his hold on her head as a cold chill ran through him. The feeling of sickness rushed over him again and he covered his mouth to stop himself vomiting again – not that his stomach seemed to have anything left in it to bring up anyway.

After a few moments of staring down at the body of what had once been his mother, he allowed the autopilot side of him to take the controls again. *Close your mind*, he told himself. *Don't think about what you're about to do. Just do it. You have to, and you know it.*

Moving as though in a trance, he left the kitchen and headed up the stairs to his mother's bedroom. She kept a gun in a drawer of the cabinet beside her bed in case any of her clients ever decided to overstep the, admittedly rather liberal, boundaries of decency she insisted upon during their visits. There had been occasions when some of her less regular clients had been overly violent during sex or had demanded their money back after an unsatisfying session (invariably their own fault). She had pulled the gun on a few occasions, but it had never been fired.

JD walked into the bedroom to be engulfed by a foul stench, and sickened by the sight of the bloodied covers on the bed in the centre of the room. Visions of his mother in agony in this room at the hands of Kione flashed through his mind, and he quickly looked away from the bed and walked over to the small wooden bedside cabinet. Pulling open the top drawer he pushed aside a few undergarments to reveal the shiny silver revolver that his mother owned. Since she had never had to fire it, it still looked bright and new. After a deep breath he picked it up and looked over it, breaking out the cylinder to check the loads. There were six, all unfired. *This is the gun I'm going to use to kill my mother.*

The thought was a vile one. It made him retch, but once again no vomit came up. His stomach was empty, his guts shrinking. *I can't do this.* Then for the first time he noticed what was standing on top of the cabinet.

A bottle of bourbon.

Snapping the cylinder back, he put the gun down on the bed beside a pool of drying blood and picked up the bottle. It was full, unopened. He stared hard at the smooth, translucent, golden-brown liquid inside. Would this stuff really take the edge off what he was about to do? It was just bourbon, after all. Just an alcoholic drink with a bit of a kick to it. Would it provide him with answers? Or strength? Only one way to find out.

The cap was screwed on tight and he was shaking so much that he struggled to twist it off. Eventually, after he had summoned just enough strength from a body that seemed hollow, it came loose and fell to the floor.

'God forgive me for all I am about to do,' he whispered aloud, holding the bottle aloft as if talking to the Lord. Then he put the neck to his lips and took his first sip.

It tasted foul.

So he took another sip. His stomach was still in knots and it was hard to keep the stuff from coming back up again. *There's but one way to keep it down*, he thought. *Pour more down after it.* So he drank more. Each sip tasted a little less foul than the one before, but no matter how many sips he took, he still wasn't ready to pick up the pistol and head back downstairs.

So he kept drinking.

The feeling of sickness soon began to pass, and adrenalin started to take over his body. Gradually the alcohol calmed his nerves. He felt it filling the hollowness inside him. A new sensation in his stomach began to take over, a burning rage as the realization of what had happened began to sink in, and the reality of what had to be done became more apparent. The autopilot was no longer in control, but nor was JD. *Something else was taking over. The thirst for blood.* Not the same thirst that a vampire has, this was an urge to kill not for food, not for sport. This was an urge to kill in order to feel alive.

Before he knew it there was suddenly just one last mouthful of bourbon left in the bottle. He took a long look at it, then sucked in one more deep breath and poured it down his throat. The thirst for blood took over completely. His shoulders arched back and his lips curled up into a sneer. His chest puffed out and he looked down at the gun he had placed on the bed. Staring down at it brought another momentary flash of the vileness that had gone before in this room, tempering his adrenalin rush a little. Suddenly the room was looking fuzzy and the gun was becoming blurred. *Better get this over with before it's too late*, he thought.

With all his might he threw the empty bourbon bottle against the wall, where it shattered noisily, shards of glass spraying everywhere. The sound it made seemed loud enough to wake the dead, and in this case it woke the undead. He heard one of the two vampires stir in the kitchen below. Taking a last deep breath, he picked up the revolver and headed out of the bedroom and back down the stairs.

When he reached the bottom he saw the still-unconscious body of Kione slumped in one corner of the kitchen. It was lying against the cupboards near the sink, the two gaping holes where its eyes had been staring blankly back at JD, but it was still unconscious. Death had not come for the creature yet and small puffs of steam were still issuing from its lips as the air was expelled from its battered lungs.

In the other corner of the kitchen, out of JD's sight, was the vampire that had once been his mother. She had climbed to her feet and was looking for some flesh to feed on. JD hardly recognized the woman as she stepped slowly over Kione and appeared in his line of vision. Her face was still caked in blood and the blue veins within it were bulging. Maria needed her first taste of human blood. Seeing him only as a potential victim, she forged a huge bloodthirsty grin at JD and charged towards him, her eyes mad with the lusting for his blood.

Standing at the foot of the stairs, JD was now struggling to maintain control over his drunkenness even with the burning rage inside him. Slowly he raised the gun in his right hand and pointed it towards the onrushing vampire. His hand had begun trembling almost uncontrollably, and the legs that had carried him down the stairs were now turning to jelly. Even to take aim was a struggle, but just as his final chance to fire came, he took it. At the last possible moment before the monster was on him, he closed his eyes and squeezed the trigger.

BANG!

The noise reverberated around the house. It was far louder than he could possibly have imagined, and it was followed by an echoing that seemed as if it would never end. Several seconds later, as the sound seemed to quieten a little, to become a mere ringing in his ears, the boy opened his eyes again. His mother's body was lying flat on its back in the kitchen doorway, smoke pouring out and upwards from a gaping hole in her chest where the bullet had entered. Her heart had been blown apart. As the smoke departed her body it floated away into nothingness, her soul passing with it.

JD's hand was no longer shaking, his grip on the gun had steadied, and for the first time he felt the wet sensation on his face where his mother's blood had sprayed over him as the bullet punched into her flesh. She lay there dead before him. Her soul had been taken, and his had been lost in the process. A window in the kitchen had somehow blown open and both their spirits had slipped out through it and vanished into the night sky.

He took two steps towards her corpse and looked down on it for a moment. The blackened eyes were unrecognizable in the bloodied face. This was not his mother any more, and he was no longer JD, the fun-loving innocent who had so recently fallen in love with Beth. He pointed the shiny silver revolver at the lifeless corpse and with a hand as steady as a rock fired the remaining bullets into its face and chest, hitting his target with great precision for a young man who had drunk so much.

When the chambers of the pistol were empty he tucked it into the back of his trousers and pulled the hood of his robe up over his head. Thanks to Kione, he had learnt a valuable lesson. When you have the chance to kill someone, never pass it up, it might come back and bite you. Kill first, worry later.

As he watched his mother's decaying body burn away into ash on the floor his anger began to build. If the men in his mother's life had not deserted her, then there was a good chance that this would not have happened. Now he was going to have to go to the house of one of those men and explain to his younger brother that he would never see his mother again. This wasn't fair. Bad things happened to good people, and it just wasn't right. He and Casper didn't deserve this.

The pain in JD's heart was agonizing. The only thing that had tempered it so far was the rush of adrenalin brought on by inflicting suffering upon others.

Fourteen

Bull wasn't best pleased. He had little tolerance for his younger half-brother at the best of times. Casper was dumb and offered nothing in the way of interesting conversation, only childish remarks. Sure, Bull understood that the kid was not quite right in the head. Deep down he felt bad for him, but at times like this he couldn't help thinking that it served the little bastard right.

Bull's mother and father had split up for a while many years earlier, and when they did so his dad, Russo, had shacked up with a hooker for a short time. The hooker fell pregnant and Casper was the end result. A retarded son of a whore. Bull's father had always suspected that the hooker, Maria, had tricked him into the pregnancy, and he had ditched her not long after the boy was born. Unfortunately for him, the law was on the side of Maria and, after a paternity test, he found himself paying her a weekly maintenance subsidy, and even occasionally having to babysit for the mistake known as Casper.

And now was one of those times. Neither Russo nor his fifteen-year-old son Bull had the patience to cope with Casper, with his overexcitable nature and moments of hyperactivity. They had been sitting in their living room in front of a warm fire enjoying a game of chess. They wore matching pairs of blue pyjamas and crimson dressing gowns in readiness for retiring to bed for the night, so an interruption from anyone was unwelcome. Particularly an interruption from a tiresome individual like Casper.

Yet here he was sitting with them in their own house,

babbling on about having to stay with them until his older brother JD came to pick him up. He was making even less sense than usual, and both Russo and Bull were convinced this had something to do with JD, whom they both despised equally. He was a troublemaker, lacking in discipline, frequently breaking the law yet always getting away with it, and he was a tough little bastard, too. He'd beaten Bull at arm wrestling countless times, which really pissed Bull off because he was very strong for his age and never lost to anyone else. JD had a slight advantage as he was a year older, but one day that would begin to count for nothing, and when that day came Bull would triumph over him, whether it be at arm wrestling or something else. That day would come. Definitely.

Casper had been drenched when he arrived. He had fought his way through the thunderstorm to their house and was now a trembling, shivering wreck, babbling on about vampires, red walls, Elvis and shotgun-toting priests. The usual crap from this little asshole.

After about twenty minutes Russo and Bull had managed between them to calm the boy down and sit him on a rug in front of the log fire. He sat there in jeans and a green sweater soaked though from the rain. His arms were wrapped tightly around his knees, hugging them in towards his chest. He was either shivering from the cold, or trembling with fear at something. Maybe even both.

Russo looked over at Bull, who had flatly refused to join JD at maria's house. His son was a handsome younger version of himself, only with more hair and whiter teeth. 'Wadda ya reckon?' he asked.

'Kid's a fruitcake. Reckon JD's s'posed to be lookin' after him and has decided to get the fuck out somewhere else and send him here. Prick.'

'Reckon you're prob'ly right. That bitch Maria. She's mos' likely on her back earnin' cash while JD's out stealin' cars. And we're stuck here with the fuckin' dimwit.' Russo was so irritated that he made no effort to hide the fact that he felt absolutely nothing for Casper.

Bull was in agreement. 'I dunno why you don't just kick him out. She says he's yours but, come on – he could be anyone's. I mean, look at the little prick. He don't look nothin' like you. He's too wimpy to be one of us.'

At that moment there came a loud knock at the back door. Bull gestured to his father to stay in his armchair. 'I'll get it,' he sighed.

He walked out of the room and into the kitchen, pulling the cloth of his pyjama bottoms out of his ass as he went. The back door was at the far end of the kitchen, and through the glass panel in the door he could see a dark, hooded figure outside.

'Who's there?' he shouted through the door.

'Is Russo home?' a husky voice filtered in from outside.

'Who wants to know?'

'Just let me in.'

'JD? That you?'

'Open the fuckin' door, will ya!'

Bull vaguely recognized the voice as JD's, though it sounded different. It had a gravelly tone to it that was unfamiliar, and not particularly friendly. He turned the key in the lock and pulled the door open.

'Russo here?' asked the voice from within the dark hood.

'You come to pick up your brother? He's drivin' us fuckin' nuts in there. Babblin' away like a two-year-old.' He paused and sniffed as JD brushed past him and in to the kitchen. '*Jesus*, man, you been drinkin'? You fuckin' stink!'

JD ignored him and strode through to the living room, where he saw his little brother sitting in front of the fireplace, drying off. For once, Casper ignored him, lost in his own thoughts. Russo was sitting in his armchair on the other side of Casper, and he looked seriously pissed. JD didn't care.

'Russo, I need a favour,' he said. It didn't sound like a request. It sounded like an order.

Russo got up from his armchair, his muscular body tensed for any confrontation. For a man in his early forties he was in pretty good shape. Only his thinning hair betrayed his age. He moved towards JD, oozing aggression in every movement. His body language spoke volumes: this man wasn't in the mood to take any shit from anyone, and he very quickly picked up on the smell of alcohol on JD's breath.

'You're all out of favours, JD. Take Casper and get the fuck out of here. Don't you ever pull this shit again. I've got two jobs. I don't have fuckin' time to keep lookin' after *him* every time you and your mother decide he's too much of a fuckin' liability for you.'

'He's not a liability.'

'He fuckin' is, an' you know it. . I ain't got the time nor the patience for him. I reckon in the grand scheme of things I've bent over backwards for that kid over the years, just 'cos I used ta feel sorry for your mother, but you an' her are both pushin' it too far. I just ain't got the time to look after a goddam retard no more. You get him out of here, and don't you ever send him back here, neither. And you can pass that on to your whore of a mother, too. I'm done with it. All. You hear me?' He took a threatening step towards JD, and added, 'Get out, take him with you, and don't fuckin' come back. Ever.'

From his place in the kitchen Bull listened intently, a smile spreading across his face. It was about time his father told these two bastards how things stood. Yet despite Russo's provocation, JD's reply was calmly considered.

'You don't understand, Russo. Something's happened. I need Casper to live here with you for a while. I can't explain right now.'

Russo pushed JD in the chest. 'You just don't get it, do ya? Why can't you leave us alone? What the fuck's wrong with you? You're a drunk, and your brother's a retard. *Get the fuck out*. Go on.'

'Russo, you don't understand.'

'What part of "Get the fuck out" don't you understand?'

'*Goddammit*! Will you just listen a minute?'

'*I said OUT!*' Russo turned to Casper. 'And you, Casper. Get your fuckin' coat on. You're goin' home.' But the boy appeared not to hear him, and continued to stare blankly

ahead of him into the flames. '*Casper. Hey! Hey you! Retard!*'
He had a way of pronouncing the last word – 'Ree-tarred' –
that made it sound especially humiliating.

In the kitchen, Bull was helping himself to a carton of milk
from the fridge. This was an argument he'd be best staying out
of. Sure was interesting, though. As he was opening the carton
in order to pour some of its contents into a pint glass on the
kitchen sideboard, he heard JD's reply. His voice had taken on
a sinister tone, like nothing he'd ever heard before.

'You call my brother a retard again, and I swear to God,
I'll drop you.'

'What?'

'Drop you. *For real.*'

'You threatenin' me, you little shit?'

Bull smiled to himself. If JD was taking a threatening
tone with his father then most likely he'd finally get the hiding
he so richly deserved. His father had been talking for years
about teaching the boy some discipline. It would be a beating
that JD had been asking for. Russo was a former Green Beret,
and a master in hand-to-hand combat. If, after all these years,
he decided to administer a beating to the boy it would be swift
and very painful.

If JD replied, Bull didn't hear him. *Hah!* he thought.
Probably shittin' himself now, and backin' down. He heard
his father making it clear to JD one last time.

'Right, now get out. You ain't welcome. Truth is, you
never were, nor your brother, neither.'

JD's voice came again, once more in the sinister rasping
tone. 'Casper. Put your coat on. We're going.' At last he seemed
to have got the message. *So much for the tough-guy act.*

Bull finished pouring the remains of the milk into his glass
and walked over to the flip-top bin in the corner of the kitchen
to dispose of the carton. He heard his father get in one last dig
at Casper, just to rile JD and remind him who was boss.

'Come on! Hurry up, for Chrissakes, you little retarded
bastard.'

Bull slammed the waxed-paper milk carton into the bin,

the noise masking the loud cracking sound that came from the living room. He was still smirking to himself as he walked back to pick up his glass of milk from the sideboard by the sink. Before he reached it he was nearly knocked over by Casper, who rushed past him and out through the back door. The look on the young boy's face was one of terror, as if he had seen a horrible apparition. The kid was terrified of something, making no attempt to close the door behind him or wait for JD to catch up with him. He ran straight out, leaving the door wide open, allowing a gust of wind and rain to blow in.

Bull took a large swig from his glass of milk. A moment later the hooded figure of JD walked out of the living room and brushed past him, deliberately knocking his arm and causing him to spill a little of his milk. His face was still hidden inside the recesses of the dark cowl. *Prick,* Bull thought as he smiled and waved at JD's departing back.

'Bye,' he said sardonically. 'See ya. Come again.'

To Bull's annoyance, JD made no attempt to shut the door behind him, so he put his milk back down and walked over to shut and lock it to keep the howling wind and rain out. With the door closed, an eerie silence seemed to settle on the house. The living room was quiet now, and Bull half expected his father to walk out and start ranting about JD. After waiting a few seconds he called out.

'Wanna drink, Dad? They're gone.'

No answer.

'Dad?'

Still no answer. Bull picked up his glass of milk again. Then he walked out of the kitchen and into the living room. There he saw a sight so ghastly that it would haunt him for the rest of his days. He was only fifteen. He had never seen death up close, but here it was. And it was his father who'd done the dying. The glass of milk slipped from his hand, bouncing off his foot and on to the floor.

'Jesus Christ! Dad! Oh fuck, no!'

His father was lying on his back on the floor. His neck had been broken and his head was twisted to one side. His tongue was hanging out and his eyes had rolled up into his skull, so that only the whites were showing.

Once Bull's initial shock at seeing his father's corpse had passed, it was replaced by rage. The hatred he had always felt for JD erupted like a volcano in the pit of his stomach, engulfing his entire body. Like a man possessed, he rushed through the kitchen to the back door, unlocked it and wrenched it open. The night sky revealed nothing to him but the heaviest of rain and a gale-force wind buffeting the house. He shouted into the darkness to make sure his voice carried as far as the wind would take it.

'You muthafucker! I'll kill you, JD! You just wait!' He struggled to hold back the tears of sadness and rage that were trying to force their way out of the corners of his eyes. *'One day, when you think it's all forgotten, I'll be waitin' for you. You fuckin' cunt. You're a walking corpse, man. I'll fuckin' kill you. Mark my words! God might forgive you one day, but when He does I'll be waiting for you! FUCKIN' BASTARD MUTHAFUCKER!'*

As if only to unleash his rage, Bull continued to howl out into the wind and rain for quite some time. He wanted to remember this feeling, wanted to be certain that the next time his path crossed with JD's he would react accordingly.

By killing the bastard.

Fifteen

Back to the Future

Captain Robert Swann, US Special Forces, had been interned in a secret maximum-security prison in the desert beyond the outskirts of Santa Mondega for almost three years. In that time he had not had one single visitor. The same could be said for most of the other prisoners. These were men who had been forgotten about, whose former lives, many of them, had been expunged from all records. Of the four hundred inmates, only a handful would ever again be lucky enough to see the sun rise as free men. These prisoners all knew something that they shouldn't, or had done something so hideous to someone they shouldn't have messed with, that they were effectively on Death Row, but with no mercy killing to put a point to their terms.

Swann's crime was a singularly unpleasant one. He was a serial rapist, and he had made the mistake of perpetrating one of his most vicious rapes on the daughter of someone high up in government. His victim had been so traumatized by the brutality of the attack that she had taken her own life shortly afterwards. As it happened, this worked in Swann's favour, for her suicide meant there was insufficient evidence to proceed with a formal court martial. Not only that, but he had been lucky enough not to have been secretly executed for his crime. Indeed, he had not even been dishonourably discharged from the service – technically, he was still a serving officer.

Swann had one thing on his side that kept him alive. It was why he was fortunate enough to be serving his time in the secret desert prison. He was a highly decorated Army veteran, a man with talents of such incredible rarity in the field of combat that it made no sense for his own government to erase him. Further, he had once saved the life of the White House Director of Communications. All this was just enough to save his neck, though even then it had been a near-run thing. Swann was an exceptional soldier, fearless and willing to die for his country; he just couldn't keep his snake in its cage. Even now, at the age of thirty-seven, he was still a rampaging sex monster, and being cooped up in prison for such a long time had made his appetite insatiable.

In the very early hours of the seventeenth morning of October, Swann was awoken in his cell by two armed guards. He was smart enough not to resist when they handcuffed him roughly, and despite his requests to know what was going on, and their refusal to answer, he made little fuss simply because he was grateful for the break from the tedium of his normal routine.

He was escorted through the prison corridors and a seemingly endless succession of security doors directly to the Warden's office. After being shoved through the door he was pushed down on to a chair in front of the Warden's desk. He had only ever been in this office once before, and that had been on his first day, when he had had the prison rules rammed home to him by Warden Gunton.

The office was twice the size of the shitty cell in which Swann had been living for the last few years. It had shelves on all four walls adorned with books and ornaments, with here and there the occasional painting hung where there were gaps in the shelving. Set between two windows behind the desk was a large painting of the grey-haired, leather-skinned Gunton, just to emphasize how vain the man was. He was wearing a smart grey suit in the portrait. This would have come as no surprise to anyone who knew him. The Warden had ten suits, all identical, all grey, all boring. That, however, summed up the man perfectly.

The only curious thing on this dark morning was that the Warden wasn't seated in the chair behind his desk, as Swann might have expected. There was another man sitting there. Not a weaselly little fella like the Warden, either, but a big, broad-shouldered muthafucker who could have passed a night-club bouncer. Same grey suit as the Warden, different face. Different aura. This man had a pale, smooth-shaved head, and a pair of dark sunglasses hid his eyes. *The shades are clearly for show, as it's night time,* Swann pondered. *Or maybe the guy is blind? Hmmm. Unlikely.*

The two guards who had escorted Swann nodded at this man and made their exits via the door through which they had come. The man stared at Swann through his dark glasses, his face giving nothing away. The prisoner wondered if maybe this man was admiring the fact that he had a full head of hair, for although his head was shaved at the sides, Swann had a thick crop of brown hair on top. Maybe the guy was envious? Probably not, though it was possible. For almost thirty seconds neither of them spoke. It was Swann who cracked first.

'Okay, I give up. What?' he said, looking out of the window to emphasize his unconcern at the intimidating stare of the man opposite him.

'Want those cuffs off?' the man asked.

'Sure. Why not?'

'Hands on the table.'

It was an order, and Swann didn't like taking orders from someone he didn't know. At this point, however, he was still an inmate, and this guy might well turn out to be someone high up in the Secret Service or some such organization, so he played ball and held his hands out over the desk. The bullish man reached over and took hold of Swann's wrists. He had a very firm grip. Quickly turning the other man's hands upside down inside their restraints, with one swift movement, during which he really didn't seem to do anything much, he made the handcuffs break in three places and fall free of Swann's wrists and on to the desk.

Swann was impressed. That was a neat trick, no doubt

about it. Even so, he didn't allow his face to give anything away, and he sat back in his chair without so much as a thank you.

'So. You want out of this place?' asked the man in the Warden's chair.

'Name's Robert Swann, since you didn't ask.'

'I know who you are, thank you.'

'And yet you haven't bothered to introduce yourself. Kinda rude, if you ask me.'

The man smiled. 'You can call me Mr E.'

'As in Mystery Man?'

'No. As in Mr E.'

'Awright, keep your hair . . . on.'

Mr E smiled. Swann could sense that this man was admiring his attitude. In this he was right. Swann had exactly the kind of arrogant, sonofabitch, take-no-shit persona that Mr E was looking for.

'I've arranged for you to receive a full pardon, Mr Swann.'

'Thanks. Guess I'll be on my way then,' said Swann getting up from his seat.

'No. You won't. Siddown. The smartass act will get you so far, but don't overcook it. It's not cool, and you're not twelve, so stop it.'

Swann sat back down. Mission accomplished. He'd pissed this guy off enough. Time now to listen and see what the deal on offer was.

'Go on then. Gimme what ya got,' he said, rubbing his hands together in anticipation of whatever might be coming his way.

'I need a guy with iron balls to work undercover for me. A tough job. Life threatening.'

'Undercover? Where?'

'Santa Mondega.'

'Go screw yourself.' Swann's reaction was instinctive.

'Hold on a second. There's something a little different about this job. The undercover agent will be infiltrating a gang of vampires, disguising himself as one of them.'

'Go screw yourself again, you baldass muthafucker! Do I look like a cunt to you?'

'Yes. But you're not listening. This job is not as bad as it sounds. Let me finish.' Mr E remained calm in the face of the insults and general shitty attitude of Robert Swann. 'A Hubal monk has returned to Santa Mondega with the Eye of the Moon, and I want you to find him, and *it*.'

Swann still wasn't quite listening. This was a mission for an idiot, and he was no idiot. 'And just how the hell am I supposed to pass myself off as a fuckin' vampire?' he asked.

'You won't. First off, I just want you to find the guy who *will* work undercover as a vampire. We have developed a serum that will allow a mortal man to walk among the undead without them being aware that he is not one of them. I need your skills as an interrogator and your undercover experience to train this new guy so that he doesn't get killed within five minutes.'

Swann breathed an inward sigh of relief. So at least he wasn't expected to be the new soon-to-be dead undercover agent.

'Who's "we"?' he asked suspiciously.

'You don't need to know that.'

'But it's official? From the Goddam highest-in-the-land, kinda thing?'

'How else would I be here, talking to you now? And where do you think a free pardon comes from?'

'Uh-huh. But only a complete and utter fuckin' brain-dead moron would take on a job like this. And I gotta tell you, I don't think I've met the moron that'll take this one.'

'Quite right,' said Mr E. 'You haven't met him. Yet. But there is such a man.'

Swann shook his head. He thought he knew everyone in the Special Forces skilled and brave enough to take on the top jobs, and this sounded like the top job in a very short list of top jobs. So it had to be someone new. Someone who had flown up through the ranks in the few years he had been away.

'Go on,' he said, smiling now. 'Enlighten me. Who's the

man with balls enough to infiltrate a gang of vampires and pretend to be one of them, with only a serum and some white foundation as a disguise? I gotta know this. And even if he's brave enough and stupid enough to do it, what exactly is his incentive? How much is this kamikaze joker gettin' paid?'

'Paid? Ha!' Mr E sat forward again, leaning across the desk, smiling at Swann. 'No, this guy will do it for free.'

Swann was now beginning to suspect that this was a joke of some kind. Maybe even at his expense, but he continued to play along nonetheless. 'Jeez, he really *is* a moron. So . . . What's his name?'

Mr E slid a stiff brown envelope over the desk. The convict picked it up. It was reasonably light, suggesting that details about this mystery man were fairly limited. He opened the flap at the top and pulled out a black-and-white five-by-eight photo of a guy dressed in a Terminator outfit. He placed it on the desk and then pulled out the remaining contents, which amounted to nothing more than a few typewritten sheets of paper containing the personal details of the man in the photo. It didn't take Swann long to scan the information and realize that this clown had no military or law-enforcement background. He pulled out the last sheet, which was headed 'Mission Details'. He scanned that, too, realizing at once that there was little danger in this charade for him. Mr E had told the truth: it was this guy who was at risk.

'What the fuck? Who the fuck is Dante Vittori? And why the fuck is *he* your man?'

Mr E surprised Swann by allowing himself a slight snigger. The bald head and sunglasses gave the impression that he didn't have much of a sense of humour.

'Actually, this man is more than qualified. Firstly, he knows about the vampires in Santa Mondega, so there's no issues with breach of confidentiality, because this guy has seen the undead in action with his own eyes.'

'Okay.' Swann sounded as unconvinced as he felt.

'And secondly, as well as being a total moron, our research shows that he's almost completely fearless, if only because he's too fucking witless to realize when he's in danger.' He paused a moment. 'Thirdly, he's got an incentive. I have with me a tape of a film made by the Santa Mondega Police Department. It's a short re-enactment of the shootout in a bar called the Tapioca during last year's eclipse, using actors. The bartender, Sanchez, gave an eyewitness account of the events as they happened, and a short film was compiled in order to try to track down the culprits. The footage shows Dante Vittori dressed as the Terminator, shooting up the place with a monk in a Cobra Kai outfit, and that well-known serial killer the Bourbon Kid. The three of them will probably all get the chair if they ever get caught alive. Here, watch.'

Mr E turned around and pointed a remote control at the Warden's portable television, which stood on a small table in a corner of the office. The screen fizzled on and after a few seconds the picture became lighter, and Robert Swann realized he was watching what was probably a fairly accurate reconstruction of the Tapioca eclipse massacre. Mr E began to narrate the action as he pointed at the TV. On screen was a scene filmed inside the bar. There were a number of mannequins scattered around the floor of the barroom, representing the vast number of corpses that had been revealed when the eclipse ended and daylight returned.

'You will see at the bottom of the screen *here* –' he pointed – 'as the eclipse ends, that Dante Vittori, dressed in his Terminator outfit, comes charging out of the toilets and joins in the action.' Mr E paused the tape for a moment. 'Now you'll see there's a young Hubal monk – *here* – aiming a gun at the Bourbon Kid, and there's a girl on the ground – *here* – who's barely alive.'

Swann was fascinated. Catching just a glimpse of some of this exciting footage was a real privilege. Since being imprisoned he had been lucky to watch any television at all, and what he had seen had all been family viewing. Mr E continued the video playback and carried on with his narration.

'Now you'll see that instead of aiming his shotgun at the Bourbon Kid, who's just killed about a hundred people, our man Vittori instead points it at the back of the monk's head. This is the first clue we have that he's an idiot. The monk then discusses something with our man before retreating out through a back entrance. Then comes the second clue that our man Dante is a total meathead. Instead of killing the Bourbon Kid, he next turns his gun on the dying girl on the floor. The Kid joins in, and the pair of them blow her pretty much to bits.'

The two men watched the footage in silence for a few moments before Mr E picked up his commentary again.

'After that it gets a bit crap. The bartender Sanchez, who's meant to be the guy – *there* – dressed as Batman, jumps over the bar and beats the Bourbon Kid in a fist fight and the Kid runs away like a coward.'

'No shit?'

'Yeah, but no one believes that part. Apparently this Sanchez guy swears it's true and wasn't willing to cooperate with the video unless it was kept in.'

'Jerk.'

'Quite.'

'So what actually happened to this Dante guy after the shootout?'

'Well, he got away and probably thinks no one knows he was involved. But he was in the bar with this broad.' Mr E slid a six-by-four-inch blowup of a very pretty, dark-haired young woman's passport headshot over the desk to Swann. 'Her name is Kacy Fellangi, and our guy Dante will do anything for her. So all we gotta do, is find Dante, find his girlfriend, and bingo! – we got ourselves an undercover vampire.'

Swann still wasn't convinced. He didn't think he was ever going to be, either.

'Yeah yeah. But if this guy is such a moron, surely the vampires will see through him straight away?'

'Sure, there's a good chance of that, but it's a chance I'm willing to take. You just find me Dante Vittori and Kacy Fellangi. Once we make him an offer he can't refuse and give him the impression his girlfriend will suffer if he doesn't do as we ask, then he'll be right on board.'

'Okay. Any idea where I'm gonna start looking for this guy?'

'It's not gonna be too hard, in fact. I've had surveillance guys tracing him for some time, just waiting for him to stick his head above the parapet and pop up on our radar.' He paused briefly, then asked, 'Now, you know how I said he's a total moron?'

Swann sensed that Mr E was placing a little more emphasis on the fact that Dante was a moron than was really necessary. The point had been established, so why keep bringing it up?

'Yeah?' he asked sceptically, intrigued in spite of himself as to what his would-be new employer was about to reveal.

'Well, we know that he and Kacy left Santa Mondega right after the eclipse. And we think they moved to Florida, which is a pretty sensible thing to do if you know that Santa Mondega is rife with the undead. Right? But guess what? Two days ago he called the Santa Mondega International Hotel and booked the honeymoon suite for a week at the end of this month.'

'You're kidding?'

'Nope. Turns out he's planning on marrying the girl Kacy and sweeping her off for a surprise honeymoon in Santa Mondega.'

Swann shook his head. 'What a fuckin' loser.'

'That same thought had occurred to me'

The two men finally shared a smile. An understanding had been reached after all. Mr E knew that Swann was smart enough to work out what was required from here on, and provided him just one more titbit of information.

'In those files is what I believe to be the current address where Vittori and Fellangi are staying. We traced it from Vittori's credit-card details. Now I want you to go and get the pair of them. Once you've got them on board, issue the guy with this mission.'

Instead of studying the paper with the mission details on it that he had pulled from the brown envelope, Swann picked up the photo of Kacy and took a closer look at it.

'This is the girl, huh?' he asked, knowing perfectly well that it was.

'Yes.'

He looked back up at Mr E. 'And you're gonna want them both killed when the mission's done, right?'

'I don't recall having said that.'

'But that's the truth of it, ain't it?'

'Yeah. Yeah, that's right.'

'Shame,' said Swann, tutting. 'I could really enjoy ruinin' this chick.'

Mr E got up from the desk and turned his back on Swann, preferring to stare at the painting of the Warden between the two windows.

'So fuck her before you kill her,' he said without emotion. 'Or . . . kill her . . . then fuck her. I don't care which. Just make sure they're both dead when the mission is over. Whether it's successful or not.' He pulled a small white envelope from the inside pocket of his grey suit and held it out to Swann. 'That's your pardon. Dated today, and signed by the President. Don't lose it – such things are not easy to come by.'

Swann took it, popped it and the photo of the girl into the brown envelope with the details of the mission and of Vittori, and got up to leave.

'Sure thing, boss.' He raised an eyebrow and smiled to himself. 'Consider it done. *All of it.*'

Sixteen

It was no great secret that Dante didn't like fortune tellers. Yet here he was again, sitting at a round table opposite some mad old crone with his gorgeous sweetheart Kacy beside him.

The premises were nothing too special this time, either. The three of them were in a tent, albeit a fairly spacious one, but it was just about the crummiest joint of any of the numerous fortune tellers they had visited. In fairness, the tent was one of many at a travelling fairground, so not much should have been expected really. 'Madame Sangria' was the name of the psychic in question. An elderly lady in a shapeless black dress, she wore her hair in a red bandanna, and affected huge gold rings in her ear lobes and at least five cheap multi-coloured beaded necklaces hanging down over her bosom.

Today was Dante and Kacy's fifth 'anniversary', and Dante had promised his girlfriend that he had a big surprise in store for her. Kacy was well aware that they weren't about to head out for a fancy meal at an expensive restaurant. If that had been the case, Dante would surely have insisted she wore something more appropriate than the blue jeans and baggy grey sweatshirt she had picked out for the day. He too would probably have made more of an effort, rather than choosing a pair of ripped jeans and a dirty white T-shirt with a picture of Foghorn Leghorn on the front.

Since Kacy knew Dante's mind better than anyone, she was fully prepared for the great surprise to be crap. *And this is crap*, she thought. They had been to many fortune tellers in the past because she enjoyed the whole experience, but that didn't mean she wanted to go to another one as a special treat to celebrate the five years they had been together. The only comfort she took from this outing was that she knew Dante had probably racked his brain for weeks before coming up with the idea. So, grateful for the fact that he had at least put some thought into it, she was happy, sort of. After all, Dante may not have been particularly sharp, but he had a really good heart, and even if what he believed was a bit of creative genius – taking her to yet another fortune teller – was actually totally lame, it didn't matter. The important thing was that he loved her enough to make the effort.

Dante had paid Madame Sangria twenty dollars to read the Tarot for Kacy. The woman had dealt out cards on to the round table in front of her. It was a small table with a dirty red-and-white checked tablecloth draped over it. After laying the cards face down on it in a line she slowly turned them over one at a time. In an attempt to create some suspense she said nothing as she did this. She allowed the cards themselves to do the talking.

> Card One – The Lovers
> Card Two – The Fool
> Card Three – The Ace of Cups
> Card Four – The Devil
> Card Five – Death
> And Card Six . . .

When Kacy saw the sixth card her heart leapt into her throat. This was no normal tarot card. This one was special. There was no other card like it in all the different sets of tarot cards in the whole world. It had no picture on it, just writing, and it said:

Kacy I love you with all my heart. Will you marry me?

She turned to look at Dante and immediately grabbed hold of his hand to steady herself. He had stolen her breath away. This man she loved, this well-renowned moron with half a brain cell, had taken her completely by surprise. She was all his.

'Yes,' she mumbled, her eyes welling up. 'I love you too, you muppet.'

'Cool,' said Dante, leaning over and kissing her full on the lips. 'Now let's get the fuck outta here and go get drunk.'

'You bet.'

Dante winked at the old fortune teller on the other side of the table, muttered a quick *Thanks* under his breath, and led Kacy out of the tent. Once they were back in the open air he pulled her tightly to him and they kissed as passionately as they had ever done. Kacy didn't want to let him go. Her heart was bursting as though it was ready to flee her chest, such was her happiness.

'I'm gonna make you so happy,' she whispered to her new fiancé.

'You already did,' he whispered back. 'You said "Yes".'

A third voice, a man's, interrupted them.

'Dante Vittori, you're under arrest.'

As statements go, it brought Dante and Kacy crashing back to earth in an instant. Dante spoke aloud for both of them.

'Oh for fuck's sake!'

Standing in front of them were two burly men in smart black suits with grey ties and very dark sunglasses. Dante pulled away from Kacy and faced up to the pair.

'So what have I done now?'

Behind the two men, a number of families and odd-looking carnival folk were wandering around the fairground, oblivious to Dante's predicament. There were a hundred more exciting things to catch their attention, like coconut shies and merry-go-rounds. Two men in suits speaking to a scruffy young couple was low on anyone's list of Things to See and Do.

The man who had spoken first, a big, heavily moustached character with an Arabic look to him, held up and then flipped open a wallet to reveal an ID card with his picture on it tucked inside. He didn't give Dante and Kacy enough time to read what was on the card before he flicked the wallet shut again.

'I'm Special Agent Baez, and this is Special Agent Johnson,' he said, indicating the other man. 'You're wanted in connection with a series of murders in Santa Mondega. It is in your best interests to come quietly. If you choose to struggle we'll be forced to restrain you with whatever force may be necessary. Don't test me on this.'

Madame Sangria popped her head out of the tent entrance to see what was going on.

Dante threw her an icy glare. 'Some fuckin' fortune teller you are,' he complained. 'Gimme my Goddam twenty bucks back, you useless old hag.'

The old woman smiled at him. 'I guess that fool card was you, then?'

'Not necessarily,' said Dante, turning back to face the smartly dressed figure of Agent Baez. 'Look at that.' He pointed to the sky behind the agent.

'I'm not falling for that old trick,' Baez sighed, shaking his head.

'You already did,' said Dante.

Special Agent Baez looked confused for perhaps a tenth of a second, which was all the time Dante needed to lunge forward and headbutt him in the face. There was a loud crack as the man's nose broke, followed by a soft thudding noise as Dante kicked him in the balls. As the agent doubled over in pain with blood spurting from his nose, Dante grabbed him by the back of the head and brought his knee up full into his face. Baez collapsed in a heap on the ground and began to vomit as he did his best to squeeze his stomach down and force his balls back out from wherever they were now situated.

Dante whirled round, looking to deal with the other guy. But the second agent was way ahead of him. As soon as he had seen Dante attack his colleague, Johnson had pulled a gun from inside his jacket and pointed it at Kacy's head.

'One more clever move from you, friend, and your girlfriend's gonna feel my pain,' he warned.

Dante recoiled. This was a fight that couldn't be won. 'Yeah, bite me, dickhead,' he said bitterly.

A third man suddenly materialized from behind Dante. Before Kacy could warn him, the new arrival (who happened to be Special Agent Robert Swann) had knocked the young man unconscious with a single swift blow to the back of the neck.

'This is definitely our guy,' he said, looking down at Dante's crumpled, unmoving form. Then he looked over at Kacy and grinned. 'Hello, missy. My, you sure are a pretty little thing, ain't you?'

Seventeen

Dante and Kacy had spent an extremely unpleasant evening travelling in the back of a security van. Both of them had suffered the indignity of having their wrists handcuffed behind their backs and black cloth bags placed over their heads and tied at the neck. When the van had eventually come to a stop, the young lovers had been taken out and separated. Dante had no idea what had become of Kacy, and her welfare was paramount in his thoughts when, after what seemed like an interminable walk guided by at least one agent, the bag he was wearing was finally removed.

He looked around and discovered he was sitting in front of a desk in a smart oval-shaped office. It had no windows, but the royal blue carpet, bright white walls and smart mahogany furniture gave the impression that it was the office or meeting room of someone who earned a lot of money. That person was most probably the guy sitting opposite him. The smooth-headed, smartly suited, sunglasses-wearing Mr E.

'Is this the White House?' Dante asked.

'Yes, it is,' Mr E said, without any expression on his face. 'And I'm the *real* President of the United States. That guy you see on TV? He's just an actor.'

Dante wasn't totally convinced.

'Is that right?' he asked warily.

'No.' Mr E shook his head. This guy Dante Vittori didn't disappoint. He was living up to his billing. The perfect fall guy. 'Have you any idea why you're here?'

Dante shrugged. 'Is it anythin' to do with sellin' pirate videos?'

Mr E rubbed his forehead with his left hand. It had not taken long for him to realize that talking to Dante was going to be frustrating; indeed, merely sitting opposite someone of such low intelligence was beginning to irritate him already. Mr E prided himself on his own high intelligence. He didn't want it sullied.

Standing behind Dante's left shoulder was Robert Swann. Mr E gestured to him with his other hand. Swann immediately twisted Dante's head around to the left a little to face a giant plasma TV screen on the wall. Then he flicked a button on a remote control in his hand and barked an order.

'Watch this. It should answer that "How much shit am I in?" question you've been asking yourself.'

Dante watched the videotape re-enactment of events in the Tapioca during and after the eclipse. The actor playing his part looked nothing like him, but watching and recollecting the events as they unfolded on the screen caused him to smile and nod to himself in approval of his character's handiwork with a gun. The actor did a pretty good job of blowing holes in Jessica the Vampire Queen.

'Pretty cool, huh?' He smiled smugly as the film ended.

'Not so much,' said Mr E, shaking his head again. 'That'll get you the electric chair, my friend. There's a hundred dead bodies there. So far no killer has been tried, let alone sentenced for their murders.'

Recognizing an opportunity to be annoying, Dante grabbed it with both hands. 'They sure don't look like no dead bodies to me. Look more like mannequins. I don't reckon it's a crime to kill a mannequin, is it?'

Mr E sighed in frustration, completely failing to realize that Dante was jerking his string. 'It's a re-enactment, you fool. The mannequins are there for show. We could hardly use the real dead bodies, could we?'

'One of 'em looks like Kim Cattrall.'

'Oh, for Chrissakes, is this guy for real?' asked Mr E, looking for sympathy from Swann.

'He's being a cock,' Swann suggested from where he

stood, just behind Dante. 'I think he wants to go to the chair, myself. Making crap jokes like he's doing is a sign of guilt if you ask me. Reckon he killed all those other folks, not just the dying girl. Be easy to try him for all their deaths too.'

Dante recognized that the time for joking had passed. 'Well, I didn't kill 'em all. It was that fuckin' crazy in the hood. He must have fired off about two hundred shots in two minutes. Me? I only shot the psycho vampire broad on the floor. And you can't murder someone who's already dead. Which everybody knows vampires are.'

Swann patted Dante on the shoulder.

'That's as may be, kid, but there's no evidence to show that it wasn't you who killed several of the other victims, is there? And we haven't ruled out the possibility that you were working as an accomplice of the Bourbon Kid.'

'Well,' said Dante, removing Swann's hand from his shoulder and turning to eyeball him. 'I reckon the video footage you just played shows quite clearly that I was in the bathroom with the candlestick and Professor Plum. If that's all you got on me, I'll be on my way, thanks.'

Mr E glanced over at Swann. The two men exchanged a quick look that was wasted on Dante. It was a look that said, *Hey, this is definitely our guy. He's got balls.*

'Dante,' said Mr E, smiling at him in as warm a manner as he could muster. 'How would you like to work undercover for the US Government on a secret mission that only you can pull off?'

Dante stopped eyeballing Swann and turned back to Mr E. He paused momentarily, as though deep in thought.

'No thanks, I gotta get home.'

'Sorry. You're not going home. Not for a while, anyway. It's either prison and then the electric chair, or complete our mission and then get a full pardon from the President.'

'Pardon?'

'That's right, a full pardon.'

'No I meant "Pardon, I didn't hear any of that." I'm deaf in my right ear.'

'Oh, I'm sorry.' Mr E actually sounded apologetic. 'What I said was . . .'

'I know what you said. I'm not *really* deaf, you moron.'

A sense of humour like Dante's was utterly wasted on someone like Mr E. It baffled him, to say the least.

'Look here, young man. Is your answer "Yes", or what?'

'My answer to what?'

'Will you take our mission and work undercover for the government?'

'What's the mission? Find you a new wig?'

Mr E sighed again, unable to hide his annoyance, not so much at the comment itself but at the childish intent behind it. Even so, he began to speak, slowly and with exaggerated care. 'We want you to go undercover as a vampire and infiltrate a ruthless gang of the undead in Santa Mondega. We believe they may have the Eye of the Moon in their possession. We have reason to believe that the young Hubal monk Peto, who was in the Tapioca with you during the eclipse, has returned to Santa Mondega with the Eye and is using its powers to conceal himself among the vampires.'

'Why the fuck would he want to do that?'

'He is looking for the Bourbon Kid. The Kid killed all of the monks of Hubal last year with the exception of Peto Solomon, the young monk you met. He escaped with the Eye of the Moon. We suspect that he has learnt how to use the Eye and is planning on exacting some sort of revenge on the Bourbon Kid. And although that wouldn't be such a bad thing, we need that stone, because the chances are if Peto and the Kid cross paths, the Kid will end up with the Eye, and we cannot allow that to happen.'

'Why not?'

'It's too complicated to explain to the likes of you, Mr Vittori. Just mingle with the vampires, find Peto, find the stone and bring it to us. My suspicion is that if Peto is disguising himself as a vampire and sees you, he will approach you. Technically, you're the closest thing he has to a friend in that godforsaken city. Once you give us the monk and the stone –

or just the stone – you and your girlfriend can go free.'

Dante laughed aloud for less than two seconds before sensing from Mr E's expression that he was deadly serious.

'You must think I'm, like, a total moron,' he grinned. Mr E and Swann exchanged another brief glance. Dante sat back and crossed his right leg over his left. 'Not a fuckin' chance. Find some other sucker,' he added.

'Nope. Can't do that,' said Swann. 'You take the mission on, or, believe me, I will personally see to it that you and your girlfriend suffer. Think of the worst thing that could possibly happen to you, and I can assure you you're not even close to what I have in store for you.'

'I dunno, I can imagine some pretty horrible stuff,' Dante replied nonchalantly.

'Like what?'

'Well, I once sat through three Nicholas Cage films in one day. That was pretty bad.'

'Smartass. This will be worse than anything you can imagine.'

Dante gasped. 'A Chris Tucker triple bill?'

Swann's patience was exhausted. 'Think about watching your girlfriend suffer at the hands of a group of my men, and you're still not close. One more smart comment from you, and I'll make it happen even *after* you've said yes to the mission we're offering you.'

'Okay, okay. You've made your point. I'll do it. Shit, man, get a sense of humour, will ya?'

Swann placed his hand back on Dante's shoulder, tightening his grip until it was just a little uncomfortable.

'Maybe this guy's not so dumb after all,' he said, raising his eyebrows.

Mr E nodded in agreement. 'Take him away and start injecting him with the serum. It'll help if he has a few days to get used to the effects before we send him in.'

Eighteen

In Professor Bertram Cromwell's office at the museum, the phone on his antique wooden desk rang only once before he snatched it up. He had been expecting it to ring, and could not contain his eagerness to answer it. The display on the telephone indicated that the call was from the reception desk, and as Cromwell knew even the smallest detail about what went on in his museum, he knew that it would be Susan Fraser on the other end.

'Hello, Susan.'

'Hi, Mr Cromwell. I have a gentleman here to see you. A Mr Solomon.'

'Exellent. Thank you, Susan. I've been expecting him. Could you get someone to escort him down to my office, please?'

'Certainly, sir. I'll send him right down.'

'Thanks again. Goodbye.'

Cromwell had not been this excited about a meeting for a very long time. The last surviving Hubal monk was, apparently, on his way down to his office. The day before, he had received an unexpected call from this monk asking for a few minutes of his time. He had agreed to the request immediately. There were things he could learn from this person, and no doubt a few pieces of his own information that he might share with his visitor.

Within a couple of minutes there came a knock at his office door.

'Come in,' he called, intrigued to see what the meeting would bring,

The door was opened by a security guard, who duly ushered a slightly built young man in and closed the door behind him. The Hubal monk took a look around Cromwell's office, marvelling at the two side walls covered from ceiling to floor in shelves full of hardback books. After a few seconds he focused his gaze upon the Professor, who had risen from the large black chair in which he had been sitting at his desk.

'Mr Solomon,' he said urbanely, 'or may I call you Peto? Please do take a seat.' He gestured politely at one of two smaller black leather chairs on the side of the desk opposite him.

As was his custom, Cromwell was wearing an exquisitely smart and extremely expensive hand-built suit, a perfectly cut charcoal-grey three-piece with an immaculately pressed white shirt underneath, and a silk tie in a soft red that was so understated that it could only have been handmade at exorbitant cost. He peered over the narrow half-moon lenses of his glasses at the monk, who was not nearly so well dressed.

Peto had on a pair of black combat trousers and a skin-tight black sleeveless wraparound karate top with a thin yellow lining to it. He had also grown a thick head of dark hair, although all of it bar the front inch or so was hidden beneath a red bandanna he had tied around his head, pirate fashion. He acknowledged Cromwell's offer of a seat by bowing his head and then walking over to the desk, his sandals clapping against the wooden floorboards as he went. Reaching the desk, he stood opposite the silver-haired museum director and finally spoke.

'I thank you again for your time, Professor Cromwell. It is much appreciated.'

'On the contrary,' the Professor replied, holding out a hand over the desk. 'The pleasure is all mine. So marvellous to meet you.'

Peto shook Cromwell's hand, and both men sat down. 'You know why I'm here?' the monk began.

'At a guess, I'd say it concerns the mummified remains of Rameses Gaius.'

'Damn right.' The monk smiled briefly. 'I heard that the mummy was stolen from your museum around the same time last year as all of my Hubal brothers were slaughtered by the Bourbon Kid.'

'You are absolutely correct. The very night the Bourbon Kid landed on your island and murdered Ishmael Taos and all of the Hubal monks, was the night the mummy went missing. I would suggest, however, that you're wrong about one thing. I don't believe it was stolen. I believe it escaped.'

There was a pause as each man waited for the other's reaction. Cromwell was looking to see whether the monk would believe him. Peto was waiting to see if the Professor was trying to make a fool of him. Eventually both settled on the idea that they shared common ground. Peto spoke up first.

'I suspected as much. So you know about the curse of the mummy?'

'Naturally,' said Cromwell, breathing an inward sigh of relief. 'It is not something that I would expect anyone other than you to believe, however. If I were to tell anyone else about it, they would quite certainly have me institutionalized. Indeed, the fact that I believe it seriously troubles me, too. I do not mind admitting to you that I have been questioning my own sanity at times.'

'Yeah,' the monk sympathized. 'I know what you mean, but last time I came to this town I saw some pretty strange fuckin' shit. There ain't much I *don't* believe in, these days.'

'You were here for the last eclipse, weren't you?'

'Uh-huh.'

'Hmm. That took place just a day after a former employee of mine turned up in this office with the Eye of the Moon.' Cromwell thought back to the moment when Dante Vittori had sat in the very same chair in which Peto was now seated. In the course of that meeting the Professor had stabbed Dante in the arm during an experiment to verify the healing powers of the Eye. The results had been fairly inconclusive, and the only memorable part of the incident was that he had been called a cunt for the first time since he had left school.

Peto pulled one side of his karate top open and revealed a blue stone hanging around his neck on a silver chain.

'You mean *this* Eye of the Moon?' he said, quickly covering it up again.

'Good Lord!' gasped Cromwell, shifting uncomfortably in his leather chair, which squeaked with the movement. 'So the Bourbon Kid didn't get his hands on it then?'

'Nope. I took it and ran. I sensed he would come for it. Then, after I found out a few things about Ishmael Taos, my faith in his teachings wavered a little. I decided I wanted some time away from the island. Fuckin' good timing, too. Every single one of my monk brothers, including Taos, was murdered the night I left.'

'The same night the curse of Rameses Gaius was lifted.'

'Exactly. Which is why I'm here. I wondered if there was anything much you could tell me about the mummy. From what I'm told, you're an extremely knowledgeable man who knows a shitload about all the displays you have in this wonderful museum.'

'You flatter me.' Cromwell smiled. 'But you are quite right. I'll take you for a look at the remains of our display later – not that there's really very much to see, mind you. Also, I am curious about something else. You said just now that you had seen some very strange things the last time you were here. Could you elaborate? Was it vampires or devil worshippers, or what? I am very eager to know.'

Peto took a deep breath. 'Well,' he began, 'I never thought I'd find anyone who would believe any of this stuff, but basically it started when me and my Hubal brother Kyle saw this fucked-up film called *Weekend at Bernie's*. We thought it was a far-fetched comedy at first, but the things we saw afterwards make me suspect that it was actually a documentary. We were attacked by vampires, and we saw a werewolf get blown to bits by a bounty hunter who claimed he was employed by God. Then the Bourbon Kid showed up and killed just about everyone else during the eclipse, albeit with a little help from a guy we met called Dante.'

'Dante Vittori. My former employee, the one who came to me with the Eye last year.'

'Yeah? Nice guy . . . I think.'

'Oh yes,' the Professor defended his likeable former employee. 'A bit rough around the edges, perhaps, but he had a lovely young girlfriend to keep him in line.'

Peto nodded. 'Oh yeah. She was hot, all right.'

Cromwell stood up from his desk and walked over to the wall of books to his left.

'I had often suspected that this city is harbouring the undead,' he said, picking a thick hardback book from a shelf at eye level. He inspected the front cover for a moment and blew a little dust off it, then moved back to the desk with it.

'Oh, they're everywhere,' said the monk matter-of-factly. 'I've recently infiltrated a gang of vampires to see if I can find out the whereabouts of the Bourbon Kid.'

'Really? How have you managed that? Isn't it rather a dangerous thing to do?'

Peto patted his chest. 'This here blue stone has wonderful powers, many of which I'm sure I have yet to learn, but one of which allows me to walk among the undead without detection.'

'Fascinating,' said Cromwell, shaking his head in bewildered awe as he sat back down in his vast leather chair. 'But why would you come back here to find the Bourbon Kid? Are you looking for revenge? Because from what I hear about that fellow, he's best avoided.'

'I want to cure him.'

Cromwell couldn't quite believe what he was hearing. 'Cure him? Of what? Killing people? I believe the cure for that is the electric chair!'

'Believe it or not,' said the monk, unable for a moment to look the Professor in the eye, 'I actually have a tiny amount of sympathy for the guy. He had it tough as a kid, from what I understand. I believe I can cure him of the disease that makes him kill without reason. Most of all, I want to look him in the eye and know that deep down he feels some remorse for what he's done. He has the blood of Ishmael Taos in his veins, so he can't be all bad. I believe he must have a good heart beating somewhere beneath all that hatred and anger.'

Cromwell raised his eyebrows just for a second. 'Well, good luck with that,' he said passing the book he had just picked out over to the monk. 'Here, you really should read this. It explains in great depth the curse of the mummy that escaped from here last year.'

'Rameses Gaius?'

'The very same.'

'In this book?'

'Oh yes. Rameses Gaius was an immensely powerful Egyptian ruler mainly due to the things he learned from using that blue stone you're wearing.'

'So it's true? He was the original owner of the Eye of the Moon?'

'No. That would have been Noah.'

'You're fuckin' bullshittin' me, surely?'

The Professor sighed. 'What is it about that stone that gives Tourette's Syndrome to everyone who wears it?'

'Fucked if I know,' Peto shrugged. 'But seriously – Noah?'

'Well, according to that book anyway,' the Professor continued. 'Take it away and read it. Since you have already made it clear that you think *Weekend at Bernie's* is a documentary rather than fiction, you shouldn't have too much trouble believing half the stuff you read in there.' Cromwell paused, lost in thought for a moment, before addressing Peto again. 'Now come, I'll show you the Egyptian Tomb display from which Gaius escaped. On the night he disappeared, two of my security guards were murdered. One of them called me in the middle of the night to say he'd seen something suspicious, and I regret to say that before he could tell me what he'd seen, I heard him being killed.'

'No shit? By the mummy?'

'Actually, I've a sneaking suspicion that he was killed by Beethoven.'

Peto frowned. 'Beethoven? The Saint Bernard?'

Cromwell was used to dealing with morons, but this was intolerable. Although Peto was generally pretty smart, he clearly watched too many shit films, and seemed to live his life away from Hubal on the basis of what he had seen in them.

'No, you fool,' he snapped. 'Beethoven *the composer.*'

Peto slapped his forehead. 'Of course. That makes perfect sense. Why on earth would I suspect a dog, when clearly a nineteenth-century composer was responsible?'

Cromwell paused for thought. Put like that, maybe he had been a little quick to judge the monk. An apology of sorts was in order. He rose from his chair and said, 'Here, let me get you some coffee on the way, and perhaps something to eat?'

'Thanks,' said Peto, tucking the book under his arm and standing up. 'There is something else you might do for me, though.'

'Name it,' Cromwell smiled, heading for the door.

'You know anywhere I can get my hands on a copy of *Weekend at Bernie's 2?*'

Nineteen

Breakfast cooked by someone else was one of the few things in life that Sanchez cherished. The Olé Au Lait was renowned as the best place in Santa Mondega to get a decent fried breakfast. Even better, the food was brought over to you by the delightful young waitress, Flake. Today she had even been kind enough to place a newspaper by the side of Sanchez's plate. He knew, though, that she treated him well only because there were no other customers in the café at that time of day – eight o'clock – anyway. The rest of the city folk were probably all hungover; in fact, Sanchez was one of the only early risers in the place.

'I'll have a good tip for you later,' said Sanchez, winking at Flake. The sweet young brunette winked back at him but said nothing, heading back behind the counter to wait for the next order. Sanchez was moderately sure, too, that as she walked away from his table she was deliberately wiggling her butt for his benefit. So he made a point of staring at it, just to be sure her efforts didn't go to waste.

When he'd finished staring, he looked down at the items on his table. A rapidly cooling cup of coffee that had arrived ten minutes before the food he'd ordered, a newspaper and an oversized white plate crammed with bacon, sausages, fried eggs, giant mushrooms, grits and home fries. Where to start?

He began with a swig of coffee, then picked up his knife and fork and dived into the nearest sausage. Picking it up on the fork he took a giant bite out of one end. *Mmm delicious,* he thought.

The front page of the newspaper had a rather dull article about a local priest being involved in some sort of choirboy-buggery scandal. An all too familiar story, and one that held no interest for the likes of Sanchez. Like many tabloids, this one featured a photograph of a nubile young woman on page 3 of every edition. He turned the front page over, ready to feast his eyes.

And when he did, he damn near choked on his sausage. As his jaw dropped open, the half-chewed bits fell out and onto the table next to his plate. Staring back at Sanchez from page 3 of the *Santa Mondega Universal Times* (or *SMUT*, as the locals preferred to call it) was a picture of Jessica. Fully clothed, mind you, but it was definitely her. When he looked more closely, he saw that it wasn't so much a photo, but a photo of a painting of her, with a caption underneath:

Missing. $500 reward for information leading to whereabouts.

Shocked, the bartender looked around him suspiciously. He was still the only customer in the Olé Au Lait, so it was a safe bet that no one had seen his sausage fall out. Apart from Rick, the chef behind the counter.

'You okay, Sanchez?' he called over. His big floppy white chef's hat was hanging over the front of his face, but in any case he bore an uncanny resemblance to the Swedish chef from *The Muppets*. He had big bushy eyebrows, tiny, almost invisible, beady eyes and a thick brown moustache. 'Something wrong with your sausage?'

'Nah,' Sanchez shook his head. 'Just felt a sneeze comin' on, is all. Seems to have passed now.'

'Okay.' Rick nodded, and turned back to the paper he had spread on the counter.

Sanchez returned to his own newspaper. In the picture, Jessica was wearing an entirely black outfit, which, from what the bartender could recall, was the only outfit she actually owned. The brief wording in the copy printed beneath the picture requested that anyone who knew her whereabouts should contact the paper. There was no mention of who had placed the advertisement, not who was offering the reward.

Now Sanchez was not averse to getting his hands on the five hundred dollars on offer, but he much preferred staying alive. If word got round that he had Jessica, in a coma, tucked away safely in an upstairs room of the Tapioca, then there was a darn good chance he'd get a visit from the Bourbon Kid. And he sure as shit didn't want that. Maybe it was the Kid who had posted the missing-persons ad? One thing was certain – Sanchez needed to know who was looking for Jessica, and why. But he couldn't risk calling the *SMUT* himself and having it known that he was taking an interest in the situation. Distractedly, he picked up the half-chewed piece of sausage from the table, slipped it back into his mouth and started chewing again. After swallowing it and washing it down with a mouthful of coffee he shouted back over to the chef.

'Yo, Rick! How'd you like to earn yourself a free bottle of liquor?'

Rick frowned. 'If I have to earn it, it ain't free.'

'Do you want a bottle of fuckin' liquor or not?'

'Sure. What's the catch?'

'Can you call the *SMUT* for me, and ask them who placed this missing-persons advert?' Sanchez held up page 3 of the newspaper for the chef to take a look.

Rick wandered round from behind the counter and grabbed hold of the newspaper, studying the advertisement.

'No way they'll tell you who's posted it. It's a confidential ad,' he said, shrugging.

'There's gotta be some way of finding out.'

'Could be. I know a friend of a friend works for the *SMUT*. Reckon I can ask him to dig around and find out, if it's that important to you.'

'It is. And it's worth a bottle of my best liquor to you if you can do that for me.'

'Tennessee whiskey?' the chef asked hopefully.

'Whatever you desire,' Sanchez replied, grandly. Anyone who knew him also knew that anything for which he was prepared to give away something that had cost him hard cash, had to be *real* important.

'You got yourself a deal. Might take a day or two to find out, but I'll give you a call, soon as I hear anything.'

'Thanks, Rick I really appreciate it,' said Sanchez. It sounded as though he meant it, too. 'Top up that coffee for me, will ya?'

The chef frowned. 'Why couldn't you call the *SMUT* yourself?' he asked.

'I don't want anyone knowin' I'm interested in this girl, is all. Let's keep this between us. Yeah?'

'Sure,' said the chef. He grinned, then added, 'You know where the coffee jug is. Top up your own coffee, you tubby bastard.'

Twenty

Stephanie Rogers had been given the most exciting assignment of her entire career in the police force. True, it had sounded like a dull exercise at first. Read a book, compile a presentation based on your findings, and offer suggestions to the hotshot detectives on where to begin investigating those findings. But this was no ordinary book, and this was no ordinary police headquarters in a city that was itself far from normal.

What Officer Rogers had been reading was an untitled book by an anonymous author. The very same book that had been read by countless other folk, all of whom were now dead. All murdered. Not one single survivor. The success of her task depended upon what she discovered within the pages of the book. It was hoped that she would find the reasons for the murders. Well, she had now completed the task. It had been a solo project, and a top-secret one at that. One that she was allowed to discuss with no one other than the select few who had assigned the task to her.

And now here she was presenting her findings to that select few. Three detectives in charge of solving the great mystery of *The Book With No Name*, its links to the murders, and, of course, its connection with the Bourbon Kid, of evil memory.

It had been drummed into Stephanie right from the day she had been given the assignment that she should present all of her findings, no matter how ridiculous they might seem. Which was a relief to her, because the findings were, frankly, utterly preposterous, and completely unbelievable.

Captain De La Cruz and Detectives Benson and Hunter each sat at a different desk in the briefing room. It was a room with the look and feel of a classroom. Windows ran along one side of it, all with the dark blinds pulled down. The opposite wall was windowless, but for a small glass panel in the door to the left of the lecture podium at the front. There were twelve desks, set out in rows of three in front of the podium.

Michael De La Cruz sat in the small plastic chair at the front-row desk closest to the window. He was a good-looking Latino, always well groomed and with impeccable taste in clothes. He was probably the vainest officer on the force, but his carefully contrived appearance was a prime example of just how meticulously he approached all aspects of his life. The minor details mattered to this man.

Certainly they mattered to him more than they did to his colleague, Randy Benson, a scruffy individual with an unwashed appearance, sitting at a desk in the third row from the podium. He still lived with his mother, and it was rumoured that he'd never had a girlfriend. Stephanie believed the rumours, because this unkempt, brown-tank-top-wearing, white-haired loser had a notoriously short fuse, probably brought on by some deep-rooted sexual frustration. He was an unattractive man in just about every way possible. He was also extremely hairy. If, God forbid, she ever saw this man without his shirt on, she thought that there was every chance he would turn out to have an afro stuck on his chest.

The third officer, Dick Hunter, sat at the centre desk in the very back row. Stephanie didn't know him well. He had only been a member of the force for eight months or so – another of the new recruits brought in from out of town to replace the dwindling numbers since last year's massacre. He was a South African with thinning, light-brown hair, and for the most part seemed to be well-educated and well-spoken in equal measure. Maybe just a little shy, Stephanie thought.

For thirty minutes the three of them listened to her talk about her findings, and not once did any of them interrupt or give even so much as a hint as to what they were thinking. Stephanie found it hard to tell whether the three thirty-something officers were taking her seriously or not, so that by the time she came to her summary she was feeling embarrassed and wishing she had never been given the assignment in the first place.

'So, to summarize,' she began, finally arousing some interest in Michael De La Cruz. She had hoped to impress him, not least because she had been involved in a brief but torrid affair with him only six months earlier, and she was rather hoping for another taste. The man was a sexual tyrannosaurus. A devil in the sack.

Hearing her announce that she was about to summarize, he sat up as though he was only now starting to pay attention. She did her best to pretend she hadn't noticed, but it broke her concentration for a moment. She paused slightly in order not to stumble over her words as she began the summary. She had dressed in her smartest and sexiest work outfit especially for this presentation. A sharp grey suit jacket with a skirt that didn't quite reach her knees and a white blouse that showed off just a little cleavage, and yet *not one* of these losers had complimented her on it. The best she had received was a slight leer from Benson, but that was nothing new. He'd leer at a woman wearing a garbage sack if he thought he could see some flesh.

Not wanting, for various reasons, to make eye contact with any of the detectives, she fixed her gaze on a computer monitor on the small side desk beside the podium as she launched into her summary.

'*The Book With No Name* is basically a hotchpotch of different stories and possible facts cobbled together in one volume. It makes hardly any sense, for the most part. The grammar and spelling are absolutely abysmal and the author is clearly a moron, which might explain why he didn't put his name to the book.' There was a polite laugh from De La Cruz, which calmed her nerves a little. She allowed herself a brief smile before carrying on. 'Although that could also be because there is possibly more than one writer. But the standout facts are these,' she pointed to a whiteboard behind her, on which had appeared the first slide in a presentation she had compiled on the computer. It was a photograph of Archie Somers. 'Detective Archibald Somers, a well-respected officer in this very department until his mysterious disappearance, was in fact the Lord of the Undead, Armand Xavier.'

She could feel her stomach tightening as the enormity of what she was saying tore into her like a bad bout of food poisoning. The three officers exchanged glances with each other. None of them gave anything away, but then, they didn't need to. So far as Stephanie was concerned they were undoubtedly thinking she was an idiot. *No use in stopping now, though*, so she brought up the second slide.

'This woman, known as Jessica Xavier, was his wife and was responsible for turning him into a member of the undead some time after he discovered the Holy Grail and drank the blood of Christ, which made him immortal . . . *obviously*.' She tried her hardest to sound as if even she didn't believe the nonsense she was coming out with, just in case they were about to laugh at her. Yet once again she received no reaction from her audience.

Slide three. A picture of a hooded man, his face concealed in shadow.

'This man, the Bourbon Kid, is believed to have killed both Archibald Somers – or Armand Xavier, whichever you prefer to call him – and his wife Jessica last year, during the eclipse. Their three sons,' she skipped to slide four, a picture of El Santino, Carlito and Miguel, three dead local gangsters, all shot to death in the Tapioca. 'They were also killed by the Kid – probably – but their bodies were recovered and their deaths have been verified.'

Slide five. A picture of *The Book With No Name*, probably from an old engraving.

'This book, the one I have been reading and researching, was allegedly made from the Cross upon which Jesus Christ was crucified. This means that it cannot be touched by the undead or it will kill them. Bit like Superman and Kryptonite, I guess.' Again, no laughs from her audience. *Shit!* 'The book positively identifies Archibald Somers as Armand Xavier, which is why he set about killing everyone who ever read it. But of course he couldn't destroy the book, because to touch it would bring about his own death.'

Slide six. A still from *Indiana Jones and the Last Crusade,* showing Harrison Ford holding a wooden cup.

'The Cup of Christ. The book says nothing of its whereabouts other than that the last people to have seen it were Armand Xavier and his friend Ishmael Taos, a monk, who, we believe, was the father of the Bourbon Kid.'

Slide seven. A photo of a monk – meant to be Ishmael Taos, but actually Chow Yun Fat from the film *Bullet-Proof Monk.*

'According to *The Book With No Name,* drinking from the Cup of Christ – or Holy Grail, as it's also known – grants the recipient immortality.' She paused. 'Well, not quite.' All three detectives looked a little more interested, just as they had done briefly when she had touched on this part of the story earlier in the presentation. 'To drink the blood of Christ grants immortality, but Xavier and Taos had already done so some hundreds of years ago, leaving nothing over for anyone else. Drink the blood of Xavier or Taos, or their descendants, and immortality can be attained also, only to a slightly lesser degree. Drink the blood of a vampire from the Cup and the effect is much the same, except that the recipient becomes a member of the undead. I think that effectively what the book is saying is that you'll get the strengths of whoever's blood you drink from the Cup. So if you drank Einstein's blood I guess you'd become a genius, or something like that. But there's also a suggestion here that I suspect has never been tried. Drink a combination of the blood of the descendants of those who drank Christ's blood, vampire blood and mortal blood, and there's every chance the recipient would become not only immortal, but all-powerful. Not just King of the Undead, but King or Lord of Everything. More powerful than Somers, Jessica, the Bourbon Kid or Ishmael Taos. In fact, probably more powerful than all of them put together. The trump card, if you like.'

With that, her presentation was technically finished, and she looked around for one of the three men to offer a reaction – a positive one, she hoped. To her relief, De La Cruz began applauding.

'Stephie, you've excelled yourself. This is fantastic stuff.'

'Really?'

'Damn right. This is exactly the kind of thing we were after.'

'Then I ought to say that there's one other thing that I didn't put in the presentation. The best part.'

Benson and Hunter sat to attention. Could Stephanie Rogers really have something, some piece of information better than what she had already provided?

De La Cruz got up from his seat and spoke for all of them. 'Go on,' he said, walking up to join Stephanie by the computer.

She took a deep breath. 'I found out what happened to Ishmael Taos,' she said, smiling.

Hunter piped up from his desk at the back of the room. 'Give her room, let her speak.'

'Ishmael Taos was murdered shortly after the eclipse. He was beheaded in his sleeping quarters.'

'Ow!' yelped De La Cruz, wincing and rubbing his neck.

'I suspect he was murdered by the Bourbon Kid, who, as I suggested earlier, was his son. The Kid killed him, and just about every other monk on the island of Hubal, and disappeared, along with a precious artefact, the blue stone known as the Eye of the Moon.'

The three detectives looked at each other. For some reason it suddenly crossed Stephanie's mind that they might already know this piece of information. They were probably only humouring her by acting surprised. So, then – time to surprise them one more time.

'You already knew that?' she asked.

'We suspected,' said Benson, getting up from his desk and rubbing his crotch a little to rearrange his genitals. Hunter, following his lead, also stood up. He picked up his briefcase from the floor by the side of his desk and prepared to leave. But the ranking officer, Captain De La Cruz, gestured to his two colleagues to wait a moment. He knew Stephanie well enough to know that she had something else to say, something important.

And Stephanie did have something else to say. She tried to be nonchalant about it, but her voice gave away how impressed she was with herself.

'Do any of you know who the Bourbon Kid is, though?' she asked with a hint of smugness. 'Or where he lives?'

'Nope.' De La Cruz shook his head. 'Nobody knows those things. And I suspect no one ever will.'

Stephanie smiled. This was a big moment for her.

'I think I know,' she said.

Twenty-One

The hotel that Dante had booked for his surprise honeymoon with Kacy proved ideal as a staging post for his undercover mission. After a quick upgrade, paid for in cash by Robert Swann, they found themselves in an impressive third-floor suite. The happy couple had a double bedroom to themselves, and as well as a large sitting room there was a spare bedroom for Swann and a female colleague who were 'babysitting' them.

Dante was sitting on the large double bed in the bedroom he and Kacy were sharing. It was a decent-sized room with the bed positioned in the middle of it, covered with a crisply laundered orange duvet. He was now only minutes away from the start of his first night attempting to pass himself off as a vampire.

Swann entered the room and approached his charge, holding a syringe full of serum. 'You ready for the injection?' he asked, sitting down on the bed.

'Stick it in me, you sorry piece of shit,' Dante growled back.

Dante had the left sleeve of his maroon shirt rolled up so that Swann could make the necessary injection of lifesaving serum. Kacy, wearing a pair of blue jeans and a pink T-shirt, was sitting beside him. She was holding his hand, making the most of the last few minutes she had with him before these cowardly Secret Service lowlifes sent him off to do their dirty work for them. She hoped and prayed with all her heart that he would make it through his first night among the vampires and survive undetected because of this serum. It had been explained to them that the chemicals in the serum would lower Dante's blood temperature enough for him to move among the undead without being eyed up for dinner.

Agent Swann looked as if he was taking a degree of sick pleasure from injecting the clear liquid from the syringe into Dante's arm. To his credit, the young man didn't flinch as the needle went in and was kept there for about fifteen seconds, far longer than was necessary. Sadistic by nature, Swann had already started to take a considerable dislike to him (as most figures in authority tended to do), so prolonging any pain Dante might be feeling gave him something of a kick.

With them in the bedroom was Swann's new colleague, Special Agent Roxanne Valdez. She was a tall black woman with scraped-back beaded hair, wearing a figure-hugging white sweater that showed off some great curves. She also wore a short brown skirt. Their clothes were all part of the façade they had created for the hotel staff – two couples on vacation together. Swann had dressed like a tourist in a blue Hawaiian shirt with knee-length chino shorts. *So much for discreet,* Dante thought, as he endured the injection at the hands of the special agent. *Talk about advertising yourself as undercover. Stupid prick.*

It was Agent Valdez who brought the inappropriately lengthy injection to an end. She could see her colleague was taking too much pleasure in his work.

'Come on, that's enough,' she snapped. 'You're just being an asshole now. *Stop it.*'

Swann cast a quick, spiteful glance at her as he pulled the needle out of Dante's arm. 'I was just taking extra care to make sure I injected the right amount of serum. Better more than less,' he said, unconvincingly.

He checked the syringe was completely empty and then got up and carried it out of the room. He passed through the large sitting room with its sofa, two deep armchairs, minibar, coffee table and television, before disappearing through a door in the corner into one of the suite's two bathrooms. When he had gone, Roxanne Valdez made her way over to the side of the bed where Swann had been sitting as he carried out the injection. She sat on the edge by Dante and took hold of his arm to check it over and ensure there was no identifiable bruising where the needle had gone in. Kacy was convinced that she gripped Dante's bicep in a manner that implied she was checking to see just how firm it was, rather than to see whether it was bruised. The agent also sneakily placed her free hand on his thigh, as if she was trying to steady herself. Not only that, but she seemed to hold on to Dante for just a second longer than was absolutely necessary as she looked him over.

'Okay, you're looking good,' said Valdez, smiling at her patient. 'How're you feeling? Ready to take on the underworld?'

Dante looked her in the eye and forced a fake smile. '*Bite me, bitch*,' he snapped.

Kacy was relieved to see that the smile and ever-so-slightly-inappropriate bicep touch had not made her man warm to the agent in any way.

'Hey, don't be like that,' said Roxanne, still smiling warmly at him and caressing his arm once again. 'Now, do you think you're ready to wear a wire tonight? Or would you rather leave it for now?'

'*Wear a wire*? Do I look like a cunt to you?'

'No,' Roxanne responded calmly. 'Nobody here looks like a cunt.'

'I disagree,' said Dante pointing at Agent Swann through the doorway. 'Look at him. Cunt.'

Swann marched back in. 'I heard that. Cut it out. We've all got our orders, right? I didn't think up this mission for you. I'm just the guy they dumped the babysitting assignment on. I'm not thrilled at having to sit in this fucking hotel room all fucking day and night watching over your whiny little girlfriend, either. So quit it with your shitty comments.'

'Boo-fuckin'-hoo,' said Dante, mocking him. 'Now, you call Kacy whiny again and I'll give you something real to cry about.'

'Is that right?' Swann asked over his shoulder as he walked

back into the sitting room.

'Yeah.'

Roxanne, deciding to put an end to the macho talk, which in her opinion was approaching kindergarten levels of puerility, stepped in to defuse the situation. She stroked Dante's arm again, then pulled his sleeve back down to cover the site of the injection.

'Look, Dante,' she said quietly, 'forget about the wire for this evening. Just see if you can get yourself into one of the vampire clans. And see if you can work out which one your buddy the monk is most likely to be hiding in. He may already be dead, in which case just see what you can find out about the Eye of the Moon, and whether any of the clans have managed to get their hands on it.'

'She's right, pal,' Swann called from the other room, where he was leaning back against an oak table outside the bathroom. 'As we discussed earlier, your best bet is to head to the Nightjar. That's where all the vampires hang out. See if you can get in there and use your winning personality to become buddies with one of the vampires who's on his own, then get him to introduce you to some of his friends. Next thing you know you'll be havin' drinks with fuckin' Count Dracula. Piece o' piss. You'll be fine.'

'If it's so fuckin' easy, why aren't you doin' it, tough guy?' Dante retorted.

'I would, but I don't know what your buddy Peto the monk looks like, do I, numbnuts?'

Swann tutted as if annoyed by Dante's stupidity, even though he wouldn't have swapped places with the young man in a million years. He walked towards the bedroom again, but stopped off at the minibar in the sitting room to get himself a drink. As he bent down to look in the fridge, Kacy squeezed Dante's arm to get his attention. Her lover stopped watching Swann and turned to look at her.

'Don't ask any questions if you think it'll get you into trouble,' she said, failing to mask the now permanently worried look on her face. 'If you think it'll blow your cover and make you look like an outsider, don't ask. In fact, don't do anything other than fit in, for now. Fuck these two and their demands. This is only your first night undercover. Take your time. Don't say anythin' stupid. Just listen where you can for something useful.'

Dante leaned over and kissed her on the mouth to reassure her, pulling his arm free from Roxanne Valdez and stroking Kacy's long dark hair in an effort to calm her.

'Trust me, baby. I know what I'm doin'. I mix well with everyone when I have to. Don't you worry, I'll be back before the sun comes up.'

'Just be careful. And for fuck's sake stop using the expression "Bite me".'

'Sure thing, babe.' Dante winked at her and stood up from the bed. 'Right, it's about that time.'

Swann appeared in the doorway and wagged his finger at the young man. 'Listen to your girlfriend, pal. Don't do anything stupid, but do try an' find out all the stuff we talked about. And I wanna know about all the different clans. And see if you can find out who the head of each clan is. It'll impress the boss, an' then maybe you'll get some reward at the end of this.'

'Like I give a fuck about impressin' your boss,' Dante muttered, walking past him and on across the sitting room. 'Your bald cockhead of a boss can find out the heads of the clans for his fuckin' self.'

He walked into the bathroom and disappeared out of sight round the door. It was a small room (there was a bigger bathroom off Dante and Kacy's bedroom), with a white porcelain washbasin to his left and a matching shower unit opposite it, as well as a toilet in one corner. Dante stood over the basin and looked at his reflection in the mirror. *You can do this,* he whispered to himself. *You've got nerves of steel. You can handle this. It's just a walk in the park.*

He clenched his fists and pulled a tough guy face at himself in the mirror. He didn't want Kacy seeing him nervous like this, having to pump himself up for action. He needed her to see the cool-as-you-like, unflinching version that had taken the injection in the other room. No sense in worrying her any more than was absolutely necessary. It wouldn't help if she knew that for the first time in his life he was absolutely petrified.

After a quick staring contest with his reflection he turned on the hot-water faucet above the basin and used both hands to catch some water and wash it over his face. The serum was starting to kick in now and he was beginning to feel the initial chills as his blood temperature dropped. The warm water helped him to deal with the initial icy shock.

After a short while the dark face of Roxanne appeared around the door. 'You okay?' she asked. 'You look a little nervous, honey. Maybe you should have a drink before you go?'

'Nah, 'sokay,' said Dante. 'These vampire fucks prob'ly drink like fish, so the smartest thing I can do is at least stay sober before I go out. I could end up havin' a skinful of beer and tequila tonight, and let's face it, the drunker I get, the more likely I am to get myself in trouble.'

Roxanne stepped fully into the bathroom and closed the door behind her. She walked over to stand beside Dante and began rubbing his back.

'You know, Dante, you're actually a lot smarter than people give you credit for,' she said, offering a comforting smile.

'Thanks.' He smiled politely back at her as she ran a reassuring hand down his arm. Maybe she wasn't such a bitch after all. So far, she had actually tried her best to keep him calm. He had to be at least a little bit grateful for that.

'I better get goin',' he said giving her a grateful pat on the back. Then he manoeuvred himself around her in the small space between the shower and the washbasin and opened the door. He smiled at her one last time, and then headed out of the bathroom, ready to face the undead world for the first time since he had left Santa Mondega a year earlier.

So it was a pity that, even with all his wits about him,

Dante hadn't been quite smart enough to notice something when Roxanne had been standing beside him rubbing his back.

The mirror over the basin had shown only *his* reflection.

Twenty-Two

The locker room below the police headquarters had been off limits for years. Officers still went down there on odd occasions to discuss things privately, but it was frowned upon, and the official line was that anyone caught trespassing down there could expect to find themselves in line for a public dressing-down.

Even so, Stephanie now found herself in that very locker room with De La Cruz, Benson and Hunter.

'What exactly are we looking for here?' she asked nervously. A stickler for procedure, she didn't like being somewhere that was officially out of bounds.

'We're not *looking* for anything,' said De La Cruz. 'We've found something, and I think you should see it.'

De La Cruz led the way through the musty, dingy locker room towards the long-disused showers at the back. Stephanie trusted Michael De La Cruz, but being in a subterranean locker room with three males (albeit police officers) was a little intimidating. In spite of this, she did her best to hide the tension she was feeling. She followed directly behind De La Cruz, while Benson and Hunter hung back a few feet, as though they wanted to whisper among themselves. Which they did.

Once they were inside the open-plan shower area De La Cruz turned to face Stephanie.

'You ready to see just why this locker room has always been out of bounds?' he asked.

Stephanie raised her eyebrows. 'Go on.'

De La Cruz hit the 'on' switch for the shower furthest from

the entrance. There was a sudden whirring sound followed by a drawn-out but very loud grating noise. The light-blue-painted wall at the back of the showers began moving to the left. De La Cruz had just opened a secret passageway. A gateway to things that were probably best left alone. Stephanie began to feel even more uneasy. What was about to be revealed to her here, exactly? Intrigued, in spite of herself, by what she might find, and allowing her curiosity to get the better of her, she peered in to see what it was that was so secret it had to be concealed behind this shower-room wall. On first inspection it didn't look like much. In the gloom of the small chamber the moving wall had exposed, she could make out only an antique wooden table on which had been placed a book and a golden chalice. She turned back from the darkened room to look questioningly at De La Cruz.

'This, my dear Stephanie,' he said softly, 'is the Holy Grail that you have been reading about in *The Book With No Name*. Or, if you prefer, the Cup of Christ. It has been here at police headquarters stashed away beneath our noses all this time.'

Stephanie, unsure exactly how to react to this bizarre statement, simply smirked. *After all* she thought, *De La Cruz had to be shitting her, surely?*

'You're kidding, right?' she asked, checking the reactions of Benson and Hunter behind her. Both looked deadly serious. 'Well, *aren't you?*'

De La Cruz shook his head. 'See that book on the table?' he said.

'Yes.'

'We believe it was written by Archibald Somers. Looks like a diary or series of memos of some sort. It confirms much of what you have told us from what you read in *The Book With No Name*.'

'Really? So why have me do all that research?' Stephanie was confused. And irritated. If they already knew so much from reading this new book, why make her read the whole of the fucking *Book With No Name*?

'Well, it kinda looks as though Somers was writing his own version. Only this is a diary of sorts, detailing all of his wrongdoing and rewriting the story of *The Book With No Name* in his own words,' De La Cruz replied. 'As a member of the undead, he couldn't touch the original book. As we've established already, to touch the book would kill him, so he appeared to be writing his own version with a whole bunch of new chapters.'

'What's the relevance of this?' Stephanie asked. This whole business was making her more nervous by the minute.

De La Cruz ran a finger inside his shirt collar to loosen it. 'Don't you want to know why it's hidden away down here?'

'Does it by any chance cause the death of everyone who reads it?'

Behind her, she heard Benson laugh briefly. She glanced at him, but his face had resumed its stern and serious look.

'It's hidden *here*,' said De La Cruz walking over to the table and flipping open the book's black leather cover, 'because *I* hid it here.'

Stephanie suddenly felt even more uneasy. What was De La Cruz driving at?

'I don't understand what you're trying to say,' she stammered.

De La Cruz sighed, then said patiently, 'This book revealed the hiding place of the Holy Grail. I came here, along with Benson and Hunter, to find it. Problem was, of course, that, as you confirmed from your findings in the original book, there's no blood of Christ left to drink from it.' He paused a moment, marshalling his thoughts, before continuing. 'So in order to achieve ultimate immortality – in essence, to become a god – an individual would have to drink the blood not just of a mere mortal, but also of a vampire and, for good measure, the blood of a descendant of Ishmael Taos or Armand Xavier. And drink them all from this very cup.' He picked up the golden chalice and held it up in front of his face, marvelling at its beauty. It wasn't much more than eight inches in height and was shaped somewhat like a brandy glass rendered in metal, only with a slightly longer stem.

'So what are you intending to do with it? Call the FBI?' Stephanie asked, not grasping where the detective's explanation was heading.

'Oh no, my dear,' said De La Cruz, putting down the cup and leaning back against the table. 'You have now told us you think you know where to find the Bourbon Kid, the son of Taos. Which means we only need to drink his blood, with the blood of a vampire and the blood of a mortal, to gain immortality. And you, my dear Stephanie, are a mere mortal.'

Stephanie turned back to Benson and Hunter to see if they were as confused as she was.

Both men stood staring at her. The hunger had overcome them, and they opened their mouths wide to reveal perfectly formed fangs, thirsty for blood. Utterly terrified, she turned back just in time to see De La Cruz move in upon her. He was clasping a six-inch silver dagger in one hand and, like his colleagues, he too now sported a set of hideous fangs. The flesh on his face had thinned to reveal the blue veins beneath, ready for their fill of her blood.

With the silver dagger the smartly dressed detective sliced Stephanie's neck wide open with a single sweep of the blade. He watched wide-eyed and with a ferocious thirst as her blood began to pour out into the cup he was pressing against her chest with his other hand.

Twenty-Three

By the time Dante arrived at the Nightjar, it was already dark. His thoughts were racing, though he looked cool enough. Would this potion that he'd been given actually work? Would he be recognized as a fraud straight away? And how many vampires were going to be inside? He had other worries, too, like how was he supposed to know the vampires from the ordinary folk? Well, he reckoned fatalistically, only time would tell. For now he just had to drag his ass inside.

The Nightjar had undergone a great many changes in the year since Dante had last been in Santa Mondega. First of all, there was a new bar manager. The previous manager, Berkley, had been shot dead by the Bourbon Kid the night before the last eclipse. A European guy named Dino had taken over and had set about refurbishing the place. Dino, a child of Italian parents, dressed immaculately in smart fashionable clothes at all times, unlike most of his clientele. Unlike all his clientele, truth be told. In order to try to raise standards in the bar (which he had extensively remodelled, redecorated and refurnished) he had also taken the opportunity to employ some security staff. Tonight, two bouncers stood at the front entrance. Dante was going to have to get past them before he even got close to meeting any vampires.

As he attempted to stroll past them and into the bar in as casual a fashion as he could manage in the circumstances, one of the bouncers, a man known as 'Uncle Les', held an arm out across his chest to stop him before he reached the front door. Les was a large man, as one would expect of someone in his line of work, and he wore a sleeveless leather vest over a black T-shirt, no doubt to show off the gallery of tattoos on his arms. He had long grey hair pulled back into a ponytail, and his craggy facial features and grey stubble suggested he was probably in his early fifties. Still not a guy to be messed with, though. Old or not, this guy looked like he was handy in a bar fight.

'What's ya name, son?' he asked in a Southern drawl.

'Dante.'

'Where y'all from?'

'I'm local.'

'Not seen you here before.'

'That's 'cos I ain't been in since Berkley got killed.'

'Okay,' said Uncle Les, looking to his colleague for a second opinion. 'Whadda ya reckon, Jericho? We gonna let this guy in?'

Jericho, puffing on a slim cigar that hung from the right corner of his mouth, took a long look at Dante. It was hard to tell what he thought because his face wore a permanent sneer, always looking as though he was only one second away from spitting on the floor. He was wearing a black denim shirt, the top half of which was unbuttoned to reveal a wispy thatch of hair on his bronzed chest. He was also wearing black denim jeans, with, on his right leg, a metal brace that ran from his ankle right up to his thigh, where it was tightly wrapped with a brown leather strap. Jericho had been shot in the leg by a monk almost a year ago, and now needed the brace to prevent his knee from collapsing whenever he put too much pressure on it. The brace was partly responsible for his permanent sneer. Anyone considering messing with him would instantly know from his face that he wasn't in the mood for it. He looked Dante up and down.

'What's your favourite song, sonny?'

'What the fuck has that gotta do with anythin'?'

'Answer the question.'

'Jeez, *whatever*,' said Dante struggling to hide his impatience, and struggling even more to think what his favourite song was.

'Hold on,' said Jericho, raising his left hand for silence. With his other hand he pushed open the solid oak doors slightly and peered inside the club. The noise from inside started filtering out. Drowning out the chatter was the sound of a band playing the opening bars of 'Whatever' by Oasis.

'The Psychics like you. Guess you can go in,' said Jericho gruffly.

'Huh? The Psychics? Who the fuck are they?'

'They're the band. If they play your song, you can come in. And they're playing your song, so get your ass inside before I change my mind.'

Dante did as he was told and walked on into the bar, unsure of what exactly had just happened. A second guy who had been standing behind him tried to follow him in. Dante heard Uncle Les interrogate him in similar fashion.

'Favourite song?'

'Anything by Michael Bolton.'

'Get the fuck outta here.'

The inside of the Nightjar was a great deal different from how Dante remembered it. It seemed to be nearly twice the size it had once been, but was a good deal darker. It was also, he thought, a shitload busier. And everyone in the place actually looked like a vampire. Fact is, they probably always had done, but until about a year ago Dante had had no idea that vampires even existed, so it was little wonder that he had not noticed them before.

There were about two hundred customers crammed into the bar, drinking and generally making merry. Most bars in Santa Mondega were rough, if not dangerous, places to be, if memory served him well, but the revamped Nightjar actually looked like somewhere you could have a good time. On a stage to his left, a girl group was belting out 'his' song. They were wearing sexy black leather outfits and showing a fair bit of flesh, too. And they could play. *Boy, could they play.* The lead singer, who had long, bright red hair flowing halfway down her back, was hot as hell. The others were playing an assortment of instruments from guitars and drums to violins and flutes. There were eight young broads in total, and one tubby fella playing a tuba. He looked a little out of place, being the only male, the only fat one, the only one with a combover, and the only one with an incongruous brass instrument. All he had in common with the others was the tight-fitting black outfit, and on him that wasn't a good thing.

After checking them out for a minute, Dante fought his way through the crowds to the bar. Since the people in the crowd were not overly keen to make way for him, it was almost inevitable that he should accidentally bump into the back of a well-built man. He heard the guy curse and saw some of his drink spill onto the floor. Unsurprisingly, the man turned around to see who had barged into him. 'You're new here, aren't you?' he said in what may have been an English accent.

Smiling apologetically, Dante looked back at the guy barring his way. Much like everyone else round these parts, he was wearing a black leather sleeveless jacket and blue jeans. He was unshaven, with a particularly narrow face beneath dark, scraggly hair and sunken cheeks accentuating the bones of his face. He too was heavily tattooed. His eyes couldn't be seen because he was wearing what Dante thought was a pretty cool pair of wraparound sunglasses. And he was holding a half-full glass of beer, the other half of which was dripping down his hand and onto the floor.

'Er, yeah. How did ya know?' Dante maintained his awkward 'Please like me' smile.

'You're not wearing an emblem, and you're on your own.'

'An emblem?'

'Yeah. Shows you're part of a clan. You should know that, though. You're a vampire right?'

'Oh yeah. Sure. 'Course I am.'

'Good, 'cos you know, we've been getting undercover cops trying to infiltrate this place just lately, and the first giveaway is that they don't have an emblem.'

'Oh shit.' Dante sensed he was in trouble already. Saying

'Oh shit' out loud probably wasn't helping his cause, either. 'Can you get me an emblem?'

'So you really don't belong to any clan?' the man asked.

'Nah. I only arrived in town this mornin'. Can I join your clan? . . . *Please?*'

There was an awkward pause amid the bustle of the noisy crowd. Dante was well aware that he had made himself sound desperate to belong, like a geek on his first day at a new school. Eventually, after looking Dante up and down for what seemed like an age, the man whose drink he had spilled responded. 'Sure thing,' he said, suddenly breaking into a smile. 'Here, have these.' He reached inside a small pocket on the front of his jacket and pulled out a pair of sunglasses, identical to his own. He handed them to Dante, who, mumbling his thanks, quickly put them on.

To his surprise, the would-be vampire found that he could still see perfectly clearly, as if the glasses weren't actually tinted. This was a relief, for the Nightjar wasn't exactly blazing with light. He could now stare at other people and not feel too self-conscious about it, since they wouldn't be able to tell for sure whether he was looking at them or not. As the guy who'd given them to him was wearing a pair too, Dante thought it was probably a safe bet that he no longer stood out in the crowd. He kept reminding himself of what Kacy had made him promise. Don't do anything stupid, and don't draw attention to yourself.

'Thanks, man. 'Preciate it.' He held out his hand to the other. 'I'm Dante, by the way. Who the fuck're you?'

'Obedience.' He took the outstretched hand and cursorily shook it.

'Excuse me?'

'Obedience.'

'Must be me. I thought you said "Obedience" just then.'

'That's right. I did. I'm called Obedience because I have a habit of always doing as I'm asked. I kinda like to please, y'know.'

'Really?'

'Yeah.'

'Great,' said Dante, eager to test his obliging new acquaintance. 'So buy me a beer and introduce me to some of your friends.'

'Sure,' said Obedience, smiling.

The helpful vampire duly led the way to the bar, where he ordered two beers. Everyone in the place looked a bit vampish, but no one appeared to have actually transformed into a creature of the night. *Which is a bonus,* Dante decided, as he waited for Obedience to be served.

When their drinks came, Dante's new friend handed him a bottle of Shitting Monkey beer, then led him through a crowd of strange-looking folk. Some were dressed as clowns, some in drag, others looked like Maori tribesmen, and there was a particularly large group of what looked like 'white Rastafarians' wearing multicoloured tie-dyed T-shirts. Obedience ignored them all, heading towards a dark corner where three men stood watching the band.

'Cool choice of song, by the way,' Obedience said, as they approached the three men.

'Thanks,' said Dante. 'It just kinda popped into my head.'

'Yeah, that happens.'

They stopped before the three men, who were all dressed similarly to Obedience. All wore the same wraparound sunglasses. Obedience grabbed the arm of the nearest man. He had a neatly combed mop of blond hair with a particularly uncool side parting and a thick yellow moustache that rested on his top lip. He also affected rather slim, effeminate blond sideburns (if sideburns can actually be effeminate), and he was very pale. *Even for a fuckin' vampire,* Dante was thinking.

'Fritz, I'd like you to meet Dante,' said Obedience, indicating his new friend with a wave of one hand. Fritz held out a hand and Dante shook it.

'IS VERY NICE TO MEET YOU, DANTE. MY NAME IS FRITZ!' the blond man shouted in a heavy German accent.

'Yeah, nice to meet you too, er . . . Fritz, is it?' Dante

replied, less vocally. Although the band was loud, there was no call for shouting at the top of one's voice as this German dude was doing.

'You'll have to excuse Fritz,' said Obedience. 'He can't help shouting.'

'MY VOICEBOX VOZ DAMAGED WHEN I VOZ BITTEN BY MY MAKER!'

'Oh yeah. Right,' said Dante uncertainly, eagerly hoping to avoid too much conversation with the loudest man in Santa Mondega. It would be hard to go anywhere unnoticed with this freak.

'And who's this guy?' Dante asked, pointing at the first of the other two identically dressed men to Fritz's left.

'SILENCE!' shouted Fritz.

'Alright alright, keep your fuckin' hair on. I was only fuckin' askin'.'

'NO NO! YOU MISUNDERSTAND!' the German barked aggressively. 'HIS NAME IS SILENCE!' He was patting the guy next to him on the back. This fellow had dark hair cropped short on top, but shaved to the bone on the sides. That aside, he looked much more as Dante expected a vampire to look. He was deathly pale, with gnarly teeth and deep-set dark eyes, coupled with two-day-old stubble.

'Why'd they call you Silence?' Dante asked. The man didn't respond so Dante turned to Obedience. 'Why'd they call him Silence?'

'Because he hardly ever speaks.'

'Oh, right. Why's that, then?'

'His maker damaged his voicebox. It's painful for him to talk so he says very little.'

Dante smiled at Silence, who offered half a smile in return. *What a coupla freaks. A shouting German and his silent buddy.*

'I guess you two are, like, the Jay and Silent Bob of the undead world, huh?' Dante joked.

No one laughed. Instead, there was an awkward silence. *Shit!,* thought Dante. 'So who's this guy then?' he asked, pointing at the third man, anxious to skate over his gaffe.

'This is Déjà-Vu,' said Obedience.

Déjà-Vu was smoking a cigarette. He took a single long drag on it, then blew a kind of smoke ring, only it came out like an uncoiling snake. It floated up through his greasy shoulder-length hair and disappeared toward the ceiling.

He nodded at Dante. 'Have we met before?' he asked.

'I don't think so,' Dante replied, unsure whether this was a joke or not.

'Don't worry,' said Obedience. 'Déjà-Vu gets that a lot.'

'So you keep saying,' said Déjà-Vu, without a hint of irony.

For the next couple of hours Dante drank beers and exchanged stories with Obedience and his three friends. They were all friendly enough, except for Silence, who said nothing to him all night. Obedience always bought the drinks, Fritz shouted along to whatever the Psychics were singing, and Déjà-Vu – well, he looked confused for the most part, and seemed to do a double-take every time he saw someone walk by.

As new buddies went, these guys seemed to be all right. They had accepted Dante into their clan, and Obedience had even promised to get him one of the sleeveless black leather jackets they all wore. The jackets all had the group logo on the back which consisted of gold-embroidered lettering reading simply 'The Shades'. So far, Dante's mission as an undercover vampire was going nicely. He had made four friends and joined an exclusive clan or club or whatever the fuck it was. Any nerves he might have had about the task that lay ahead of him evaporated further with each beer he downed. He felt integrated already. Only time would tell if that was a good thing.

As it happened, what Dante had not noticed was that more than one of the other drinkers in the Nightjar had already recognized that he wasn't a vampire.

Twenty-Four

Peto sat alone in his apartment after yet another evening at the Nightjar among the undead. He still hadn't picked up any information about the Bourbon Kid, but curiously enough he had seen the young guy, Dante Vittori, whom he had met the previous year. On Peto's last visit to Santa Mondega Dante had offered to help him and his fellow monk, Kyle, locate the Eye of the Moon. Technically, he had kept his part of the bargain, but crucially he had turned on Peto at the last minute, aiming a gun at his head just as the monk had been about to fire at the Bourbon Kid. Had Peto managed to kill the Kid he would have unwittingly saved the lives of all of his Hubal brothers, brutally murdered shortly afterwards.

Yet still Peto had a feeling that Dante was a good guy. Cromwell had said as much, and his opinion seemed to carry some weight around these parts. Peto remembered how, after the previous year's eclipse, Dante had sent him from the Tapioca with the Eye of the Moon and the promise that he would deal with the Bourbon Kid. From what the monk had discovered since, Dante had actually done nothing of the kind. Instead, he had joined the Kid in pumping hundreds of rounds into the prone body of the young lady dressed as Catwoman.

His feeling about Dante had been confirmed when he spotted a picture of a woman bearing a striking resemblance to Jessica the Catwoman in the volume Bertram Cromwell had lent him. The book, entitled *Egyptian Mythology*, carried a full-page reproduction of a painting of her, giving her name as Jessica Gaius.

Now that he had finally found something in the book

worth reading about, Peto made himself a mug of coffee and settled into the single bed in the corner of his dingy, unheated apartment. Naked apart from the Eye of the Moon hanging around his neck, he lay under the single cotton sheet with his head propped up against the headboard. It made no sense to take the precious amulet off at any time. Any night-prowling intruder who sought to kill or wound him as he slept would be unsuccessful so long as he had that stone on him. Its healing powers were, quite simply, phenomenal. (It was also particularly useful for allowing its wearer to wake up hangover-free after a night on the booze.)

The gentle glow that emanated from the Eye when out in the open was bright enough to allow him to carry on reading, even after he had switched off the bedside lamp. So, as he lay in bed with his cooling coffee and the precious Eye, he read more about Jessica. What he discovered was extremely interesting. It was also extremely disturbing.

According to the dry and somewhat academic text, she was the daughter of Rameses Gaius, the Egyptian ruler whose mummified remains had allegedly escaped or been stolen from the Egyptology display in the Santa Mondega Museum of Art and History. As Cromwell had explained, Gaius had not only owned the Eye of the Moon, but had mastered the full use of its powers. Engrossed, Peto read on, learning that Gaius had been the chief monk of an Egyptian temple in the first century after the death of Christ. From that position of enormous power he had controlled everything, including the appointment of the Pharaoh. He was known to the people as 'The Moon' because he only ever came out at night.

As a young man, Gaius had lost an eye in a fight. Some years later he had discovered, hidden in one of the Great Pyramids, a blue stone known once to have been owned by Noah. Centuries earlier, the great Old Testament patriarch had used the stone to control, among other things, the tides during the Great Flood. Once Gaius realized the stone's power he wore it not around his neck, as many before and since had done, but in his empty eye socket, and so was born the name 'The Eye of the Moon'.

Through that Eye, Gaius learned to orchestrate many things. His most impressive power was an ability to control inanimate objects with his mind – *such as a mannequin of Beethoven*, Peto thought quietly to himself. Nor was that all for, using the Eye for the purposes of black magic, he had also created his own, corrupted version of the Egyptian *Book of the Dead*. Taking the basic premise of a book devoted to recording the rites necessary for safe passage into the afterlife, he created *The Book of Death*, his most powerful weapon. Whenever he suspected treachery from one of his council, he would simply write the person's name, with a date, on one of the pages in the book. As fate would have it, the life of the person in question would end on the exact date stated. The victims all died in different ways. Some were murdered, others simply dropped dead from heart attacks or died peacefully in their sleep. The existence of *The Book of Death* ensured that Gaius remained unchallenged as the true ruler of Egypt, whoever may have reigned as Pharaoh (and whose appointment was in any case decided by Gaius). For safekeeping, he entrusted the volume to a loyal subject, who kept it locked away out of sight.

Gaius's fall mirrored that of many tyrants. Like many extremely powerful people, he became paranoid and untrusting of those around him, as Professor Cromwell's book recorded. He had quarrelled with his daughter Jessica after she had recognized, and he had emphasized, that she could never rule in Egypt herself, for he had achieved immortality by wearing the Eye of the Moon at all times. He would never die, and therefore could never be succeeded, so Jessica's desire for the throne of Egypt would never be realized. Furious, she had fled the country and disappeared for several years.

In her absence, two of Gaius's early followers, Armand Xavier and Ishmael Taos, returned from a search for the Holy Grail. They claimed to have drunk the blood of Christ, thereby acquiring for themselves immortality similar to that enjoyed by Gaius through the Eye. This was extremely unwelcome news to the Egyptian ruler, particularly when they demanded a share of his power.

In order to rid himself of them, Gaius planned to write their names in his book. Xavier and Taos expected as much, however, and one night before he slept they sneaked into his private chambers and, while one held him down, the other removed his precious Eye from its socket. Then the pair of them wrapped him as a mummy and buried him beneath his own temple, placing a cheap green stone in his empty eye socket to complete his humiliation.

Gaius eventually died from starvation within the tomb in which they had encased him. The Egyptian chief monk had always known, however, that the day would come when someone outwitted him, and had taken out an insurance policy. Deploying one of the Eye of the Moon's many powers, he had created a curse which had later become known, to the few people who learnt the story down the centuries, as 'the Curse of the Mummy'. In the event of his murder and the theft of his precious Eye, a spell of sorts would ensure that he would be reborn the moment his killer or killers eventually died themselves.

Peto took his final sip of coffee. *Hmm. Well, that has now happened,* he mused. Armand Xavier and Ishmael Taos had both been killed by the Bourbon Kid shortly after the last eclipse. And now the mummy exhibit in the museum had come to life and escaped. *This could be bad,* the monk thought. *That mummy is gonna be after the Eye of the Moon. And that means it's after me.*

From what Peto had learned from an intensive study of Hollywood movies during his time away from the tranquil Pacific island of Hubal, the mummy was the Daddy of the Undead. Not someone you wanted in your life, and even less so on your tail.

At first, the long-winded prose and tortuous constructions of *Egyptian Mythology* had threatened to send Peto to sleep. Yet as he had read on, the story of the Eye of the Moon had begun to grip him, and he was now wide awake. He read on for just a few more minutes before finally settling to sleep. There was nothing else of note in the book, and he was disappointed not to learn more about what became of Taos and Xavier after the mummification of Gaius.

Peto did not sleep well after all his reading. His mind was troubled. What had become of Jessica? Was she dead now? And if so, would she be reunited with her father Rameses Gaius, now that he was free again? One thing of which the monk was certain was that the two of them would be after the Eye of the Moon.

He was certain of something else, too. Once he had completed his mission of finding the Bourbon Kid and using the Eye to cure him of his evils, he was getting the fuck out of town.

Twenty-Five

Sanchez was having a shitty day. And not for the first time, either. He'd had hardly any sleep for about three months now, and he was starting to look paler than the vampires he so often refused to have in his bar. The Tapioca was still the one place in town that wouldn't tolerate bloodsuckers.

Sanchez could generally sniff out a vampire better than anyone in Santa Mondega. Yet in the upstairs apartment of the Tapioca he had the most dangerous vampire of all, Jessica the Vampire Queen. And Sanchez had no idea she was a bloodsucker. Not a fucking clue. He just thought she was really cute, and he was desperate for her to come out of her latest coma and finally show him some gratitude. Last time, after he'd spent five years secretly keeping her safe with the help of his late brother Thomas and Thomas's late wife, Audrey, she had regained consciousness and been pretty rude to him. Then she'd jumped in the sack with a notorious bounty hunter named Jefe. Well, now Jefe was dead, so effectively there was currently no competition for her affections from anyone else. Sanchez had a head start, and intended to take his chance this time.

Jessica had been in her current coma ever since that bastard the Bourbon Kid had shot her to pieces again. The Kid had been helped by the Terminator – well, a guy in fancy dress who had turned up as a T-800. Sanchez wanted the pair of them dead, though he would happily settle for not seeing them again. These days, he didn't have the contacts he'd once had with people who might be capable of offing someone like the Bourbon Kid, or a Terminator. His two best hopes would have been Elvis and Rodeo Rex, but both had been brutally murdered. No one was really sure by whom.

So Sanchez had lived the quiet life for almost a year since the last massacre in his bar. He wasn't sleeping well, and he was unwittingly harbouring a Vampire Queen while she healed, but aside from that everything was just peachy.

Until now.

Things had just taken a turn for the worse. The minute they walked in Sanchez knew that their appearance would be followed by all kinds of trouble. The members of a vampire clan known as the Filthy Pigs arrived in the Tapioca, three of them to be precise. They were in plain clothes. One of them, the senior officer, Captain Michael De La Cruz, was smartly dressed in a pair of casual black trousers with a bright white shirt and a trendy, loose-fitting brown leather jacket. His hair was impeccable, slicked back with some fashionable spikes here and there, and a little bit of growth at the back. *Oh great*, thought Sanchez, *another one of these New Age pricks with three haircuts going on all at once.*

Mind you, De La Cruz was nothing compared to the second guy, a dirty-looking bastard whom Sanchez knew as Detective Randy Benson. This guy was far worse. He was wearing a fluorescent blue short-sleeved shirt and a pair of knee-length, fluorescent yellow shorts. And he could have done with having De La Cruz lend him at least one of his hairstyles because he didn't appear to have any of his own. A mad-professor's haircut was the only way to describe this loser's mop of white hair.

The third guy, whom Sanchez had never met before, was Detective Dick Hunter. He struck the bartender as a pathetic, weaselly-looking individual with a queerboy look about him, wearing a tight white T-shirt that revealed a pair of inappropriately pointy nipples. More than enough for Sanchez to take a dislike to him. He was a stranger, after all; not much more was needed to make Sanchez hate the prick.

De La Cruz swaggered up to the bar, flanked by the other two. He knew how uncooperative the bartender could be, so he didn't mince his words. 'Sanchez, you miserable son of a bitch, we wanna see upstairs,' he snarled. 'And get us three whiskeys to take up with us. On the house.'

Sanchez was cleaning a glass by wiping the rim of it on his dirty white sweatshirt, and doing his best to act uninterested, at which he excelled. 'You ain't going up there without a warrant,' he promised in his usual pissed manner.

De La Cruz retaliated. His response was programmed, much like Sanchez's. 'Don't fuck with me, Sanchez. If I have to come back with a warrant I'm gonna wipe my ass on it. And then I'm gonna rub it in your face.'

'Guess it won't be the first time I've been shitfaced in my own bar,' the bartender replied with a sarcastic smile.

The detective leaned a little way over the bar, just enough for Sanchez to get a waft of his foul breath, and a glimpse of his protruding fangs. 'Then I'm gonna rip your throat out with my teeth. Now let us upstairs, you porky little fuck.'

Sanchez sighed and put the half-cleaned glass down on the shelf directly beneath the bartop. He didn't mind making enemies of vampires or cops, but vampire cops, well, that was kinda different. These guys could really make his life miserable. They could harass him every day if they wanted, and basically put him out of business in next to no time. He was worried about Jessica, but he knew when he was beaten. No point in fighting a battle you were never going to win.

'Let me get you those whiskeys,' he said.

'Good man. I knew you could be relied on to assist a police officer in the pursuit of his duties.' De La Cruz winked and patted Sanchez patronizingly on the cheek before settling down on a stool at the bar. His two colleagues remained standing either side of him while Sanchez reached for a bottle at the back of the bar and poured shots into three of his cleanest glasses.

'Make mine a double . . . *Fatso*,' Benson growled. He had sensed the bartender's resolve weakening, and his natural bully's instincts made him demand a double even though he didn't particularly want one. Like De La Cruz, he was also pointing out the obvious. Sanchez was getting heftier, and there was no hiding it. The newly grown thick black sideburns that covered the sides of his face did nothing to disguise the folds of flesh that merged his chin into his neck.

Ignoring the insult as best he could, Sanchez placed the three shot glasses on the bar in front of the undead officers. Then he used a dirty white rag to wipe the bartop around the drinks. The sun had been out all morning and the place was hot, so every time Sanchez spilt something on the bar the surface grew sticky as the liquid evaporated in the heat. The massive propeller fan on the ceiling over the bar area was working overtime to keep the place cool. It wasn't having much success.

'You gonna tell me what you're expectin' to find upstairs?' Sanchez asked nonchalantly as he swabbed away with his cloth.

'Sure,' said De La Cruz, picking up his glass of whiskey and chinking it against the glasses of his two colleagues as they picked up theirs. There was a two-second pause before the bartender spoke. He actually asked the same question again.

'Whadd're ya expectin' to find upstairs?'

'A pretty lady in a coma. But don't you worry, Sanchez. We're not gonna take her with us, so you can rest easy. She's still all yours.'

The three men downed their drinks in one. De La Cruz and Benson immediately began retching, spitting the liquid onto the floor. Hunter seemed to be savouring the taste, but after seeing his colleagues' reaction he joined in, pulling a disgusted face of his own.

'What the *fuck* is that?' asked De La Cruz, trying to spit every last drop of the fluid from his mouth.

'That's my finest whiskey,' Sanchez shrugged. 'I gotta say it's an acquired taste, though.'

'No shit,' gasped Benson, who was still retching. 'It tastes like piss.'

'Yeah, a lotta people say that,' smiled Sanchez.

'I can see why,' remarked Hunter, staring at his empty glass in disgust. 'What's this stuff called? Just so's I can avoid it in the future, you understand.'

'It's a homebrew.'

'You got any more?'

De La Cruz and Benson both threw questioning looks at Hunter. Was he serious? Did he really want more of the stuff? He picked up on their incredulity and quickly covered his tracks.

'I believe I ought to confiscate some. Y'know, health an' safety an' all that?' Seeing that the others didn't look convinced, he turned back to Sanchez. 'You got much of this in stock?'

The bartender offered a beaming smile. 'Sure. There's an unlimited supply. Reckon you can have the rest of this bottle on the house. Here y'are.' He handed the bottle over to the detective, who took it willingly.

'Okay. That's enough of this,' De La Cruz interjected. 'Show us where the girl is, Sanchez.'

'You can find what you're looking for up this way.' The bartender gestured behind him to the stairs in the room that led off the bar.

The three vampire cops made their way around the bar and through the back room to the foot of a bare stairway. Two of them were still spitting the remains of the foul taste from their mouths. The other, Hunter, took a swig from the bottle he'd been handed by Sanchez and swilled it around in his mouth to savour the taste as he passed by the bartender on his way to the stairs.

Sanchez didn't follow them up. The further he could keep away from them the better. Besides, he had four customers sitting at one of the tables in a corner of the bar who might require his famed service at some point in the next hour or three.

Once they were at the top of the stairs, where they were faced with a sturdy wooden door, De La Cruz pulled the golden chalice from an inside pocket in his jacket.

'I sure fuckin' hope she's still in a coma, or this could get pretty hairy,' he said, turning the handle on the door.

'She must be pretty hairy herself by now,' remarked Benson. Seeing the others' looks of disgust, he tried to explain. 'I mean, you know, her legs must be getting real hairy. Might even have a moustache. Hell, it's been a year, hasn't it?'

'Oh shut up, you deviant,' said Hunter, pushing him in the back.

Led by De La Cruz, with Benson in the middle and Hunter bringing up the rear, still swigging from his bottle of Sanchez's homebrew, they made their way into the room at the top of the stairs. Sure enough, in the middle of the room was a bed in which Jessica lay fast asleep, looking peaceful, if somewhat dead to the world. It was a small single bed with a thick brown mattress on it, and a single white sheet covering the young woman's body. It was warm enough up here that there was no need for anything more than a thin sheet to cover her while she slept.

De La Cruz crept over to the bed like a parody of someone trying not to wake her. He put a finger to his lips to signal the others to be quiet, knelt down by the side of her bed, moved the sheet aside slightly and took hold of her right arm. Then, negating whatever purpose there may have been in keeping quiet, he slid his favourite six-inch silver dagger from his sleeve and sliced through a vein in Jessica's lower arm, just above the wrist. Surprisingly, this didn't wake her. He held the chalice beneath her arm where he had made the incision. Blood spurted out of the cut and he did his best to catch as much of it as possible in the cup.

'You think she felt that?' Benson asked softly.

'Doesn't matter,' whispered De La Cruz, frantically moving the cup around to catch as much of the spurting blood as possible. Some sprayed on to his fingers and he licked it up immediately. His two colleagues gazed longingly at the blood feast before them. 'She'll heal up in next to no time. Won't even know we were here.'

When he judged that there was sufficient blood in the cup,

De La Cruz took a mouthful and handed it back to Benson. Then he pulled a length of white bandage from his pocket and began to wrap Jessica's wound. As he did so, and as Benson was taking his fill of blood from the cup, De La Cruz suddenly felt a huge rush of adrenalin surge through his body. Every bone, every muscle, every cell suddenly took on a life of its own. He was tingling all over. A feeling of power rushed through him. *Incredible power.* This is what it felt like to be a Vampire King, a purebreed, a daywalker and a god. Within thirty seconds Benson and Hunter, having downed their own share of the blood, were experiencing that same feeling. It was a sensation far more intense than than that they had enjoyed after drinking Stephanie Rogers's blood the night before.

'Oh . . . my . . . God,' said De La Cruz, standing to his full height with his shoulders back. 'This is awesome!'

'Isn't it just?' Hunter agreed, washing Jessica's blood down with another swig from the bottle of homebrew.

Benson seemed oblivious to the others. He was enjoying the feeling too much to waste breath sharing the experience with anyone else. After a few moments, with them all struggling to come to terms with this second, much greater rush of body and mind enhancement inside twenty-four hours, De La Cruz recovered his senses, snapping out of what was almost a euphoric trance.

'Next stop Dr Moland's Mental Hospital,' he grinned. 'Bring on that Bourbon-drinking freak. The three of us are a match for anyone, and once we've gotten the blood from that sonofabitch we'll be ruling the fucking world.'

Hunter was blinking frantically, taking in this whole new, overwhelming sense of superiority. At last he snapped out of his own self-indulgent trance.

'You know something, De La Cruz? I'm in the mood to party all day and all night. Starting right now.'

De La Cruz nodded. 'Sure you are. We all are. But let's go hunt first. Then tomorrow we can go get the Bourbon Kid.'

'I sure do want some fresh young blood tonight,' grinned Hunter. 'I wanna nail some good-lookin' babes right now.

Come on, let's go. I'm not sure I can hold this in. Not for long, leastways.'

'I'm right with you, buddy,' said De La Cruz, running his tongue over his lips in the hopes of licking up any last traces of Jessica's blood that might be around his mouth.

'Let's get out of here right now and head straight to a brothel. Last night's feast is gonna seem tame compared to tonight's.'

Hunter led the way, polishing off the bottle of whiskey as he went, looking to screw another out of Sanchez on the way out. De La Cruz followed hard on his heels. A newfound hunger and lust was already taking them over. It was uncontrollable. Benson could feel it too.

'I'll catch up with you in a while,' he called out after them. 'I'm just gonna rebandage the cut on her arm. I don't think it looks tight enough.'

'Whatever,' De La Cruz yelled back as he disappeared down the stairs.

Benson looked around. No one in sight. This was the perfect moment. He was alone in a room with a Queen who was out cold. Opportunities like this didn't come along every day. His heart was racing as he undid the belt on his yellow shorts. Jessica was gonna be an amazing fuck, coma or no coma. He looked down upon her sweet pale face. Those luscious lips, that perfect skin and beautiful long dark hair. Not forgetting the breasts and legs and all the rest hidden under the thin white sheet.

Panting, he pulled his yellow shorts and filthy off-white underpants down to his ankles, then reached for the sheet. Slowly he peeled it back, savouring the moment. Beneath it, Jessica was naked, and as he laid eyes on her silky white flesh Benson was unable to contain his excitement. He tentatively reached a hand towards her right breast, almost salivating as he prepared for his first squeeze.

Then she opened her eyes.

'You wave that cock anywhere near me and you're gonna lose it,' she hissed. 'Now get the fuck out!'

Benson reeled back in shock. Somehow he managed one last quick look at Jessica's naked body before wisely taking to his heels and heading for the exit. With his shorts and pants around his ankles he resembled a penguin as he waddled in terror towards the stairs as fast as he could. Eventually, after tripping over once and frantically pulling his shorts back up, he reached the head of the stairs and took a look back. Jessica had closed her eyes again. Maybe he had imagined it? Even so, this woman was the Vampire Queen. Raping her while she was unconscious was one thing, but doing it after she'd seen his face and was fully awake was not an option.

Not just yet, anyway.

Twenty-Six

When Dante arrived at the Nightjar for his second night with the Shades he was relieved to find Obedience and Fritz standing at the bar. He had on the trademark wraparound shades they had given him the previous night, and he'd come out in just jeans and a thin black sweatshirt, hoping they would supply him with one of the cool black leather jackets that marked them out as members of their particular clan.

Tonight the place was fairly quiet, at least in comparison with the previous night, but even so he still didn't manage to make it to the bar without knocking into someone. This time, however, it didn't seem to be his fault. One of the white Rastafarians appeared from nowhere and banged into his shoulder.

'Whoa! Sorry, man,' said Dante instinctively.

The Rastafarian was a fairly short guy in a baggy black karate-style outfit. His dark dreadlocked hair hung at the same length all around his head, hiding most of his face.

'Why're you here?' he asked Dante in a half whisper.

'Havin' a drink with the guys,' Dante replied, throwing the fellow a confused look. *What did this guy expect? He was in a fuckin' bar, fer Chrissakes. Why else would he be there?*

Anxious not to get caught up talking to a member of another clan he turned his back on the Rastafarian and carried on making his way to the bar, where he could see Obedience and Fritz were waiting. He couldn't help thinking that the guy's voice sounded familiar, though. Still, it wasn't worth dwelling on. Right now he had more important things to worry about. Like trying to find Peto the Hubal monk. And staying alive.

The Nightjar's owner, Dino, was sitting at the far end of the bar in a smart blue suit, sipping at a glass of red wine, while two young bartenders in black trousers and pristine white T-shirts did the work. One of them was behind the bar polishing glasses and the other was cleaning a table in the far corner. There were no more than thirty customers scattered around, most talking quietly among themselves. Tonight, everyone seemed to be dressed more or less normally. No clowns. No Maori tribesmen. And as far as Dante could tell, no drag queens.

'Hey guys, how's it going?' he asked as he approached Fritz and Obedience.

'What did Chip want?' Obedience asked. He sounded suspicious.

'Who?'

'That Rastafarian you were just talking to.'

'Oh, him. He was just tryin' to get me to join his clan.'

'Yeah?' asked Obedience. 'Even though you don't have dreadlocks like the rest of them?'

'Yeah,' said Dante, pulling a surprised face. 'What a moron.' He hurriedly changed the subject. 'So, anyone wanna beer?'

Despite the unsettling questions about Chip, the two members of the Shades seemed pleased to see him, which was a good start. Dante dimly recalled that the previous evening had gone well enough. He seemed to have fitted in okay, so unless he had misjudged the whole thing through that night's excessive intake of alcohol, all was well.

Responding to his offer of a beer, Obedience spoke for both vampires. 'We were just about to head into town and pick up some young meat, actually,' he said.

'Young meat?'

'Yeah, we were gonna head down to a strip joint in town and feast on a couple o' hookers for supper. You in?'

This was not at all what Dante had in mind. Not even close. It was one thing to be able to blend in with the vampires thanks to the serum he had injected in to his bloodstream, but if they were expecting him to sprout a pair of fangs and bite a hooker's neck in order to drink her blood . . . well, they were going to be mightily disappointed. And he was going to be mightily dead.

'Er – I dunno, guys. I've got a bit of gut ache. Reckon I'll just hang out here an' have a few beers. Thanks for askin' me, though.'

'NONSENZE!' yelled Fritz. 'YOU VILL COME VIZ US. VE HAV SOMEVON WHO VISHES TO MEET VIZ YOU!'

'Yeah? Who?'

'ZE BOSS! VANITY, ZE LEADER OF ZE SHADEZ, VISHES TO MEET VIZ YOU TO DISCUSS YOUR INITIATION INTO ZE CLAN!'

The whole bar fell silent, it being impossible for anyone not to have heard what Fritz had said. The thirty or so customers all waited to hear Dante's response, and since The Psychics were on a break there wasn't even any background noise to distract them.

'Oh, right. Okay,' said Dante. 'I'll pass on supper, though.'

'You're not hungry at this time of night?' Obedience was clearly baffled.

'Nah, I had a Chinese before I came out,' said Dante, rubbing his stomach.

'Aaah.' Obedience and Fritz nodded in unison. They had both suffered from bad guts due to feasting on Chinese in the past. They were tasty, but hell on the digestive system.

'So, where's the other guys?' Dante asked, tactfully changing the subject.

'NEVER MIND ZEM!' bellowed Fritz. 'VE HAV CLEAVAGE UND MOOSE VIZ US ZIS EVENING!' He pointed at two female vamps who were just making their way over from the rest rooms at one end of the barroom. One was a fairly stunning brunette with enormous breasts wedged tightly together inside a tiny white T-shirt. *At a guess*, thought Dante, *that's gotta be Cleavage.* Her friend was a tubby unattractive blonde with a huge nose and one eye much bigger than the other. *Moose*, Dante thought. The two of them attracted a number of admiring glances as they trotted back to the bar in their short skirts.

'Hi Fritz, is this Dante?' asked Cleavage as they reached at the bar.

'YES, ZIS IS ZE YOUNG MAN VE MET LAST NIGHT. VE ARE TAKING HIM TO OUR LEADER. YOU COMING?'

'Sure,' said Cleavage, eyeing Dante as though he was a piece of meat. 'Hi Dante, I'm Cleavage. People call me that 'cos I have a great cleavage. Or mebbe you didn't notice?'

Dante hadn't noticed much else. He was staring right down at her breasts as if they had him in a trance.

'Great cans,' he said out loud instead of in his head.

'Excuse me?'

'Nice to meet you.' Dante reached out and shook hands with her, finally making eye contact.

Cleavage smiled back at him. She was used to people talking to her boobs all night, so she was pleasantly surprised to meet someone who even looked up. 'This is my friend Moose,' she said, pointing to her hideous companion.

Dante shook hands with Moose, who beamed a ridiculously gummy smile back at him.

'People call me Moose because I put loads of the stuff in my hair to keep it like this,' she said, patting her enormous blonde bouffant, which looked as though it was held in place with marine varnish.

'Ha ha! Yeah, right,' laughed Dante. A confused look came over Moose's face, and Dante realized immediately that he shouldn't have laughed at her. She hadn't actually been kidding.

'What's so funny?' she asked.

'Great to meet you. You have great hair.' Dante offered his most winning smile.

'Aw, thanks,' she simpered, beaming back at him. The compliment had the desired effect, erasing the previous gaffe from her memory.

In the course of all the meeting and greeting, Uncle Les, the older of the two bouncers, had made his way over to the group. Tonight, he was wearing blue jeans and a matching sleeveless denim jacket with a white T-shirt underneath. It showed off a rippling set of muscles and a six pack that was moulded by the thin T-shirt. He was in need of a shave, but no one was in a hurry to mention it.

'If you folks ain't gonna be buyin' any drinks in here tonight I'm gonna have to ask you to leave,' he said sternly.

'We were just leaving, actually,' said Obedience. 'We're heading for Vanity's place. If Silence or Déjà-Vu turn up, can you tell 'em where we are?'

'I might.'

'Thanks.' Obedience turned to the others. 'C'mon. Let's get outta here, before things turn ugly.'

Uncle Les took a look at Moose. 'Bit late for that, ain't it?' he quipped. Fortunately Moose was incredibly thick-skinned, and was so certain of her attractiveness that his spiteful remark went over her head.

The group made their way out of the Nightjar, Fritz leading them down the quiet street towards the Swamp, a strip club owned by Vanity. Dante hung back with Obedience.

'Reckon that bouncer's a Grade-A prick, ain't he?' Dante ventured.

'Yeah, but he's a real badass. You wouldn't wanna mess with him, trust me,' the vampire replied.

'Yeah?'

'Oh yeah, he's a hardass, all right.'

'He ain't no Wade Garrett, though, is he?'

'Who the fuck's Wade Garrett?'

Dante shook his head in disgust. 'It don't matter.'

'Well, maybe they should employ this Garrett character down here. Lord knows we could do with someone to keep all the fuckin' werewolves out.'

'You don't like werewolves?'

Obedience was clearly surprised that Dante even had to ask. '*Shit no!* Do you?'

'No.'

'Good. Those hairy stinking muthafuckers should stick to their own side of town. Last thing we need is the likes of MC Pedro in the Nightjar trying to rap with The Psychics. Fuckin' nightmare, that was.'

Dante carried on walking along at the rear with Obedience. It was unnerving that every question he seemed to ask had an answer that he felt any vampire worth his salt was supposed to know. How the hell was he going to find out anything about the Eye of the Moon or Peto, or any crap about the clans, without sounding like a fool? Or, worse, an impostor.

Well, there was probably no way of asking without looking stupid. And since he was never normally one to worry about making an ass of himself, he just asked.

'So tell me, Obedience. Any idea where the Eye of the Moon is these days?'

'*What?*'

'The Eye of the Moon. Y'know, that blue . . . '

'I heard what you said.' Obedience stopped dead in his tracks in the street and grabbed Dante by the arm, holding him back until the other three vampires were safely out of earshot. 'Don't let Vanity hear you ask any shit like that. In fact, don't you let anyone else hear that kind of talk, either. Talk like that'll get you killed quicker than a silver crucifix will. People here don't talk about that stone. Brings nothing but misery with it. And if you're asking about it, people are gonna think you have it, or know something about where it is. And that ain't good.'

'Shit, man, I'm sorry. I didn't know.'

'Don't worry about it.' Obedience started walking again. 'Just don't ask anyone any questions, man. Ever. I introduced you to the clan. If you show me up I'll be in deep shit. Just be polite when Vanity asks you anything and keep your answers brief. Don't ask any questions yourself. Keep it simple and he'll initiate you into the clan. Okay?'

'Okay. I can do simple. Simple's my middle name.'

Obedience stopped again and took off his shades to reveal

deep-set dark brown eyes. 'Man, you're nervous tonight, Dante. You were cool last night. Now you're like a bag of cats, all fucking edgy and shit. What the fuck's up with you?'

'Aah, y'know, I just haven't had a drink yet, and I wanna make a good impression when I meet this guy Vanity. Just a bit of nerves, I guess. Nothing a few shots of tequila won't cure.'

'Right. Fuck it,' said Obedience. 'Let's stop in at the Painted Lady and have a few drinks there first. You can ask me all the stupid questions you like, get them out of your system. I'll prep you on what not to say when you meet Vanity, and we can get tanked up while we're there. How's that sound?'

'Yeah! Sounds great, man. The Painted Lady, I ain't never heard of that place.'

'It's an underground joint. They got all sorts there. Alcohol, drugs, gambling, strippers and tattoos.'

'Tattoos?'

'Yeah, it's a tattoo parlour by day, which is why it's called the Painted Lady. How about getting a cool tattoo on your arm? I know Vanity's got one of our jackets waiting for you at the Swamp. It'd be kinda rude not to have some ink on your arm to show off when you're wearing it.'

'Cool. I've always wanted a tattoo.' Dante had visions of surprising Kacy by getting her name tattooed on his arm. She'd love that. Might even cheer her up a bit.

What actually happened when they got to the Painted Lady wouldn't have pleased Kacy at all. Dante and Obedience stayed a little too long. They drank too much. They dabbled in some drugs and they watched the strip shows.

And when they were done with all that, Dante, in his drunken state, made a horrific error of judgement.

Twenty-Seven

The report compiled by Stephanie Rogers contained all the information that De La Cruz, Benson and Hunter required on the whereabouts of the Bourbon Kid. She had dug deep, and where so many others had failed, she had come up with an answer. For almost eighteen years a man with no name had been resident at the local mental hospital. He was living there not as a patient, but as a lodger, having checked in there shortly after Halloween eighteen years earlier.

Although the three detectives were scared of no one, they saw no need to go and collect the Bourbon Kid themselves when they could pay someone else to carry out the task for them. Muscle for hire. Specifically, the two most reliable contract musclemen in Santa Mondega: Igor the Fang and MC Pedro. They weren't just strong, they were super strong. And supernatural. Werewolves, sent to do a vampire's job with the promise of a few sips of blood from the Holy Cup in exchange for their services. De La Cruz had briefed them, but, lowlife that he was, he hadn't mentioned to them that the man they were to break out of the mental hospital was in fact – if their information was correct – the son of Ishmael Taos. A man also known as the Bourbon Kid.

Igor parked their camper van in the far corner of the main parking lot outside Dr Moland's Hospital. The top half of the van had been sprayed blue, but the lower half was a pea-green colour, due to a botched respraying job a few weeks earlier, when they had run out of paint halfway through. It was nearly midnight, but even in the dark the two-tone effect was clearly visible.

The parking lot wasn't well lit, and with a bone-chilling wind coming in from the ocean it was unlikely that too many people would be loitering around outside a hospital that happened to be situated in the middle of an area of deserted wasteland. The lot had just over forty spaces, but there were only three other vehicles in it and they were all parked out front in the special 'reserved for staff' slots. Now was as good a time as any to break a patient out.

Both men pulled balaclavas over their faces, then tiptoed their way up to the glass doors of the hospital's front entrance. Igor led the way, his huge, six-foot-five-inch frame hardly the best qualification for a discreet approach. MC Pedro, shorter by nine inches, followed, stooped over and trying to keep his face out of sight of any hidden cameras by covering it with his thin hairy hands. He was the smart one of the two, although only in terms of self-advancement and self-preservation. Igor was fearless because of his size, so being seen and identified bothered him less. Pedro was sneakier, and happily allowed his partner to take the lead, letting him be the first to deal with any problems they might encounter.

Pedro's sneakiness had allowed him to climb the ladder of power among werewolves. He stuck to the simple-minded Igor like glue, using the giant as a kind of unofficial personal bodyguard. It wasn't that Pedro couldn't handle himself, it was just that he liked to work his way up the ladder unnoticed, picking off his enemies by first gaining their trust. Whereas if Igor ever chose to try to better himself, all he had to do was use his fists. As things currently stood in the undead world, he was unwittingly using his fists to help Pedro advance himself.

The light from the moon shimmered down on them as they crept along. Luckily it was not yet a full moon, so there was no chance of them turning hairy halfway through the operation.

The main hospital building was three storeys high, the outside painted from top to bottom in a calming light blue colour, although they could not see that in the fitful moonlight. The huge glass double doors at the front entrance were closed, which was normal not just for this time of night, but at any time. The winds in this region were biting and the place was exposed to the elements, so the doors were almost always kept closed. Igor sized them up as he approached. It was going to take a superhuman effort to knock them down. But then, he *was* superhuman, so there shouldn't be any problem.

In order to help them sneak in unseen, the pair of them had dressed in black jeans and black sweaters that matched their balaclavas. The effort they had put into dressing themselves as shadows was entirely wasted, however, when one of the massive doors was suddenly shattered by a single kick of the big black boot on Igor's right foot. Before the glass had even hit the floor, he was striding menacingly through the frame and up to the reception desk. Pedro, spotting the word 'Pull' on the undamaged door, was pleasantly surprised to find that it opened easily. He stepped over a few shards of glass on the tiled floor and proceeded to follow his partner into the building.

The desk was manned by a forty-something, bored-out-of-his-mind former doctor named Devon Hart. He had worked as receptionist there for over six years and had seen all kinds of crazy shit go on at night, so this intrusion didn't particularly faze him. He was reading a book called *The Mighty Blues* by Sam McLeod, and was enjoying it too much to care about the shattered glass and the two thugs who had approached his desk.

'We're closed, you know,' he sighed, without looking up. 'And if you don't leave immediately I'll call security.'

'Thatta fact? Well, I got news for ya, homeboy, we *are* security,' snarled MC Pedro.

'*Excuse* me?' Devon finally looked up, frowning. These two clowns clearly weren't security. Security didn't generally wear black balaclavas, or call him 'homeboy'. Come to think of it, they didn't usually smash in the glass doors at the front of the hospital.

'Yo, white boy, word to your mother. I'll excuse you on the other side of your face in a minute, you ain't careful,' the smaller thug responded. Pedro was beginning to talk as if he were rapping. It made him feel in control, and he firmly believed it intimidated other people. Besides, anyone who said it didn't scare them was clearly unnerved by it – in his opinion, anyway.

'What the fuck are you talkin' about?' Devon asked, failing to hide his bewilderment.

Igor the Fang thrust an arm out across Pedro's chest, as though he thought his buddy was about to lunge at the aloof receptionist. If either of them did decide to attack Devon, he'd be dead long before security arrived. Apart from the three of them, the lobby was empty of people. There were several large terracotta plant pots on the floor containing small trees, and a waiting area with two leather sofas and a small wooden coffee table in between on which lay a few tired-looking magazines.

After a quick look around to make sure no one was hiding behind the sofas or plants, Igor took over the questioning.

'We're lookin' for a patient with no name. He lives here. Where can we find him?'

'I'm afraid I can't give out that sort of information,' Devon replied. 'I'm going to have to ask you to leave and come back tomorrow, during official visiting hours.'

Pedro lunged at him, only to be held back firmly by Igor's huge muscle-bound arm.

'Oh yeah?' Pedro snapped. 'Well, I'm gonna have ta ask *you* to leave an' come back tomorrow. How d'ya like that?'

Devon looked at Igor quizzically. 'Is your friend a patient here?' he asked.

'Just tell us where we can find him,' Igor growled, his face screwing up into a wolfish snarl.

Devon sighed wearily. 'Come on, then,' he said. 'At least make it worth my while.' He held out a hand, palm upwards. Igor knew the drill and pulled a roll of banknotes from an inside pocket. He slipped a twenty-dollar bill into Devon's hand, then, seemingly from nowhere, with his other hand he slammed the blade of a pocket-knife through the note and straight through Devon's hand. It sliced clean through the receptionist's palm and lodged itself in the wooden desk below, pinning the hand down so that only the fingers could move.

'Yeeeoooowww! SHIT!'

'Don't make him ask again, man,' Pedro suggested to the stricken receptionist.

'Fuck, *fuck*, FUCK!' Devon stared, open-mouthed and wide-eyed, at the blood spurting from his hand. '*Room Forty-Three, second floor. FUCK!*'

'Can I have my blade back?' asked Igor.

Devon nodded frantically. 'Take it out!'

Igor obliged by forcefully pulling the blade back out. Then the huge wolfman snatched back the bloodied twenty-dollar bill and slipped it into one of the front pockets of his black jeans. 'Thanks.'

Having relieved Devon of the key to Room 43, Igor and Pedro pushed through a pair of double doors into a long narrow hallway and set about finding the staircase to the second floor. In less than two minutes they found themselves standing outside a grey door with a small square window in it at head height and the number 43 just below it. Igor peered through the window and saw inside the room a single bed with the body of a man lying asleep in it.

'That's our guy,' he said. 'He's sleepin', so this oughta be easy.'

Pedro also peered in to get a look for himself. Then he slipped the key into the lock and turned it. It was definitely the right key, which meant this was definitely the right guy. Pedro turned the doorknob and looked at Igor.

'You wanna go in first, or shall I?'

Twenty-Eight

Vanity, the leader of the Shades clan, was not a vampire who enjoyed being kept waiting, so his mood was fairly dark by the time Dante and Obedience arrived at the pool hall. The hall was on the third floor of the nightclub aptly named the Swamp. The Swamp was a shithole that attracted the sort of lowlifes that weren't even welcome in the Tapioca. It was a rundown building that had once been a multi-storey car park, but a shoddy revamp had turned it into what was now a distinctly unclassy five-storey club that attracted as many rodents as it did paying customers.

Fritz, Moose and Cleavage had arrived at about ten o'clock, but it was another two hours before Dante and Obedience showed up.

When they arrived they were both extremely drunk and noisily boisterous. That, however, was not the reason why their entrance caused quite such a stir. They had made their way up two flights of stairs to get to the pool room. On their way up they had passed a number of bikers, hookers, drug dealers, clowns and Depeche Mode fans, and every single one of them had stared hard, first at Obedience, and then at Dante. They had all seen something that they didn't like. Word was spreading round the joint fast that something was amiss.

Vanity was in a game of pool with Déjà-Vu and Fritz when he saw the two drunkards stagger through the doors at the end of the hall. '*Finally*, they're here,' he grumbled, slamming his cue into the white ball and pocketing a tricky red.

There was no mistaking why he was called Vanity. This guy was one handsome dude. He had long dark hair and an immaculate goatee. His dress sense was sharp, too, tonight running to a smart black suit with a perfectly pressed black shirt underneath. His eyes were his most distinguishing feature, however, and by a very long way. They flickered between three different colours. This may have been a trick of the light, but rather like a rotating disco ball they changed from gold to black and then silver to black before repeating the routine. Each change was a mere flicker, but to look into his eyes for too long was simply hypnotic, which certainly helped him to attract all the female company he could possibly handle. He had formed the Shades because of this affliction. He had found that he fitted in better when he was wearing a pair of sunglasses, because he could hold a conversation with someone without freaking them out, or, indeed, hypnotizing them. So cool shades had become the clan's emblem.

Fritz and Déjà-Vu had been standing at the far end of the pool table watching Vanity take his shot. There was a long bar counter stretching along the back wall with a bartender standing behind it preparing cocktails for Cleavage and Moose. The two female vampires were buying a round of drinks with some money that Silence had handed them. The quietest of the vampires was out of sight, however, having taken himself off to the men's washroom in the far corner of the hall.

As Dante and Obedience staggered merrily over to the pool table, a small crowd of disparate characters they had passed on the stairs was assembling behind them, following them at a short distance as they made their way towards Vanity. As they passed Cleavage and Moose at the bar, Dante heard the pneumatic brunette squeal something that sounded like 'Oh my *God*! That's not good . . . '

When they were no more than six feet from the table, Vanity threw his pool cue to the floor. 'What the fuck have you done?' he demanded. He was staring at Obedience.

The English vampire sobered up very suddenly. Taking on the look of a disobedient puppy, he stared meekly at his boss's feet. Vanity snarled at him, 'Look at me when I'm talkin' to you!'

Dante was blissfully unaware of the serious displeasure in Vanity's tone. 'Hi, my name's Dante, you must be Vanity, huh?' he said, offering his hand.

The vampire leader turned his attention to this potential new member of his clan. He looked Dante up and down with a stare that suggested he wasn't at all pleased by what he saw. 'Are you responsible for this?' he bellowed. His voice caused the floor to shake, and it finally snapped Dante into a moment of sobriety. It suddenly began to dawn on him why Vanity sounded angry.

'VOT ZE FUCK IZ ZAT?' Fritz's ordinary speaking voice boomed out as he and Déjà-Vu approached from the pool table behind Vanity.

Just an hour earlier, Dante had made a terrible error of judgement. After getting extremely drunk with Obedience the pair of them had decided to get a tattoo each. Dante had chosen to have the word 'Kacy' tattooed around a bright red heart on his right bicep, but this wasn't even on show beneath the sleeve of his black sweatshirt. It was Obedience's tattoo that was responsible for all the stares they were getting.

Somehow, Dante had not quite been able to come to terms with the fact that Obedience would always do as he was asked, no matter how preposterous the request. He was also not familiar with an unwritten rule among the vampires that Obedience's eagerness to please was not to be abused. Dante had broken that rule. Not believing for a moment that Obedience would go along with it, he had ordered his new vampire friend to have a tattoo across his forehead. And it was this that had attracted everyone's appalled stares. The rapidly sobering Obedience was standing alongside Dante in the middle of the pool hall with the word 'CUNT' tattooed across his brow in large green capitals.

For an awful moment there was a terrible disheartening silence. It was broken, ironically enough, by Silence, who reappeared from the men's room, allowing the door to slam behind him. Even so, the sound of the door banging to only distracted everyone for half a second.

'Was this your fuckin' idea?' Vanity asked Dante, prodding a long bony finger into his chest.

'Hey, we – er – y'know? – we wanted to get some tattoos,' the other stammered.

Vanity looked at Obedience again. 'Did you want that tattoo on your face? 'Cos I'm takin' a wild guess it wasn't your first choice.'

Obedience took a deep breath. 'Dante suggested it,' he muttered.

Just then Silence arrived on the scene, curious to see what all the fuss was about. Straight away he registered Obedience's new tattoo. His initial reaction was one of surprise. Then amusement. The normally mute vampire couldn't help himself and began to snigger, and as all the others turned to see who it was that was finding the situation funny, he burst into a full-on howling laugh, one that a werewolf would have been proud of.

For a few seconds he was laughing on his own, oblivious to the shock on everyone else's faces. Then the surprise of hearing anything come from his mouth started a few of the others off, and pretty soon almost everyone was laughing hysterically and pointing at Obedience's new tattoo. Even Obedience began to laugh, just so he could feel he was in on the joke.

By now the only two people not laughing were Dante and Vanity. The former was on the verge of suffering a panic attack, realizing that he had to all intents and purposes made an enemy of Vanity on his first meeting. As for the vampire leader, well, he just didn't think the joke was that funny. Fortunately, being extremely vain, he was desperate always to be at the forefront of fashion, and the current trend was to laugh at the prank Dante had played on Obedience. Eventually he too began to laugh along with the others, albeit rather unenthusiastically.

Dante could have hugged Silence for saving his ass. As it turned out, the quiet vampire just liked a good joke. In fact, he had just returned from carrying out a practical joke of his own in the men's room – a practical joke that was about to backfire spectacularly and cause no small degree of bloodshed.

The Eye of the Moon

There were two things Silence lived for: practical jokes, and massive bar brawls. In that respect he was less than a minute away from his perfect night out. Things were about to turn seriously, if not ridiculously, ugly in the Swamp. And Silence's new comrade Dante, in his drunken state, was about to get his first taste of a vampire bar fight. The relief he was feeling at having escaped any punishment for the tattoo incident would be over all too soon.

Twenty-Nine

Kacy could barely stomach any food. She was worrying herself sick thinking about what Dante might be up to. Robert Swann had been a real sweetheart, convincing his colleague, Agent Valdez, that it would be good to allow Kacy to eat in the hotel's restaurant with him. So while Dante was out drinking in town with a horde of the undead and hoping not to be unmasked, Kacy was eating a three-course meal with Swann.

The hotel dining room was huge, an imposing space that was often used for the most exclusive weddings and other social events in Santa Mondega. There were at least fifty tables of varying sizes, and at least half of them were in use while Kacy and Swann were sharing their intimate dinner. Each table had a spotless white tablecloth draped over it, and all of those in use were lit by smart pink candles in elegant two-branched candelabra. Light classical music played discreetly from hidden speakers, and there was always a member of the waiting staff on hand to cater to diners' every need, such as adding more ice to the bucket that held the wine on the table Kacy and Swann were sharing. If a gentleman in Santa Mondega wanted to impress a lady, this was the place to come.

The food was exquisite too, but Kacy was struggling to force it down. Beneath the elegant, if rather abbreviated, black dress she was wearing, her stomach was tying itself in knots, so that trying to swallow anything too dry, like the bread that they had been offered on sitting down, was all but impossible. She had forced down a couple of prawns from her shellfish salad, only for her palate then to reject anything that tasted of fish. The only thing that she seemed able to swallow easily was the wine, and Swann, as if he could sense her tenseness, was regularly topping up her glass. He wasn't just acting like a gentleman, either. For once, he actually looked like one, too. The hotel manager had provided him with a smart grey suit and a red tie for a small charge. The effect of it was that this serial rapist and all-round scumbag was able to pass himself off as a man of taste and manners. He'd even slicked his hair back with some sort of gel spray he'd borrowed from Valdez.

By the time the main course of chicken and pasta arrived, Kacy was actually feeling better than she had at any time since she and Dante had arrived back in Santa Mondega.

'There's nothing like a few drinks to calm your nerves and put everything in perspective, is there?' smiled Swann, as he took up their second bottle of Chardonnay from its silver ice bucket.

'I'm not much of a drinker, normally,' said Kacy, forcing a smile. 'But this is going down real easy. Thanks for getting your partner to let us eat down here. That room was starting to drive me crazy. I'm a bit of an out-and-about girl as a rule, so sitting around with nothing to do but watch crappy movies was really starting to do my head in.'

Swann smiled back at her. 'It's the least I could do. You've got a lot on your mind. It's only fair that you get a chance to relax, instead of sitting around worrying about your boyfriend Danny all night.'

'It's Dante.'

'Whatever. Try and forget about him for a few hours. He'll be fine; he's a tough kid. He wouldn't want you sitting around stressing yourself about him, would he? Besides, he's probably steaming drunk again, so there's no harm in you having a few drinks too, is there? Why should he have all the fun, right?'

Kacy watched him top up her glass, and although she knew she was getting a little tipsy – she could hear herself babbling slightly – the alcohol really was helping to ease her concerns about Dante. Then, of course, Swann was turning out to be quite a nice guy. At least he was paying her some attention, something Dante hadn't been able to do much of in the last few days.

'You're right,' she said picking up her wine glass and chinking it against the one Swann was holding. 'I reckon I might get drunk, too. That way, when Dante gets back tonight, we'll be on the same wavelength for the first time in ages.'

'Oh dear,' said Swann solicitously, setting his glass back down. 'Things with you and him not going so well these days, huh?'

Kacy took a large sip of her wine and thought for a second. What the hell – there was no one else to talk to. The other agent, Valdez, seemed to have an unhealthy interest in Dante, so Swann was the closest thing Kacy had to a trustworthy friend right now. So for the rest of the meal she got more and more drunk, telling him all about the fears she had for Dante and the mission he was on, and how much he annoyed her with his foolhardiness and regular rushes of blood to the head that invariably landed him in trouble. True, she loved Dante more than she believed she could ever love any person, but he still had all these annoying habits that she had to iron out to prevent him from getting himself killed. It was his minor imperfections that made him such a challenge, and such fun to be with. And for tonight she could confide her fears about all these things to Special Agent Swann over dinner and fine wine.

For his part, Swann feigned interest and continued generously to provide glasses of wine as though it was on tap. All the while, as he became drunker, he was listening less and less to what Kacy was saying and staring more and more at the cleavage she had on show. And if he wasn't mistaken, she was purposely letting him get an eyeful. By now he had convinced himself that she was deliberately leaning forward over the table with increasing frequency as the evening wore on.

When at last they finished their meal and the time came for them to go back to their suite, Swann had reached a stage at which he was struggling to control his sexual urges. Kacy was a fantastic flirt, and after finishing off her dessert, a rather provocative-looking Banana Surprise, she was drunker than she'd been in years.

Feeling cheerful and ridiculously horny, Swann stared longingly at her across the table, eyeing up any and all of the flawless skin she had on show. Ever since Mr E had somehow secured his release from a life term in prison as a serial rapist, he hadn't even had so much as the sniff of a fuck. Now here was this young beauty flirting openly with him, practically inviting him to take advantage of her. He knew that he couldn't take her back to their shared suite because Valdez was still there, and Dante might come back at any point. But if he could get a key from reception for one of the other rooms then he was pretty sure Kacy was up for a fuck. He'd probably have to trick her into it, but he could tell that, secretly, that's what she wanted. Once he had her alone in a bedroom, he bet she'd be more than willing to let him screw her. In fact, just thinking about it was getting him seriously aroused, so much so, that in order to get up from the table without showing off the huge bulge in his pants, he was going to have to think about Barbra Streisand for a few minutes.

He'd done this for just about long enough when, at the most inconvenient of moments, Roxanne Valdez appeared. She had on a pair of black leggings and a black sweater, and looked positively fearsome as she strode through the dining room. Valdez was no fool. She knew full well what he was up to because the boss, Mr E, had warned her to watch out for exactly that sort of behaviour from Swann. In one swift move, perfectly executed to look like an accident, she knocked over the ice bucket on the table and watched with a grin as the freezing water and chunks of ice splashed down into her colleague's lap.

'JEEESUSSS!'

Swann sprang to his feet and began frantically rubbing his crotch, pulling his pants away from his skin to lessen the shock of the ice-cold water. Kacy, in her drunken state on the other side of the table, pointed at him, giggling hysterically. Valdez, meanwhile, continued to control the situation, pulling back on Kacy's chair to get the girl to her feet.

'Come on Kacy, it's time you came back to your room,' she said, throwing a hard look at Swann, who was too busy mopping his soaked and frozen groin to notice.

As Agent Valdez guided Kacy back up to the suite on the third floor, Swann seethed. Valdez was a bitch. He'd worked that out within minutes of meeting her. But Kacy, well, he had wined and dined her and been on his best behaviour, only for her to laugh like a hyena when his partner had tipped the ice bucket over him. She had revelled in his humiliation. She would suffer for that later, the dirty little cockteaser.

All he had to do was get her on her own.

Thirty

Once the laughter over Obedience and his new tattoo had died down, Dante was invited by Vanity to join him in a game of pool. With his confidence returning after he had so carelessly landed himself in trouble, he was relieved to have the opportunity to play. Dante was actually pretty handy with a cue, so it was a chance to impress. He knew a few trick shots, too, that he could show the other guys if things went well.

Déjà-Vu tossed a coin. Dante called heads. The coin landed on the table, heads up.

'I knew it. Heads again,' Déjà-Vu remarked.

Dante elected to break. Unfortunately, correctly calling heads was where his luck at the pool table ended. As it turned out, he only had time to play his first shot. The cue ball smashed into the pack of colours at the other end of the table, and as it did so another ruckus started up. A clown named Jordan came staggering out of the men's restroom. His white romper suit was soaked through with water, and he didn't look at all happy.

There were still three other clowns in the pool hall who hadn't left right away after the hilarity of Obedience's tattoo had died down. They were at another pool table, practising trick shots, completely engrossed in what they were doing. That changed when they saw their fellow clown and the state he was in. It was immediately apparent to them that all was not well.

'What the fuck happened to you?' shouted the largest of the three clowns. His name was Reuben and he was hard to miss, due to the enormous green curly wig he wore at all times. His face was painted white with a big red smile slapped across it and a solitary black tear below his right eye. The leader of the Clowns clan, he was not a vampire to be messed with. His black romper suit he had on cleverly disguised a buff, muscular torso underneath, and his apparently good-natured clown's face concealed a vicious nature. His two companions, Ronald and Donald, who had moved to stand on either side of him, wore yellow wigs and white romper suits, a look that was almost identical to that of Jordan, the clown who had just emerged from the men's washroom. Aside from the fact that his clothing was extremely wet, there was one other glaring difference that immediately distinguished Jordan from his friends Ronald and Donald. Where they both had the trademark oversized red smiles painted across their faces, Jordan had none. And without it he looked extremely angry.

'Someone's wiped the fuckin' smile off my face!' he ranted, waving an angry finger around at everyone in the bar area. There were now only Clowns and Shades left, apart from the bartender Hank, and he was readying himself to duck down out of the way.

All eyes turned to Silence, the last person to have come out of the men's room. The quiet vampire shrugged his shoulders, and smiled.

'You . . . you fuckin' sonofabitch!' Jordan raged, storming towards Silence. 'I was only asleep for a fuckin' minute. What the fuck? How would you fuckin' like it if I did something to you while you were asleep?'

The sight of him storming towards Silence, who was standing by the pool table, only served to set off everyone else. Like a pride of lions homing in on a wounded antelope, Clowns and Shades swarmed in from all directions, ready for a fight. Dante was glad to see that the Shades outnumbered the Clowns by six to four, or even eight to four if you included Cleavage and Moose, who for the time being remained seated at the bar. Unfortunately, his relief was short-lived, for it soon became apparent that the Clowns were carrying weapons.

Reuben whipped a heavy knife with an eighteen-inch blade out from the sleeve of his clown suit, and his two yellow-haired minders did likewise, revealing equally large bone-handled knives that verged on being long enough to be classified as swords.

Jordan had squared up to Silence, unveiling a blade of his own that he had drawn from under a flap on one leg of his sodden white romper suit. He stood, tensed and ready for trouble, no more than two yards away from his enemy, waiting for the go-ahead from Reuben.

Vampires generally wait for the nod from their leader when there's a rumble, and the Shades were looking to Vanity, who was standing at the pool table with Dante. Fritz, Obedience and Déjà-Vu had all made their way around the table to square up to their knife-wielding opponents.

Vanity spoke calmly in the direction of Reuben. 'There's no need any joking around here, Reuben. This can be sorted out without any bloodshed.'

Reuben sneered at Vanity, his bright red grin broad across his face. 'Do I look like I'm jokin' around?' he asked.

'Well, yeah, you kinda do,' Vanity replied, gripping his pool cue, ready to use it in his defence.

This only served to rile the clown further. 'Your buddy Silence has played one too many stupid tricks. This time he's gone too far. You hand him over to us and the rest of you can walk away. That's the deal.'

'NO FUCKING DEAL!' bellowed Fritz from the place he had taken up just behind Silence. 'VE SHADES, VE SCHTICK TOGEZZER!'

'Then you'll die together.'

That was the signal for it all to kick off. The Clowns waded in, swinging and jabbing their blades at anything that didn't look funny. The Shades all grabbed whatever weapons they could, which was mostly pool cues, and set about fighting them off.

Except for Dante.

Unusually for him, he froze at seeing a fight develop.

He'd never been attacked by bloodthirsty clown vampires before, and wasn't quite sure how to react. More importantly, however, he had an image of Kacy flashing through his head. In his mind, he saw her crying, begging him to run away at the first sign of trouble. He hated to see Kacy cry, even if he was only imagining it, but he knew that if he stayed and fought, there was a damn good chance she'd be crying soon enough, because he was liable to get killed or at the very least lose a limb. He heard her tearful voice in his head screaming '*Run you idiot! Run!*'

So as the fight got under way, with everyone watching out for whatever weapon was being swung or stabbed in his direction, Dante rolled beneath the pool table out of harm's way. He soon spotted a gap at one end where there seemed to be no one wielding a weapon, so he crawled over to it and then rolled out and ran towards the bar. Reaching it, he wasted no time in diving over the counter. Ducked down on the other side were Hank the bartender and Moose and Cleavage. Dante came crashing down alongside them.

'Hi,' he said, smiling a nervous smile.

All three of them looked at him in a manner that suggested that they thought his action in joining them somewhat cowardly. But before any of them could say anything judgemental a clown's head appeared, looking over the bar above Dante's head. The fearsome smiling face beneath the bright yellow wig was bad enough, but the figure was also brandishing a large blade above its head, ready to swing it down at Dante cowering below the bar.

THWACK!

The blade missed Dante's head by a few inches and embedded itself in the bartop. The clown struggled to reach fully over the bar to get at its target. Dante, terrified by the sight above him, pressed himself as far back against the wall behind the bar as he possibly could, desperate to avoid the next swing of the blade.

Somehow, Hank, Moose and Cleavage managed to manoeuvre themselves out of the way, running along the space behind the bar and out towards the staircase, away from danger, where they could watch the proceedings from a safe distance.

Dante could hear all manner of crashing and yelling coming from the area around the pool table as his new vampire buddies fought with the horrific clowns. His immediate concern, however, was the clown Ronald, who was leaning over the bar, leering at him, and drooling blood from his mouth, no doubt from a wound recently picked up at the end of someone's pool cue.

Ronald quickly realized that Dante was just a few inches too far away to be caught with a swing from where he was standing, so he sprang up on to the bartop. He stood up tall, his bright yellow curly hair touching the ceiling as he loomed over the cowering figure of his enemy. He was smiling inanely, eyes wide open, blade at the ready and, more significantly, his fangs on full display. He had morphed into a vampire in the space of half a second.

For a moment the clown looked as if he would simply dive down on Dante and attack him with his blade, but he hesitated for just a moment, and Dante saw in his eyes an expression of mild surprise.

'You're not even a vampire,' the clown hissed. How he had come to this conclusion was anyone's guess. Perhaps it was just the terrified look on Dante's face. More likely, it was the fact that Dante wasn't morphing into anything. He was just cowering on the floor as most humans do when faced with a vampire clown wielding some kind of machete.

Whether or not anyone else heard the clown's exclamation was hard to tell because of the clash of blades and pool cues and the occasional cry of pain, fury or triumph.

Then a loud bang silenced everything.

Dante was still staring up at the terrifying figure on the bar, but the clown's expression had suddenly changed. Where blood had been dribbling from his mouth, it was now also pouring out from a hole in the centre of his face. For no more than a second the nightmarish creature swayed first backwards and then forwards, before toppling down off the bartop and on to Dante on the floor below. The long knife fell with him and missed Dante's arm by a whisker before clattering on to the floor.

There followed a second loud crashing sound, that of breaking glass somewhere, and it was succeeded by the whoops of the inrushing wind.

Dante pushed the dead clown off himself and watched him disintegrate slowly into smoke and ash on the floor beside him. It was an unpleasant sight, accompanied by a rotten stink that hastened his desire to get up. Screwing up his nose and trying to breathe through his mouth, he climbed to his feet to peer over the bar.

The pool hall was in a state of absolute carnage. There were two more dead clowns on the floor between the tables. One was definitely Jordan, his soaked romper suit and lack of smile identifying his corpse. The other dead clown also had a yellow wig, but there was no sign of Reuben the green-haired leader. He had escaped by crashing through a window at the end of the hall and vanishing into the night sky. The window was now letting in an icy wind through the clown-sized hole where the glass had once been. As Dante watched, both clown corpses began to smoulder and smoke, before flaring briefly into flames which reduced them to two handfuls of greasy ash.

The members of the Shades were all on their feet and staring at Dante, who was still standing behind the bar, dumbstruck by the carnage.

'Did you shoot that guy?' Vanity asked.

Dante shook his head. 'Wasn't me. Thought one of you guys did it.' The Shades all looked around at each other. None of them was holding a firearm.

'That's weird,' said Vanity suspiciously. 'Somebody shot that clown in the head. Who the fuck was it?'

The others all took it in turns to shrug. Obedience was holding his left arm just below the elbow where he appeared to have been cut, and Déjà-Vu was rubbing his chin as if he'd been caught by a punch. Fritz, Vanity and Silence were all covered in the blood of the two dead and now disintegrating clowns. But no one was owning up to having a gun, let alone firing it at the head of the clown whose remains were now lying behind the bar at Dante's feet.

The first person to break the silence was Cleavage, who was making her way back into the pool hall, followed by Moose. 'I think we oughta get the hell outta here before Reuben rounds up a bunch of his friends and comes back here in greater numbers,' she suggested.

'Fuckin' good idea,' said Vanity. 'He'll turn this place into a fuckin' circus. Come on, people, let's roll. Head home for the night and we'll meet up again tomorrow in the Nightjar.' He looked over at Dante. 'You done okay, my friend. Come to the Nightjar again tomorrow night and we'll talk some more.'

Dante nodded, breathing a huge sigh of relief. Somehow he'd made it through another night undercover with the Shades. One thing was bugging him, though. He was only alive because someone had saved his ass by firing a bullet into the skull of the clown who had been about to kill him. And they had done so just after the clown in question had announced that Dante wasn't a real vampire. Everyone had heard the gunshot, but had anyone heard what the clown had said?

Above all, why was no one owning up to the shooting?

Thirty-One

Igor parked the two-tone blue-and-green camper van right outside the front of the police headquarters. It was late and the streets were largely deserted, and as most of the folks who were out at that time of night were criminals this was the last place they would be hanging around. After a quick check up and down the street Igor and his companion made their way round to the double doors at the back of the van. Pedro opened them carefully. They were relieved to see the body of the patient they had brought back from Dr Moland's Hospital was still there, not moving. No doubt still unconscious from the blow to the head received back at the hospital as he slept. He hardly looked threatening, either. He was wearing a pair of dark blue jogging bottoms and a thin blue pullover with red sleeves, the same clothes that he had been sleeping in when they ambushed him.

Igor dragged the body out by the feet and threw it over his shoulder. Pedro closed and secured the van doors behind them as the big werewolf carried their prisoner up the steps at the front of the headquarters and in through the glass doors to the reception area. After making sure the van was locked, Pedro followed on behind, checking round to see if anyone had noticed them.

They had successfully surprised the sleeping patient in Room 43 at the hospital, and after Igor had violently slammed him over the back of the head with enough force to knock him into a different kind of sleep, Pedro had pulled a cloth bag over his head. It had been all too easy. De La Cruz had warned them that this guy could be highly dangerous. That might still turn out to be true, but they had caught him unawares, and he had let himself be taken without any kind of fight at all.

It being the middle of the night, the reception desk was manned by just one officer. His name was Francis Bloem, a cautious, rule-bound, red-haired officer in his late twenties. He recognized the two wolfmen, and wasn't in the least bit fazed by the sight of one of them carrying a body.

'That the package you picked up from the hospital?' he asked, nodding at the hooded figure.

'It might just be,' Igor replied. 'Mind if we come on through?'

'Knock yourselves out,' the officer replied.

As Igor lugged the body through reception to the elevators at the far end, MC Pedro stopped and gave Officer Bloem an evil stare. Then he launched into one of his stupid and pointless raps. 'Who's gonna knock who out? I'm gonna knock you out, hear what I say, homie?'

Bloem sat with a quizzical look on his face, unsure how to respond, and by the time he realized that Pedro's rap made no kind of sense, the werewolf pair were stepping into the elevator and heading down to the locker room beneath the headquarters. He shook his head, then buzzed Captain De La Cruz using the speeddial on his switchboard. The Captain answered after one ring.

'De La Cruz.'

'Hey, it's Francis on reception. Those two dogs you sent on an errand have just returned with a body for you. They're on their way down now.'

'Thanks.' De La Cruz hung up.

In the locker room, De La Cruz, Benson and Hunter waited excitedly for the elevator to arrive. When it did, the doors hissed open and the body of Patient Number 43 came flying out on to the floor. Igor had obviously grown tired of carrying it, and had launched it straight out in the direction of the three officers waiting in front of him in the middle of the locker room. The captive with the bag on his head let out a muffled yelp, indicating that he had regained consciousness.

Pedro and Igor, still looking like a couple of mismatched cat burglars in their all black-outfits, stepped out of the elevator and stood triumphantly over their prisoner. Without their balaclavas to cover their heads any more, each was sporting the kind of deranged hairstyle that follows a particularly bad night's sleep. Pedro's hair looked like something that might be found on a Lego character, which was particularly unfortunate because his skin was an unpleasant yellow colour at the best of times. And this was not the best of times. Unaware that the removal of the balaclava had given him the World's Stupidest Hairstyle, he stood with his hands on his hips and a smug smile on his face. His oversized companion stood with his arms by his side, wearing a witless toothy grin dominated by one particularly large fang in his top row of teeth.

'There he is,' growled Igor, pointing at the hooded figure on the floor. 'That's your guy. The man with no name from Room Forty-Three at the hospital.'

De La Cruz stepped forward and grabbed a fistful of the cloth bag still tied around the captive's head. 'So this is the son of Ishmael Taos,' he said with a contented smile. 'At last we meet. Thought we wouldn't find you hiding out in an asylum pretending to be a fruitcake, huh? Well, you thought wrong, buddy.' He kicked the hooded man in the back, forcing another muffled yelp. 'Benson, bring the cup here. Let's get a taste of this guy's blood.'

The concealed entrance at the back of the showers was already open, revealing the secret room behind it. Benson, as vilely dressed as ever, mostly in brown, sprang up off the heels on his pointed black boots and began to float over to the large wooden table in the room. Reaching it, he swooped gracefully down and picked up the golden chalice that was resting on the table next to Somers's book. Then, as though bored with floating through the air, he merely walked back over and handed it to De La Cruz. The third officer, the weaselly Hunter, took station at Benson's side, eager to see what was about to happen.

Still holding the chalice, De La Cruz knelt down, untied

the rope around the captive's neck and pulled the bag from his head. This revealed the terrified face of a man who was probably in his late twenties, but which had a childlike quality on account of his babyfaced looks and scruffy dark hair. He was breathing erratically, as if the shock of his abduction was inducing a panic attack, and his eyes were bulging, unable to hide the fear that had undoubtedly gripped him.

If he had needed a spur to his terror, De La Cruz provided it as he began his transformation into a creature of the night. His face paled and thinned to that of a blood-lusting, merciless vampire, and his fingers turned to claws with razor sharp talons where once his nails had been. Long, pointed fangs sprang from both his jaws, forcing his lips into an obscene parody of a smile. For a moment he stood there, a dapper vampire in a smart dark blue shirt and pressed jeans, ready to begin the killing. As he licked his lips and readied himself for the murder of the terrified victim before him, Pedro stepped forward.

'Hey! We had a deal, De La Cruz,' he snarled.

'Sure we did,' the detective hissed back. 'And I intend to honour it. You two have done well. As agreed, you shall have the first taste of blood.'

Hunter, meanwhile, had been taking a long hard look at their prisoner, soon to be the meat of their feast. Unlike the others, he was studying the terrified man's face. 'You sure this is the right guy?' he asked. 'This bozo don't look so tough to me.'

Suddenly alarmed, De La Cruz turned to Benson. 'What do you reckon?' he asked.

'Let me get the artist impressions,' the other replied. He floated over to the book on the desk behind them, opened it and picked out a selection of sketches on rough paper that had been folded up and tucked inside. These were artists' sketches that Archie Somers had compiled over the years from people who claimed to have seen the Bourbon Kid and lived. Most of them had actually been based on descriptions provided by Sanchez Garcia, so they weren't considered particularly reliable; nor would they ever be admissible as authentic pieces of evidence. He studied the pictures closely, glancing up to compare them with the panic-stricken face of their prisoner, who looked up at him, desperately hoping the scruffy cop would clear him. Benson could see the fear in his eyes.

'Reckon it's him,' he said, smirking. 'Let's get a taste of his immortal blood. Then we'll know for sure.'

'Please! No! Don't . . . *please*,' the terror-struck young man pleaded, looking up into De La Cruz's hateful eyes. It was too late. De La Cruz turned to Hunter and nodded. The latter reached inside his jacket and pulled out a bone-handled machete, the blade of which was almost two feet long, and wickedly sharp. He raised it above his head, then swung it down towards the man's bound wrists. Hunter's face had blood lust written all over it as he watched the blade slice right through the man's left wrist. The severed hand fell to the ground as blood spurted everywhere, accompanied by the agonized screams of the victim.

De La Cruz picked up the severed wrist and held it over the golden chalice, trying to catch every last drop, ignoring the screams of the prisoner, now half mad with fear and pain. When he was done he stood and passed the almost full cup to Pedro, who accepted it eagerly, immediately swallowing a huge mouthful of its contents. As he allowed the bittersweet, copper-tasting blood to slide down his throat and so into his veins, he felt the power of it engulfing him. It was a moment to savour, and he became so wrapped up in the enjoyment of it that he barely noticed Hunter and Benson begin their transformation into vampires. They were lusting at the sight of the blood spurting from the arm of Patient Number 43, longing for a piece of the action.

Pedro's already limited self-control deserted him. His eyes came alight, and the quickening brought about by drinking from the chalice caused his transformation into a werewolf to take effect almost instantaneously. This was not normally possible other than during a full moon, but he now had heightened powers. The drinking of blood from the cup had different effects on its beneficiaries. Pedro's was the new-found ability to transform into his more powerful self in the blink of an eye. With a roar from deep within his being, he handed the cup to his giant companion, who followed his example, drinking deeply, and in his eagerness even wastefully allowing a little of the precious liquid to dribble down the side of his mouth.

The screaming man on the floor began to sob like a baby, incomprehensible pleas for mercy mingling with his anguished howls. De La Cruz looked down at him, smiling in satisfaction, enjoying watching their captive's suffering. The man rolled onto his right side and lay in the foetal position, wailing and sobbing in equal measure. Yet unremarked by his tormentors, he was also seeking escape. He had only one hope of getting out of this situation alive. And he had had one piece of luck, for the blow that had removed his hand had also cut the rope binding his wrists. With his good hand he reached into the pocket of his pants and slowly drew out a cell phone. He had successfully kept this phone hidden about his person during his stay at Dr Moland's Hospital. It was his most prized possession, a recent gift from his best friend as a reward for his good behaviour at the hospital. His only chance of survival was to call on that friend. The one and only person he could count on. His brother. His *elder* brother. The brother who had fought the vampire that had savaged their mother all those years before. The same brother that had since become known as Santa Mondega's most feared killer.

The Bourbon Kid.

De La Cruz spotted the phone almost at once, and as soon as he saw the wounded man pressing buttons on it he kicked it out of his hand.

'No use calling the police, you fuckin' retard. We're already here,' he scoffed. Benson and Hunter both allowed themselves a howling laugh. These were high times indeed. Who did this moron think he was? *Trying to call for help. What a fuckin' loser.*

The two werewolves, however, were too busy revelling in

their newfound strength to join the laughter. They were dimly aware of the cup being refilled and passed to each of their vampire accomplices in turn, but in their own euphoria they saw these things as though in a dream. After the last of the detectives had finished drinking his share of the blood, the golden chalice was passed around until it found its way back into the hands of Michael De La Cruz. Once again the senior detective and chief of the Filthy Pigs vampire clan roughly grabbed hold of the distraught prisoner's truncated arm and held its bloody end over the cup. He pumped the arm violently to increase the output of fresh blood to fill the chalice once again.

'Stick around, guys. There's gonna be plenty more blood for everyone,' he said, smiling hideously through his great gash of a mouth, now stained crimson.

For the next five minutes the three vampires and two werewolves ripped their wretched prisoner to pieces, prolonging his agony by keeping him alive for as long as possible before finally tearing out his heart, so putting an end to his fading screams and cries for mercy. It was an end he welcomed with all his being.

The locker room was now a bloodied mess. The dead man's blood and entrails were smeared all over the floor and walls. The mess they had created meant nothing to his tormentors, who were too hyped-up to care. Invigorated after such an enjoyable kill, and with their blood lust sated for a while, all five sat around contentedly on the floor, occasionally looking at each other, sharing the acknowledgement of the beauty of their kill. It was a wonderful feeling. For the three members of the Filthy Pigs it was reminiscent of what they had felt when killing Stephanie Rogers, and also when drinking the blood of Jessica Xavier in the upstairs room at the Tapioca. For Pedro and Igor, the blood from the cup had brought a new sensation, and one they were both relishing. This was better than an orgasm by the light of a full moon.

As the seconds ticked on, however, it began to dawn on the three vampires that this feeling, though intense, was actually no better than when they had killed Stephanie. It was good, sure, but shouldn't it be better? Shouldn't the blood of a descendant of an immortal have taken them to even greater raptures?

As he looked around the room, Benson was the first to notice the white glow backlighting the screen on the cell phone that De La Cruz had kicked from their captive's hand during the blooding. The phone was on the floor within distance of his left hand, so he leaned over and picked it up.

'Looks like our guy called someone,' he said, noticing that the call-duration time on the display was still ticking along. It changed from 04:53 to 04:54 as he watched. Shrugging at the others, he put the phone to his ear and spoke into the mouthpiece.

'Hi, this is Detective Benson of the Santa Mondega Police Department. Who am I speaking with, please?' he said, smirking at his bloodied companions. He was an immortal now, so it didn't matter who was on the line. There would be nothing they could do to harm him.

Whoever was on the other end of the phone was breathing heavily, yet very slowly. The sound had a *gravelly* quality to it, and after a few seconds its unnerving resonance began to cause the smile to fade slowly from Benson's face. 'Who is this?' he repeated, more sharply. The others looked on, noting the concern on his face and in his voice. The undead have a heightened sixth sense, and it was telling all of them that something was wrong.

The breathing coming through the earpiece stopped a few seconds later when the recipient of the call hung up. The display on the phone showed the call duration timed at 05:25.

'Who was that?' De La Cruz asked, not attempting to mask the mild concern in his voice.

Benson flicked through the menu options on the cell phone.

'CALLS MADE – BIG BRO – DURATION 05:25'

Thirty-Two

Devon Hart's evening had been shitty right from the moment the two men dressed in black and wearing balaclavas had walked in, smashing one of the front doors as they did so. He'd been stabbed in the hand by the larger of the two and bullied into giving them the information they required. That wasn't the worst thing about his evening though, not by a long way.

From the minute he'd witnessed the two intruders carrying out the unconscious body of Patient Number 43 he knew he was going to have to quit his job at the hospital and get as far away from Santa Mondega as possible. That patient was not to be messed with. Everyone in the hospital knew that. All of the other inmates there were either murderers who had pleaded insanity, or crazies predicting the end of the world and trying to ensure it happened. The only likeable patient they had was Casper, better known around the place as 'Forty-Three'. He was a simpleton, very pleasant and well-mannered, but deeply paranoid and with a mental age of about eight. He was almost certainly the least aggressive of all the patients, but no one would *ever* have messed with him. No matter how mad or disturbed the other inmates were, there was one thing they all knew not to do: upset Casper. Do that, and you got a nocturnal visit and a nasty pummelling from his brother, a man whom no one wanted to fuck with.

Casper's brother didn't visit the place often, dropping by maybe once every six or seven weeks. He'd always make sure his younger brother's stay was paid up a few months in advance, and he'd insist on asking whoever was on reception whether anyone had upset Casper since his last visit. Because the receptionists were all too scared of him to risk lying about it, they sang like canaries, giving up anyone who'd made off with Casper's crayons, given him a Chinese burn, or simply just changed the TV channel when he was watching *Sesame Street*. The culprits all paid for their actions and there were no repeat offenders, so generally Casper's stay at Dr Moland's Hospital had been quite a pleasant one. But that stay had ended, and as a result Devon Hart's now had to.

Right now, Hart was sitting in Cubicle 3 of the ground-floor men's rooms with his head in his hands and his trousers round his ankles. His stomach had been in knots ever since he'd seen Igor and Pedro sling Casper's body in the back of their camper van. It was now three a.m. His shift had just three more hours to go, and then he was never coming back. He'd made his mind up. Fuck whether he got paid or not, he just wasn't going to show his face round these parts ever again.

After thirty minutes of trying to take a crap and failing miserably he finally decided he'd had enough. He pulled his pants back up, flushed the toilet and headed to the row of basins to wash his hands.

The mirror above the white plastic washbasin confirmed his deepest fears to him. He looked like shit. He felt like it, too, and not just because he was nursing a ragged hole in his now heavily bandaged hand. Truth was, he'd given Casper up too easily. It was not only that he feared the retribution of the kid's big brother, either. He would have to live with the knowledge that he'd allowed two obvious thugs to ambush and kidnap a total innocent. That would prey on his conscience for ever.

As he pulled a variety of different grimaces at himself in the long mirror above the basins he tried not to think about what might have happened to Casper. The condensation on the glass seemed to spell out the word 'Guilty' right across his forehead. *Guilty* was how he felt. It was hard even to look himself in the eye, and eventually the sight of his reflection looking back and feeling sorry for itself made him feel sick.

His mouth filled with saliva as if he were about to throw up. Suddenly overwhelmed by self-hatred, he spat it at his reflection, the fluid covering much of the pathetic face that was staring back at him.

Devon didn't have to stare at his reflection for much longer, because as the spittle started to slide down the mirror, the bathroom was suddenly plunged into darkness. It awoke him from his trance-like state and he snapped out of it in an instant.

Power cut? Oh shit, he thought. *What the fuck else can go wrong tonight?*

There wasn't a glimmer of light anywhere as he staggered, arms out in front of him, towards where he thought the door was. Once he felt the painted wood of the door he swept his hands around until one of them settled on the doorknob, which he turned. The door swung open easily, but he was disappointed to find that the hallway outside was just as dark.

Hart knew there was a flashlight in a drawer in the staff kitchen so he took a left turn into the hallway and walked slowly down it, with one hand on the wall and one out in front of him to keep him from walking into anything. He managed to make it about ten yards down the hallway in the silence and darkness before something sent a shiver down his spine. For a few moments he had been getting a taste of what it was like to be blind, and to some extent deaf. All he had been able to hear were his own quiet footsteps. Then he heard someone else take a step in the corridor behind him. He spun around in panic and called out in the darkness. 'Hello?'

No answer.

'Hello,' he called again, more softly this time. 'Is someone there?'

Still nothing. Must have imagined it. He turned back and walked on towards the kitchen, pressing his hand hard against the wall to steady himself.

Then he heard it again. Another footstep behind him. He stopped dead, frozen to the spot. And listened. There was definitely someone behind him. He could hear breathing. He could, *couldn't he?* Of course he could. Devon Hart knew what breathing sounded like. He held his own breath for a few seconds to be certain it wasn't himself he could hear.

'Hello,' he said again, this time not looking back. 'Listen, I know there's someone there. I can hear you.' Dreading what he might be getting himself into, he turned round again and stared into the dark abyss of the hallway that led back to the reception area.

And then there was light, although only a little. Ten yards in front of him Devon Hart saw a flicker of light. A tiny flame, even, the size of a fingernail on someone's little finger. It confused him momentarily, before he realized what it was. *A cigarette.* Strangely, though, it appeared to have lit itself.

'Hello,' he called out yet again. Terror was now really beginning to grip him, squeezing the air from his lungs. Someone was there. They had made it known by smoking, but they weren't speaking. 'Who *is* that?' he called out once more, straining his eyes in the hope of seeing a figure behind the tiny glow at the end of the cigarette.

After what seemed like an age, Hart saw the end of the cigarette flare brightly one last time, and then whoever was holding it dropped it to the floor. He stared at it, watching it burn away on the floor, expecting to see it extinguished by the person who had discarded it. But it stayed lit. Then the sound of footsteps came again. His unwelcome visitor began to move towards him, the sound of his boots getting louder and the steps quicker with each passing moment.

Finally the footsteps came to a stop. Devon Hart felt a hand seize him around the throat.

Thirty-Three

Sanchez was tired of this same old bullshit. Barely a month went by without him being dragged down to police headquarters to look at mugshots of criminals who might be the Bourbon Kid. In the past it had always been the worn-down old cop Archie Somers who had forced him to endure this ritual. The results were always the same; the familiar faces would be brought up on the computer screen. Sanchez knew them all, and none of them was the Bourbon Kid.

On this occasion he had been called in by Detective Hunter, one of the three cops who had visited the Tapioca the day before. With uncharacteristic kindness, Sanchez had brought him a bottle of his finest 'homebrew', seeing as how the detective had enjoyed the stuff so much on his recent visit to the bar. Hunter had taken the bottle eagerly, and was now enjoying frequent sips of the dark yellow liquid. He had even succeeded in spilling a few drops on his sweater in his eagerness to get the bottle to his lips.

Sanchez wasn't sure what irritated him more, being dragged down to look at the same old mugshots, or the fact that Hunter was enjoying drinking this morning's fresh piss. 'Look, man, this is a fuckin' waste o' my time,' he sighed. Hunter ignored him, clicking his mouse again to bring another face up on screen.

The interview room they were in was a shithole, to the say the least. It had once been the office that Archie Somers had shared briefly with Miles Jensen before the pair of them had perished in unusual circumstances on the night of the last eclipse. Hunter was sitting behind the desk in front of the window with the blinds pulled down for maximum interrogation effect. His computer monitor was turned around so that Sanchez, sitting on the other side of the desk, could get a good look at the mugshots coming up in the slideshow. It was obvious even from the bartender's clothing that he wasn't into the whole process. His grubby white T-shirt carried a simple logo, its message aimed directly at Hunter. 'FUCK OFF!' it read in large black letters.

'That's Marcus the Weasel,' said Sanchez, looking at the latest picture on the screen. 'He's fuckin' *dead*, man. Been dead for about a year. *Jesus!* Don't you ever update these things?'

Hunter clicked the mouse and another photo appeared on screen.

'Dead.'

And another.

'Dead.'

And another.

'Dead,' said Sanchez again.

'Bullshit,' Hunter snapped. 'That guy was in here last week.'

Sanchez shrugged. 'If you say so.'

Another mugshot appeared on screen.

'Dead.'

Hunter released his grip on the mouse and pursed his lips, glaring furiously at Sanchez. 'Are you saying "dead" for all of them now, just to be annoyin'?'

'Yep.'

'You fuckin' porky prick. You think I enjoy having you waste my time?'

'Look, buddy,' said Sanchez leaning across the desk. 'You're wasting both our time. There are no fuckin' pictures of the Bourbon Kid in your database, okay? Never have been. Never will be. I've given E-fit descriptions of him to your artists plenty of times.'

'I've seen 'em,' said Hunter. 'You're a real fuckin' comedian, you know.'

What the detective was referring to was a particularly

annoying habit that Sanchez had. On no fewer than five occasions he had given descriptions to police artists and successfully tricked them into drawing pictures of themselves instead of the Bourbon Kid. It was a lousy gag, but it was the only way to get back at the bastards for repeatedly dragging him down to headquarters. He sat back in the chair and folded his arms. 'We done?'

'Nope.'

Hunter flicked another mugshot up on screen. This one grabbed Sanchez's attention and he leaned forward, unfolding his arms.

'My God!' he whispered. 'It's *him*.'

Hunter brightened. 'The Bourbon Kid?'

'No, my paperboy. That bastard's been late three times this week.'

'Right. That does it.' Hunter roared. 'I'm going to kill you. I mean it.' He was just about to lunge across the desk at Sanchez when the door in the wall behind Santa Mondega's most annoying bartender opened. Michael De La Cruz walked in, wearing a crisp red shirt buttoned to the neck and a pair of smart loose-fitting black pants.

'Any luck?' he asked.

'You kiddin'? This guy's a fuckin' joke. He's not gonna tell us shit.'

De La Cruz grabbed hold of Sanchez's shoulder and squeezed it tightly. 'You know the Bourbon Kid is gonna be dropping by your bar again some time soon if we don't catch him? Only, this time he might not let you live. And as you're the only person alive who knows what he looks like, technically you're the only person who can save himself from being killed by him next time he comes in.'

Sanchez turned around to face De La Cruz. 'Is that supposed to be ironic?' he asked.

'No. It *is* ironic.'

'Look,' said the bartender, already tired of the conversation. 'There's two things in life I never wanna see. And one of them is the whites of that man's eyes. Not even in a fuckin' photo.'

'Well then, maybe you'll start being more cooperative,' De La Cruz suggested. 'This is for your benefit as much as ours, okay?'

'Sure.'

'So – you said there were two things you never wanted to see, right? What's the other thing?'

'How meat pies are made.'

De La Cruz shoved Sanchez in the back of the head. 'Useless prick.'

'Can I kill him?' Hunter asked.

'It's tempting. But we've got bigger problems. There's been an incident.'

'An incident?'

'Yeah. You know the Dr Moland's Mental Hospital on the edge of town? The one where Igor and Pedro snatched the Bourbon Kid's brother?'

'Yeah.'

Sanchez butted in. 'The Bourbon Kid has a brother? You're fuckin' kiddin' me! Who is he?'

'None of your goddamn business,' snapped Hunter.

Sanchez wasn't finished with his own line of questioning. 'He the guy you an' the werewolves killed last night after drinkin' his blood from the Holy Grail?'

The two officers stared at him.

'How the fuck do you know about that?' asked Hunter.

'I don't. It's just a rumour. In fact, it's a rumour I haven't even heard yet. Forget I said anythin'.'

'You know what?' said Hunter. 'That wagging tongue of yours is gonna land you in some trouble you can't weasel out of one day.'

'Least my tongue knows what whiskey tastes like.'

'What the fuck's that supposed to mean?'

De La Cruz had heard enough bickering. 'Will you two shut up a goddamn minute?' he barked. 'You wanna hear about what happened at the hospital, or what?'

'Sure. Sorry. Go on,' said Hunter.

'The hospital burned to the ground last night.'

'*What?*'

'Burned to the ground. Fire Department found a hundred and twenty-five dead bodies inside.'

'Fuck,' Hunter shook his head. 'Those crazy werewolves. They set the place on fire?'

'Nope,' De La Cruz wagged a dismissive finger. 'It wasn't them. The place was still right as rain when they left. This fire happened in the early hours of this morning. Long after they'd gone.'

'So it was an accident? Or what?'

'Nope. This was no accident.'

'Many survivors?'

'None.'

'None at all?'

'None at all.'

Sanchez remained sandwiched between the two officers, listening intently. First-hand gossip – a rarity indeed. And De La Cruz looked like he had a whole lot more information to pass on.

'Not one single survivor. Wanna know why?'

'All the fire escapes were blocked?' Hunter ventured.

'Nope.'

'So you're tellin' me all one hundred and twenty-five people that were in the hospital when it went up in flames were burned alive? Not one fuckin' person managed to get out?'

De La Cruz shook his head. 'Nope. No one burned alive. This was a cremation.'

'Huh? I don't get it.'

'All one hundred and twenty-five victims were dead before the fire started.'

Hunter recoiled in his seat and arched his shoulders back. 'What the fuck? How come?'

'Take a guess.'

The thin-haired South African detective frowned for a few seconds before coming up with an answer. 'Gas leak?'

'You ever heard of a gas leak gouging out people's

eyes? Decapitating them? Blowing off kneecaps, ripping out throats?'

'Say again?'

'You heard me.'

Hunter's jaw dropped. 'You're sayin' that someone killed all these people first? *Then* set fire to the place?'

To get the attention of the two officers Sanchez cleared his throat and pointed at the picture of his paperboy on the computer screen. 'Well, it won't be him,' he said.

De La Cruz slapped him across the back of the head again and turned back to the other detective.

'Hunter, it's gonna be the Bourbon Kid. That's who's done this.'

'Yeah, but why? None of the people in that hospital did anythin' to him. Except maybe any security guards who let Igor and Pedro through. That's just a motiveless killing of a hundred and twenty-five innocent people. What the fuck's the point in that?'

De La Cruz shrugged. 'Don't know. Who knows why that guy does anything?'

'I do,' Sanchez offered.

'What?' asked De La Cruz.

'I know why he killed all those people. And why he did it so brutally and mercilessly, too.'

'This guy's a fuckin' clown,' said Hunter. 'Come on, Sanchez, crack your funny joke and get out. Why's the Bourbon Kid killed all these people this time? C'mon – what's the punchline?'

'There's no punchline,' said Sanchez soberly. 'This is for real. You wanna know why he killed all these innocent people, and made each of them suffer horribly in many different ways before they died? Or not?'

'Go on,' De La Cruz was taking more interest than Hunter. For once he was right to, because for once Sanchez wasn't kidding around.

The bartender stood up and picked his dirt-brown suede jacket from the back of the chair he'd been sitting in. He started to put it on as the two officers waited for his response. Having slipped his arms into the sleeves, ready to leave, he finally answered.

'He killed these people to make a point. And that point, my detective friends, is this: the biggest mass murderer in livin' history doesn't need a motive to kill people. He does it for fun. But you guys – well, you killed his brother and gave him a motive. I reckon the point he's making is that you guys are gonna suffer way worse than those hundred and twenty-five folks that never did *anythin'* to piss him off.' Sanchez squeezed round De La Cruz on his way to the door. 'I gotta head outta town an' do some shoppin',' he smiled.

'Hold on a goddamn minute!' Hunter shouted from his seat behind the desk. 'How come he never kills you, huh? You've encountered this guy twice and survived both times. What are you? Friends with him, or somethin'?'

Sanchez stopped, reflecting on what Hunter had asked him. Both officers waited for him to offer up an explanation.

'Y'know,' said Sanchez, after considering his answer for a moment, 'the reason I'm still alive is 'cos I don't overstep the mark with that guy.'

Hunter waved a dismissive hand across his face. 'Bullshit! "Overstep the mark?"' he sneered. 'You don't even know what it means.'

'I know where the Bourbon Kid's mark is,' the bartender said quietly.

'Yeah? An' where's that?'

'Take a look behind you.'

Thirty-Four

Elijah Simmonds was not exactly Bertram Cromwell's favourite employee, but he was exceptionally good at his job. He was the Operations Manager at the museum, and where Cromwell was a man of the people, Simmonds was all about profit margins, and how to increase them. The two of them had been sitting in Cromwell's office going through the museum's accounts for over two hours, and what Simmonds had made abundantly clear to the Professor was that cuts were going to have to be made or profits were going to be severely hit.

Cromwell had sat in his vast leather chair looking through the profit-and-loss columns in the accounts as Simmonds, who was seated on the other side of the desk, regularly leaned over to explain some minor detail to him. Simmonds was a high-flyer in his late twenties. Young as he was, he already had an eye on one day having Cromwell's job overseeing the whole museum. He had no love for the art and historical artefacts held within the museum, but he did love earning money, and he was addicted to power.

Cromwell was well aware of his Operations Manager's ambitions, and wasn't fooled by his fake enthusiasm for the pieces in the museum. But he respected the fact that, for reasons he didn't quite understand, the younger employees seemed to like Simmonds. Maybe it was his trendy hairstyle and cheap but flashy dress sense? Personally, Cromwell thought a man in a suit sporting bleached blond hair tied back into a ponytail looked a little slimy, but he kept his opinions to himself. In his view, judging people by their appearances was foolish, and if it had been a rule he lived by it would have prevented him from meeting some truly wonderful people over the years.

'So this is the sixth consecutive month that profits have fallen, then?' Cromwell asked, peering over his glasses at the younger man as he looked up from the book on his desk.

Simmonds was in a smart blue suit over a white shirt that had the top two buttons undone. He wore no tie, something that Cromwell would never consider. And he was scratching his balls a lot when he spoke to the Professor, something he did regularly but to which he appeared to be oblivious.

'Yep, six months straight,' Simmonds confirmed. 'Since the initial burst of interest we had after the theft of the mummy, things have just gotten steadily worse.'

Cromwell took off his glasses and put them down on the desk. All this staring at numbers had made his eyes tired. 'It's hardly surprising is it? The Egyptian Tomb was our centrepiece, after all. We're going to need to find something particularly special to replace it I suppose. Thing is, a genuine Egyptian mummy is a pretty tough act to follow.'

'Well, yeah,' Simmonds agreed as he continued to tug at his crotch. 'But in the meantime we're going to have to cut costs.'

Cromwell shifted uncomfortably in his massive leather chair. His expensive grey made-to-measure suit from John Phillips in London could withstand all manner of fidgeting without ever creasing, unlike Simmonds's cheap off-the-rack number.

'I take it you have something in mind already?' Cromwell ventured.

'Yessir,' said Simmonds, sitting up straight and placing his hands on the desk where Cromwell could see them. Which was a relief to him. 'We can afford to lose at least one member of staff, as a start.'

'Really? Are you sure? Because the last time I checked we were already pretty thin on the ground.'

'True, Professor, true. But we can afford to get rid of one of the under-performers.'

'We have under-performers?' The older man laughed gently. 'How did this happen?'

'Well, actually there's only one, sir. I'm afraid your track record for picking employees isn't the best.'

Cromwell was taken aback. 'Excuse me?'

'I'm not showing off or anything,' Simmonds replied, 'but all the staff I take on are impeccably behaved and work extremely hard. The last few people *you've* employed, largely as an act of charity, haven't exactly fitted in well here, have they? Remember that guy Dante Vittori?'

'The one who smashed a priceless vase over your head?'

'Yes, him. He was useless.'

'Nice guy, though.'

'Come on, Professor, he was an idiot!' Simmonds protested.

'Granted, but calling him an idiot while he was holding a priceless antique vase above your head was hardly *your* finest hour, was it?'

Simmonds sat back in his seat again and began fidgeting with his crotch as the cheap suit crowded his nether regions once more.

'You should have let me press charges and send that loser to jail. He might finally have learnt something. Anyway, you get my point. I'm suggesting we fire your other charity-case employee.'

'The only other person I've employed is Beth Lansbury.'

'That's who I mean.'

'Why on earth would you want to fire her? She's a delightful young woman.'

'She doesn't mix well with others. Eats lunch on her own in the canteen. And, of course, she has a criminal record.'

'I'm well aware of her criminal record, thank you, Elijah. That girl had a very tough time of it as a child. I believe she deserves a break. That's why I employed her. And her father, God rest his soul, was a friend of mine many years ago.'

'Wasn't Dante Vittori's father a friend of yours too.'

'Yes.'

'Well then.'

'Well then what?'

'Well then, that's not a great reason for employing people, is it? I mean, don't get me wrong, sir, I think it's very noble of you to employ kids of your old friends, but it's not good business sense. You know the rest of the staff are frightened of her? They call her "Mental Beth". No matter how you dress it up, tough childhood and all that, she still murdered someone in cold blood, and that scares people. More work gets done when she's not around. When she's here it puts everyone else on edge. And what about that horrible scar across her face? Ugh! You must have noticed the reactions of many visitors when they see her. See? She's even scaring off paying customers. Trust me, getting her off the payroll and out of this building can only be good for business.'

Cromwell picked his narrow-rimmed half-moon spectacles back up from the desk and put them on. He rubbed his forehead for a moment, frowning as he did so. Then he closed the accounting book in front of him. 'Very well,' he said, pushing the ledger back across the desk to Simmonds. 'Send Beth down here when you get back upstairs. I will speak to her myself.'

Thirty-Five

Igor was still feeling the exhilaration of the previous night, when he had gorged on the blood of Patient Number 43, otherwise known as Casper. Now, while his companion in the blood feast, Pedro, had chosen to spend the afternoon with a hooker, Igor had decided to go for a drink downtown. An opportunity to flex his new immortal muscles was required. His first port of call was the Fawcett Inn right in the centre of town, the most popular drinking haunt for werewolves. Where the local vampires had taken control of the Nightjar, the wolfmen had claimed the Fawcett Inn for themselves.

From the outside, the place looked reasonably quiet when he arrived. The front door was open, no doubt due to the humidity in the air. It was not an especially big bar; in fact, lightly modelled as it was on an English pub, it had the appearance of an old thatched cottage of the kind that one might find in northern England.

Once inside, Igor was disappointed to find that the Fawcett Inn was not particularly busy. He was looking to show off a bit, and so would have appreciated a larger audience. No more than fifteen paying customers were sitting around at tables to the left of the bar. As was often the case there was just the one bartender, a grey-bearded black guy named Royle. Royle doubled as the doorman in this place. He was big enough and tough enough to handle any of the customers that came in looking for trouble. In the past that had just about included Igor, but now the newly self-appointed head werewolf was ready to put that to the test.

'Royle, get me a bottle of moonshine. And I'll have this

one on the house,' he snarled in a confrontational manner. He was hoping Royle would be offended by his arrogance and challenge him to a test of physical strength. Sadly, he was disappointed. Royle did not oblige. He'd obviously heard about Igor's new, improved and higher level of undead-ness.

The bartender picked up an unopened bottle of his best moonshine from under the bar and placed it, together with an empty shot glass, on the bartop in front of Igor.

'Congratulations,' he said, deadpan. 'I hear you and Pedro killed a handicapped guy and drank his blood from the Holy Grail.'

Igor was not in the mood for any attitude from anyone. He had come dressed to kill in a bright white silk shirt unbuttoned to halfway, showing off an abundance of coarse black chest hair. Around his neck he wore a gold chain with a crocodile tooth hanging from it. And he'd been out that day and bought some pretty sharp black leather pants in which he was now only too happy to strut around, somewhat like Tom Jones. (Or so he hoped . . .)

'Take caution in your tone,' he snarled archaically at Royle, picking up the bottle of moonshine and uncorking it. 'That sounded for a second like you might be mockin' me, and if there's one thing I don't gotta take no more, it's patronizing, shitty remarks from you or anyone else in this goddamn place.' His voice rose as he spoke, to be certain that everyone heard. With no music playing, everyone *did* hear; indeed, they had all stopped having conversations of their own in order to show the necessary level of respect.

Igor looked around for a customer to eyeball as he poured himself a full glass of the moonshine and then downed it in one. No one seemed to be eyeballing him, so he poured himself another. 'There's a new sheriff in town,' he called out, again loud enough to make sure everyone heard. He knew they were all hanging on his every word, but right at the moment no one wanted to look him in the eye. Instead, all of them were gazing in fascination at their drinks, or their shoes.

Eventually, irritated by the lack of confrontation, Igor

shifted his giant frame around to face everyone full on and finish shouting out his announcement about the new sheriff. 'And his name is Igor the Fang. No longer are us werewolves gonna be seen as second-class citizens. We're not gonna take no shit from no vampires no more, neither. We're gonna be equals.' He paused for a pull at his drink, then went on. 'The first three men in here to pledge their allegiance to me, right here and now, will be my lieutenants. Sign up now, guys, this is a once-in-a-lifetime offer to become a part of the number-one wolf crew in Santa Mondega. Women and riches will follow. Come and be a part of a clan that's movin' up in the world. A clan of wolves to match all the vampire clans put together. The baddest clan in the land.' He took a step towards the occupied tables and shook a fist in the air. 'Now, who's with me?'

There was a pause as the lowlife wolfmen in the barroom absorbed what he was saying. The fifteen or so young males sitting at the various tables were all exchanging uneasy glances, each waiting for one of the others to say something. Eventually one brave young guy in a sleeveless blue denim shirt stood up from one of the nearby tables and walked over to Igor. He was the bravest of the bunch, all right, a scruffy young werewolf with thick, unkempt auburn hair, who went by the name of Ronnie. He was looking to move up in the world quickly, and if it meant taking a risk and showing he was braver than the others, then fuck it, that's what he was going to do.

'I'll pledge my allegiance to you, Igor,' he stated solemnly. 'What would you have me do?' Archaic language seemed to be catching on.

Igor looked him up and down, and nodded approvingly. This guy had balls.

'What would I have you do? Simple. I want a drinkin' partner, for a start. Royle, gimme another bottle of moonshine. On the house.'

Royle threw a dirty look at Igor behind his back, then rolled his eyes as he watched two more scruffy young men get up from the table at which Ronnie had been sitting. They hurried over to stand by their friend. Neither of them was quite as brave as Ronnie, so to be on the safe side they both hung back a foot or so behind him. All three of them stood facing Igor, who was now leaning back against the bar, looking full of himself.

'Better make that another two more!' the big wolfman bellowed without bothering to turn and look at Royle.

'Fine,' the bartender growled, smiling a sarcastic smile. 'Reckon I'll just head out back get a couple more bottles for you.' He shuffled out through the open door at the back of the bar.

Igor took a long look at his three new lieutenants, running the rule over them. They weren't exactly well built, any of them, but they were all undoubtedly proud of their heritage as werewolves because each of them sported a good degree of facial hair, a sign of pride in a wolf.

'So, what are your names?' he asked them.

The first guy to have gotten up, Ronnie, who was still standing slightly in front of the other two, took a step back and trod on the feet of one of the guys behind him.

'You know what?' he said. 'I changed my mind.'

'Yeah, me too,' said the other two in unison. They too each took a step back. All three of them had turned pale and were staring wide-eyed at the bar behind Igor. The newly self-proclaimed head wolf's first instinct was that they were a little nervous, maybe even intimidated by him, fearing that he might be about to make an example of one of them. Then his sixth sense kicked in. *Something's not right.*

'What's goin' on?' Igor asked, wiping his nose and then inspecting his fingers. 'Have I got a booger hangin' or somethin'?'

All three young wolfmen shook their heads in unison. They had seen something behind Igor that warranted a retreat of sorts. The rumours that Igor had killed the retarded kid brother of the Bourbon Kid were being verified for them. For behind Igor was a sight they had hoped not to see. It was that of a hooded man rising up from behind the bar, his face shielded from them by the shadow of his cowl.

The dark figure held its gloved hands in front of it and almost two feet apart, fists clenched. Wrapped around these black-gloved hands and stretched tightly between them was a silvery length of cheesewire.

By the time Igor's instincts kicked in and told him he was in trouble, the cheesewire had been whipped over his head and wrapped tightly around his throat. Within a second the hooded man had dragged him over the bar and out of sight, kicking and choking as he went.

The Fawcett Inn emptied of customers in less than five seconds. No one was going to hang around to see the outcome of this. They had already seen more than they wanted to.

The Kid was back. And he hadn't even had a drink yet.

Thirty-Six

Captain De La Cruz was sitting at the desk in his office, tapping away at the keyboard on his computer. He had stretched the buttoned-up collar on his red shirt quite significantly by tugging at it consistently for the last hour. Pulling at his collar was something he did when things were bothering him. And right now something was bothering him.

The blinds on the window behind him were closed, keeping out the last of the day's sunlight. The thin shafts of pale blue light that did filter in through the slats lit up the dust motes all around his face, which were almost as much of an irritation to him as the computer screen he was frowning at. His frustrated look hinted that he wasn't making much progress with whatever he was doing. With that in mind, Hunter knocked tentatively on the glass-panelled door of the office and waited for his captain to gesture for him to enter. De La Cruz duly did, and after kicking at the base of the sticky door, which had never opened easily, Hunter made his way in, pushed it almost shut behind him and then stood behind the chair on the near side of the desk, resting his hands on the chairback.

De La Cruz looked up at him. 'Why does everyone have to kick my door, huh?' he asked. 'Why can't people just push a little harder? I mean, how fuckin' difficult is that?'

Hunter offered an apologetic, yet also sympathetic, smile. 'You sound kinda agitated. An' I gotta tell ya, I'm feelin' it too.' He took off his brown tweed jacket and hung it on the back of the chair, then sat down and tugged at the neck of his brown sweater. In doing so, he was inadvertently mimicking his superior officer.

De La Cruz slapped his keyboard one last time and turned his attention away from the computer's monitor and fully on to his partner.

'Feelin' what?' he asked.

'I'm feelin' bothered by what happened with the retarded guy,' Hunter replied, scratching his chin.

'Oh that,' De La Cruz grimaced. 'Nah, matter of fact that's not what's bothering me. Not exactly, anyway. It *is* bugging me, but not as much as what happened right afterwards. It's bugging me more that Benson gave his name to the person on the other end of the guy's cell phone. What the fuck was he thinking?'

'Yeah, that's pissin' me off too. You reckon it was the Kid on the phone?'

'You even doubt it?' asked De La Cruz, tapping the space bar on his keyboard a few times to make a pointless little tune.

'Yeah, I know. Benson's ego is gettin' totally out of hand. Discretion's not exactly his middle name, is it? You think we should be doin' somethin' about it?' Hunter already knew the answer.

'Yeah. He's becomin', like, a liability. I got absolutely no doubt in my mind that the Kid's gonna be after him now. And he may already be after *us,* too. We've lost our element of surprise here, Hunter, and we've killed the Kid's fuckin' retard brother. If he's not after us yet, he soon will be, once he's tracked down Benson. I mean, *fuck* . . .' De La Cruz had succeeded in winding himself up, and he made it obvious when he smacked the space bar a bit harder. 'Benson gave away his own name easily enough. He'll give up our names to the Kid too, once he's put under a bit of pressure. This is fuckin' serious, man.'

De La Cruz's mood was visibly darkening as he spoke aloud what they had both been thinking, but not saying, ever since the previous night's kill.

'You want me to make Benson disappear?' Hunter offered.

'I do, yeah, but there's a problem. I can't get a hold of him. The slimy bastard has fucked off somewhere. We'll deal with him all in good time, but I think our first plan is to try and get to the Bourbon Kid before he gets to Benson and our beloved buddy starts singing like a goddamn canary.'

'You don't reckon Benson could handle the Kid?'

'Hunter, *you* could handle the Kid and *I* could handle the Kid, but Benson's just too much of a loose cannon. If our new strength is as great as we think it is, any one of us should be able to wipe the floor with that bourbon-drinking sonofabitch. But let's not take any chances by sending Benson after him.'

'Okay. So what you got in mind?'

'Take a look at this,' said De La Cruz spinning the monitor part-way around so that Hunter could get a good look at what was on screen.

'What's this?' the other asked, checking out the black-and-white video image on the Captain's screen.

'CCTV footage.'

'Of what?'

'The massacre here at headquarters on the night of the eclipse last year, when the Bourbon Kid killed all the on-duty cops, as well as that good-lookin' receptionist Amy Webster.'

Hunter took a look at the flickering CCTV footage, which was currently paused and hard to make out. 'What part is this?' he asked.

'This is the bit where he kills Archie Somers by sticking that fuckin' book into his chest.'

'How in hell did you come by this?' asked Hunter. 'I didn't know there was CCTV in the station.'

'I found it on YouTube.'

'You don't say!'

'No, dumbass. It turns out Internal Affairs secretly installed CCTV cameras some time ago in order to check up on all of us.'

'But surely that's illegal?'

'They did it in *Lethal Weapon 3*,' said De La Cruz, shrugging.

'Oh well then,' said Hunter, grimacing. 'If they can do it in the movies, I guess they can do it here.'

De La Cruz shrugged again. 'You got it, Dick.' He tapped the space bar and the video started running again. Hunter watched the last few moments of Archie Somers on screen as the detective first attacked the Bourbon Kid and then, after a brief struggle and an exchange of words, staggered back in a ball of flames and finally turned to smoke and ash. Once Somers was gone, the Kid (who had his back to the camera) made his way out of headquarters and the tape ended.

'Nice,' said Hunter. 'We learnin' anythin' from this?'

'Well, actually, yeah – I think we are,' said De La Cruz, tugging nervously with one finger at his shirt collar. 'You see, the Kid's not what you think.'

'Well, I think he's a mass murderer. Is he a mass murderer?'

'Well, yeah . . . '

'Then he's exactly what I think.'

De La Cruz faked a smile. 'Funny guy, huh? But here's the thing. I've seen this clip a hundred times before, and one thing has always bothered me.'

'What's that?'

'Why does the Bourbon Kid leave *The Book With No Name* behind? Is it just because he's not bothered about it, or is it because of this?' He used the computer's mouse to drag the 'play' bar on the screen back a little. Then he hit the space bar again and the video started playing again. 'Look at this.'

Hunter looked more closely at the screen. He watched the footage unfold, and concentrated hard on trying to spot something he'd missed before. Nothing jumped out at him as once again he watched in fascination as the old detective departed for the depths of Hell in a fireball. As the clip drew to an end he watched the Kid put his hand up to his neck and then pull it away again to look at his fingers. A second or two later he pulled his hood back up over his head and walked out.

'Well, he's clever enough never to let his face be seen by

the cameras that *we* didn't even know we had hidden in this place,' Hunter observed. 'But we've always known he's smart like that. We don't have any footage of his face anywhere. Guy's too smart, always knows where the cameras are. Even if *we* don't.'

'You missed the key moment there,' said De La Cruz, once more resetting the 'play' bar on the screen. This time he went back a little further, pausing on the struggle between Somers and the Kid just before Somers began to smoulder and smoke. Hunter stared at the screen for a few seconds, then picked up on what De La Cruz was showing him. His captain was nodding.

'Yep, you got it. Our old buddy Somers planted a bite on the Kid's neck. Count to ten from there and the Kid's halfway to becoming a bloodsucker. He can't touch the book any more because Somers has turned him. He's a fuckin' vampire, like the rest of us.'

'Holy shit!' Hunter whispered aloud, his jaw dropping open, betraying his utter astonishment. 'I can't believe we missed that before.'

De La Cruz was deep in thought, staring hard at the glass-panelled door of the office, which wasn't quite shut properly. 'Well, you know what,' he mused. 'I don't think it was ever that important before. Kinda an irrelevance, really, but I just got to thinking. Y'know, the Kid's now got a little more than he bargained for. This helps us in a big way. We can track him down now. I'm certain of it.'

'How so?' asked Hunter. 'How'll this help us find him?'

'Think about it. The Kid now has all the same vampire instincts that we have, right? That's only natural.'

'Okay, yeah, so he's gonna have the thirst, the hunger for human blood, and he can be killed by things like the book, right?' Hunter paused. 'I'm not gettin' it, am I? What are you drivin' at?'

The other detective continued to stare ahead at the glass door, but leaned forward over the desk a little to make his point. 'Think a tad more laterally, my friend. If he has *all* of the vampire instincts, he's gonna have suffered one major personality change that you haven't mentioned.'

Hunter shook his head, baffled. 'Which is?'

'Companionship. The Kid has always been a loner right?'

'Fuckin' A!' It finally dawned on Hunter what his captain was trying to say.

'You think he'll have joined one of the clans?'

'Yep,' said De La Cruz, looking back at the monitor and smacking the keyboard's space bar again, before watching the Kid being bitten by Somers once more. 'Our boy will have been living amongst us for some time. 'Course, the big question is, what name does he go under? And, just as importantly,' he said, shaking a finger at his colleague, 'which clan is he hiding in?'

'My God! If he hasn't worked out that you and I were involved in the killing of his brother by now, it won't be long before he does find out. Word has flown around the clans already, and *fuck,* even Sanchez knows, or guessed, and he's just a fuckin' bartender.'

De La Cruz nodded, frowning. 'Yeah, I know. But I have a plan,' he said, reaching into one of the drawers on his side of the desk. He pulled out the cell phone they had taken from Casper after they had slaughtered him. 'Take this phone with you to the Nightjar. Press redial, and see whose phone rings. That's when you find out who the Bourbon Kid is and which clan he's in. Just kill the person whose phone rings.'

'What if no one's phone rings?'

De La Cruz sat back in his chair, exasperated. 'I dunno. Don't kill anyone. Or better still, kill everybody.'

Hunter could see that his senior officer's patience was wearing thin, but he didn't appreciate the sarcasm. 'You know, with that kind of attitude, Captain, you should consider a career in the Church.'

'Damn right I should. I think they're missing out on some great ideas. Now just take this phone, will you, and get the fuck outta here.'

He tossed the phone over to Hunter who caught it and stood up from his seat ready to go.

'You comin' with me?' he asked.

'No. By all means call me if you need me. But for now I'm gonna try and find out what the fuck has happened to Benson.'

Thirty-Seven

After his visit to police headquarters, Sanchez had headed out of town to a shopping mall for the afternoon. After an exhausting few hours traipsing around clothes shops and stumbling into the back of other shoppers who insisted on stopping dead in their tracks for no apparent reason, he had finally managed to get a cab back to Santa Mondega in the early evening.

The shopping trip had been a success, more or less. He'd picked up some pretty decent new clothes for Jessica, having discovered that morning that she had woken from her latest coma. He had been awoken by the sound of her coughing in the early hours, and had been delighted to find her wide awake. She was still too weak to get out of bed, and she couldn't speak much, but with her phenomenal healing powers it would only be a matter of time before she was up and about.

He had bought quite a selection of items of clothing for her, ranging from miniskirts and stiletto-heeled shoes to tracksuits and Hawaiian shirts. He'd even gone to the trouble of having a white T-shirt specially printed for her, bearing the legend 'I WAS SHOT BY THE BOURBON KID AND ALL I GOT WAS THIS LOUSY COMA'. Then, because he hated shopping so much, he'd also done a lot of his own clothes shopping, just to get it all done in one go and save himself from having to make another trip out of town that year. He stuck to the basics for his own clothing. Three pairs of baggy black trousers and a selection of short-sleeved shirts in different colours. He'd also bought some dark hair dye specially made for men. He was starting to show signs of going grey (as well as thinning out on top). Restoring his once-thick black locks to their former glory seemed like a smart idea, particularly as Jessica was now back in the world of the living.

The cab had dropped him at the edge of town. The driver, an annoying, tough-talking Frenchman, had refused to drive into the city centre because he was too fucking scared. He had claimed he was in a rush, but this was a blatant lie, as Sanchez well knew. Out-of-town drivers had heard all the rumours about the undead within the city, and just didn't have the balls to cross the line marking the city limits.

The two carriers full of clothes he was carrying were making the slightly overweight Sanchez sweat excessively, and after walking for fifteen minutes or so he felt in need of a serious breather. His white 'FUCK OFF' T-shirt, now sporting large sweat patches on the back, front and under the armpits, was beginning to stick to him. His heavy black pants were making his ass sweat to the point that his buttocks were starting to make slurping noises as he walked. He trudged on through Santa Mondega's dusty streets under the glare of the setting sun, and as he did so he began to feel an incredible thirst coming on.

As fortune would have it, Sanchez's arduous journey home took him past the Fawcett Inn. Not a pleasant establishment, and well known as a local werewolf hangout, but seeing as there wasn't a full moon anywhere in sight he figured it wouldn't hurt to stop in there for a quick, refreshing glass of moonshine.

Barely had he made up his mind to call in at the pub, than something happened to make him rethink the idea. As he was approaching the place he heard a god-almighty commotion, and then a whole bunch of folks came rushing out of the front door of the thatched building, barging each other aside in their attempts to get clear of the place. *Bomb scare?* thought Sanchez.

Nah.

Fire, mebbe?

No. No sign of any smoke.

So what else could it possibly be?
One other possible cause sprang to mind.
Uh-oh. It couldn't be?
Could it?

One of the last of the fleeing customers, a fat Mexican nicknamed Poncho, ran towards Sanchez, eyes bulging. He looked as though he'd raced straight out of Trap Two in the pub's men's room, because he was holding his baggy brown pants up with one hand and trying to buckle his belt with the other. His half-undone white shirt was hanging out, and he had a length of white toilet paper coming out the back of his pants, and trailing along behind him. As he drew near he shouted the warning that the bartender most dreaded.

'HE'S BACK! FUCKIN' BOURBON KID, MAN!'

Poncho barged heavily into Sanchez's shoulder as he charged away down the street. The slight impact reminded Sanchez of just how tired he was. He stopped walking and let his shopping bags drop to the ground. His legs had turned to jelly a few minutes earlier simply from exhaustion (and because he was unfit). Now they had turned to spaghetti, so it was a miracle he was still standing at all. He stared at the front entrance of the Fawcett Inn, watching to see if anyone else came out. Or any stray bullets, for that matter. Up to this point, he hadn't actually heard any gunshots, which was unusual if the Kid was back.

Sanchez had survived two previous encounters with Santa Mondega's most prolific killer. Now, for some inexplicable reason that would probably one day see him handing a blank cheque to a psychiatrist, his curiosity had got the better of him. He wanted one more look at the face that so often hid beneath that dark cowl. He took a few steps towards the entrance. The large wooden door was open inwards, shuddering a little in the wind. Through the gap in the doorway he could see that it was too dark inside to make out much. Even so, it seemed safe enough to step a little closer, because up to this point he still hadn't heard any gunshots or screams from inside. At least, none that he could hear from where he was. So he took another step. Then another.

Then he heard something behind him.

He turned sharply and saw Poncho. The tubby Mexican who was an infamous local thief had run back and grabbed the bags of shopping that Sanchez had set down. After picking them up he stopped, shrugged at Sanchez in an apologetic fashion, then ran off with all the bartender's new stuff. *Bastard.*

Sanchez turned his back on the thieving little shit. Yet he had to respect Poncho's initiative. The opportunity to acquire some free shopping was there and the guy had taken it. Besides, Sanchez had more pressing matters at hand. As carefully as he could, he took a few more tentative steps towards the entrance of the Fawcett Inn until he was little more than ten feet away. And finally something happened.

A sudden movement made his heart miss a beat and his stomach tighten, as though he'd just taken a pineapple up his ass. The door of the pub opened a little more and a body appeared, crawling desperately along the ground. It was Igor the Fang. He was clawing his way along the dusty flagstoned floor and out of the bar as if he had lost the use of his legs and was relying solely on his upper body to get anywhere. He looked up at Sanchez, his face a bruised and swollen mess, his neck seeping blood from a deep cut. For just a moment it looked as though he was about to plead for help. That moment passed all too quickly, for a second later his body was dragged back inside the pub. His fingernails were damn near ripped out as he tried desperately to embed them in the dusty gravel outside, in a failed bid to maintain some kind of grip on the civilized world.

And then, just for a split second, a hooded figure appeared in Sanchez's line of vision.

Then the door was slammed shut.

It was the cue for Sanchez to make himself extremely scarce. Without another moment's hesitation he hurried on down the street as fast as his tired legs would carry him. The next bar in the direction he was heading was a mile away. It was the Tapioca, and Sanchez needed to get there and board the place up before the Kid arrived.

And he needed to warn Jessica.

Thirty-Eight

Beth felt horribly nervous. She didn't like the corridor that led down to Bertram Cromwell's office. It was creepy, and had a number of very dark paintings on the walls either side. Sinister characters within the paintings seemed to be staring down at her as she passed them. It didn't get much better when she reached the tall black door at the corridor's end. She found that creepy, too. It had a gold-coloured doorknob at waist height on the right-hand side, and a small silver nameplate screwed to it at eye level with the word 'CROMWELL' engraved on it in thin gold letters.

In the ten years she had spent in prison she had learnt to hate, respect and fear authority in equal measure. Being summoned to the office of a figure in authority, be it the prison warden or the director of a museum, had always spelt trouble for her, so she was more on edge than usual. After counting to three to try to calm herself she knocked twice on the door. A moment later she heard Cromwell's voice call 'Come in' from the other side.

She turned the doorknob to the left and pushed. The door didn't open. So she turned it to the right and pushed. Still the door wouldn't give. Beth remembered being in Cromwell's office once before, some months earlier, but she couldn't recall how the door opened, or indeed whether it was even she who had opened it. She tried turning the handle in each direction several times, even pulling the door instead of pushing it, and the longer she went without it opening the more nervous she became. After about twenty painfully long seconds she started to feel humiliated. It would be obvious to the Professor that she was a fool who couldn't open the door. Each second that ticked by brought her ever closer to having to call out to him through the door to explain her predicament.

Eventually, just as she was about to break out into a nervous sweat, the door opened, courtesy of Bertram Cromwell pulling it from the other side. He stood there, immaculately dressed as always, smiling back at her.

'I'm sorry, I couldn't . . . The door . . . It just . . . I turned the knob, I mean handle . . . but . . .'

'Think nothing of it,' said Cromwell courteously. 'Lots of people have trouble with this door.'

Beth sensed that he was saying that simply to make her feel better. The chances were high that no one had ever struggled with the horrible door before. She was probably the first. What an idiot, and what an awful start to her meeting with the Professor. Particularly awful because she had a sneaking feeling that she was about to be fired. She'd been fired from every job she'd ever had since her release from prison. Everywhere she went, at least one of her colleagues, if not all of them, would invariably complain to management that they didn't feel comfortable working with her. She had done well to last six months in this job, and that was probably because Cromwell had known her father many years earlier. Or so she'd been told.

She had been working as a cleaner at the museum since Cromwell had been kind enough to employ her, but she hadn't managed to make a single friend in her time there. Invariably, every time she got to know one of the other members of staff and began to think they were hitting it off, someone would inform the other party of her colourful past, and pretty soon the friendship would peter out. She'd grown used to it over the years; in fact, it was one of the reasons why changing jobs so often didn't bother her too much. It wasn't nice to stay at one place for too long when you knew everyone hated you.

Cromwell took his seat in the black leather chair behind his desk, while Beth stood and admired the shelves of books on the walls to her left and right.

'Please sit down,' Cromwell said, indicating one of the two chairs on her side of his nineteenth-century oak desk.

Beth smiled politely and sat down in the chair on the left. 'I suppose you're going to want this back?' she said, tugging at the shoulder of her navy blue dress. It was one of the three standard cleaner's uniforms she had started her job at the museum.

He gave her a sympathetic smile. 'You did well to last six months, right?'

'It's better than usual,' she replied. She could feel a tear welling up in her right eye. Despite the fact that no one at the museum spoke to her, it had been one of the better jobs, and she was dreading the thought of preparing for interviews in order to find some kind of employment elsewhere.

'So, Beth. I've been hearing that you have not been mixing well with other staff here? Apparently you take lunch on your own each day?'

'Well, yes, but I . . . it's just that . . . I don't have any friends.' It hurt to say it out loud and she felt the tear in her eye doubling in size.

'No friends? Hmmm,' Cromwell drummed his fingers on the desk for a few seconds. 'You've booked the rest of the week off, haven't you?'

'Er . . . yes. Should I . . . ? Erm . . . is this it, then? Should I not come back to the museum after my vacation?'

Cromwell reached down to the floor to the right of his chair and picked something up. Beth peered across to see what it was. He placed the object, a package wrapped in brown paper, on the desk directly in front of her. It was about the size of a pillow and seemed to contain something soft.

'What plans do you have for your vacation?' Cromwell asked. His line of questioning was beginning to unnerve Beth a little. She was nervous around most people, but figures of authority like professors made her even more so.

'Excuse me?'

'Your vacation. You have booked three days off. I was just wondering what you had planned.'

'Oh, nothing really. Nothing interesting, that is. Looking for a new job, probably.'

'Don't do that just yet,' said Cromwell, smiling.

Beth couldn't make out whether or not he was telling her that she wasn't fired, or if he was having a joke at her expense. Since she didn't want to seem presumptuous, she decided that he must be joking.

'Okay. So when do I finish working here?'

'When *you* choose Beth. Or when you smash a valuable antique vase over Simmonds's head.'

'I'm sorry, but I'm not following you.'

'I'm not firing you, Beth. You're a hard worker. And on your first day back from your vacation you and I are going to meet for lunch in the canteen.'

Beth, astonished, said the first thing that came into her head. 'Really? What time?' she asked.

'*Lunchtime.* I don't know – any time. Just come and get me when you're ready. Lord knows I've been lunching on my own for so long now I could use some company once in a while. I don't think anyone else wants to sit with me at lunchtime, so in exchange for not firing you, even though I've been advised to by the pony-tailed one, I expect you to invite me to lunch once a week from now on. If that's okay with you, of course?'

Beth fiddled nervously with her long brown hair. The Professor was such a gentleman, and, she thought, probably quite a ladykiller in his day. And although she knew that he had made his lunch suggestion out of pity, it was a kind enough gesture to ensure that the tear in her right eye slid down her cheek. She discreetly wiped it away, camouflaging the move with her hair twiddling. She thought that the Professor probably hadn't noticed.

'Thank you, Professor Cromwell. I'll do that.'

'Good, but you still haven't told me what plans you have for your three days' vacation.'

'Oh. Well, nothing really.' Beth continued to fidget uncomfortably with a few long strands of hair hanging just in front of her ear.

Cromwell smiled at her again and then nudged the brown-paper parcel over the desk to her. 'It's eighteen years today, isn't it?' he said quietly.

Beth stared down at the floor. 'Yes.' Her voice was a whisper.

'Halloween, eighteen years ago. That must have been a terrible night.'

'Yes. Yes, it was.'

'So, I've bought you this gift,' said Cromwell, nodding at the package. 'Open it, please.'

Beth reached tentatively for the package as if expecting him to snatch it away. When it was in her hands she set about unwrapping it. It had been sealed at each end with thick industrial tape. Not exactly girly wrapping, but who was she to complain.

After peeling the tape from the parcel she tore it open and saw within it a soft but very warm-looking blue hooded sweatshirt with a zip-up front. She lifted it out of the packaging and held it up. As she did so something else fell out and clattered on to the desk.

'Oh, I'm so sorry,' Beth gasped, fearing she had scratched the wood on the desk.

'Don't worry,' said the Professor, amused, but anxious to reassure her. She really was extraordinarily self-effacing, he thought.

Beth smiled shyly and held up the blue hooded sweatshirt. 'Thank you so much for this,' she said. She sounded genuinely pleased.

On the desk in front of her, where it had fallen from the package, lay a silver chain with a large crucifix hanging from it. The crucifix was also silver, but a small blue stone had been set in the centre of it.

'Is this for me too?' she asked.

'Yes. I want you to wear the sweatshirt and the necklace when you go to the pier tonight.'

'What?' Beth's confusion was all too obvious, and she

blushed furiously.

'You go to the pier every Halloween night, don't you?'

'Yes, but how did you . . .'

'Let's just say that I like to know a little bit about the people I employ. You know, the personal details. As I understand it, you go to the pier every Halloween night and freeze half to death, and I can't have that. I would hate to think of you coming down with a cold, spoiling your three days off. And the crucifix? Well, that's just in case any evil spirits come your way. It may help to ward them off. The blue stone in the centre is in fact a tiny vial. It contains holy water from the Sistine Chapel in Rome.'

Beth was overcome with gratitude. 'Thank you so much, Professor Cromwell. I don't know what to say. These are lovely.'

'You don't have to say anything, Beth. I am very glad that you're pleased. But I am curious about one thing. Why the pier every Halloween? It's very dangerous down there. Is it because that's where you were arrested that night eighteen years ago?'

'Kind of,' said Beth, fastening the chain around her neck and adjusting the crucifix so that it hung centrally. 'I was supposed to meet a boy there at one o'clock on the night – well, morning, I guess – I was arrested. I think I missed him because I was late getting there, but a fortune teller who lived by the pier said he would come back. So I wait there from midnight till one every year. I know it sounds silly, but ever since I left prison it's kind of become a tradition.'

'A fortune teller, you say? Was that the Mystic Lady?'

'Yes, Annabel de Frugyn. She was murdered last year.'

'I remember reading about it. You know, that woman was undoubtedly a little eccentric. She predicted all kinds of strange things. She claimed that puppets could see, and that there would be an earthquake in Santa Mondega on the fourth of March about three years ago. Caused quite a panic at the time, and she was totally wrong, of course. Strange woman. Bit of a con artist, too. Always looking through the obituaries and stuff.'

'I know, Professor Cromwell, but I just like to pretend to believe it all. You probably think I'm being silly, and I know everyone calls me "Mental Beth", but I just have to live with those things. Spending an hour at the pier every Halloween is better than Christmas for me. That may sound mad, but it's true. In spite of all the horrible things that happened on that night eighteen years ago, it was still the best night of my life, and if people think that makes me "mental" then so be it.'

Cromwell got up from his chair. 'I admire your spirit, my dear,' he said generously. 'Take the rest of the day off. Wrap up warm in that sweatshirt, and keep the crucifix on, where it can be seen, and I'll say a prayer that your young man comes back for you tonight.'

'Thank you,' said Beth, standing up and picking up the blue sweatshirt. 'Thank you for everything, and see you in three days.'

'I hope so.'

Thirty-Nine

After his brief flirtation with danger brought on by the reappearance of the Bourbon Kid, Sanchez had rushed back to the Tapioca in double-quick time. He burst in through the front door like a man possessed, sweating and panting for breath. The barroom wasn't exactly how he liked to see it, either. To his dismay there was a clan of six werewolves and a hooker sitting at one of the tables right in the centre of the room. The werewolves were a scruffy bunch, like most of their kind. All unkempt, unshaven and a good deal hairier than the average customer. And the average customer in the Tapioca was usually pretty hairy, but these guys stood out to Sanchez. Apart from the hooker, they were the only drinkers in the bar, most likely because any others would have cleared out at the sight of them.

Sanchez recognized the leader of the clan first – it was MC Pedro, the useless rap-star wolf. A Grade-A idiot (like most werewolves, if truth be told) who was blissfully unaware of just how shit his rapping and lyrical flow was. On this occasion he had come dressed appropriately for a wannabe rapper, wearing an oversized yellow LA Lakers basketball shirt bearing the number 42. The hooker was sitting on his knee, which was not an attractive sight. She looked distinctly rough in a scarlet-coloured dress that left little to the imagination, and her jet-black hair was a mess, suggesting she'd already carried out a few of her services in the men's room out back. Sanchez was livid at the sight of this loser, his hooker and his loser friends sitting in the bar area.

'Hey, I thought I told you guys never to come in here!'

he yelled at them, in a manner far braver than even he had expected.

'Hey, man,' said Pedro, standing up from the table and causing the hooker to fall off his knee and on to the floor. He approached Sanchez with an arrogant strut that looked particularly stupid because his basketball shirt was hanging down past the knees of his black combat trousers and wasn't quite wide enough to accommodate the long steps he was trying to take. When he was little more than two feet away, in an attempt to impress his comrades and intimidate Sanchez, he burst into one of his infamous raps. '*Wassup you bitchass muthafucka? The moon ain't bustin' out just yet, so there ain't no need for you to fret. Let me break it down for ya, we're legit for one more sip, 'cos for you my homeboy we're too legit. One more sip is all it takes, and then my brother we'll all do the shake!*'

Sanchez didn't like rap at the best of times, but when it was done as poorly as this and made absolutely no sense, it turned his stomach. Had this MC Pedro guy heard any rap music by anyone other than MC Hammer and Vanilla Ice? Probably not.

When, a moment later, the idiot werewolf rapper patted him on the shoulder in a slightly intimidating manner, Sanchez could actually feel himself getting angry. He didn't have the time or the patience for this shit. Normally, Pedro's threatening manner would have made the cowardly bartender feel more than a little uncomfortable, but on this occasion it didn't have the desired effect. Sanchez had bigger things on his plate right now. The Bourbon Kid was heading their way, and all of these pansy-assed werewolves were likely to perish if Santa Mondega's most feared decided to look in for a quick snort.

'I gotta go upstairs a minute,' said Sanchez, pushing past Pedro and heading behind the bar towards the stairs to the apartment above. 'I want you lowlifes gone by the time I get back.'

'Sure.' Pedro smiled. '*You'll just hear one more sound.*

An' it'll be me orderin' one last round.'

Sanchez was appalled, not just by the rapping but by the news that the werewolves planned to order another round of drinks. Unfortunately, he didn't have time to argue. He needed to get to Jessica before the Kid showed up.

Working behind his bar on this most unpleasant of early evenings was a fairly new employee named Sally. She was an attractive would-be Baywatch babe, only with just a little bit more meat on her bones than a lifeguard should really have. She usually wore low-cut tops to show off her generous cleavage, and today was no exception – a skimpy, tight red top with a plunging neckline was twinned with a tiny pair of black leather hotpants. This outfit was similar to the one that she had worn to her job interview with Sanchez, and which had been the main reason he had employed her. She had no previous experience as a bartender, and she was fairly dumb, but she had it where it counted when it came to the customers, who liked her. A lot. Behind the bar, Sanchez made a quick stop by Sally and quickly whispered some instructions into her right ear as he stared down her cleavage. The instructions were only too familiar to Sally already, although she didn't relish carrying them out. After making sure she understood exactly what he wanted her to do, he bounded on up the stairs to the room where Jessica was staying.

MC Pedro strutted up to the bar and leaned over the wooden counter to get as far into Sally's personal space as he could. And to sneak a look at her tits, or as much of them as was on show.

'Seven whiskeys. Now,' he growled.

'Sure thing.' Sally offered a half-hearted smile. There were two things she didn't like about her job at the Tapioca. The first was having to serve dangerous bastards like MC Pedro. The second was always having to serve them piss instead of what they actually ordered, because Sanchez insisted on it. So it was with a great deal of reluctance and after an almighty deep breath that she picked up the special bottle from under the bar and poured out seven glasses of the stuff.

There was a stained copper tray on the bar, and she set the glasses down on it one by one, shaking very slightly as she did so, fearing what might follow once the werewolves tasted their drinks.

'That'll be twenty-eight dollars, please,' she smiled nervously at Pedro.

'*Yo bitch. This place is a fuckin' rip-off! Change the price or I bite your lip off!*' Pedro rapped, even louder and more angrily than usual. Though there was no sign of the full moon due that night his rage was starting a semi-transformation into his werewolf persona. This wasn't something that would normally have been possible, but Pedro had tasted blood from the Grail. Since then he could turn at will, or just instinctively. Luckily, this was not a full turning. He merely sprouted a little more hair around the face, and a minor ripple ran through his arms as his biceps enlarged a little. His new strength was hard to control when he felt even the slightest rage inside.

'You know what?' said Sally nervously. 'Have these on the house. Just don't tell Sanchez, okay?'

The beast within Pedro calmed a little and his appearance returned to its more normal state. At that moment another man walked in through the front entrance and joined him at the bar. Pedro recognized him immediately.

'Hey man, how ya doin'?' he asked.

'I'm good,' was the newcomer's abrupt response. He was wearing a long dark robe with a large hood hanging down around his shoulders.

'Yo, barmaid,' Pedro snapped. 'Get my buddy here a whiskey too. Stick it on my slate.'

'Sure.' Sally picked up the piss bottle once more, but the Tapioca's new customer quickly stopped her.

'I'll have a shot from that bottle over there,' he said, gesturing to a bottle of bourbon that was gathering dust at the back of the bar. 'On the rocks.'

'Yo, wassup? You don' like the whiskey in here, homeboy?' Pedro asked his suspiciously.

'That's stuff's piss.'

'*It may taste like it's full of piss, but it don't mean . . . you can't touch this!*' Pedro rapped.

'It's piss.'

From the back of the bar where she was pouring bourbon over a couple of ice cubes, Sally was picking up on a distinct touch of gravel in the newcomer's voice. She hadn't seen this guy in the Tapioca before, and she already had a feeling she wouldn't want to see him again.

Pedro hadn't really got the point of his companion overemphasizing the *It's piss* joke, so he picked up his tray of drinks and carried it over to the werewolves' table and set it down. The hooker now had nowhere to sit because Pedro wanted his chair back, so she stood up and proposed a toast.

'To Pedro, the new boss!' she called out.

'To Pedro!' the others chimed in unison. There was a chorus of chinking glasses as they all toasted their leader. Their mood was buoyant and the drinks were free. What more could a werewolf or a hooker ask for?

Their cheeriness was soon drowned out, however, by the sound of Sanchez charging down the stairs. When he made it to the bottom he grabbed Sally's arm as she was placing a drink down on the bar.

'Hey, you see the girl from upstairs anywhere?' he demanded, tugging hard on his employee's arm.

'No, why? She not upstairs?' asked Sally.

'No she ain't. *Jesus, woman,* she's gone. How the fuck did you miss her? She must have walked out this way? Aw, fuck!' Sanchez was unable to hide the anger in his voice He was furious with the barmaid. She had been made well aware of how precious Jessica was. The beautiful woman upstairs wasn't a secret Sanchez shared with many people. Unfortunately, Sally had wandered upstairs once and seen Jessica asleep, so he had been forced to divulge a little information about the woman he had secretly been in love with all these years. He also issued a simple instruction: never let anyone up there, and never let Jessica out without him knowing about it.

Before he could tear into his hapless employee, Sanchez

heard a voice that made his stomach flip and his blood run cold..

'Hey, barmaid. Fill the glass.'

He looked over at the man sat at the bar. Now Sanchez hadn't shit himself since he was a kid, but he very nearly lost control of his ass at the sight of the Bourbon Kid sitting in his bar with a glass of the gold stuff in front of him. *Holy-fuckin'-shit-I-don't-need-this*, he thought in his terror.

Before Sanchez could speak, or even reach out to try to grab the glass of bourbon from where it sat on the bar, a glassful of warm piss was thrown in his face. It went in his eyes, mouth, nostrils and ears, and then began to drip down his nice white 'FUCK OFF' T-shirt.

It wasn't the first time he'd been soaked in his own special brew, and it probably wouldn't be the last. Karma had a habit of catching up with Sanchez at times like this. As the shock subsided he took a moment to wipe his eyes to try to rid himself of the stinging sensation that was now making him weep a little. Standing at the bar was one very angry wannabe werewolf rapper, with a furious snarl distorting his face.

'You fuckin' scumbag, Sanchez!' Pedro was shouting. 'That ain't the first time that fuckin' bitch has pulled that piss trick!'

The five other werewolves and the hooker remained at their table, fuming. Each had taken a swig of the piss in their glasses, and somehow each had managed to spit some of the foul liquid over whoever was sitting opposite them at the table. They were all trying to brush the stuff of their faces with their hands, spluttering and hawking as they tried to rid themselves of the taste.

Sally stepped back out of range of the angry werewolf. She clearly felt safer topping up the glass of bourbon on the bar than dealing with the angry figure of Pedro. For a moment the stunned Sanchez didn't know where to look or what to say. Then he just blurted out the first thing that came into his head.

'That's the *Bourbon Kid!*' he yelled, pointing at his newest customer.

Pedro turned sharply and looked at the Kid who was sitting at the bar. He still hadn't pulled his hood over his head.

'Don't talk fuckin' stupid, Sanchez, I know this guy, his name's . . .'

Before he could finish his sentence the Kid sprang from his barstool and grabbed the thick black hair on the back of the rapper's head. Then he smashed his face down on to the bartop.

CRACK! – The sound of Pedro's nose breaking echoed around the bar. The Kid pulled his victim's head back up. It was already slick with blood and his nose was no longer in the middle of his face.

ROAR! – A new sound. That of Pedro instinctively turning into a werewolf. Ready for a fight.

SMASH! – Face down on the bartop again.

And again.

And again.

This werewolf had taken great pleasure in the slaughter of Casper, an innocent whose brother had not been there to save him. He had to be made to pay. No quick death for this piece of filth. Seven times in succession the werewolf's face was cracked down on to the bartop and hauled back up again. Each time it came back up it looked twice as bad as before. The seventh time the wolfman's face hit the bartop it yielded a loud cracking noise as a set of huge fangs shattered and flew out of his mouth and over the bar.

The Bourbon Kid pulled Pedro's battered wolf face back up from the counter one last time and dragged him a foot back from the bar, once more pulling him by the thick hair on his head. The werewolf was unsteady on his feet, utterly dazed by the savage speed of the attack, which had taken him completely by surprise. While he was still struggling to regain his senses, his attacker shaped his free hand into a half-clenched fist. Then, in one sudden move of unimaginable violence he plunged his sharp clawed fingers into the wolf's soft neck. They pierced the skin and flesh with horrible ease. An unpleasant squelching sound followed. The Kid's hand wriggled and pulled at the wolf's throat for a few brief seconds and then snapped back, leaving a gaping bloodied hole where the front of Pedro's neck had been. In the Kid's grip was a pulsating lump of bloodied gristle that had once been Pedro's Adam's apple.

For a few seconds he held the bloodied flesh out in front of the werewolf, allowing the dying eyes to stare at it as they slowly began to roll upwards in their sockets. After checking that Pedro's pupils had disappeared up into his skull, the Kid released his grip on the dying body, and watched it crumple to the floor. He then tossed the bloody Adam's apple nonchalantly over the bar, where it hit Sanchez in the face and slipped to the ground.

The five other werewolves and the hooker at the table in the middle of the barroom had remained motionless all through the attack, paralysed by the fear that had gripped them. All had desperately hoped that Pedro would fight back and triumph. Now, one look into the eyes of the Bourbon Kid as he turned slowly to face them was all it took to convince them how matters stood. None of them wanted to hang around, and they rapidly came to their senses, threw their chairs back and charged for the exit. Only the hooker remained seated, hoping to be left alone.

The wolves were not quick enough. The Kid produced a wooden-handled knife with a bright ten-inch blade from within his dark robe, raised it above his shoulder and then launched it at the partly open door. It effortlessly penetrated the open door, the tip coming out on the other side. The door was struck with such ferocity by the blade that it swung on its hinges and slammed shut, embedding the pointed end of the knife in the side of the door frame, thereby bolting the door shut and trappping everyone inside. *That blade is going to take some shifting*, Sanchez thought, his mind fixing on trifles at the moment of greatest danger.

The werewolves all stopped dead. Turning to face the bar,

they watched in open-mouthed horror as the Kid lifted his dark hood up over his head. He then pulled one of his trademark Skorpion automatic pistols from inside his robe, pointed it down at the lifeless bloodied mess of the body on the floor by his feet, and blasted a silver bullet through Pedro's face. Gobbets of blood and matter sprayed everywhere, making splashing noises as they hit the walls. The Kid looked back up at his audience and focused his glare on them once more. All that was could be seen within the dark cowl were the whites of his eyes.

Fearing for their undead lives, the wolfmen began to back away. Their tormentor raised his free hand to indicate that they should remain still.

'Bartender,' he snarled in his unmistakable gravelly tone, without even looking over at Sanchez.

'Yeah?'

'Top up my drink while I redecorate your bar.'

Forty

Robert Swann wanted this mission over and done with, and he wanted to get his hands on Kacy. There were two things that could bring this case to a close. The first was if Dante found and identified the monk Peto. To Swann, that didn't look like it was going to happen any time soon because Dante was too much of a loser. The second thing that might bring the case to an end would be if Dante was identified as an impostor by the vampires and killed as a result. One of those two things would happen tonight, Swann was convinced of it. As he pulled the syringe out of Dante's arm after the usual early-evening injection of the blood-cooling serum, he took a long look at Kacy. She was gazing like a love-struck teenager at her moron boyfriend. Swann longed for the day when a woman might look at him like that. Especially a hot one, like Kacy. He had put on his smartest grey chino trousers and a clean black shirt after remembering how she had seemed to warm to him when he'd worn a suit the previous night.

'Have a good night, buddy,' he said to Dante as he took the empty syringe into the bathroom to clean and sterilize it.

Dante ignored Swann and pulled the sleeve on his black sweatshirt back down. He was sitting on the double bed in their room next to Kacy, with Roxanne Valdez hovering over them. She had relayed to Dante the whole story of the previous evening when Kacy and Swann had got drunk together over dinner. It hadn't gone down well so Kacy wasn't about to rile him further by dressing in anything sexy that might get Swann's eyes popping out of his head. She had just thrown on a pair of jeans and a white sweatshirt. Dante tugged at the sleeve of her shirt and pulled her towards, him planting a kiss on her lips.

'This is all gonna be over tonight, babe, I can feel it,' he said confidently. 'I'm startin' to get used to the feel of this serum and now that I'm well in with these vampire guys I can start askin' a few more questions. I feel good about tonight.'

Kacy got to her knees on the bed and kissed him on the forehead.

'I'll stay up and wait for you. Be good.'

'Love you, Kace.'

'Love you too.'

Valdez stepped towards the couple on the bed. 'C'mon now, Dante,' she said. 'No time like the present. The sooner you get going, the sooner you'll find the monk. I've a good feeling about tonight, too. It's Halloween and everyone will be drunker'n hell and in good spirits. So there's a good chance the monk will make contact with you if he gets plasterered like everyone else.'

Dante kissed Kacy on the lips once again and got up from the bed. Roxanne tossed his sleeveless black leather Shades jacket over to him and he caught it on his way out of the room, slinging it over his shoulder as he went. He walked through the sitting room and into the hall. Reaching the front door of the apartment, he pulled it open and looked back at Kacy one last time. She was still sitting on the bed on her knees gazing lovingly back at him, so he gave her a quick sexy wink and stepped out into the corridor.

As Dante was closing the door behind him, Swann was coming back out of the bathroom with the sterilized syringe in his hand. 'Gone has he?' he asked, smiling broadly.

Kacy nodded back at him from the bed, a sad look spreading across her face at the thought of Dante out in the perilous world of the vampires once more. She would have looked a good deal sadder if she'd known what Swann was so happy about. When he had given Dante his nightly injection of the serum, he had actually filled the syringe with water instead of the blood coolant.

Swann wanted Dante out of the picture, and by injecting him with nothing more than water, he had ensured the vampires would finally recognize him for the impostor he was.

Forty-One

Detective Randy Benson stopped in at the Olé Au Lait for a quick caffeine fix. He was on his way to a secret appointment in an hour's time. It was an important one, but he was a tad early for it. He hadn't wanted to hang around at police headquarters because he had discovered something that he didn't want De La Cruz or Hunter to know. And he was only too aware that the building was the perfect setting for an assassination attempt courtesy of the Bourbon Kid, so a quiet coffee on his own in the always peaceful environment of the Olé Au Lait was perfect. Or at least, it should have been.

Flake was kind enough to bring his latte over to him, along with a selection of doughnuts on a silver plate. He pointed a couple out and the pretty young waitress placed them on a white china dish set beside his coffee on the small circular wooden table at which he had seated himself.

As she walked back behind the counter he took a moment out to admire her pert little ass as it wiggled away beneath her short black skirt. It really was a miracle she hadn't been bagged by one of the local vampires by now. Maybe if things went well for him tonight he'd pop back and give her a nibble. For the time being he would have to make do with the sticky chocolate ring or the frosted bun she had left him.

Just as he was about to take a bite out of the chocolate-covered doughnut his evening took an unexpected turn. A previously overlooked but extremely burly man in a suit who had been sitting at the counter stood up and walked over to Benson's table. The man had a smooth-shaved head and was wearing a pair of dark sunglasses. His suit was a shiny silver colour and looked expensive. As he approached Benson his true size became more and more apparent. Every step that brought him closer made him look larger, until finally he was standing well over six feet tall and a fair few feet wide right in front of the detective.

'Can I help you?' asked Benson.

There wasn't another chair at Benson's table so without looking, the man reached out with his left hand and pulled a chair from the next table. The fact that there was a young man sitting on the chair didn't bother him. The fresh-faced, long-haired student who had been sitting and sharing some pleasant conversation with his girlfriend was sent sprawling to the floor as his seat disappeared from under him.

'What the fuck?' he shouted, startling several of the café's other customers. He was tensed up and ready for confrontation, but all it took was a single glance at the face of the man who had removed his chair to make him wisely choose to find an unoccupied chair from somewhere else. Benson had coolly observed what the burly man had done and watched as the giant sat down opposite him.

'You know, some people don't like that,' he advised his visitor.

'We all have things we don't like,' the man replied, barely moving his thin, colourless lips.

'True enough. You know, one thing *I* don't like is strangers sittin' themselves down at my table when I'm havin' coffee. Why don't you find somewhere else to sit?'

'I want to sit here.'

Benson wasn't troubled by the man's size. It didn't matter how big he was. The undead detective was more than capable of dealing with just about anyone these days. He leaned across the table a little and took a bite out of his chocolate ring.

'Doughnut . . . ' It was one of those comments that might have been construed as a statement or a question. The burly man took it as a question.

'No thanks. Bad for your arteries, you know. Now put the fucking thing down. You take another bite out of that while I'm talking to you and I'll rip you a new asshole.'

Benson sensed real conviction in the man's tone. Although caution wasn't overly necessary he chose to exercise some anyway, more out of curiosity than anything else. He put the doughnut back down on the china dish.

'Okay, big boy. Just who the fuck are you?'

The man leaned over the table a little until their faces were only six inches apart.

'I'm your superior.'

Benson wasn't in the least bit impressed. 'You know, I answer directly to the Chief of Police in this town. And I can assure you, he's not my superior either. That's all for show. I'm pretty much top dog in Santa Mondega, so no matter how superior you think you are, I'm just that little bit above ya. Ya get me?'

The burly man sat back and smiled. A confident smile. It didn't worry Benson, but it confused him. Who the fuck was this guy?

'You're looking to take over from Archie Somers, or Armand Xavier, whatever the fuck he called himself, aren't you?' said the man.

'I've already taken over from Archie Somers, thanks, buddy. Don't need no help from you for that.'

'Somers and I used to be friends, you know, back when he called himself Armand Xavier.'

'Well, bully for you.'

'Then he double-crossed me. I wouldn't let him marry my daughter, so he and his partner in crime, Ishmael Taos, set me up. Pretty nasty business. Imprisoned me in a mummified state in a tomb for quite a while. I'm talking a lot of centuries here.'

Benson's stomach tightened. 'Say again?'

'That's right.' The man removed his sunglasses to reveal the final, incontrovertible evidence. He had a bright green translucent stone where his right eye should have been. 'I'm the boss. Call me Dark Lord if you like. You could try calling me Mummy, but I wouldn't advise it. Some people call me

Mr E, but that name is fast becoming redundant. Now if you wanna wipe that smug bacon-sandwich smirk off your face, you can call me Rameses Gaius. That's what my friends call me. And you, young sir, have the chance to be my friend.'

'Gaius? But how?'

'Never you mind. I've been watching you, Benson. You and your two friends De La Cruz and Hunter – bunch of fucking idiots you are, the lot of you. Dragging werewolves in with you to do your dirty business. Have you no self-respect?'

'Well . . . '

'Hush. I'm talking.'

'Sorry.'

'Yes, you are. You and your cronies meddled in my business. You went looking for the Bourbon Kid without my blessing.'

'I didn't realize we had to . . . '

'Hush.'

Gaius spoke softly but firmly and Benson sensed that another interruption would be most unwise.

'I already had a plan in place to find the Bourbon Kid, and it didn't involve stirring him up like you've done. You now have to take care of your mistake. I could have finished him off in his sleep, but now you and your crew have made the whole thing a sight trickier. So you're gonna have to pay me back.'

Benson waited long enough to be sure it was his turn to speak.

'Go on. Whadda ya want me to do?'

'All I need from you is the Bourbon Kid's name and the Holy Grail.'

'*That's all?*'

'That's all.'

'Well, that's easy. I can give you his name right now.'

'Really?' Gaius betrayed his surprise that Benson had such information to hand.

'Yeah. He's a John Doe.'

'What?'

'A John Doe. Accordin' to research by a woman named Stephanie Rogers who was on the case, his mother never gave him a name. She didn't want any evil sorts coming after him when he was a kid, so in order to keep him out of any national records he was never registered at birth.'

'How could he have gotten by without a name, though?'

'Shit, man, I dunno. Maybe they called him John Doe when he was around the house? How the fuck should I know?'

Rameses Gaius thought for a while before speaking. 'Fascinating. Good work, Benson. Now all I have to do is what his father and Xavier did to me.'

'Which is?'

'Mind your own business.'

''Kay.'

'Good. So far you've done moderately well in righting your mistake. That's half your job done already. Now all you have to do is get me the Holy Grail. Do not mistake me – I know you have it. Once you deliver it to me I'll make you my High Priest.'

'Which means what, exactly?'

'You don't know what comes with serving as my High Priest?'

'I get to polish your eye once a week?'

A second figure that Benson hadn't previously noticed approached from the counter area. A much smaller figure than that of Gaius, but one with a magnificent physique. This was the woman all male vampires desired above any other. Jessica, the Angel of Death. She was dressed in her traditional all-black attire, a pair of tight-fitting black leather pants and a thin black silky blouse that was unbuttoned to about halfway down.

Reaching the table, she stood to the right of Gaius and leaned over until her face was barely a breath away from Benson's, and her cleavage was practically under his chin. And what a beautiful face it was. Smooth as silk, with enormous, beautiful brown eyes, and shiny dark shoulder-length hair that perfectly framed the creamy white skin of her face.

'I could be all yours, honey,' she whispered in what was without a doubt the sexiest voice he had ever heard. 'Think about it. You and me, a four-poster bed, some whipped cream and a set of handcuffs. Whadda you say, huh? I know you wanted me before, but now I'm offering you the chance to have me when I'm conscious.'

Holy Shit! The Angel of Death was a goddess, instinctively coveted by all vampires, though only accessible to the most powerful. Benson could feel his trousers tightening already. The power was there for the taking, and all he had to do was go and fetch the Holy Grail. Child's play.

'So, are you up to it?' Jessica asked.

'Fuck, yeah. I am,' Benson replied eagerly.

'Then what are you waiting for?'

Benson downed his still-steaming coffee in one mouthful. 'I'm right on it,' he said, standing up and knocking the china dish off the table with the unexpected bulge in his pants as he turned to get past Jessica. She threw him an admiring glance. 'Don't be all night,' she cooed.

Benson, slightly flustered and hugely excited, rushed out of the coffee shop. He knew that in order to get the Holy Grail he might have to take on the Bourbon Kid. That would no doubt be a very tough proposition, but he had a little something in his favour. A secret weapon he had chosen not to share with his buddies De La Cruz and Hunter, or now with his new friends Rameses Gaius and Jessica. He just had to go pick it up. Then all the power he craved, and the woman he desired would be his for the taking.

In fact, he might even be about to become more powerful than Gaius.

Forty-Two

Dante arrived at the Nightjar in the nick of time. As he approached, the big bouncer, Uncle Les, was preparing to close the front door for the night.

'Yo, new boy,' the bouncer called out when he saw Dante heading along the deserted street in the bar's direction. 'You better hurry your ass up if you wanna get in. We're shuttin' the doors early.'

Dante took off his wraparound sunglasses and broke into a polite jog to show the bouncer that he was hurrying his ass up, as requested.

'Wassup, Uncle? Private party or somethin'?'

'Nah. Trouble headed this way. Bourbon Kid's back in town, 'pparently. On another killing spree, if reports are true.'

Dante reached the entrance and stepped inside the bar. Uncle Les secured the door behind him.

'Thanks, man. Could be an early close tonight, then?' Dante asked hopefully.

'Or a lock-in. Literally,' the bouncer replied.

Taking a look around the bar area, Dante could see that the place was buzzing tonight, packed wall to wall with vampires. It seemed like they'd all heard the bad news about the Kid's return and decided to congregate in one place. *Safety in numbers,* he supposed. Either that, or they just loved Halloween.

In a corner of the bar he could make out two of the familiar Shades jackets. The vampires wearing them were Fritz and Obedience, which was a relief because they were the two he found easiest to get on with, simply because they were the most talkative, even if one of them was a bit shouty. As he headed over to join them he picked up the tune being played by The Psychics on stage to his left. They were banging out a pretty decent cover of *Loser* by Beck.

Making his way through the crowds towards the undead buddies whose respect he had earned over the last two nights, he couldn't help but notice that he was attracting some strange looks. As he sang along to the chorus of The Psychics' song – 'I'm a loser, baby, so why don't you kill me?' – he put all the funny looks down to the fact that these vampires were in awe of how cool he looked in his new jacket. It felt good to be accepted.

After struggling through the crowd he eventually reached Fritz and Obedience, who had their backs to him. He tugged at Fritz's jacket. 'Hey fellas, anyone wanna 'nother drink?' he asked.

Fritz turned and smiled at him. Obedience did likewise, but very quickly both their smiles turned to frowns. Their sunglasses hid the look of confusion in their eyes.

'VOT ZE FUCK?' shouted Fritz reflectively, staring hard at Dante.

'What?' asked Dante, confused. 'Have I got 'cunt' written across my head, or somethin'?' He laughed at his own joke and shoved Fritz playfully, nodding at Obedience, who was standing just behind the German. Neither vampire laughed. Instead, Obedience stepped forward, reached out a hand and grabbed Dante's face, squeezing his cheeks. *Checking his temperature.*

'Fritz, are you thinking what I'm thinking?' he asked his buddy. His voice was cold.

'FUCKING RIGHT I AM! I AM FUCKING SINKING ZIS SING ALSO!'

Dante sensed a touch of hostility from Obedience and put it down to his bad joke. 'Hey, sorry, man. I was just kiddin', y'know?'

Obedience released his grip on Dante's face, but then

immediately grabbed his left arm and pulled it towards him. Roughly, he rolled the black shirtsleeve back and scanned up and down the arm. He twisted the limb a little, making Dante flinch, and gestured for Fritz to take a look.

'Fritz, our man here's been injecting something into his arm. Look at these needle marks in his veins.'

Fritz studied Dante's arm closely and saw a few marks where Swann had injected the serum each night. Dante sensed that he was in a spot of shit, and that some quick thinking was required. 'Shit, man. Ain't nothin' bad,' he mumbled. 'Just H.'

Obedience sneered. 'Quite a regular intake of something, I'd say. These marks are all pretty fresh. Myself, I don't reckon you've injected yourself with this much H in the last few days. Must be something else.'

'Nah, it's heroin,' Dante protested. 'The stuff's very moreish, y'know.'

'So's the serum that they pump into undercover folks who try and walk among vampires,' Obedience snarled. His fangs were coming out on display. Both he and Fritz knew they'd been duped. Dante had been an impostor all along. Obedience, in particular, was seething at the betrayal. He had a ridiculous tattoo emblazoned in green across his forehead because of Dante. To discover that his new comrade wasn't really one of them had obviously upset him.

Fritz finally stated the obvious, letting Dante (and the rest of the crowd in the Nightjar) know that the game was up.

'HE'S NOT A FUCKING VAMPIRE. HE'S UNDERCOVER! SCHWEINHUND!' the German barked, his voice sounding more furious than ever.

Obedience gripped Dante's arm a little harder. He wasn't about to let his grip loosen and risk letting the undercover mole escape.

'He may not be one of us,' Obedience growled. 'But he'll make for a fine supper.'

Forty-Three

Hunter arrived at the Nightjar to find the large wooden door at the front bolted shut from the inside. A glance through one of the tall, narrow, dark-tinted windows showed that, inside, the place was heaving with drinkers. *That's odd,* he thought.

He leaned into one of the inset window frames and tapped on the glass to try to get the attention of the nearest reveller on the other side of the glass. The first person he laid eyes on was Santa Mondega's most fearsome clown, Reuben. The green-wigged, pale-faced, broad-smiling bloodsucker was standing on the edge of a group of clowns. Unbeknown to Hunter, they were plotting a way of exacting revenge on the Shades for the misunderstanding that had taken place at the Swamp the previous night. In the barroom beyond the clowns, all of the Nightjar's other customers seemed to be watching The Psychics perform a hip song-and-dance routine on the stage.

Reuben heard Hunter's tap on the glass over the noise of the band and immediately turned to see what it was. His painted white face looked over at the Filthy Pig at the window, acknowledging him with a nod and a big painted red smile that conveniently hid the look of contempt beneath it. Hunter gestured with his hand and a nod towards the entrance, indicating that Reuben should open the door and let him in. In response the clown simply stared back at him, and then gave him the finger.

'Once I get in there, you won't think it's so fucking funny, you circus freak!' Hunter yelled through the window. To his further annoyance, the clown turned his back on him. 'Fuckin' bastard.'

At that moment another of the Nightjar's regulars arrived at the front entrance. He had sneaked out of the shadows and sidled up alongside Hunter without making a sound. It was Silence. He was wearing the obligatory trademark black sleeveless jacket of the Shades, but with no shirt underneath and a pair of ripped blue denim jeans above a pair of shiny black boots with pointed toes. He stared at the Filthy Pig from behind his sunglasses.

'Whassup, man?' Silence inquired in a husky voice. 'What's with the shut door?'

Hunter couldn't recall ever hearing Silence speak before, and was mildly impressed that the normally wordless vampire should choose to unleash several of his precious words upon him. It wasn't foremost in his thoughts for long, though. Getting into the Nightjar was top priority.

'Dunno. But I'm gonna get it sorted,' Hunter finally responded, sliding one hand inside his brown tweed jacket. He pulled a cell phone from his inside pocket. It was the one De La Cruz had given him earlier. The one that had once belonged to Casper. 'I'll call Dino. He'll let us in.'

Silence took a look at the phone in Hunter's hand as the Filthy Pig started tapping in the number for the Nightjar.

'Nice phone. Where'dja get it?' he asked.

'Since when did you get so fuckin' chatty?' Hunter snapped as he finished keying in the number, pressed the 'call' button and put the phone to his ear. It rang a couple of times before it was answered. Dino's voice spoke.

'Nightjar.'

'Hey Dino. It's Hunter. Let us in, for fuck's sake.'

'How many of you are there?'

'Just me an' Silence.'

'Hold on.'

Dino hung up at the other end, so Hunter put the cell phone back in his pocket and stood waiting impatiently outside the entrance with Silence. The quiet vampire took off his sunglasses and the two men eyeballed each other while they waited. Hunter didn't like Silence, and didn't want to waste any effort in talking to a man who was renowned for having poor social skills. Unfortunately, Dino was taking a long time getting to the door, and the uncomfortable quiet began to irritate the detective.

'So what exactly is wrong with your voice anyway, huh? That's why you don't say much, ain't it? 'Cos it hurts to talk, or somethin' like that?'

Silence nodded. 'Yeah, hurts to talk.'

'Yeah,' said Hunter, nodding. 'Sounds like you swallowed a bucket of grit.'

Silence reached inside his jacket.

'Hey! Whatcha doin'?' Hunter asked aggressively. He sounded rattled. The long wait outside was making him paranoid. A feeling, he thought, that he shouldn't have, now that he was more powerful than any of the other vampires.

But Silence simply pulled a soft pack of cigarettes from his inside pocket and held them out towards Hunter. 'Smoke?' he asked.

'Yeah. Yeah, thanks.' Hunter reached out and took one. He placed it between his lips. 'You gotta light?'

Silence nodded and with his free hand reached inside his jacket again. This time he produced a Zippo lighter. He held it out, flipped the top open, and flicked the wheel to ignite the flame. Hunter leaned in to the flame and sucked on the cigarette. It duly lit, and Silence replaced the lighter in his pocket.

'You ain't havin' one yourself?' Hunter asked.

Silence put the pack of cigarettes to his mouth and pulled one out with his teeth. He then slipped the pack back inside his jacket and took a drag on the cigarette, which lit itself.

'Wow,' remarked Hunter, impressed. 'How d'ya do that?'

'Friend showed me.'

There was a loud grating sound as the bolts on the other side of the door were slid to one side and the door slowly opened. Jericho, the bouncer with the leg brace, peered round it and eyed the waiting vampires warily.

'Just you two?'

'Yeah,' said Hunter, pushing the door further open and barging in past the doorman. Silence followed him in with a bow of the head by way of thanks to Jericho.

By the time the bouncer had bolted the door shut again, Hunter had forged a path to the bar. The other vampires seemed to be picking up on his new aura and they parted to let him find space. Silence followed on behind him.

'Dino, gimme a beer,' Hunter shouted over to the bar owner, who was helping out his staff.

'What?' Dino was having trouble hearing over the noise of the band. The Psychics were performing the Kaiser Chiefs hit 'I Predict a Riot' and were currently belting out the chorus.

'GLASS O' BEER!' Hunter shouted. Dino shook his head and put his hand to his ear. He was still engaged in filling the glass of one of the Dreads a few feet further down the bar. The Rastafarian was watching the bartender like a hawk to make sure he wasn't given a short measure. Dino (unlike Sanchez) wasn't one to upset his customers, but there were just too many distractions for him to pick up clearly what Hunter was yelling.

'GLASS O' FUCKIN' BEER!' Hunter shouted again. It was no good. Dino couldn't hear him. A new approach was required, and by good fortune Hunter spotted Fritz standing behind him. The German was with his buddy Obedience and their new clan member Dante, who Hunter could see was quite clearly not even a vampire. Obedience had a firm grip on Dante's arm and seemed to be holding on to him. Silence joined them. Hunter thought they all looked agitated about something. He wasn't interested in what they were doing, however. He was just hoping to get Fritz's attention.

'Hey, Fritz! Help me out, will ya? Order me a beer,' he yelled at the German.

'SURE!' Fritz bellowed back. 'DINO, GET ZE MAN A FUCKING BEER, VILL YOU!'

Surprisingly, given how loud the German shouted, it was still not working. Dino was oblivious to the request. A new approach was required. Hunter pulled his pistol from its holster under his jacket, pointed it at the ceiling and squeezed the trigger.

BANG!

The sound was deafening, and was followed by a few small chunks of white plaster and a lot of white dust falling from the ceiling. Skeins of blue smoke swirled above Hunter. The place fell into a deathly quiet. The Psychics stopped playing 'I Predict a Riot'. All that could be heard was the echo of the gunshot ringing in everyone's ears.

'Why don't you fuckers take a break?' Hunter yelled aggressively at the band, who looked as startled as everyone else.

They were a six-piece on this particular evening. Mandina, the lead singer, was wearing a short purple dress and the rest of the 'almost all-girl group', two guitarists, a drummer, the tubby male horn player and a dancer were all laced up in nothing more than matching sets of skimpy black underwear. They made a fine sight (with the possible exception of the tuba player), so most of the audience were still able to enjoy them without hearing the music. Now that they were no longer blaring out a tune and the bar was totally hushed Hunter was able to order his drink. He turned his attentions back to the bar. 'And I'll have a beer, Dino.'

Dino picked a glass from behind the bar and began to pour Hunter a beer. He had a chunk of white plaster on the shoulder of his suit jacket. He could see that Hunter was clearly rattled, and as the Filthy Pig had already pulled his pistol out and used it once it was in the bar owner's best interests to keep him happy. Hunter was a 'made' man, after all, despite the fact that his geeky appearance might suggest otherwise. His hair was as neatly combed as ever and looked as though it had recently been blow-dried. With the thick brown sweater he wore beneath his tweed jacket, he looked like a reject from *The Cosby Show*. But he was undeniably dangerous.

Since a hush had now fallen on the bar, and everyone's conversation had stopped, Hunter realized he had the perfect opportunity to call the 'Big Bro' number. He picked the cell phone out of his pocket again and flicked through the menus to find the number. Once he'd found it he barked out a last reminder to the rest of the customers in the bar.

'Now listen up! Everybody just sit tight for one more minute, will ya? I've got an important call to make. So can you all keep your fuckin' mouths shut for just a little longer while I call someone that you may all have heard of, huh?' He looked around at his audience, who were at best feigning interest in what he had to say. 'Yes, folks, I have the phone number for the Bourbon Kid. An' I'm gonna call him right now, so keep it buttoned.' He put his left index finger to his lips for emphasis, then used his right thumb to press 'Call' on the cell phone.

Amused to see that everyone in the bar was now paying him full attention, he put the phone to his ear and waited for it to ring. The dialling tone kicked in after about three seconds. Half a second after that, the silence in the bar was broken by the sound of someone's cell phone ringing.

Someone standing no more than three feet from Hunter.

Forty-Four

Josh had only been working at the Santa Mondega City Library for a month, and it had been hell. The head librarian, Ulrika Price, was a severe taskmaster, and she made him nervous. And when Josh was nervous he had a tendency to lose control of his bodily functions. This could happen in many different ways, such as a sudden burst of snot shooting out of his nose, a mouthful of spit flying over the person he was talking to or, in extreme cases, pissing his pants just a little.

From day one Ulrika had taken great pleasure in making him feel uncomfortable and in wielding such power as she had over him. Intimidating a fifteen-year-old boy like Josh gave her a real buzz, of a kind that was all too absent from her otherwise sad and lonely existence.

Today had been one of those days when she was more uptight than ever, and it had pushed Josh to the brink of quitting. He had a second job anyway, so he could just about afford to lose his job as a trainee librarian. The only responsibility with which he was entrusted was placing the returned books back on the shelves where they belonged, and by Miss Price's reckoning he was shit at doing even that. Already that day she had berated him for placing a Dan Brown novel in the Non-Fiction section and, even worse, a Barbra Streisand biography in with the Humour titles. It seemed he could do little right, certainly in Ulrika's eyes. Of course, it was her own fault for putting him under intense pressure to replace books the minute she logged them back in. One thing she wouldn't stand for was a pile of returned books mounting up on her reception desk.

The black school trousers Josh was rapidly growing out of were starting to creep up his ass due to all the sweat he was working up on his jaunts back and forth to the shelves, and his plain white shirt was close to becoming transparent. After placing a book entitled *Dieting for Midgets* on the top shelf of the Cookery section he returned to the reception desk to find out what Ol' Misery Guts had for him next.

When he got there she was on the phone, and knowing how she valued her privacy he stood and waited patiently for her to finish her conversation. She was sitting in the padded plastic seat right behind the reception desk, facing the entrance so she could see everyone who came in and went out. She was always checking to make sure no one tried to creep away with a book without signing it out first.

Josh knew better than to get caught listening in to her phone call. Ulrika Price took some highly dubious calls from some very unsavoury characters sometimes. Josh knew this because, on one occasion when she had been away from reception, he had impersonated her when answering the phone. A man with a deeply unpleasant voice had spoken on the other end and given him a list of four names and a date, then slammed the phone down. The junior librarian had thought nothing of it, but when, a few days later, Ulrika had found out what he had done she had gone ballistic and pinned him up against a wall with a hand at his throat. After that, he had made a point of never impersonating her again.

And now, this late in the day, she was busy peering over her spectacles and scribbling something down in a book on a shelf beneath the counter as she 'umm-ed' and 'aah-ed' on the phone. Josh, unsure whether she'd seen him waiting on the customer side of the desk, cleared his throat to let her know he was within earshot. The sound elicited an evil stare from Ms Price and she pulled her grey cardigan tighter over her shoulders, turning away from him just enough to be sure that he couldn't see what she was writing. Eventually, after another ten seconds of nodding and 'uh-huh-ing', she replaced the handset on the chunky, old-fashioned white phone and turned to her junior.

'Are you all done now?' she grumbled at him, frowning so much that the front of her fair hair, which was tightly scraped back into a severe bun, clawed its way forward down to her eyebrows. For a woman in her thirties, she was not ageing well.

'Yes, miss. I've just put the midgets' diet book back.'

'Did you remember to put it on the bottom shelf?'

'Not as such. No.'

Ulrika's face screwed up into a contorted snarl, and she got up from her padded plastic chair.

'I despair,' she sighed. 'I really do. I'll go and move it myself.' She walked around the desk and came through the reception counter via a hinged wooden flap by the wall. She came over to where Josh was standing.

'Sorry,' he shrugged as she barged past him towards the cookery section right at the back of the giant hall of bookshelves. She heard his apology and stopped in her tracks for a moment with her back to him. He could see that the awful blue veins, which ran down her calves beneath the hem of her blue knee-length skirt, were twitching. After a slight pause she turned to face him.

'Don't worry about it. You'll get better at this one day . . . probably. In fact, you can start by putting that *Sesame Street* annual back on the shelves. Then go home. I'm sick of the sight of you.'

'What *Sesame Street* annual?'

'There's one behind the counter somewhere. It's really not at all hard to recognize. *Honestly!*' Ulrika Price was exasperated, and not bothering to hide it.

'Okay. I'll do that and be off, then. Thanks. G'night, miss.'

Ulrika didn't respond and simply strode off towards the cookery section, looking for any young people on her way whom she could berate or accuse of stealing.

Josh leaned over the counter to look for the *Sesame Street* annual. The only book that caught his eye was a black volume on the lower part of the desk in front of which Ulrika had been sitting when she was on the telephone. He reached over and grabbed it. It was a heavy hardback book and it took all his strength to lift it with the limited leverage he could apply from his position leaning over the counter. Once it was in his hands he took a look at the title. *The Book of Death*, it read.

Holy shit! he thought to himself. *These Sesame Street annuals have changed a bit since I was younger.*

Not wanting to upset Ulrika further, he decided to give some thought to where he should put this book. It didn't seem right to place it in the Children's section. That wouldn't be appropriate. So where?

Reference – *when in doubt always put a book in the Reference section.* It was a rule that had served him well during his time in the library. Why change it now? Not wanting to be around when Ulrika returned from the Cookery section, he hurried on over to Reference. He slipped the book on to one of the shelves, then hightailed it out of the library to get something to eat before heading off to his late-night job.

When Ulrika eventually returned she was alarmed to find that *The Book of Death* had gone missing, along with Josh. *This was serious.* That book was not meant for public consumption. It was a special book that she kept locked away in a safe, only ever taking it out when she was instructed to do so. Her master, the great Rameses Gaius, had bestowed upon her the honour of being the keeper of the most powerful book in the history of mankind. And tonight had been one of those nights when he had instructed her to take it out and enter some names into its pages.

If she wanted to carry on as his mistress, and achieve the immortality and everlasting beauty he had promised her in return for her services, she had to find it before it fell into the wrong hands. And if Gaius was to ever find out how careless she had been with it, she feared that her time on earth would come to an abrupt and painful end.

Forty-Five

Hunter turned around. After calling the number for 'Big Bro', he had heard a nearby cell phone ring almost immediately. He still held Casper's phone to his ear. And standing almost directly in front of him was a member of the Shades, holding in one hand a ringing cell phone. It was the gullible one who always did as he was told, Obedience. Hunter swiftly drew his gun back out from its holster over his ribcage on the and aimed it directly at Obedience's head. The latter held up a finger to gesture to Hunter to wait a moment as he answered his phone.

'Hello, who's calling please?' he asked the caller.

'Me, you asshole,' Hunter replied, ending the call.

Obedience, looking confused, also hung up. The whole bar was watching, wondering what was going on.

'This, my friends, is the Bourbon Kid,' Hunter announced, pointing at Obedience as he spoke to the onlooking crowd.

Dante, who was standing next to Obedience, spoke up on behalf of everyone. 'Are you nuts?'

'No, I'm deadly serious. This phone I'm holding here has the Bourbon Kid's cell-phone number in it. I just dialled it and this dumb fuck has just answered. He's the Bourbon Kid. He's been livin' in amongst us for some time, plotting to kill us all.'

Fritz stepped forward in defence of his friend, ready to square up to Hunter physically if the need arose. A vampire should always be willing to stick up for any fellow member of his clan, and Fritz was as loyal a friend as any vampire could wish for.

'BULLSHIT!' he barked in Hunter's face, spraying him with only a little saliva.

'Look, I'm not the Bourbon Kid,' said Obedience with an impressive degree of calm. 'And this isn't my phone. I'm holding it for someone else.'

Hunter cocked his pistol and kept it fixed on Obedience's forehead, aimed right at the unfortunate 'CUNT' tattoo.

'Don't fuckin' lie to me.'

'I'm not lying.'

'ZIS IS TRUE!' Fritz spoke up again for his friend. 'HIS MOMMY TOLD HIM NEVER TO LIE, UND AS HE ALWAYS DOES VOT HE'S TOLD, TECHNICALLY HE MUST BE TELLING ZE TRUCE!'

'So who's fuckin' phone is it?' Hunter asked, straightening his arm and inching the gun closer to Obedience's face.

'I'm not allowed to say. The owner swore me to secrecy.'

'You got three seconds to tell me or I'm putting one right through your fuckin' face!'

'Y'know,' Dante interjected. 'You remind me of that guy from *Sesame Street* . . .'

'Shut up, fuckwad,' Hunter growled, swivelling the gun in Dante's direction. Dante raised his arms and backed away a step. He quickly reminded himself that Kacy wouldn't approve of him relating his favourite *Sesame Street* insult again, and that it wasn't his life in danger, but Obedience's. There really wasn't any need for him to get involved unnecessarily, particularly as Obedience had potentially been about to kill him before Hunter's intervention. Besides, Fritz and Silence would no doubt stick up for their buddy.

'VAIT!' yelled Fritz, as if on cue. 'IF YOU DO ANYSING TO OBEDIENCE I ASSURE YOU VE SHADES WILL HUNT YOU DOWN UND EXACT OUR REVENGE!'

'See this?' said Hunter pointing at his feet. His left shoe was tapping the floor gently. 'That's me quakin' in my fuckin' boots. Hunt me down all you fuckin' like, I couldn't give a shit. I could kill you with both my hands tied behind my back. Yeah, an' that gives me an idea . . .'

He pulled a pair of handcuffs from inside his jacket and threw them to Silence, who calmly caught them in his left hand.

'You, *Motormouth*. Cuff your buddy Obedience.'

Silence gave Hunter a hard stare for a second, but then did as instructed, cuffing Obedience's hands in front of him rather than behind his back to give his friend at least a small amount of comfort. Hunter let the hammer on his gun back down and holstered it once more, then grabbed hold of Obedience, spinning him round and then pushing him towards the Nightjar's front door.

Loyalty was a supreme virtue as far as Fritz was concerned. Seeing that Hunter was now no longer holding his pistol he made his move. The German lunged forward and took a swing at the detective. His right fist swung through the air with blinding speed, aimed at his enemy's jaw. But Hunter was made of sterner stuff these days, and saw the punch coming before it was even thrown. He moved out of its path with childish ease. His retaliation was swift. For the merest fraction of a second he released his grip on Obedience, then hit Fritz in the stomach with a counter-punch of such ferocity that it sent the German flying thirty feet across the bar, his feet a good six feet off the ground. The crowd parted as if a fireball was passing through them, allowing Fritz to journey unimpeded through the air. He moved at such pace he might have ended up halfway across the street, had it not been for the wall on the other side of the barroom by the entrance, into which he crashed. The impact caused him to bounce violently back, and he landed face down on a table with three members of the Punk Ladies clan sitting at it. The table split in half and Fritz fell through it, with the Ladies' drinks spilling down on top of him.

Silence didn't wait for an invitation. He burst forward and seized Hunter in a bear hug from behind. The muscles on his arms bulged as he exerted all his strength on tightening his grip around the Filthy Pig's chest. To no avail. Hunter had far superior strength these days, and easily shrugged him off.

He broke free from Silence's grip, then turned and sneered at him before picking him up by the throat and throwing him in the same direction as he had thrown Fritz. Silence followed the same trajectory as the German, crashing into the wall and then sinking to the floor by the three Punk Ladies' feet, landing on Fritz as his friend tried to stand upright.

Dante felt distinctly uneasy, for with neither Vanity nor Déjà-Vu present everyone would be looking to him to make the next move. Fortunately for him, Chip appeared behind him, dressed in his usual black wraparound karate outfit. He grabbed Dante's right arm, which he had been lining up to take a swing at Hunter, and whispered in his ear. 'Now's not the time. Be smart.'

Dante recognized the voice this time. He turned and looked closely through the dreadlocks and the painted veil that covered so much of Chip's face. Just as he'd thought. He liked this guy, and he trusted him – just about – so he had earned the right to tell Dante what to do. At least once, anyway.

So Dante lowered his half-clenched fist and backed away. Even though he was standing down and failing to support his fellow clan members, it was quite unlikely that anyone would berate him for this. Hunter had proved himself to be a real hardass. Right now every vampire in the Nightjar was deeply concerned at the thought of such an unpleasant, bullying character having gained such an increased level of power. It seemed that things in Santa Mondega were about to get ugly, and not just tonight either. Hunter, and whatever he signified, could be a long-term problem.

Everyone watched in silence as Hunter prodded Obedience in the back and followed him to the exit, aggressively eyeballing anyone who looked as though they might make trouble as he went. When they reached the Nightjar's front door, Jericho unbolted it and let them out, before shutting the door again and securing it behind them. The crowd in the bar heaved a huge collective sigh of relief.

It didn't take long for the chatter in the place to start up again. Everyone began discussing the events they had just witnessed, debating whether or not Obedience was the Bourbon Kid. They muttered, too, about just how worrying it was that a vicious prick like Hunter had become so incredibly powerful, effortlessly hurling two pretty hard dudes like Fritz and Silence thirty feet across the barroom.

In the general relief that the incident was over, Dante lost sight of Chip. He searched around for him in the crowd, still very aware that, for some unknown reason, the blood-cooling serum hadn't worked that night. With that in mind he needed to keep out of sight of Fritz and Silence, and indeed any other vampires with twitching fangs. He needed to get out. And soon.

No more than two minutes had passed before the place fell to a hushed silence again. An almighty ruckus had started up outside. There was shouting in the street, and it sounded like another fight had broken out. A few people rushed to the tinted windows and peered out. Something big was going on out there, but no one could quite make out what it was. It was too dark in the street and too bright inside to be able to see clearly what was going on. It was clear, though, that whatever was happening, it was developing fast.

And then there came an almighty bang.

Something, or *someone,* hit the huge bolted wooden entrance door from the outside, making it shudder violently. The people at the windows stepped back. In fact, even the people not at the windows stepped back.

THUD! – the door took another pounding blow and shook some more. Everyone stepped back another six inches, and well away from the entrance. This door, this solid, thick oak door was in danger of coming off its now creaking hinges. Best not to be in the way. Or even close.

The Psychics, who could never resist playing a tune when there was some action about to go down, attempted to lighten the mood by kicking off a new song, breaking into the old classic by The Animals, 'We Gotta Get Out Of This Place'.

THUD! – the door creaked loudly as its massive metal hinges began to bend under the strain of the repeated pounding.

Something was hitting that door with the force of a battering ram manned by a dozen burly men. Whatever it was outside, it was trying to get in.

By now everyone had scurried as far away from the door as they could. Backs were literally up against walls. That door was coming off its hinges and into the bar at any second.

CRASH! – that second arrived.

At enormous speed, the door flew off its hinges and, still upright, carried on through the barroom. Plastered to the outside of it was Hunter. Something had hit him so hard that he had slammed into the door and knocked it off its hinges, and then flown through the bar with his back pressed hard against the oak. The door's journey came to an end when the lower half of it hit the bartop and toppled up and over it, catapulting Hunter over the bartop and into the shelves of bottles and glasses on the wall behind. Slowly he crashed down on to the floor, with shelves and broken glass collapsing down on top of him with a sound like an express train hitting a glazier's truck. The nearest person to him was Dino, who had been lucky enough, or sensible enough, to duck well out of the way in the far corner of the bar.

For a moment all the customers stood and stared open-mouthed at the bar area, watching as the shocked and dazed figure of Hunter slowly clambered to his feet behind the bar, covered in glass and alcohol and various other small pieces of debris. He didn't look quite so fucking tough now. Then, in unison, like a crowd at a tennis match, everyone turned their heads and looked back to the massive hole where the Nightjar's front door had been.

A figure appeared in it.

An unsavoury sort of figure, looking extremely disgruntled, and ready to carry on the fight.

Dante's mouth was as open as anyone's. Maybe more so. He'd seen this guy wipe out a bar full of people a year earlier during an eclipse. It looked as though it was about to happen again, too. He had that all too familiar feeling.

Déjà-Vu.

The member of the Shades in the doorway was wearing a long dark robe with a hood hanging around his shoulders. Once he had everyone's attention he pulled the hood up over his head, just to confirm exactly who he was. Just in case anyone was in any doubt.

There was no mistaking it. This was the Bourbon Kid. Dante had never managed to get a good look at his face during the eclipse a year earlier, but now, with the cowl covering much of it, he was all too recognizable. And he was ready to fight.

Hunter, however, still fancied his chances. Moreover, he could not afford to lose face in front of the vampires he intended to rule over in the future. He dusted himself off and stood to his full height, sneering at anyone who dared to make eye contact with him. Then he sprang in to action. In one fluid move he leapt back over the bar and charged at the Kid, who had walked down into the centre of the room.

'You fuckin' scum! YOU'RE A DEAD MAN!' he screamed, lunging at his hooded foe with unprecedented speed and strength, even for a vampire. But he swung and missed. The Kid managed to duck, and then in response threw a punch back with equal speed but far greater precision. Hunter might well have been as fast and as strong as the Bourbon Kid, but in terms of skill and prowess as a fighter he was a mere amateur in a professional bout.

The Kid's fist landed in his opponent's ribs with a sickening crunch, momentarily doubling him over. Yet Hunter's resilience and tolerance for pain were exceptionally high and his recovery was impressively rapid. He straightened up and swung another haymaker in the Kid's direction. Missed again. Once more the Kid showed him and the watching audience just how to throw a good punch. This one was aimed higher, but with equal speed and accuracy.

CRACK! – broken nose.

Ignoring the pain, Hunter instinctively swung again. And missed again.

CRACK! – another blow to the ribcage. Hunter now had at least three broken ribs that were pushing deep into his stomach and lungs, closing off his oxygen supply and causing no small amount of internal bleeding.

He swung again, but this time much of the speed and strength of his punch was gone. Once more, the Kid easily ducked out of the way, then stepped menacingly closer to his fading opponent. Whatever his intentions were now, it was clear to everyone present that this fight would have been stopped if there had been a referee present. Unfortunately, for Hunter there was no man in black-and-white stripes at hand to enforce a stoppage, and no second to throw in the towel.

The hooded killer grabbed his wounded victim by the throat and squeezed hard. Then, one-handed, he lifted Hunter off his feet and charged towards the half-demolished bar, holding the by now terrified detective-vampire out in front of him. As they approached the bar at high speed, the Kid leapt up on to the counter, hauling the beaten cop up with him. Holding his captive's head up, he pushed it towards the huge metal blades of the propeller fan revolving over the far end of the bar. Hunter took a glance up, only too aware of where his scalp was heading. But he had shot his bolt. There was nothing he could do to stop it.

The Kid found a decent foothold on the bartop and, heaving his victim upwards, pushed Hunter's head into the path of the rapidly spinning blades. The entire bar watched, as though they were witnessing a car crash, all wanting to look away in horror, but all allowing their morbid curiosity to get the better of them.

For around ten seconds the Kid slowly heaved Hunter's head further into the fan's razor-sharp blades as they zipped around. He watched the consequences without emotion.

To begin with, the Filthy Pig's thinning, fair-coloured locks were sliced away and blew out into the bar area like wisps of smoke. And when the hair was gone, the scalp followed, dislodged by one blade and then ripped clean off by the one that followed it. The top of the skull went next and finally the brain. Hunter's head was filed down at high speed into thin bloodied slices by the propeller blades. Blood, brain matter and pieces of eye splattered all around the bar.

When the head had been sliced right down almost to the neck, the Kid released his grip and Hunter's body spun round with the fan, some part of it still tenuously attached to one of the blades. Then, after one full three-hundred-and-sixty-degree turn, it detached itself from the fan and flew off and down onto the bartop, where its momentum caused it to slide along the polished and bloodied surface, scattering glasses and bottles as it went.

Too late, the Nightjar's occupants realized that the Kid's killing was only just beginning. It was time to get rid of *all* the undead this time. Without exception, and without mercy. He pulled two Skorpions from inside his long robe and jumped on to Hunter's torso as the corpse slid slowly along the surface of the bar. Pointing his guns at the onlooking crowd he began using the torso like a surfboard, gliding on down the bartop as he loosed bullets in all directions. *Hitting his target with every shot.* Vampires fled for the shattered doorway in droves.

No one made it. Every shot was fired with Casper in mind. The hooded gunman fired his automatic weapons, his aim driven by an intense hatred for the undead. His desire to kill each and every vampire was etched into the face beneath his cowl. For what their kind had done, every last one would suffer.

When the Kid reached the end of the bar counter, he stepped from Hunter's hideous corpse and allowed it to slide off and crash into an empty table in the corner, sending several abandoned glasses of beer crashing into the wall. Then he began walking back along the bartop, picking out his targets with cold deliberation. With an automatic weapon in either hand, he fired at anyone who dared to try to escape. By the time he was halfway back down the bar he had used up all the ammunition in the Skorpions. Dropping them to the floor, he drew two smaller automatic pistols from concealed holsters within his robe barely a second later. As he began firing off rounds from these two pieces he jumped off the bartop and on to the floor in the middle of the room, shooting into the backs of a number of fleeing customers, most of whom were vampires. Naturally, there was always the possibility that some of them were merely innocent civilians, but it was not something that overly concerned the gunman.

By the time he had finished his latest bout of killing, the barroom was littered with smoking corpses turning slowly to ash, with here and there the body of some unfortunate who was not a vampire.* All that remained, apart from the Bourbon Kid himself, were the shocked, part-deafened figures of Dante, Dino the bar owner and Chip of the Dreads clan.

Dante was busy checking himself for holes, and was relieved to find that, somehow, all of the bullets had missed him. Chip, on the other hand, had been shot twice in the chest through his black wraparound top and was bleeding a little, but, strangely, seemed to be okay. His loose-fitting black karate pants were also spattered in blood, not all of which was his own.

The Kid, with his hood now pulled back and resting on his shoulders once more, secreted his two pistols somewhere about his person then bent and retrieved the Skorpions, which also vanished inside his robe. He stepped over a few broken glasses and decaying corpses towards Chip. He stopped just two feet in front of him and for a few moments the two of them stared each other out. The white Rastafarian in the karate outfit didn't seem in the least bit afraid of the man in front of him. Eventually, just as the Kid was about to speak, Chip whipped out a pistol of his own that had been tucked away in the back of his pants. In one easy movement he pointed it at the Kid's head and fired. The bullet zipped past the killer's left ear.

Wielding a machete, Reuben the clown had sneakily jumped to his feet behind the Kid. For the last minute or so,

---

* It is a curiosity of vampire physiology that their corpses do not always decompose in the same way. After the slaughter in the Nightjar, some remains smoked and flamed briefly before being reduced to ashes; others deliquesced, stinking horribly, melted and seeped through the floorboards; still others simply lay where they had fallen, awaiting the course of natural decomposition.

the clown had been lying on the floor, playing dead in the hope of surviving until the hooded man had run out of ammo. He had managed this successfully, but had then made the mistake of assuming that the greatest danger was past. As he attacked the Kid from behind, Chip fired a single round right into his face. Dead centre. In the blink of an eye the clown was back on the floor again, only this time he was not playing dead.

The Bourbon Kid didn't bother to look back to see who Chip had just fired his gun at. Instead, he pulled a soft pack of cigarettes from inside his cloak. He held the pack to his mouth and extracted a cigarette with his teeth.

'Aren't you gonna thank me for that?' Chip asked, nodding at the smoking body of the green-wigged clown on the floor behind the Kid.

'I had it covered.'

'*Bullshit!*' Chip snapped. 'He was about to cut you in half!'

'You think I didn't see those feet?'

Chip looked down and spotted a pair of brown boots on Reuben's feet. Each was almost three feet long, sticking preposterously up from the floor like a large 'V'. In getting within machete range, the clown would have had to place them so that the toes must have jutted a few inches past the Kid's own black boots.

'Oh, I see,' Chip said sheepishly.

The Kid looked him up and down. 'I just pegged you,' he said, nodding. 'You're that monk.'

'Name's Peto,' replied the dreadlocked former Hubal monk.

'When I'm done here, I'm gonna wanna borrow that blue stone you're wearin' round your neck.'

Peto nodded in turn. 'I know.'

He watched as the Kid performed his trick of sucking on the cigarette and allowing it to light itself. Peto was keen to learn the trick himself, but before he started sharing smoking tips and such with this guy he needed to know a few things. Like why he killed innocent people? And did he feel remorse for what he did? Maybe in return for trading secrets, like how to light a cigarette without a flame, the Kid would listen to reason and allow Peto to teach him about morals and ethics. He hoped this man's soul could be saved. After all, although a mass murderer, he was the son of Ishmael Taos, so he had to have some good in him, right? Peto knew that Taos would have wanted his son to know right from wrong, and to feel remorse and strive for repentance when he sinned. He owed it to his former mentor to try to teach the son these things. The precious Eye of the Moon would be a superb resource for this task. Its healing powers could rid the Bourbon Kid of all his evil thoughts. First, however, Peto wanted to know just how evil those thoughts were, and whether there was any regret hidden within that creepy dark cowl.

'One thing I gotta say to you, mister,' the monk began, wagging a finger at the Kid as he tried to establish some sort of eye contact. 'You shouldn't have killed Ishmael Taos.'

'So?'

Peto was instantly annoyed by the other's seeming lack of concern at having murdered the greatest monk that had ever lived. He had learned enough about the Kid in recent times to accept that he had his reasons, and that he was worth teaming up with because of his hatred of the undead, but he really couldn't get to grips with the guy's total lack of conscience.

'You just shouldn't have killed him. That's all I'm trying to say.'

'Okay. Anything else?'

'No.'

'Good. Let's get some drinks.' The Kid turned to Dino, who had just poked his head up from his hiding place behind the bar and was brushing some stray shards of glass out of his dark hair. 'You. Get me three bourbons. And fill the glasses to the top.'

'Sure,' sighed the Nightjar's shaken owner, limping to the shambles behind the counter to look for unbroken bottles and glasses. His bar was a wreck, and almost all his regular customers were dead. But, somehow, he wasn't. He decided that this was a positive.

The Kid turned to Dante and Peto again. 'You two want anything?'

'I'll have a beer, please, Dino,' Dante called over to the bartender.

'Beer for me too,' said Peto. 'And put a shot of bourbon into it.'

Dante had been a stunned bystander in the recent series of life-threatening events, which had exceeded anything he'd been involved in before, and that was *really* saying something. Surveying the carnage all around him, he took a deep breath. The events of the last few minutes were going to take a while to sink in. There were questions to be answered, that was for sure. For a start, the hooded man in front of him had just killed at least a hundred people, and some of them were supposed to be Dante's friends. Sort of. Fritz, Silence and a fair few other undead folks had just perished at the Kid's hands. And that was another thing. Who the fuck was this guy, anyway?

'So whaddo I call you now? Déjà-Vu, or Bourbon Kid, or what?' Dante asked him.

'I don't give a fuck. Call me what you want.'

'Okay Dave. Thanks for not killin' me, by the way.'

The Kid blew out a lungful of smoke and picked up a stool from the floor to seat himself at the bar. 'I seem to recall tellin' you I owed you one when you helped out during the eclipse last year. That was you in the Terminator outfit, wasn't it?'

'Yeah. Thanks, man. Guess that makes us even, then?'

'Not likely. I shot a clown in the head for you the other night. *You* owe *me* one now'. He paused, looking hard at Dante and Peto in turn. What he said next surprised them both. 'I want you to help me out with some other shit I gotta do. Coupla real badass vampire bosses need wipin' out. You guys in?'

The Bourbon Kid wasn't generally given to asking for help from others, but a Hubal monk with the Eye of the Moon and a guy who had helped him kill Jessica the Vampire Queen were useful allies to have. And with him currently being a vampire himself, he wasn't going to be able to use the old *Book With No Name*-strapped-to-his-chest routine when it came down to killing whoever the chief bloodsucker might be.

'I'm in,' Dante shrugged. He was up for a fight, as always. Besides, he wasn't sure what would happen if he turned the kid down.

'Has this got anything to do with Rameses Gaius?' Peto asked, quietly.

The Kid frowned. 'What the fuck would it have to do with him? He's been dead for centuries.'

'He was,' Peto agreed partially. 'But he was mummified, and from what I hear, he rose from the dead when you killed Ishmael Taos and Armand Xavier, which lifted the curse upon him.'

'You fuckin' Rastas man. You should stay off the fuckin' weed.'

'I'm serious.'

'I don't give a shit.'

'Well, you should. There's a mummy on the loose somewhere in this city.'

'So why don't you go fuck your mummy?'

'That's not very nice,' Peto said defensively.

'Do I look nice to you?'

It was a fairly open question that didn't really need answering. The Bourbon Kid was covered in blood and dressed like the Grim Reaper, so no, he didn't look nice.

'Look, I was just telling you,' Peto protested. 'But if you don't care about Gaius, then that's fine. But yeah – you can count me in to help you kill these vampires, but then I seriously suggest we get the fuck out of town before this mummy shows up.'

'Thanks,' the Kid said in his unmistakable gravelly tone. 'Now let's have us some drinks to wind down. And, *Monk Boy*, put somethin' on the jukebox, will ya? I seem to have killed the band.'

The corpses of the dead band members were smoking away into dust and ash on the stage amidst all their instruments, which were riddled with bullet holes. Peto was sorry to see the end of them, as he'd rather enjoyed their habit of playing a song to fit any occasion. Ruing their violent end, he walked over to an old Wurlitzer jukebox in the far corner to the left of the stage. The machine had remained surprisingly undamaged in all the gunfire. It was a fairly battered old unit that had seen better days, and it had been turned off for at least six months since The Psychics had showed up and insisted on playing nightly for free. Dino had switched it off in the middle of a song, with no intention of ever turning it back on.

Peto stood next to it and faced the others. Then he elbowed it once, much as he had seen the Fonz do in the TV show *Happy Days*. It kicked into gear, and by the time he'd taken a seat at the bar alongside Dante and the Kid, Thin Lizzy were well into a chorus of 'The Boys Are Back In Town'.

Forty-Six

De La Cruz, understandably, was in a state of abject panic. Not least because he still had no idea where the hell Benson had got to. His colleague had not been seen since early morning, when he had left headquarters without saying a word to anyone about where he was headed. On top of that was the small matter of the stories he was hearing about the Fawcett Inn, the Tapioca and the Nightjar. All had received an unwelcome visit from the Bourbon Kid. Massacres had taken place in each of them. The next stop for the hooded maniac would no doubt be police headquarters.

De La Cruz was extremely tempted to make a run for it, but he knew that would leave him on his own, looking over his shoulder for the rest of his days, waiting for a visit from the Grim Reaper. He was going to have to call in as many officers as he could and make a stand right there in the building. His main problem was that it was getting late, and the only cops that liked working the late shift were the ones who happened to be vampires. One such officer was the red-haired receptionist, Francis Bloem. He was doing his damnedest to find available colleagues of the undead kind to come and help protect De La Cruz (and Benson, if he showed his face again any time soon).

As it happened, Bloem was going nuts as he sat at his desk in reception. Trying to track down any available officers was proving all but impossible. Many of those he had tried to contact were no longer answering their cell phones or responding on the police networks. The reasons why weren't exactly clear, but there was a distinct possibility that many of them were unable to respond because they were dead. He was shifting uncomfortably in his chair, flicking through his own small black personal address book in the hope of getting some alternate contact details for any of his fellow officers, when De La Cruz came bounding over. It was obvious the detective was badly spooked. His smart red shirt was practically glued to him by the wet patches of sweat that made it look as though he'd taken a shower in his clothes.

'You found anyone yet?' he asked urgently, unable to hide the panic in his voice.

'The only two guys who have responded to the call are Goose and Kenny, sir. They're on their way here now,' Bloem responded.

De La Cruz's jaw dropped open. Only *two* officers available? And two absolute deadbeats, to boot. His disappointment was all too evident.

'Goose and Kenny?' he groaned.

'Yessir.'

'We are *so* fucked.'

'I'll keep trying to get hold of some of the other guys, sir, but no one seems to be responding. Reckon they know what's coming and don't want any part of it. Or they're already dead.'

De La Cruz frowned and picked up a piece of foolscap-sized scrap paper from Bloem's desk. It had a handwritten list of officers on it and all of them had crosses next to their names, with the exception of Goose and Kenny, who had ticks. What if Benson had decided to back away as well? Or had been killed? If the reports that were trickling through were true, then Hunter had just been given an absolute pounding at the merciless hands of the Bourbon Kid. So much for immortality. In spite of what they had come to believe, drinking blood from the golden chalice didn't seem to be making too much difference. If the Kid got his hands on you, you were still fucked either way. Not good. Not good at all. *Damn you, Benson,* he thought. *You'd better not have bailed on me. Not now.*

***

At that precise moment Randy Benson was standing at the reception desk in the local clinic just two miles down the road. The clinic had been reopened that evening at his request. Having closed at the normal time of 5 p.m. the key members of staff had been dragged back in, courtesy of Benson. They weren't overly happy about it, either, but a police emergency warranted – indeed, demanded – their cooperation.

Benson had a book in his hands and was reading some details aloud from it to the woman at the reception desk. The nurse in question, Jolene Bird, scribbled down the numbers he read out to her. She was a little nervous at being in the presence of a senior member of the local police, and was struggling to hide it. With her free hand she fiddled constantly with her curly blonde hair, and when she wasn't doing that she was adjusting her wing-framed blue spectacles. Anything to keep her hands busy. She'd worked at the clinic for a good twenty years, and she could recognize a serious visit from the police when she saw one. They were usually linked to a murder. This looked like one of those times. The mere knowledge that she could make a mistake that might result in a murder investigation being compromised made her seriously edgy.

'Do you have the warrant with you, sir?' she asked Benson, making only fleeting eye contact.

'Sure,' Benson smiled, in an attempt to put her at ease. He pulled a piece of yellow paper from the breast pocket on his shirt and handed it over the desk to her.

'Great, thanks,' Jolene smiled back nervously as she gratefully accepted the warrant. She proceeded to do her best to concentrate on its main points for a few moments to ensure it was all in order, then she folded it in half and placed it in a large pocket on the front of her long white coat.

'This all appears to be in order,' she said. 'If you'd like to follow me I'll take you down there now and fetch it for you.' She opened a metal cupboard behind her, looked around inside it for several seconds, selected a key, which she pocketed, then closed the cupboard door and stood up.

Benson followed Nurse Bird through a set of double

doors and down a couple of corridors, staying a yard behind the whole time so that he could admire her neat little backside. If he'd needed to know the way back in an emergency he'd be in all kinds of trouble. He took little notice of where he was being led; keeping his eyes focused on the swivelling cheeks beneath the nurse's white coat. She eventually led him down several flights of stairs to the basement, and by the time they arrived at a locked vault guarded by two bulky security men in blue uniforms, he still hadn't been able to work out whether she was wearing any underwear.

The huge grey door to the vault in front of them had a sign above it which read 'CRYOPRESERVATION CHAMBER'.

'May we go in, please?' Nurse Bird asked.

'Sure thing, Jolene,' said one of the guards. He turned and typed a six-digit code into a keypad on the wall behind him. Jolene then stepped forward and typed in a code of her own. Next, she looked into a retina-scanning device placed at head height just above the keypad. A white light flashed in the unit. The scanning software duly recognized the retina in front of it and the vault door hissed a little then automatically began to open outwards. It came open slowly, moving just a few inches before suddenly stopping. It was a thick steel door and the release of the locking mechanism was only powerful enough to nudge it open a little way. One of the two guards pulled it the rest of the way open and held it back, ushering the two visitors through it. Jolene Bird walked in first, followed by Benson.

'Phew, it's cold in here,' the detective remarked. He wasn't actually feeling the cold at all, but the bright white walls made the chamber look as though it should be cold. His own blood temperature was low enough for the cold not to bother him, but as he was wearing a short-sleeved shirt it seemed an appropriate comment to make in the circumstances.

'Yes,' smiled Nurse Bird. 'We tend not to have the heating on down here.' She reached into her pocket and withdrew the yellow paper.

Inside the cryopreservation chamber was a series of

long aisles flanked by numbered deposit boxes from floor to ceiling. To the left of the door as they entered was a six-runged stepladder, in case anyone should need to reach one of the deposit boxes high up. There were about thirty aisles stretching the length of the room. Each aisle was long enough and tall enough to hold approximately a thousand of the small metal-fronted boxes.

Once again the nurse led the way and Benson followed, past about ten aisles before they eventually stopped by one with the code 9N86 in black letters on the near face of the aisle. Jolene checked the piece of paper in her hand and confirmed to herself she had the right area, then she turned into the aisle and followed it down for about sixty feet. She came to a stop at box number 8447, which was situated just below head height on the left-hand side of the aisle.

From a side pocket in her lab coat she produced the key that she had brought with her from reception. Despite the cold having numbed her fingers she managed to insert it cleanly into the lock on the box, which was set just below the number. Once she was satisfied that she had pushed it in far enough she turned it easily to the right and a clicking sound followed, much to her relief.

'To be honest, I doubt we would ever have needed this one anyway,' she said, pulling the small door open and beginning to slide out the box behind it. 'It's such a rare blood type. We've never seen its kind before.'

She reached into the box and pulled out a one-pint plastic package of frozen blood, which she handed to Benson. He took a look at it and smiled at her once more.

'Well, Archibald Somers was no ordinary guy, was he?' he replied.

Forty-Seven

Peto took a drag on his cigarette and surveyed the carnage around them. The Nightjar was a spectacular, bloodied mess. There were limbs and other body parts strewn across the floor and wedged between tables and chairs, detached from their owners' bodies by the Kid's heavy dum-dum rounds. By now, quite a few decaying remains of vampires were already little more than dust and ash. Smoke and steam was rising from so many of the chunks of flesh on the floor that the place was beginning to look like an indoor swamp. Reflecting on what had gone before, Peto blew the smoke out from his lungs and turned his attention back to the man at the bar with him, the Bourbon Kid.

'I gotta know. Did you kill Kyle? Or was that someone else?' he asked. The Kid was sitting to Peto's left, but with Dante in between the two of them, although it was obvious that it was the Kid that Peto was speaking to. On the counter stood three bourbon glasses, two of them empty and one still half full. Beside them were two glasses of beer, still almost full.

'Who the fuck's Kyle?'

'He was my best friend. He got killed in the Tapioca during the last eclipse.'

Dante butted in.

'I think Gene Simmons or Freddie Krueger shot Kyle. The cops just blamed our man here, probably because it was convenient.'

'Yeah,' said the Kid, shrugging as he took a drag of his own cigarette. 'They've pinned hundreds of murders on me that I can't really take credit for. If you believe all you hear, I'm responsible for shooting everyone from Liberty Valance to Nice Guy Eddie.'

'Who?' asked Peto.

'Doesn't matter.'

Dante decided to speak up on a small matter that was bothering him somewhat.

'You did just kill the guys from the Shades, though, right?'

'Yeah.'

'Weren't they friends of yours?'

'I don't have friends.'

'I can't think why,' Peto chipped in.

'Believe it or not, it's my choice.'

'Sure.'

'Look, dumbass, if I get close to someone, then that person is gonna get hunted down by vampires and werewolves and all kinds of other scum. I've had to distance myself from anyone I ever cared about. Seems I didn't distance myself enough, though, because now my kid brother is dead. They killed him to get to me. Count yourselves lucky I don't consider either of you two as friends, or you'd both be dead within a week.'

'Your brother's dead?' Dante blurted it out.

'Yeah. Killed by that Hunter fucker and four of his friends. Two more of 'em still have to suffer yet before my work is done. So you ask me if I was friends with some of these vampires and my answer is no. I hated every fuckin' one of them. I been waitin' for fucknuts over here to show up with the Eye of the Moon so I could get rid of this vampire blood that's contaminatin' my veins. Maybe then I could lead a normal life. And then – *and only then* – will I consider having friends.'

'So you didn't even like the other members of the Shades?' Dante persisted, unnecessarily.

The Kid looked at him, bemused. He chose to answer the question anyway, although not before he blew a lungful of smoke past the young man's inquisitive face.

'Those guys would have killed you in the blink of an eye if they'd spotted you for a fake. How d'you manage to fool 'em anyway? I clocked you right away, man. You stood out like a fuckin' lighthouse.'

'It's a serum I'm taking. Some Secret Service guy gave it to me. Lowers my blood temperature, an' helps me to pass myself off as a vampire. Though tonight it didn't seem to be workin' so well.' He shuddered, remembering what Obedience had said about supper for him and Fritz.

'You work for the Secret Service?'

'Only while they've got my girlfriend hostage.'

'Want me to kill 'em?' asked the Kid casually.

'Wouldn't mind.' Then he added hastily, 'Not her, though.'

'Sure thing. I got two more vampires to kill, then we can sort them out. What about you, Monk Boy? How've you managed to infiltrate so well? You even had me fooled.'

'No shit?' said Peto, scratching one of the now almost healed bullet wounds in his chest, just below his left shoulder. 'I've learned a few things about how to use the Eye of the Moon. It's a very powerful stone, you know. Has more than just healing powers.'

'Glad to hear it,' said the Kid, stubbing his cigarette out on the bartop and blowing the last lungful of smoke out through his nostrils. 'When we're done tonight I'm gonna borrow that stone and use it to cure a few ailments I've got. Not least of all the one that makes me turn into a fuckin' vampire at random inconvenient times.'

'I guess it's a job to keep under control?' Dante asked.

'Well, along with a minor drink problem and some anger issues I got, it ain't a fuckin bed o' roses, y'know.'

The Kid finished off his last mouthful of bourbon and threw the glass over his shoulder to smash on the floor behind him. Then he placed another cigarette between his lips. Hearing the crashing noise of the glass on the floor, Dino, who'd been in the back room, reappeared behind the bar.

'Is that really necessary?' he asked.

'What's your favourite colour?' the Kid asked him, reaching inside his robe.

'Blue. Why?'

BANG!

The Kid pulled out a heavy, nickel-plated revolver, pointed it at Dino and blasted a hole through the bar owner's head. Blood sprayed all over Dante and Peto, who recoiled in horror. The body remained upright for a second or two longer than the laws of physics properly allowed, mainly because Dino had very large feet and he had been standing up straight. But then, after a few moments of staring blankly ahead into the barroom sporting a huge hole in the middle of his forehead, his knees buckled and he slumped backwards, crashing into a shelf of glasses he had only just reset a few minutes earlier.

'Jesus!' Peto shrieked. 'What's so wrong with *blue?*'

'Nothin'. I just wanted to distract him while I pulled out the gun.' The Kid took a drag on his cigarette. 'What's *your* favourite colour?'

Peto paused for a moment.

'Can I tell you later?'

'Sure.' The Kid concealed the revolver about his person again. 'Now I reckon it's time we got outta here. You two look like you could use a trip to Domino's.'

'Great,' said Dante, getting up from his stool. 'I could murder a pizza.' Carnage and mayhem always made him hungry. (So did sex.)

'Not the fuckin' pizza place. The fancy-dress store. Change of clothes.'

He had a point. Both his companions were covered in blood. None of it really their fault. All *his,* in fact. Still, it probably didn't need to be said.

The Kid led the way out of the bar, Peto and Dante following. He paused only momentarily to draw his revolver again. This time he drew down on the jukebox and blew a massive hole through the middle of it. The damage was enough to stop the old Würlitzer from playing any more of the song 'I fought the Law' by The Clash.

Once outside, he walked over to a sleek black sports car parked by the opposite kerb. The streets were unlit, so with the night sky now at its darkest it was initially hard to tell what sort of car it was, although the bulge on the hood suggested that the engine was more than a little powerful. The only light came from the clear blue moon, but that was partially hidden behind a dark grey rain cloud. Eventually, as the Kid opened the driver's door, Dante made the car.

'Is this a V8 Interceptor?' he asked.

'Sure is. Cool, huh?'

'Fuck, yeah. I had a DeLorean once, y'know?' *Christ!* Dante thought. *Me and the Kid bondin' . . . Who'd evera thunk it?*

'Good for you.'

'Crashed it into a tree, though. Totalled it.'

'Doin' eighty-eight?'

'Fuck, yeah. How'd you guess?'

'Long shot. Now shut up and get in.'

Dante called 'shotgun', so winning the front passenger seat, meaning that Peto had to squeeze into the confined space provided by the narrow back seat. The monk had learnt a lot in his time since he'd left Hubal, but there were still a few customs that caught him unawares. Some of the time he was convinced people invented new customs like shotgunning when it suited them, just so they could take advantage of him. Seething a little, he took his place in the cramped area in the back of the vehicle, positioning himself in between the two front seats to get the maximum out of the limited leg room available.

As the car powered off down the deserted street towards Domino's he heard a tapping noise behind him. It sounded like it was coming from within the trunk. It was followed by a muffled voice.

'You got someone in the trunk?' Peto asked the Kid.

'Yep.'

'Can I ask who?'

'Nope.'

Forty-Eight

Officer Bloem had become as concerned as Captain De La Cruz at the complete lack of police officers available to them, so he was greatly relieved when he saw two guys in standard blue uniforms arrive at the glass doors at the front of the headquarters. The wind was blowing hard outside and both of them were looking a little ragged as a result. No sense in keeping the poor bastards waiting, so he rushed out from behind his desk in the reception area and pressed a security button on the wall by the doors to allow them to enter. The nearest of the two officers pushed the glass door open and Bloem was quick to pull it from his own side so that he could hold it open for them.

'You're Goose and Kenny, I assume?' he asked.

'That's right. I'm Goose, this is Kenny,' said the first officer, a young fellow with windswept dark hair. He stepped through the open door and pulled his nightstick from its loop on his belt. 'Where's everyone gone?'

'Benson's done a runner, and De La Cruz is hidin' down in the basement. But he'll be glad to know you two are here. I guess the initial idea was that you would each act as a personal bodyguard for one of them, but bein' as De La Cruz is the only one here right now, you can both do a job watching his back for now. If Benson comes back then one of you will be reassigned to him.'

'Great,' said Goose. 'We head straight down to the basement, right?'

'Knock yourselves out.'

The two officers made their way past Bloem and into the

main reception area. As Bloem went to double check that the glass doors were closed and locked securely, Goose turned back and swung his nightstick viciously.

THWACK!

The nightstick crashed into the back of Bloem's skull.

'Ow! *Fuck!* What the fuck didja do that for?' Bloem asked holding his head, where a large lump was already beginning to appear. Goose raised his arm back over his shoulder and then swung it back down forcefully to hit him with the nightstick again, this time catching him on the shoulder and a part of the neck. 'Ow! Cut that out, will ya?' He fumbled at his belt for his pistol.

The other officer, Kenny, stepped in and chopped Bloem on the back of the neck, knocking him out cold.

'Thanks,' said Dante, who had been pretending to be Goose. 'I can't understand how this didn't knock him out,' he said sourly, looking at the nightstick. It had come with the cheap imitation police uniforms they'd bought at Domino's.

'Well,' said his colleague Kenny (whose role Peto had taken). 'It helps if you *hit* him with it, rather than tickle him.'

'I fuckin' did.'

'You didn't. You totally wimped out on it.'

'I did not.'

'Did, too.'

'Did not.'

There was a tap on the glass doors. The hooded figure of the Bourbon Kid stood outside, impatiently watching the bickering going on inside. Their argument was going nowhere and there was no sense in continuing it if it was going to darken the Kid's mood further. He had been parking the car and stocking up on ammunition, and would probably be disappointed that he had missed the action. Peto made the smart decision not to keep him waiting any longer than necessary. He quickly stepped over the unconscious body of Francis Bloem to press the button on the wall to open the glass doors for his new partner in crime.

The hooded killer pushed the doors open and stepped

inside the building. The place had not changed much since the last time he'd popped in and slaughtered all the on-duty officers. And Somers.

'This guy seems to be on his own,' Peto said, pointing at the body on the floor. The Kid looked down at the unconscious red-haired lawman and pulled out his sawn-off double-barrelled shotgun (something of a favourite of his). '*Hey, wait,*' said Peto, reaching out and grabbing the other's arm. 'This guy's unconscious. There's no need to kill him. Jesus, not everyone has to die, okay? Sometimes, when a guy isn't a threat any more, you can just let him be. He could have a family, y'know? Wife, kids, pet terrapins, the whole ball of wax. Take a deep breath and let's go find this De La Cruz guy. According to this fellow on the floor he's down in the basement. See? I acquired the information we need, which was easier to do because I didn't kill him first and ask questions afterwards.'

'You finished?' the Kid asked, eyeing the hand Peto was using to grip his arm.

Peto wisely removed his hand. 'Yeah. Now listen, the other guy, Benson, has done a runner, so we've only got the De La Cruz fella to deal with right now. So just be cool, okay?'

'Okay.' The voice was pure gravel.

The monk turned and led the way into the main reception area. Dante followed, with the Kid bringing up the rear. The hooded mass murderer, however, was still caught in two minds about the whole killing-Officer-Francis-Bloem issue, so he let the others walk a few steps ahead then turned back.

BANG!

The Kid fired a round into the prostrate police officer's head.

Peto spun around instantly. '*Jeesus!* Fuckin' stop that, will you? Did you not listen to what I just said? I said *be cool!*'

'That *was* cool.'

'No it fuckin' wasn't.'

'Look, man, the gun just went off,' said the Kid coldly. 'Lucky I wasn't pointin' it at you. Got a mind of its own, this thing.'

Peto paused for a moment, taking in the sight of the

bloodied mess of the body on the floor, and the hooded figure with the shotgun standing between it and him.

'Good work,' he said. The Kid seemed to mutter something else, which sounded suspiciously like 'Never could stand fuckin' terrapins.' Peto wisely let it go.

The switchboard on Bloem's unmanned reception desk suddenly lit up and the phone began to ring. Dante reacted first and headed over to it. He picked up the headset on the untidy desk and pressed 'answer' on the switchboard's keypad.

'Hello, ten-four . . . roger. Er, Police Department . . . this is . . . '

'Who the fuck's that?' asked a voice on the other end of the line.

'Er, Officer Goose? Who the fuck's this?'

'De La Cruz. Where's Bloem. He busy?'

Dante looked over at the bloodied mess by the door. 'He's gone, sir. Reckon he lost his head.'

'Huh! Typical.' De La Cruz could be heard tutting on the other end of the line. 'You got the other guy with you? Kenny, is it?'

'Yessir. We need you to come up here, sir.'

'Why?'

'Bender ordered it, sir.'

'Who?'

Peto, picking up on Dante's mistake, mouthed the name 'Benson' to him, overemphasizing the 'son' part.

'Benson, sir. Said he's got a safe place for us to take you. Gotta hurry, though. Bourbon Kid's on his way.'

'Fuck! All right. I'm on my way up.'

Dante took off the headset and gestured towards the elevators at the far end of the hall. The Kid began walking towards them.

Pretty soon the light above the elevator in the middle showed that it was moving up from the basement to the ground floor.

Forty-Nine

Sanchez wasn't much of a one for going to libraries. He ventured to the Santa Mondega Library maybe two or three times a year, and that was usually only to borrow a few books to give to friends as birthday presents. Knowing that most of his friends couldn't read, he was normally able to steal the books back without them noticing, and return them to the library within a week or two anyway.

One of the many things he didn't like about the library was the woman who worked behind the counter. She was the chief librarian, Ulrika Price, and she was a shitty, vindictive bitch with a deep-rooted hatred for men, based on some, admittedly unpleasant, sexual experience she'd had inflicted upon her as a teenager.

From behind her desk near the entrance she had eyeballed Sanchez as he entered, and he could feel her eyes burning into the back of his head as he made his way over to the Non-Fiction section. The library wasn't busy at such a late hour, particularly with it being Halloween, so Sanchez had free rein of the multitude of ceiling-high bookshelves stretching out in aisles over the huge floor space.

His reason for heading to the library had been a matter of gut instinct, if he were honest. With Jessica's disappearance and the Bourbon Kid's return, he had decided to do a little investigative work. The local police force wouldn't do it, for two reasons. One, they were lazy bastards, and two, they were as corrupt as fuck, so if there was anything to be found in the library they'd probably find a reason not to see it anyway.

What Sanchez was looking for was a book with no

name by an anonymous author. His reason for looking was something of a long shot. After the last Bourbon Kid massacre during the previous year's Lunar Festival, the newspapers had run an article about all the murders being linked to a book with no name by an anonymous author. Everyone who had ever borrowed it from the Santa Mondega Library had been killed, including the detectives on the case. Now, although Sanchez wasn't by any means a brave sort, he'd invested a lot of time in caring for Jessica over the years, and if this book (or indeed a new copy of it) was by some chance back on the shelves, then it might provide some clues as to what the hell it was that the Bourbon Kid had against people who read the damn thing. Even more importantly, it might reveal what the hell he had against Jessica, and maybe even some information about who she was. What Sanchez found was another book by the same author.

He had stumbled upon it by chance. Simply by looking in the Reference section under A for Anonymous he had surprisingly quickly found a book entitled *The Book of Death*. No author was cited. He pulled it from the shelf, thinking to take a quick look at the blurb on the back to see what it was about. It weighed heavy in his hands, such was the thickness of it, and it felt old. The thing seemed ready to crumble in his hands, it was so frail.

The blurb on the back, such as it was, wasn't actually half as exciting as the title had hinted, either. A handwritten label pasted to the back cover simply said, in faded ink, that the book listed the names of a bunch of random dead people and the dates on which they had died. *Guess it's a log from a morgue somewhere,* he supposed.

He flicked to the first few pages and came across a bunch of handwritten, stupid-sounding names, the first two of which were Ra and Osiris. This was almost enough to suggest he should immediately stick the book straight back on the shelf, but having traipsed halfway across town Sanchez felt the need to give it some benefit of the doubt. So he flicked forward towards the pages at the end, in the hope of seeing the names of anyone he knew. The later pages were still handwritten, but each page was now dated at the top.

He was just about to put the book back on the shelf when it struck him that he would be interested to see just how up-to-date it was. Flicking right to the back, he came across a whole bunch of blank pages. So he flicked backwards until he found the current date, 31 October, at top left on one of the pages. To his surprise, the day's deaths had already been included. '*Holy shit,* that's quick!' he whispered, a little too loudly by library standards.

Aware that he was drawing attention to himself, he sneaked on down the aisle and hid himself away in a quieter corner of the library by a shelf of books that rarely attracted browsing customers. He reopened the book and took a look at the names in the current day's entry.

There were listings for Igor and Pedro and a few of the other werewolves whom Sanchez recognized as having been in the Tapioca when the Bourbon Kid had turned up. *Fuckin' werewolves. Dirty scum. The town's better off without them anyway,* he mused. This was hugely impressive, though. These wolfmen had only died a matter of hours earlier. *How the hell had someone managed to update this so quickly?*

Scouring the list of names, Sanchez suddenly felt a cold shiver come over him. 'Now that's fuckin' weird!' he said, much too loudly. Immediately realizing he might be attracting unwelcome attention, he looked around. Through the gaps between the bookshelves he caught sight of Ulrika Price. She was sitting behind her desk, looking in his direction. She had obviously heard him break the golden rule of silence. Their eyes met for a moment and she squinted at him through her glasses. Then she got up from her chair. *Fuck! That crazy bitch is coming over here!*

Sanchez couldn't prevent the sudden feeling of paranoia that came over him. That spiteful old spinster had been a prime suspect in the questioning over the murders of all the people who had read *The Book With No Name.* It was suspected, but never proven, that she had been supplying the names of all its readers to the killer.

Speed of thought was required. There wasn't time to put *The Book of Death* back where he had found it without her seeing him, and there was no way he was signing the damn thing out and having his name logged against it. He took one last look at the open page before closing the book. His eyes had definitely not deceived him. The list of the names of the dead carried right through to 1 November, tomorrow's date. These were the names of people who weren't even dead yet.

Before he had time to digest the short list of names set under the following day's date, he heard Ulrika Price bounding over towards the aisle he was in. She was in a hurry, too. *Fuck it!* He closed the book and thought frantically about where to hide it. Up his shirt? Nope, too obvious. There was no time to come up with much of a better solution, so he quickly tucked it down the back of his trousers. It was a damn good job, Sanchez thought, that he was wearing sweatpants because the sheer size of the book would have made it impossible to slip down the back of any normal pants. As it was, anyone standing behind him would have seen that he had an enormous ass, shaped like a book. As opposed to just an enormous ass, which was the usual state of affairs.

Knowing that the chief librarian was about to appear at the end of the aisle, Sanchez blindly grabbed the nearest thick hardback book from a shelf to his left and began to walk awkwardly towards where he thought Miss Price was most likely to appear.

Sure enough, no more than a few seconds later her face appeared around the corner of the aisle. She looked as irritated as ever as she peered over her spectacles at him. 'Sanchez, what are you doing back here?' she snapped. 'Are you masturbating?'

'No!' Sanchez bridled in disgust. 'How dare you even suggest such a thing?'

'Hmm. Well, good,' said Ms Price, though with a note of suspicion in her voice. 'We close in fifteen minutes, so could you *please* hurry up and choose a book?'

'Already got one,' smiled Sanchez, holding up the book he had just snagged from the shelf.

'Very well, then. Come on. Get it checked out and be gone. I want you out of here. It's Halloween, and I want to be home before the drunken hooligans show up.'

'Sure thing.' Sanchez breathed a sigh of relief and followed the librarian back to the reception desk. The book stashed down the back of his sweatpants made his walk look rather unnatural, potentially giving the impression that he had just shit his pants.

He allowed Ulrika Price to get a fair way ahead to ensure that she would be less likely to notice his curious walk. After making her way around to the reception desk via the raised counter flap in the corner, she sat herself down in her usual seat next to the computer. Sanchez stood on the other side of the desk smiling broadly at her, and congratulating himself on concealing the large book so cleverly down the back of his pants. His only problem now was that he was going to have to walk out backwards so Ms Price wouldn't see his book-shaped ass.

He placed the book he had picked from the shelf down on the counter and waited for her to log back in to her computer. He hadn't actually bothered to check what sort of book he'd picked up, and when he saw the title on the cover, and saw that Ulrika Price had also seen it, he cringed.

The Gay Man's Guide to Anal Sex

Dammit. How unlucky is that? he thought.

Purse-lipped, the librarian logged the book on to the computer under Sanchez's name and gingerly nudged it back across the counter to him. To his annoyance, he could feel his face burning with embarrassment. There was nothing for it, though, so blushing heavily, he picked the book up and then, smiling like an idiot, he slowly backpedalled all the way to the exit, maintaining eye contact with the judgemental librarian the whole time.

Fortunately, she was so appalled by his choice of book, and so disconcerted by the fact that he was grinning at her like a demented baboon while holding such a book, that she didn't take time to wonder why he was walking out backwards. If she had, she might well have considered the possibility he had a large hardback book concealed in the seat of his pants.

Sanchez now just needed to get back home and check the evidence of his eyes. He had seen some names he recognized in *The Book of Death*. Was it possible that the book was predicting that these people were going to die on 1 November?

Tomorrow.

Fifty

The dark figure of the Bourbon Kid stood motionless, loosely holding the sawn-off shotgun at the level of his waist. It was aimed at the elevator doors, waiting for them to slide apart and reveal the face of Michael De La Cruz. Dante watched on nervously from his position behind Bloem's reception desk, ready to duck down in the event of any gunfire. Eventually there was a rather quiet pinging noise, and then as expected the automatic doors parted. The Kid's trigger finger twitched, but as the doors opened it was immediately apparent that there was nothing for him to shoot at. The elevator car was empty. Where had De La Cruz gone? He was supposed to have come up in the elevator and then promptly taken a charge of heavy shot in the chest. Things weren't going according to plan.

As the Kid stood frowning at his reflection in the mirror at the back of the vacant elevator car, Dante and Peto decided it was safe to join their partner, and took station on either side of him.

'Where the fuck is he, then?' Dante asked, staring into the elevator, looking for any corners that might conceal the missing detective.

'Basement,' said the Kid, stepping inside the car.

Dante and Peto exchanged shrugs and followed him in, once more taking up their flanking positions beside him. The sight of the Bourbon Kid standing, shotgun at the ready, with two uniformed officers watching his back was not the sort of image the local police department wanted to promote, but it was what any passerby would have seen.

As the elevator doors closed, the Kid pressed the button

marked 'B' to send the elevator to the basement. Then the three of them stood waiting in silence for it to start its descent. The Kid was armed to the teeth. Strapped about his person was an arsenal of weapons, all extremely well concealed in holsters and pockets and sheaths beneath his robe. Dante and Peto each had a nightstick. Given the Kid's record for slaying enemies, it was probably best that he had all the firearms anyway. He might only be able to fire two at a time, but he would achieve more by keeping any spares for himself than he would by lending them to his comrades.

All three of them were staring at the elevator doors in front of them, ready to react to whatever might greet them on the other side when they reached the basement.

BANG!

The noise of the gunshot inside the small elevator was deafening. Dante imagined it to be what the sound of a bomb going off was like. It was immediately followed by a piercing scream and a clattering from above. Then, suddenly, a brown-booted foot appeared from nowhere, kicking Dante in the face.

The Kid had fired his shotgun upwards and was now reloading it. The charge of buckshot had blown a huge hole through the service hatch on the roof of the elevator. More than an ounce of heavy lead shot had seared though it and into the foot of De La Cruz, who had been crouching quietly on the roof above them. With the latch on the hatch now blown to pieces, the hatch door had fallen open and the lower half of De La Cruz's body had slipped through it. One of his feet was dangling around by Dante's face, but the other was flailing around wildly. It was missing all of its toes and all of the boot that had previously covered it. What remained of it was a bloodied stump that was spurting the red stuff around the elevator and over the Kid's face.

Wedged in the hatchway was the backside of the unfortunate De La Cruz. His upper body was still above the elevator's roof and he was trying desperately to haul his lower half up with it. He was screaming and cursing, hanging precariously on to the thick cable attached to the elevator's roof. Then the car came to a stop as they reached the basement.

The doors opened and both Dante and Peto leapt out into the locker room outside. The secret panel was open, but there was nothing much to see save for a curious room at the back of the shower area, in which there was a table with a golden cup standing on it. Otherwise the locker room was empty, so both turned their attentions back to what was going on in the elevator, where the Kid was trying to pull De La Cruz through the service hatch by his trousers. The detective, however, was clinging to the cable above the elevator for all he was worth, his long vampire fingers wrapping themselves around it as tightly as he could manage. He was rapidly transforming into a creature of the night, but was it already too late?

In a rather undignified moment, the Kid succeeded in pulling De La Cruz's trousers and underpants down to his ankles. The vampire wasn't coming down with them, though. His only hope was to break free of the Kid's grip and try to climb or leap his way out of there.

Realizing that he needed to take his chance where he could, the Kid took aim at the target presented to him. Without worrying himself about the consequences, he aimed the shotgun up at the crack in De La Cruz's ass. Then after briefly hesitating for maybe half a second, he forced the muzzle of the gun up between the unfortunate vampire's butt cheeks as far as it would go. The screaming abruptly stopped, no doubt replaced by a wide-eyed look of panic and dread on De La Cruz's face.

BANG!

The report wasn't as loud as the earlier one. After all, this time the Kid had a large ass-shaped silencer on the end of his weapon.

SPLAT!

Blood, guts, shit, bits of corn, internal organs, bone splinters, the whole bloody mess sprayed out all over the elevator. A fair amount of it went over the Kid and out into the locker room, spattering the onlooking Dante and Peto. The remains of De La Cruz slipped through the hatch to land soggily on the floor, and the Kid pulled his gun clear, shaking off the sloppy mess that began sliding down the barrels towards his hand. The stench was overwhelming, and the sight of all the matter sprayed everywhere was even worse. Typically, the hooded gunman was unaffected by any of it. Brushing a piece of corn from his left shoulder, he casually stepped out of the elevator and held the end of his shotgun beneath Peto's nose. The monk recoiled in disgust.

'Fuck off! I don't wanna smell that!'

The Kid walked on past his two companions. He had set his eyes upon the wooden table in the secret room at the back of the shower area. Normally the room was concealed behind the shower wall, but right now the sliding panel was out of sight, and there was nothing to keep him from heading over to the table.

'Four down. One to go,' he said, as much to himself as to the others. 'Then the job's done and we can all go home.'

'Amen to that,' said Dante, flicking a small amount of brown matter off his shoulder and on to the back of Peto's thick dreadlocked hair. The monk tutted and quickly brushed it off.

'This last one's gonna be the hardest though,' said the Kid, without looking back to see if Dante and Peto were paying attention. 'The first two were just fuckin' lowlife dogs. Now the two lieutenants are down. All that remains is our new Head Vampire. The new Dark Lord. I don't know how tough this guy's gonna be, and this is where I might need your help. There's a book in this headquarters somewhere that can kill the chief bloodsucker. It's a book with no name, and it's made from the cross they crucified Jesus Christ on. It'll kill any fuckin' undead folks, no fuckin' messin'. Only problem is I can't touch the thing 'cos I got vampire blood in my veins at the moment.' He finally turned around. 'Can you two head upstairs and hunt through all the offices until you find it?'

'Sure,' said Dante and Peto in unison. 'What are *you* gonna do?' Dante asked.

'I'm gonna wait here for the big badass boss man Benson to come back. Now hurry the fuck up, 'cos if he gets back here and I'm taking him on by myself, I might only be able to kick his ass for a few minutes before things get tricky. If he really is the new chief bloodsucker, then without that book to kill him he'll keep on getting back up every time I knock him down.'

'Meaning what?' Dante asked.

'Meaning get the fuck upstairs and start searching for the fuckin' book, dumbass.'

Fifty-One

After Benson's departure, Jessica and her father, Rameses Gaius, remained in the Olé Au Lait to discuss the rest of the evening's plan. Neither of them had bought anything to eat or drink, but neither Flake nor Rick the chef were about to give them any grief about it.

Not long after Benson had left, hell bent on his mission to return with the Holy Grail, Jessica made her feelings about him known. 'I'll tell you what, Father,' she grumbled across the table to the looming figure of Gaius. 'There's no fuckin' way in hell I'm letting that lecherous slimeball anywhere near me. Now, I know we've agreed that you can pick my new life partner for me, but if you think I'm having his filthy hands on me you can think again.'

Her father allowed a smile to break out across his face. If he hadn't been wearing his dark sunglasses, she would have seen his good eye visibly lit up, in appreciation.

'You don't disappoint, my dear,' he said. 'Feisty as ever. It's no wonder you've lasted as long as you have. Do not fear, however. Randy Benson isn't the only candidate I have picked as your future partner, and if I'm honest he's my least favourite. He reminds me of your last husband, Armand, a vile, treacherous, untrustworthy maggot. I've a feeling he'll perish at the hands of the Bourbon Kid before he ever gets his hands on the Holy Grail again.' He paused reflectively, before going on, 'You know, this has actually worked in our favour. Those three idiot Pigs killing the Kid's brother has distracted him and allowed us to gain a march on him.'

'How do you mean?'

'Think about it, my dear. He doesn't appear to know that you're back on the streets. And he wouldn't know me if he saw me. He's too busy chasing after Benson and his buddies to worry about us. If, as I suspect, he kills Benson, then one of the other candidates I have shortlisted to be your new partner will kill him for us when he least expects it.'

'So who are these other nominees?' Jessica was eager to know.

'Robert Swann, the guy I picked out to be the guardian of those two idiot kids, Dante and Kacy, is your second choice. I picked him because he is a direct descendant of an old friend of mine. He doesn't know it, of course, but he has royal blood in his veins. Add your vampire blood to it and I think you'd make a fine couple.'

Jessica sat and stared hard at her father, wondering if he was serious. He picked up on her look of disdain. 'What?' he asked, sounding baffled.

'Are you shitting me?'

'Look, he's a fine male specimen and a ruthless killer,' Gaius protested.

Jessica shook her head. 'I don't believe it. My father is a retard.'

'Excuse me?'

Jessica stood up and made an announcement to the entire clientele and staff in the coffee shop. 'Everyone, I would like to make it known that this man, Rameses Gaius, is a retard. Thank you.' She smiled at her father, who snapped angrily back at her.

'Sit down will you, for fuck's sake.'

'*You* sit down.'

'I *am* sitting down.'

Jessica shook her head. 'Do you even know what "Sitting down" means? 'Cos you obviously don't know what a rapist is!'

'What?'

'You have to be fucking nuts. Benson and Swann, they're both serial rapists, for fuck's sake! What kind of father tries to fix his daughter up with a rapist?'

'One who's giving her a very fine wedding gift.'

'Which is?'

'The corpses of all your enemies. By the end of the witching hour tonight, the Bourbon Kid will be dead, that fool Dante Vittori who helped him shoot you down last year will also be dead, and so too will the last of the Hubal monks. In exchange for this, I get to pick your husband for you.'

'Well pardon me if I don't dance for joy. You couldn't have gotten me flowers?'

'Don't be cute.'

'I can't help it.'

Jessica was standing with her hands on her hips, working the naughty child routine on her father, and it was beginning to piss him off. '*Jessica Xavier*, sit down and behave,' he ordered. 'I didn't spend the last nine months trying to track you down just to fix you up with someone you cannot abide. Now SIT DOWN!'

For once, the Vampire Queen did as she was told, sitting back down at the table opposite her father. The watching crowd of seated coffee drinkers returned to their hushed conversations now that the drama seemed to be over.

'I'm serious,' she said in a much quieter voice, almost hissing. 'They're both rapists.'

'Come on,' said Gaius, defending his choices. 'They both have their flaws, I admit, but rape aside, they're both good candidates, wouldn't you say?'

'No, I fucking wouldn't. I'm agreeing to this arranged-marriage thing simply because my last husband betrayed you. I mean, imprisoning you in a tomb as a mummy for several hundred years was a bit off, I admit. But if you're not going to take this seriously then I'm gonna have to reconsider my position. If you insist on fixing me up with either of those two serial sex offenders, I can assure you I'll be a widow by the end of the wedding night.'

Gaius sighed. 'You're *so* fussy. But fortunately there is a third candidate, and he's not a rapist.'

'That's a start.'

'In fact,' her father went on, 'you and he share a bond of sorts.' He paused for dramatic effect. 'A mutual hatred of the Bourbon Kid.'

Jessica, intrigued in spite of herself, raised an eyebrow. 'Go on, tell me more. But if you say it's Sanchez the bartender, I'm walking out right now.'

'What's wrong with *him,* then? He likes you, doesn't he?'

'You're kidding, right? It's not Sanchez? Tell me it's not Sanchez.'

'No. It's not Sanchez, my sweet. It's someone much better suited to your taste. A well-respected individual. Big muscular fellow, too. Wanna see a picture of him?'

'Sure.'

Gaius pulled a six-by-four colour photo from the inside pocket of his suit jacket and handed it across the table to Jessica. She snatched it away from him and studied it for a moment. Her face betrayed her thoughts. 'Yeah, I like the look of *this* guy,' she said, smiling.

'Good, because I suspect that he'll be the one who kills the Bourbon Kid for you tonight,' Gaius replied.

'How can you be so sure that the Kid will die tonight?'

'I've taken care of it, my dear. The Kid and his accomplice, Dante Vittori, will die tonight, along with that Hubal monk.'

'So you keep saying, but how can you know?'

'Because, my dear, while you've been busy sleeping for the last few months, I've been travelling. I relocated my old book, *The Book of Death.* Their names are now in it. They die tonight. The only question is *how* they die, and, perhaps, *who* kills them.'

Jessica's jaw dropped open. She looked as if she were about to hug her father, such was her excitement. 'Can I kill one of them?' she asked.

Gaius shook his head slowly and smiled. His daughter was such an evil bitch, and he loved her for it. 'I'll tell you what. You can go after the monk. If you kill him before anyone else gets to him, then you can also get my Eye back from him. Do that, and I'll let you choose your partner yourself. How about it?'

'Oh, it's a deal all right, Father.'

'Good,' Gaius slipped a finger behind his sunglasses and tapped his green emerald eye. 'The sooner I can get rid of this filthy green eye and get my real Eye back, the sooner we shall get rid of daylight for ever. Then the undead will rule the world. And I will be all powerful once again.'

Fifty-Two

Randy Benson arrived at police headquarters fully expecting to find a trail of dead bodies leading down to the basement. What he found was one dead body. Francis Bloem (with most of his head missing) was the only victim he came across. Never liked him anyway. Not a problem.

The blood trail didn't end with Bloem, however. Streaks of blood intermittently led the way toward the elevators at the far end. He trod carefully on his way over there, alert to any potential ambush. The middle elevator was waiting for him, doors open. He could see inside that the walls of the car were covered in blood, and something that looked distinctly like shit. And smelled like shit. Because it *was* shit. Fresh, too.

Benson felt no need to enter the smelly elevator. *How can I get down to the Grail?* he pondered. *The Bourbon Kid is no fool. He may well have set a trap for me. But he's the one with the score to settle. He'll know I'm here. To follow his trail all the way down to the basement would be naive. All I have to do is wait.*

Benson's highly developed instinct for self-preservation had served him well over the years. All the drug busts and gunfights he had been involved in had seen him come out unscathed, thanks to his habit of always holding back, and usually hiding somewhere. The Bourbon Kid would know that he had come to collect the golden chalice, Benson was becoming ever more certain of it. But the Kid wanted him dead, and probably couldn't wait to kill him, so if he waited long enough, his enemy would come to him.

He was right, too. After a wait of about ten seconds the

doors to the fouled elevator closed. Moments later, Benson was able to see from the indicator that the car had reached the basement. There was some noise from below, and then the elevator machinery churned into action and the car began its ascent back to the ground-floor level where he was waiting. The fear and expectation rushing through him ensured that his vampire fangs grew to their fullest extent, and his skin began to harden as his veins bulged in anticipation of the coming bloodshed. And so he lay in wait, with an automatic pistol pointed right at the doors, ready and itching for them to open.

The elevator came to a stop and the doors slid apart. There, standing before him, was the hooded figure he had expected to see. As always, the cowl covered much of the face, and the figure stood dead centre in the elevator in front of a rather bloodstained mirrored wall behind. A lot of blood had been shed in that elevator already. It mattered not; Benson was ready. He had knelt down, in case the Kid had been ready to fire at him. This was exactly as he had expected. *God, I'm good*, he told himself. Holding his pistol out at arm's length he fired twice, and then twice again, in quick succession into the elevator.

Four accurate shots flew straight into the target's chest, dead centre. Blood sprayed out, some of it far enough to land at Benson's feet. He watched with horrible glee as his hooded foe fell to the floor in a heap, his back slumping against the mirrored wall behind. It was clear that, beneath the cowl, he was gasping for breath.

In his excitement, Benson now found himself unable to control his own breathing. He felt as though he'd just run half a mile at sprinting speed. His heart was pounding and he was undergoing a surging rush of adrenaline. Had he done what so many others had tried to do and failed? Had he really fatally wounded Santa Mondega's most wanted?

Exhilarated, the corrupt-cop-cum-vampire-boss stepped tentatively towards the open doors of the elevator. The bloodied body of the hooded man lay motionless on the floor.

Only his chest was moving. It was expanding and contracting erratically because he was still breathing. Choking, even. Benson stepped into the car and looked down at his dying victim, aiming his pistol at the face staring up at him from within the cowl.

'I really thought you'd be more of a challenge,' he said. His enemy, this Bourbon Kid of whom he had heard so much, was mortal after all. 'You know, this was too easy. Your screaming retard brother put up more of a fight than this. You're not so much Bourbon Kid, as Milkshake Kid.'

For a second, Benson thought about what he had just said. *This really was too easy. Something wasn't right. No time to figure out what's wrong though. Just shoot the guy in the face and be done with it.*

THUD!

Something landed on Benson's head. Something heavy. From above. *Something hot.* He heard a hissing sound, and then whatever it was that had landed on his head slipped off and plummeted down past him on to the floor. It was a book.

The book.

The one with no name.

Someone had just dropped it on him through the open service hatch overhead and the effect of it was causing his hair to melt away. He reached up to pat out the small flames consuming his white hair. Then, as he raised his head to see where the book had come from he received a kick full in the face from a black leather boot. Someone dressed in full police uniform followed through, dropping from the service hatch to the floor of the elevator.

Benson was taken completely by surprise. Who the hell was this guy? Before he had a chance to react, much less to find out, the officer kicked him squarely in the crotch, doubling him up in pain. Next thing he knew, the elevator doors had closed and they were moving downwards once more. And his head was still burning up. It felt as though his scalp had been shoved on to a steaming hot iron from which he could not pull away. The only consolation was that the flames appeared to have gone out.

The hooded guy on the floor was still breathing, although no longer choking. Of far greater concern to Benson was the aggressive stance of the uniformed officer in front of him in the confined space of the elevator. The officer, a young man in his twenties with thick dark hair, was wearing a standard blue police uniform covered in blood and shit. And he looked like he was about to start a run-up for a field goal. What he was actually doing was preparing his right boot for another swing at Benson's balls. Before Benson could react, a second more powerful kick followed, and he fell back against the side wall of the elevator. This time he lost his footing, and the only thing that stopped his ass from hitting the floor was *The Book With No Name*, on which his ass landed squarely.

'FUCK! OW!'

Benson's ass went up in flames and he jumped back up, patting out the small flames on the seat of his pants. His attacker wasn't finished yet, though. Not by a long way. He was back in the field-goal stance and before Benson could compose himself he received another hard kick in the crotch. The pain this time was even more agonizing, and he felt as though his balls had relocated to somewhere off the south coast of his stomach. Fatally weakened by the book, ready to vomit at any second and with the wind well and truly knocked out of him, the suffering vampire-cum-detective fell forwards at the feet of his attacker.

'Fuck! Will you stop doin' that, fer fuck's sake!' he retched, trying desperately to prevent the contents of his stomach from reaching his throat.

Then came the moment he feared most. The elevator came to a halt, and the doors opened to reveal another man outside. He was wearing dark combat trousers and a white singlet, and Benson could see he was one fuckin' angry-looking dude. He had been waiting patiently in the locker room for the detective's arrival, and he wasted no time in reaching in and dragging the vampire out by what remained of his once greasy but now scorched white hair. Like an animal carcass in a slaughterhouse, Benson's body was thrown across the floor of the locker room, sliding over its smooth grey vinyl tiles. The scene was not dissimilar to the recent occasion when the cop and his grinning chums had thrown a terrified young man named Casper around on the same tiles as they prepared to slaughter him. He skidded face first in to the wall five feet away.

CRACK! The impact of Benson with the concrete wall made a sickening sound. He felt a tremor within his gums and then watched in horror as two of his front teeth and a spattering of blood flew out and over his head. *Ouch.* This was painful. Not like having a dentist inflict pain on you. Not unless your dentist refused you anaesthetic, set fire to your hair and ass, then kicked you in the crotch a few times before pulling your teeth out.

Benson mustered enough strength to roll himself over and managed to look up at his attacker. The muscled man in the singlet who had dragged him from the elevator and slung him so forcefully across the floor was the one he feared the most. He looked down at Benson with utter contempt and spoke slowly and purposefully to him.

'When we were kids,' he began, 'people used to say me and my brother looked enough alike that you wouldn't know we had different fathers. 'Course, once you spoke to either of us it was obvious who was who. My brother was what you might call simple. A trusting, innocent fool who'd do anything for anyone if he thought it would make them like him. A lot of people took advantage of that, and as a kid I spent a lot of time looking after him every time some scumbag upset him.'

The man stopped and looked away to the secret room, lost in thought. 'All my life,' he finally continued, 'I've had to listen to my brother cry when people picked on him. I could hear him cry when I was thousands of miles away, that's how strong the bond was that we shared. But what you did, you sick fuck, I heard every second of that out loud. I heard him begging for mercy, screaming for me to come save him.

And I heard him wailing in pain, pleading with you and your fucking laughing buddies to let him be. And I'll hear that in my head over and over for the rest of my life. The only thing I can do to drown it out is to hear the screams of his killers for a few minutes here and there. And you're the last one. *So your screaming is gonna have to last a while.*'

This man, standing over him in a bloodstained singlet, muscled, bronzed and toned, was the Bourbon Kid. That much was only too obvious.

Benson swallowed a mouthful of blood along with a few chunks of vomit that surged into his mouth. He didn't want to look the man in the eye. He was getting a taste of the pain and terror that he and his friends had inflicted on this guy's brother. He didn't really know where to look, but as his eyes began to fill with bitter tears he caught sight of movement within the elevator. The hooded man into whom he had ploughed four bullets, the one he had wrongly assumed was the Kid, had climbed to his feet and pulled his hood back.

'Chip?' Benson mouthed quietly in astonishment, dribbling blood down his chin as he did so. He recognized the newest member of the Dreads from a recent visit he'd made to the Nightjar. A look at the officer in the elevator with Chip, the one who had repeatedly kicked him in the balls, revealed a wholly unfamiliar face, for Benson had never met Dante. His major concern was centred on the face staring down over him. He knew that one all right. It was only too familiar.

'*Déjà-Vu?*'

'Ever get the feeling you've been here before?' asked the Kid. 'Only last time you weren't on the receiving end.'

Benson swallowed another small amount of vomit that had just spurted into his mouth.

'*Oh God!* It wasn't my idea, I swear. I tried to be merciful.'

The Bourbon Kid leant over his panic-stricken enemy. 'Last time my brother called me, I listened to you torture him for five minutes and twenty-five seconds before he finally died.'

To the right of the Kid, Benson saw the dreadlocked figure of Peto moving. He was still wearing the Kid's long dark robe, and he was opening it up as if he were about to take it off. Within it, two things were immediately evident. The four bullet wounds to his chest were healing nicely, courtesy of the blue stone he was wearing around his neck. And, secondly, and of greater concern to Benson, the inner lining of the robe held a plethora of sharp instruments of different shapes and sizes.

Peto walked towards the Kid, who for a moment took his gaze away from the pathetic shambles of Randy Benson. Inside of the robe Peto was wearing was one weapon he had saved especially for this moment, a wooden-handled M3-style bayonet. He pulled it out of the narrow pocket that neatly housed it and turned back to face his victim. This blade would be just the first of many weapons he would use in the course of the torture and eventual killing of Randy Benson.

With his face showing barely a hint of emotion, the Bourbon Kid reached down and pulled Benson up by his white hair.

'Your idiot friend Igor squealed and told me exactly what you all did. And I believe it started with one hand being sliced off at the wrist.'

'Hunter did that! It wasn't me!'

'Like I give a shit.'

'It's true, I swear. I begged the others to let him be. I could see it was wrong.'

'Admit what you did.'

'I didn't do nothin', I swear.' Benson was weaselling for all he was worth. It wasn't working. It was only ensuring that he left the world without a vestige of dignity or self-respect.

'So you're innocent?'

'Yes, yes! I'm innocent, I swear.'

The Kid took a look at the blade on the bayonet and gazed at his reflection in it. 'You're innocent, huh? Y'know somethin'? My brother was an innocent too. And there are only so many ways you can torture a total innocent in five minutes and twenty-five seconds. Let's go through them together. When we come to one that you remember from my brother's death, just scream it out.'

Fifty-Three

Many times Dante had to look away during the torture and eventual execution of Detective Randy Benson. No doubt about it, it was a cruel, gruesome and unpleasant business, to say the least.

He and Peto had hoped not to become too involved, but after the Kid used the bayonet to slice off one of Benson's hands at the wrist, their involvement became essential. They had followed the Kid's instructions and held Benson down flat on his back while the Kid exacted his vengeance. It had started with a small knife being used to remove the screaming vampire's eyelids, no doubt to ensure he was able to see everything that was done to him thereafter. Blood had begun spraying out right from the start, and Dante had turned away when the blade was next used to cut off Benson's lips. He had looked back occasionally when the level of Benson's screaming changed, but he had probably missed seeing half of what happened. It was clear that the vampire had had his nipples sliced off, but the worst part Dante actually witnessed was the removal of the vampire's fingernails on his remaining hand as the Kid stuck a blade underneath them and hacked them out. The navel suffered next. By this time it was obvious that the Kid's attentions were heading below Benson's waistline. The agonized screams from their victim ensured that both Dante and Peto kept their eyes averted from that point on.

Now, Dante knew that Benson was evil and a vampire and all that, but whatever he'd done to the Bourbon Kid's brother surely didn't warrant the kind of disgusting, vile punishments inflicted on him. *Did it?* Dante liked the Bourbon Kid, in so much as you can like someone who is liable to kill you without reason at any moment, and who has probably killed a vast number of people who didn't deserve it. People with families. But he was growing increasingly anxious to get the hell out of there and get Kacy back from the Secret Service people. He hated the thought of her left alone with Swann and Valdez all this time. Particularly Swann. What the hell would that scumbag be doing with her while Dante was out doing his dirty work for him? Taking her out for dinner and getting her drunk the other night may have just been the first part of some seedy plan to seduce her. Still, Dante told himself hopefully, it wouldn't be long now before he showed up with the cavalry and got Kacy away.

The undead existence of Detective Randy Benson finally came to an end after the five minutes and twenty-five seconds of pure hell that the Kid had promised him. The last thirty seconds involved no weapons other than the Kid's fists repeatedly pounding his victim's face into a pulp. The last act came when, as instructed by the Kid, Peto rammed *The Book With No Name* into the stricken vampire's chest. They watched as his remains turned to flame, smoke and then ash. Benson's screams were replaced by sighs of relief as the final moments of his time on earth ebbed away.

With their mission now seemingly over, Dante and Peto were both eager to get out of the place. No sense in hanging around in a police headquarters when you're wanted cop killers, right?

Peto had retrieved a sealed plastic container of blood from the inside pocket of Benson's jacket, which had been tossed aside with the rest of his clothes during his drawn-out execution at the hands of the Kid. 'What do you want to do with this?' he asked the weary-looking torturer, who had removed his white singlet and was using it to wipe clean the various knives and other implements he had bloodied during the extermination of Randy Benson.

'What is it?' the Kid asked.

'Just a bag of blood, by the looks of it. Like for transfusions and things.'

'Fuck it. Leave it here.'

'Yeah? What if it's important?'

'Fine. Take it home with you and put it in your freezer if you want.'

Peto took the hint and tossed the bag of blood on to the floor. It landed with a soft thump and bounced once, then slid along the tiled floor until it disappeared under one of the long wooden benches that ran along the wall beneath a row of lockers.

'So what now?' the monk asked.

The Kid ignored him and made his way over to the secret back room. The golden chalice shone brightly in the centre of the antique wooden table within the room. He picked it up and tossed it over to Peto, who caught it with one hand.

'What am I supposed to do with this?' asked the dreadlocked monk.

'Take that and *The Book With No Name* somewhere where no one will get them. Bury them somewhere. In fact, why don't you fuck off back to Hubal with 'em? That's where the Eye of the Moon, the Holy Grail and all that shit *should* be kept. It's where they belong, and it's where you belong.'

Peto bridled. He didn't much care for being spoken to like this, not by anyone. He'd fought hard to fit in in Santa Mondega, and he didn't like the implication that he didn't belong.

'You think I should go back to Hubal, huh?'

'Yeah.'

'That'd be Hubal, the island that's currently uninhabited since someone,' he glared at the Kid, '*Someone* turned up a year ago and killed all the monks?'

'Yeah, that Hubal.'

'Well, I'll decide where the fuck I'm goin', thanks. I don't need your cheap-ass useless fuckin' opinion. Anyway, it was pissin' down with rain when we got here. I can't carry that damn great book around with me in torrential rain.'

'So stick it in one of these lockers an' come back for it

tomorrow when it's stopped rainin'.'

Peto let out a deep sigh. 'How did you ever conquer Hubal? Do you ever think anything through? This book is incredibly valuable. It can kill the fiercest of vampires, for fuck's sake.'

'Yeah, but that was the new Head Vampire we just killed. The book no longer serves a purpose. In fact, I'm not even sure we needed it to kill that guy. He was practically dead when you used it on him anyway.'

'Yes, but still...'

Tiring of the bickering, Dante picked up *The Book With No Name* from where it was sitting atop the charred remains of Randy Benson. He carried it over to the lockers on the side wall and tucked it safely in locker number 65 on the top row. The other two looked on, slightly disappointed that their quarrelling had to come to an end.

'Okay. We ready?' Dante asked.

'I'm ready,' said the Bourbon Kid, shrugging.

'Wait, one more thing,' said Peto, pointing at the bare-chested killer. 'Do you still wanna borrow this blue stone I'm wearin' while the blue moon is up, or what?'

'Yeah. Yeah, I do. Let's go do this outside,' said the Kid. He picked up his robe and draped it over one arm, ramming the bloodstained singlet into a pocket somewhere inside the robe. Then he stepped past Dante and into the elevator.

Dante cleared his throat. The time had come to remind the others of a matter that was of burning importance to him. 'Uh - you ain't forgotten we're goin' to rescue my girlfriend, have you?'

The Kid sighed. 'Of course. Let me just use the stone to get rid of these vampire urges I'm getting, 'cos right now I feel like bitin' that dickwad over there,' he nodded at Peto. 'You comin', Monk Boy?'

Peto shrugged. 'Yep. Be clear though: I'm only goin' to let you borrow the stone. I get it right back the moment you're done with it.'

The three of them stepped into the befouled elevator and headed up to the ground floor. Dante was keener than ever to get back to Kacy now. She needed him, and he needed to be back with the woman he loved.

Who, as things stood at the current time, was probably the only sane person he knew.

Fifty-Four

Sanchez was pretty fucked off, even by his own usual fucked-off standards. It had been a crap day all round, what with the reappearance of the Bourbon Kid and the trip across town to the library. But now, having been all round the Tapioca and cleaned the place up, washed the blood off the walls and sent Sally home for the evening, four goddam customers had walked in.

The tubby bartender wasn't in the mood for serving anyone, but he also hadn't wanted Sally hanging around, in case any cops showed up. There was no need for her to be giving any statements to them and landing him in trouble. Of course, not one cop had shown up to take so much as a statement or fingerprint anyway. What was pissing him off most of all, though, was the fact that he wanted some peace and quiet so that he could take a look through *The Book of Death*. In particular, he wanted to run his eye over the names entered under tomorrow's date.

So now here he was with the bar area clean(ish) again and four customers seated on stools at the bar. Nasty tough-looking bastards they were, too. Not the normal-looking tough guys you got round these parts. These guys were military men, Sanchez could tell that from the minute they walked in. They had that swagger about them, and a manner that would have intimidated most other customers, if there had been any. Their presence was enough to ensure that Sanchez kept *The Book of Death* hidden away under the bar.

Upon entering they had immediately acted oddly. One man went straight ahead to the bar while the other three hung back a while, scoping out the corners of the barroom, very obviously checking for any potential danger lurking in the shadows.

In fact, Sanchez recognized one of them as a former resident of Santa Mondega, though he had left the city as a much younger man. His name was Bull, and he was the leader of this crew. This crew, had Sanchez known it, was Shadow Company, a team of highly decorated soldiers specializing in clandestine operations behind enemy lines. During their well-earned time off, however, they were available for hire on any muscle or rescue job, as long as the price was right. All four of them were fiercely loyal to each other, and it was this loyalty that was the principal reason why they were in Santa Mondega. They had a special job to do.

An unpaid job.

A revenge mission. One that Bull had waited many years for.

And tonight was the night.

The four of them were dressed in matching combat jackets, black pants, brown belts, tight black T-shirts, sunglasses with very dark lenses and black army assault boots. None seemed to have any headgear. What distinguished them from each other was a differing array of styles above the neck. Bull's jet-black hair was worn in a military-style flattop. He sat at the end of the bar chewing on a thick Cuban cigar.

To his right was the distinctly eccentric Silvinho. His head was mostly shaved down to the skin, save for a four-inch-high bright pink mohawk running fore-and-aft down the middle. He also had a distinctive teardrop tattoo below his left eye, and a thin gold ring through his right nostril.

The man next to him was Razor, whose close buzz-cut was upstaged by a diagonal scar across his face from just above the right eye, through his nose and down to the left corner of his mouth. The damage had been inflicted upon him many years earlier in a fight to the death with a terrorist wielding a samurai sword.

The last man, sitting furthest from Bull but closest to

where Sanchez was standing behind the bar, was Tex. At six-foot-seven and broadly built to match, he was a giant with greasy, shoulder-length black hair and a goatee that hung down a few inches below his chin. Yet even though Tex was the biggest of the four, there wasn't much to choose between them. Silvinho was the shortest at a mere six-foot-two, although once his mohawk was taken into consideration he was more like six-foot-six.

Each of the four soldiers had a glass of beer in front of him. When Bull took a sip, the other three would follow suit. He was clearly the pace man, and no one else's glass was ever less full than his. He would be the first to finish his drink, and the others would then do the same. Each was now working his way through his second cigar of the day. Again, when Bull lit up, the others did so as well.

To Sanchez's annoyance, it had been over half an hour since any of them had spoken. Bull had ordered the drinks and then the four of them had sat there in silence, staring straight ahead. Normally this would have given Sanchez the shits, but since the earlier events of the day when he had survived his third Bourbon Kid massacre, he was past soiling himself in public.

With the vile weather and it being Halloween, no one was walking the streets outside or poking their head round the doors to see if the Tapioca was open for business. That is, until an unaccompanied woman walked in. She had the walk and figure of a woman in her early twenties, but the tired look on her face suggested she might be a good few years older. Her long brown hair seemed to be dry, although the rest of her was drenched right through to the skin. A dark blue skirt covered her legs down to the ankles, but had done little to keep them dry. Sanchez noted that her similarly coloured dark-blue sweatshirt had a hood at the back, which she had obviously worn up over her head to keep her hair dry but had been smart enough to lower before she walked in.

Although Sanchez didn't particularly like this woman, who had a colourful past and a facial disfigurement which made it hard to talk to her without staring at it, he decided to make her welcome (insofar as he was capable of making anyone feel welcome), simply because he was becoming irritated by the lack of conversation.

'What'll it be?' he asked.

'Orange juice, please, Sanchez,' she replied.

'Sorry. Fresh out.'

'Pineapple juice then, please.'

'Fresh out o' that too.'

'Oh. Okay, what soft drinks do you have?'

'Fresh out.'

'Water?'

'Sure. It's kinda a yellow colour, though.'

'In that case I'll pass, thanks.' She pulled up a stool next to Tex. 'Mind if I just sit here till the rain eases up?'

The four soldiers paid her no attention, but Sanchez smiled. 'Sure, as long as you abide by the smoking ban.'

'It's okay.' She smiled back politely. 'I don't smoke.'

'Then you're outta here. The Tapioca is for smokers only. Non-smokers are banned.'

The woman looked across at the four men sitting on stools to her left. Each of them was staring straight ahead and puffing on a thick brown cigar.

'You serious?' she asked.

''Fraid so,' said Sanchez.

'Really?'

'Really. You're gonna have to start smoking or leave.'

Tex turned to the woman and blew a lungful of smoke in her face. He then looked her up and down before staring her in the eye and saying in a slow Southern drawl, 'Take the hint, lady.'

The woman got down from her stool and pulled her hood up over her head. She threw a disappointed look at Sanchez and then made her way back out into the rain.

Sanchez saw an opportunity to lighten the mood with his four customers. 'Strange broad, that one,' he said, hoping for some reaction from one of them. They all ignored him, but he carried on regardless. '"Mental Beth", they call her.'

At the far end of the bar Bull glanced over and fixed the bartender with a glare. It was meant to suggest that Sanchez button it, but the thick-skinned server of dubious drinks misinterpreted it as a sign of interest and continued his tale. 'She went mental as a teenager because her mother wouldn't let her see some boy. Killed her mother in cold blood one Halloween. Slit her throat from ear to ear.'

Silvinho, the spiky-pink-haired dude sitting next to Bull, looked over at Sanchez as if the story had piqued his interest.

'Where to where?' he asked.

'Ear to ear,' Sanchez replied, using his finger to draw an imaginary cut around his throat from one ear to the other.

'Where to where?'

'Ear to . . . oh, cut it out!'

Sanchez saw the pink mohawk quivering slightly and realized the man was making fun of him and inwardly sniggering at him. As it happened, however, the mood lightened a little. From having seemed to be in a virtually trance-like state the four men were all now smirking and exchanging knowing looks.

'Finish your fuckin' story, barman,' Bull called out from the end of the bar. The story involved bloodshed so the four of them couldn't help but be somewhat interested.

'Well, she killed her mother by slittin' her throat from ear to ear.'

'Where to where?' all four men chimed.

'*Ha-fuckin'-ha*. Well, anyway, her mother wouldn't let her meet this boy at the end of the pier that night. So she goes mental 'cos she's promised the boy she'll be there at a certain time, and in her rage she kills her mother. Then the dumb bitch rushes back to the pier and it turns out the boy wasn't even there. He never fuckin' showed up. She then got arrested and spent ten years in prison for murder. Ever since she got released she comes down here every Halloween and stands at the end of the pier until the end of the witchin' hour, hopin' that this boy will come back. That's why everyone calls her

"Mental Beth". Reckon the kid probably figured out she was crazy and got the hell out. Still, she ain't bad-lookin' though.'

'I'd do her,' Tex announced.

'That scar's kinda off-putting though, ain't it?' Razor remarked. The other three members of Shadow Company paused a moment and then nodded in agreement.

'I remember that story from the papers,' said Bull, as if talking to himself. 'Eighteen years ago today. Same night as my father was murdered.'

Sanchez felt the mood turn again. *Shit!* What could he do to prevent that horrible, awkward silence from returning? A witty comment was required. 'Cut her mother's throat from ear to ear,' he joked, drawing the imaginary cut again.

Bad timing. All four men shook their heads to show their distaste at his joke. Then, as if programmed, they all returned to staring soullessly ahead like statues once more.

The awkward silence did not last for long this time. After less than a minute Bull's cell phone rang, the sudden sound making Sanchez visibly jump. None of the men paid him any attention, however, and Bull quickly pulled his phone from the pocket of his pants and answered it within two rings.

'Yeah this is Bull . . . Got it . . . Thanks.' He disconnected the phone and slid it back into his pocket, then he got up from his stool.

'It's time, fellas. We've got him.'

Fifty-Five

Dante, Peto and the Bourbon Kid made their way out of the police station without having to kill anyone else, *which was nice*, Dante thought. Word had obviously spread around town that the Kid was back and killing for fun and, as it happened, for personal reasons as well, for a change. Santa Mondega's most wanted was now wearing his dark robe again. The hood rested down around his shoulders, leaving his bloodied face and hair on show for once. Dante and Peto looked little better dressed in their shit-stained and bloodied police uniforms.

The black V8 Interceptor was parked where the Kid had left it, fifty yards from the station. The darkened streets were now deserted, partly because no one wanted to be out while there was a chance of being shot and killed for no reason, and partly because the rain was getting a lot harder. Several hanging baskets outside a flower shop on the other side of the street from the police station were swaying violently in the wind. Many of the plants and much of the soil that had filled the baskets were disappearing down the street along with the usual litter of old newspapers and food wrappers, all being blown along the wet roadway and sidewalks towards the centre of town. From time to time the moon, full and blue, appeared from among the rain clouds racing through the sky. Even when it did, the rain continued, as hard as ever.

The three of them approached the car in a fairly sombre mood, each reflecting on the gruesome violence that had recently taken place. Peto was the one to break the mood. 'Hey, Déjà-Vu, or whatever the fuck your name is. You might as well use the stone now,' he shouted above the wind. 'The moon is out so best do it now, before it goes behind a cloud for the night.' He made the suggestion just as the Kid was about to open the driver-side door.

His robed companion hesitated, his hand itching to pull the handle and flick the door open. After a second he relaxed and took his hand away. 'Yeah, sure. Fuck it. Now's good.'

'Great. But listen: I'll let you have it in exchange for letting me sit in the front seat of the car this time.'

'Deal.'

Dante had made his way over to the passenger door, but, hearing that he would now have to sit in the back, he looked over at Peto, who was still standing on the sidewalk. 'What are you, like *eight years old?*' he asked in disgust.

'Hey, it's cramped in the back of that thing. There's barely room enough for a dog back there.'

Dante shook his head. 'You big fuckin' fag.'

'Yeah,' Peto smiled. 'But I'm a big fuckin' fag who'll be sitting in the front!'

The Bourbon Kid looked Peto up and down. 'You're a fag?'

'No.'

'Then why did you just say you were?'

Peto was rattled. Working with a couple of morons was seriously beginning to irritate him. 'Do you want the Eye of the Moon or not?' he snapped.

The Kid shrugged. 'Sure. Hand it over.'

Peto lifted the silver chain from around his neck, allowing the blue stone to be on show from its place of concealment beneath his standard blue patrolman's shirt. As soon as it was out in the open air it began to glow a brighter blue from within, as if a flame had been lit inside it. The Bourbon Kid walked over to him and held out his hand. With only the slightest hesitation, the former monk handed over the glowing blue stone on its silver chain.

'You know what to do with it?'

The Kid looked at him quizzically. 'What? You mean do I know how to put a fuckin' necklace on?'

'No,' sighed the monk. 'Look. Here, stand in the middle of the street, and hold the stone up so it's got a direct line to the moon. To get rid of the traces of vampire blood in your veins you need to be pointing it at a blue moon.'

'How d'ya know all this?' the Kid asked suspiciously, suggesting he doubted the monk.

'Teachings of the elders. I haven't tried it, obviously, but centuries ago a guy called Rameses Gaius – that mummy I was telling you about – discovered numerous things that this stone is capable of. Many of them are dependent on the state of the moon. You want to purify your blood and become a mortal, you gotta do it under a blue moon. I warn you, though, this is gonna wipe out your drink problem and all those fuckin' twisted evil thoughts you have. You're about to become a regular guy.'

The Kid looked long and hard at the stone. 'A regular guy, huh?'

Peto, regretting his earlier irritation with this strange and dangerous man, placed a hand on his shoulder. 'Hey, I'm proud of you. This is a big thing for you, I know.'

The Kid eyed him suspiciously. 'You really are a fag, aren'tcha?'

This invoked a childish snigger from Dante, and although he was standing a few feet behind the others it was loud enough for Peto to hear. 'You two are pathetic,' the monk grumbled.

The Bourbon Kid placed the necklace over his head and dropped it around his neck, then walked out into the middle of the street. The wind was still whipping up and the rain was now falling harder from the heavy clouds above. The Kid stood still, holding his arms out in a crucifixion pose, looking up at the moon. Dante and Peto watched in awe as the blue stone began to glow even brighter. Then suddenly, as if taking energy from the blue rays of the moon, it glowed so brilliantly it seemed almost to turn white.

The Kid was now engulfed in the bright blue and white rays, which were so intense that both Dante and Peto had to look away. For about ten seconds their comrade stood in the middle of the street shaking and fighting hard to stay on his feet as the power of the stone consumed him, sucking all the evils and impurities from his bloodstream, and from his very being. The soul of JD, the innocent teenager who had witnessed great evil at Halloween eighteen years earlier, was returning.

The sky above them let out a gentle rumble of thunder. The brief flash of lightning that had preceded it went virtually unnoticed amid the brightness of the glow around the Bourbon Kid. Seconds after the lightning flash, the glow faded from the blue stone. Only a tiny flickering light inside it, like a dying ember, betrayed the power it had just awakened. The Kid stood blinking, looking startled, if not stunned, by what he had just inflicted upon himself.

'You okay?' Dante called.

For a few moments the Kid did not respond. He seemed to be extremely dazed, until eventually he pulled a face as though he'd just drunk a glass of sour milk. 'Man, I feel like shit,' he said unsteadily.

'You feel cured?' Peto asked.

The Kid shrugged. 'I guess so. Feel kinda weak. The vampire urges have gone, but so's just about every other urge I ever had, I reckon. Is this how you feel all the time?'

'Welcome to the real world,' Peto smiled. 'This is what it's like to be a regular guy.'

The Kid took off the necklace and tossed it over to the monk. 'Here, you can have that back. Think I'm gonna go home.'

'Hey,' Dante intervened. 'Don't forget we've gotta go get my girlfriend. She's bein' held by the Secret Service, remember?'

'Fuck that,' said the Kid, heading back to the driver's side of the car. 'My killing days are over. Sorry, man. I don't wanna get involved. Fresh start for me. I just don't feel like killing right now. You'll be okay.'

'WHAT?' Dante couldn't believe what he was hearing. He took his frustration out on Peto. 'You, you fuckin' moron,' he raged at the monk. 'You couldn't wait 'til we'd got Kacy back, could ya? You had to go and give him the fuckin' stone now, didn't ya? You fuckin' idiot. Now what are we gonna do? You've turned him into a fuckin' wimp when we've gotta go an' rescue my girl from the fuckin' Secret Service. Christ, you are such a fuckin' loser.'

'Oh can it, will you? We'll be all right. I'll help you get your girlfriend back.'

'You'd fuckin' better.'

Neither of them had paid much attention to the Bourbon Kid during Dante's tirade. He had climbed into the car and shut the driver door behind him. The rumbling noise of the engine starting up grabbed both their attentions.

'Well, I'm sittin' in the front, then,' said Dante, making for the passenger-side door. Unfortunately for him, before he could get a hold of the door handle the Bourbon Kid released the handbrake, hit the accelerator and sped off.

Peto and Dante both chased the Interceptor down the road for about twenty yards as the rain fell harder and the wind blew stronger towards the city centre. But it was no use. The black car wasn't stopping. The Bourbon Kid was gone.

'Oh fuckin' great,' Dante moaned. 'Well done, well fuckin' done.' He applauded Peto sarcastically.

The monk offered an apologetic look. 'Hey, come on. Let's just walk. It won't take long. I promise I'll make it up to you. We've still got the Eye of the Moon, my deadly fists and your nightstick. It'll be plain sailing from here. Who needs him and his fuckin' car, anyway?'

Dante let out a frustrated sigh. 'Could things get any worse?' he thought out loud.

As if to answer his question there was another flash of lightning followed seconds later by an astonishingly loud clap of thunder. What, only moments earlier, had seemed like an extremely heavy downpour now seemed like a mere trickle in comparison with the sudden torrential storm that followed the thunderclap. The rain began to sheet down on them like nothing they'd ever known. Dante gave Peto one last angry look, then started trudging off down the middle of the street towards the Santa Mondega International Hotel. Peto followed on behind. The pair of them were completely drenched already and Peto's dreadlocks were beginning to go a bit Sideshow Bob. The blood and muck on their clothes and faces and in their hair, diluted by the rain, streamed down their bodies to wash away into the gutters.

'Hey Dante, don't worry,' Peto called out. 'This will all be over in less than an hour.'

Fifty-Six

Kacy sat on the comfortable cream sofa in front of the suite's television with Roxanne Valdez alongside her. Robert Swann was in the bathroom, and had been for about fifteen minutes. He had been complaining of stomach pains for much of the evening and it seemed they had finally gotten the better of him. His fellow agent had discreetly turned up the volume on the TV just a little in an effort to drown out the trumpeting noises coming from the bathroom.

They were watching a George Clooney flick called *Burn After Reading*. Valdez seemed to be enjoying it, but Kacy had been unable to keep her attention on it. She was preoccupied with the hope that tonight would be the last they had to spend in the hotel. If Dante could make it back in one piece with the information the special agents required, then maybe they would be allowed to go home. *Or would they?* She wasn't too sure. She didn't like or trust Valdez at all, and Swann had taken to staring at her and smiling whenever he saw her, which was beginning to creep her out.

About an hour into the film Valdez's phone rang. She was quick to answer it, barely allowing it to ring for half a second, which was not long enough for Kacy to identify the ring tone.

She had hoped it was Dante calling. It obviously wasn't, but whoever was on the other end clearly had important information to convey, because Valdez stood up and walked into the smaller of the two bedrooms to ensure that Kacy couldn't hear what the caller might be saying. Being a nosy sort, Kacy grabbed the TV remote and muted George Clooney in mid-sentence. Then she listened hard, doing her best to catch anything that Valdez was saying.

'Déjà-Vu? . . . Seriously? . . . Yeah, I know him . . . I can get you an address for him in five minutes . . . I know he lives somewhere on the South Side . . . Sure. Leave it with me.'

None of it made any sense at all to Kacy, but she tried to store it all in her head in case it might mean anything to Dante when he returned. Then, finally, she overheard Valdez say something that was worth listening to.

'What about this couple? . . . Thanks . . . And what about the girl? . . . Sure. I'll let him know.'

Kacy heard the female agent coming back and flicked the TV volume back on. Fortunately there wasn't any sudden loud noise from the film, so the transition back to sound was relatively seamless. Anyway, Valdez appeared not to notice it when she walked back in.

'Did I miss anything?' she asked.

'No. Nothing much happening, really.'

'Well, in that case I'm going to go out for a while. Let me know what happens at the end, huh?'

'Sure.'

Roxanne Valdez slipped into a tight-fitting brown leather jacket that she had brought back from the bedroom and headed for the door. Before she opened it she pulled her cell phone from her pocket again and began tapping away on the keys. Then, without looking back at Kacy, she slipped out through the door and into the corridor.

Kacy felt uncomfortable and paranoid. Something not good was about to happen, she reckoned. She looked over at the hotel phone in the room, thinking furiously. She could call Dante, tell him the job was done and ask him to meet her somewhere. With Swann in the bathroom and Valdez off somewhere else doing Lord knows what, she had a chance to escape. And for the first time since she had been brought here she was seriously considering it, because it made considerable sense. If, as she suspected, Valdez had taken a call telling her that the mission was over, then it would make no difference if Dante and Kacy escaped at the last minute. If they didn't escape, then in true B-movie style she and Dante were likely to be offed. With the mission over, they no longer served a purpose.

She tiptoed over to the phone on the small table outside the bathroom and carefully picked it up. When she put it to her ear she heard no dialling tone, and after pressing a few buttons it dawned on her that the phone had been disconnected. *Shit.*

She felt a warm flush wash over her, brought on by her feelings of paranoia. Then she heard a beeping noise from the smaller bedroom. Swann's cell phone was receiving a text message. He must have left his phone in the bedroom when he'd gone for the world's longest dump. She tiptoed, a little more hurriedly this time, into the bedroom. Swann's cell phone was on the dressing table in the corner.

She sneaked over to it, her heart racing with fear and anxiety. After a deep breath she picked it up, her hands beginning to shake as the fear that she might be caught by Swann gripped her. On the display was an alert telling her that the phone had just received a text from Valdez. *This could be a text worth reading*, she thought.

It was.

Kacy opened up the text message and read it. *'Job done. Girl is all urs. Dispose of body when ur done.'*

Kacy nearly vomited. She needed Dante, big time, something her instincts always told her when she was in trouble. He could fix this if he was with her. The sooner he got back to the hotel the better. It didn't matter how tough Agent Swann was, Dante could take on a tank in a fistfight and beat it, if it meant rescuing Kacy from harm.

She flicked frantically through the menu on the phone, knowing that Swann had Dante's number stored in there somewhere. She found it quickly and pressed the 'call' button. A deep intake of breath calmed her momentarily as she put the phone to her ear. *Don't let me down, baby. Please answer.* The words ran through her head, repeating themselves over and over like a broken record.

The phone rang three times and then Dante's voice came through loud and clear.

'Whadda ya want, cunt?'

'Baby, it's me!' Kacy squealed.

'Oh shit! Sorry, Kace, I thought you were Swann.'

'He's in the bathroom. I'm using his phone.'

'Okay. Sit tight, babe, I'm comin' to get ya! I got help with me. We're gonna get outta here okay. Ya hear me?'

Kacy was so overjoyed at hearing Dante's voice that she burst into tears, letting out all her fears in one surge of emotion. 'Honey, I'm scared. I heard Valdez say the job's over. I think they're going to kill us. She's gone, and she sent Swann a text telling him to dispose of my . . . ' Her terror finally got the better of her and her voice cracked completely. Telling Dante brought home the reality of the situation. It was just too much to take. Her sobbing became uncontrollable.

At the other end of the line her lover could tell that she was in a bad way and needed guidance. He knew that when she panicked she became indecisive, so he took a firm line in the hope of giving her some focus.

'Kace, listen to me. Get the fuck outta there and head to the reception desk, somewhere public. I'm two minutes away, baby. I'll see you there.'

Dante's voice gave away the fact that he was running because his speech was punctuated by deep breaths and the volume of it went up and down.

'I love you,' Kacy sobbed.

'Love ya too. Now get the fuck outta there.'

The phone went dead as Dante hung up. The next thing Kacy heard was the sound of the toilet flushing in the bathroom. It stopped her crying instantly, but threw her into an even greater state of panic. Could she get out of the bedroom and then to the main door into the corridor before Swann came out of the bathroom? And what about his phone? Should she put it back where she found it?

Her hesitation was costly. Swann wasn't one for washing his hands after using the toilet and she heard the lock on the bathroom door click as he prepared to come out. Then she remembered what Dante had said. *'Get the fuck outta there!'* He always knew what to do in a crisis. *Do what Dante says,* she thought. She took one more deep breath through her nostrils and ran for the front door.

Unfortunately, her timing was poor. Swann stepped out of the bathroom, saw her charging for the front door and instinctively reached out, grabbing her by the left arm.

'Where the fuck d'you think you're going?' he asked, looking somewhat confused.

'Umm.' Kacy was stuck for words.

'Where's Roxanne gone?'

'Umm.'

'And what are you doing with my phone?'

Swann's face was suddenly masked with concern. He could tell something was amiss. He reached over to Kacy's right hand and wrested his phone from her grasp. Her face was betraying her. She was terrified, and he could see it in her eyes.

Still gripping her arm tightly, he began flicking through the menus on his phone. He quickly found the text from Valdez and as he read it Kacy saw his eyes light up and his jaw slacken. Then a huge, ugly smile slowly broke out across his face.

'Well, well, well,' he grinned. 'I hope you've shaved your legs . . . '

Fifty-Seven

From his private quarters in the small building to one side of the church Father Papshmir watched a black V8 Interceptor pull up and come to a halt right outside the front of the church. The driver switched off the engine and stared hard down at the steering wheel for a few moments, deep in thought. The rain was still hammering down, and the windows of the car were tinted slightly so it was difficult to make out his face. Santa Mondega's streets had been quiet since the word had spread that a mass murderer was in town on a killing spree, and since the thunderstorm had started there had been even fewer people about. So who was this? And why was he here?

The driver's-side door opened and a hooded figure stepped out into the rain. There were no streetlights on and no lights showing in any of the nearby buildings. From high above it would have looked as though the town was in the middle of a blackout. That was not the case, however. It was a tradition in Santa Mondega that on the night of a blue moon the only light permitted in town would be moonlight. And, of course, it was still the witching hour, and those not tucked up safely in their beds were asking for trouble, openly advertising themselves to the undead, offering themselves as food for the vampires and werewolves. Not a wise thing to do. Especially not on Halloween.

The shady hooded figure closed the car door and walked up to the front doors of the church, head bowed to keep off the worst of the rain. He had not set foot inside for many many years. Tonight was an important night. It was time to confess.

The church doors opened with a gentle push. It was no warmer inside than out, but at least it was dry, and welcoming. The Kid walked down the aisle in the centre of the nave, passing row upon row of pews until he reached the altar. He knew his way around the church from years ago, when he had often escorted his younger brother to Sunday school. As if he had last set foot inside these walls only yesterday he took a left turn and walked around a large pillar to where the confessional was situated. He made his way over to it and stepped inside the public booth, to await the arrival of whichever man of the cloth was on duty.

In the event, he waited for less than a minute before he heard the door on the priest's side of the box open. Then the curtain over the grille separating the two sides of the booth was pulled aside. It was far too dark to make out any features on the holy man's face, but a voice spoke softly, almost at a whisper, through the grille.

'Welcome, my son. I will hear your confession now.'

'Thank you, Father,' was the response. The voice had a gravelly quality to it. 'Where to begin?'

'When was your last confession?'

'Fuck, I don't know. Coupla decades ago, I guess.'

'Decades?' there was a gentle yet polite laugh from the priest. 'You have been busy, then?'

'Yes, Father. I've been killing.'

'Excuse me?'

'Murders, Father. Massacres. I've killed many men. Many, many men.'

'Oh dear, that is unfortunate. Is this what . . . '

'And women.'

'And women?'

'Children, too. Vampires, werewolves, kids, animals. I've killed pretty much every creature God ever created. And I did it all without any remorse. For a great many years. And now I've come to confess.'

There was a pause, during which it sounded very much as if the priest was holding his breath. Eventually he exhaled as slowly and calmly as possible and spoke, again.

'Is this a joke?'

'No, Father. I've committed every sin you can possibly imagine, and a good many you could never even have dreamt of.'

'I see. And what do you think has made you do all these wicked things?'

'It all started when I killed my mother.'

'Your mother?'

'Yes. I shot her a half a dozen times after I drank a bottle of bourbon.'

There was a pause, during which all that could be heard was the constant hammering of the rain on the church roof and against the windows.

'Bourbon? Did you say bourbon?'

'Yes, Father.' A gravelly pause. 'I was *that* guy.'

There was a silence of deathly proportions for a second, followed by a loud squelchy farting noise from the priest's side.

'Please excuse me,' he mumbled nervously through the grille. 'You caught me cold there. I apologize.'

'I forgive you, Father,' said the gravelly voice calmly. 'But are you able to forgive me? Will God forgive me for these terrible things I have done?'

'Do you feel remorse for these things that you do?'

'Did, Father. *Did.* My killing days are over. I intend to lead a sin-free life where possible, but I need to know if God will forgive me for all the souls I have destroyed, for the evil that I have done.'

The sound of a door opening near the back of the church interrupted them, and succeeded in imparting a sense of urgency to both men. Both wanted the confession over as quickly as possible. The arrival of a third party was more than enough excuse to hurry matters along.

'Yes, my son, go on into the night. The Lord will forgive you.'

'You're sure? Should I feel any different now?'

'You will feel different in the morning, my son. If you wake tomorrow morning, then you will know the Lord has forgiven you.'

'Thank you, Father.'

'Peace be with you, child.'

A gust of wind blew through the church as Father Papshmir walked towards the confessional. He caught sight of the hooded figure he had seen outside leaving by the front doors through which he had entered only a few minutes earlier. Papshmir let out a deep, irritated sigh. After going to all the trouble of dressing in his full robes the man had not stayed to make his confession. Or had he?

Showing beneath the curtain on the priest's side of the confessional Papshmir saw a pair of white trainers. A pair he recognized only too well.

'Josh,' he ordered wearily. 'Come on out.'

The curtain was pulled aside and the pale, terrified face of a fifteen-year-old boy looked out at him. He was trembling, but he managed to haul himself to his feet and step out of the booth. The terrified kid could barely speak. He had managed to control his fear during the revelation that he was sitting next to Santa Mondega's most prolific mass murderer, but now he was in a terrible state. He looked as though he was in shock, so the sight of the balding priest standing before him in his dark church robes and white collar was probably a calming one.

'Have you been listening to people's confessions again?' Papshmir asked, unable to hide the annoyance in his voice. 'How many times have I told you about that? Altar boys cannot absolve people of their sins. That man's confession counts for nothing when it's you listening.'

'Sorry, Father.' The boy looked abject, standing, shivering, in his school shirt and pants.

'You're the one who should be confessing. It is a sin to impersonate a man of the cloth, you know.'

'That was the Bourbon Kid.' The words came out in a

sudden rush.

'What?'

'That man. It was the Bourbon Kid. He confessed to all his murders and stuff, Father.'

'Oh, for Christ's sake! You heard confession from the Bourbon Kid? You stupid cunt!' He looked up to the heavens. 'Forgive me, Lord,' he whispered, then he turned his attention back to Josh. 'What have I told you, eh? See what happens? You've now taken confession from someone with no soul. Well, I hope you didn't tell him his sins would be forgiven. That man is beyond redemption.'

'Well...'

'You absolved him? You dumb fuck! *Forgive me Lord.* So, that man – no, monster – is now walking the streets believing that God has forgiven him for all the murders he has committed? Well let me tell you, if he thinks that, he's very much mistaken.'

'I told him if he woke up tomorrow morning it meant God had forgiven him, so technically it's in God's hands now, right?'

The priest looked down into the frightened eyes of the teenager, and relented a little.

'I guess so,' he said, shaking his head. Then he sniffed the air. 'What on earth is that smell?'

'I've shit myself, Father.'

'In *my confessional*?'

'Yes, Father.'

'Holy shit!'

Fifty-Eight

Robert Swann was an extremely strong man. He was also superbly well trained in how to deal with a struggling captive. And as struggling prisoners went Kacy was pretty feeble. It didn't take much for him to drag her in to the bedroom in which he had spent the last few nights. With considerable aggression he threw her like a rag doll on to the nearer of two single beds. She landed flat on her back on top of the orange duvet, her head thudding gently into the white pillow below the headboard. The right-hand side of the bed was pressed up against the wall, meaning that her only escape route would be to roll over to her left into the space, no more than six feet wide, that separated the two beds. In between, against the wall, was a small dressing table with a mirror above it. Before Kacy could make any attempt to roll off the bed, however, Swann had lurched on top of her, his heavy muscular body pinning her down beneath him. It knocked the wind right out of her, so that she found she couldn't even scream. As she saw his leering face come pressing towards hers with his tongue out and his eyes bulging she turned her face sideways. The move ensured that he missed any chance of kissing her on the mouth, but only encouraged him to lick the side of her face with his wet, slobbering tongue.

His hands moved fast, one of them grabbing her left breast, the other sliding down towards her crotch. Kacy was ready to be sick, but somehow she held it back, knowing that she would be unable to fight back if she was busy retching. Just about the only part of her body that wasn't pinned under the panting figure of Robert Swann was her left arm. With it she reached out towards the dressing table, trying to find and grab hold of anything she might use as a weapon. What she found was a bedside lamp. Not a great weapon, but all she had at her disposal. She seized it by its base and swung it at Swann's head as he pressed it against hers. The lamp crashed against his ear and the flimsy orange shade fell off. The impact of it barely registered with her attacker. Swann merely sat himself up, keeping Kacy prisoner by squeezing her waist tightly between his knees. His eyes were everywhere, eagerly anticipating the sight of her naked flesh, and he wasted no time in grabbing her grey sweatshirt and pulling it up over her head. It lifted her arms back with it and she dropped the bedside lamp on to the floor. A crashing sound followed as the light bulb shattered.

While Kacy struggled to free her arms and head from her sweatshirt sleeves so that she could fight back, Swann quickly took the opportunity to unbelt and unzip his trousers. His speed was impressive, not that Kacy would have noticed. Her face was still trapped inside her sweatshirt as he pulled his pants and underwear down to his knees. His penis was already erect – and now all he had to do was rip the girl's jeans and underwear off, so he could put it to use. He went straight for the thin black leather belt on her jeans and frantically began unbuckling it. His fumblings were reminiscent of a teenage schoolboy, so out of practice was he, and by the time he'd unbuckled it and was ready to rip her jeans open at the fly, Kacy had freed her left arm from the sleeve of her shirt. Swann was too slow to react when she lunged at him. He had been so transfixed by the sight of the smooth skin of her stomach, and so aroused by the thought of the rest of her body, that he hadn't noticed her left hand scrabbling around on the floor. Kacy had managed to grab the metal end of what remained of the light bulb and swung it at him as he knelt over her, in the manner of a boxer's upper cut. Only she wasn't aiming for his chin. She went for his crotch.

'AAAAAAARGH!' Swann screamed as loud as he'd ever done, as the jagged ends of the bulb ripped into his ass and part of his scrotum. His hands reached straight down and cupped the wound, hoping that nothing was permanently damaged. Kacy let go of the bulb and tried to wriggle free. It proved easier than she'd dared hope, for in his agony Swann lost his balance and fell sideways, collapsing off the bed and on to the floor, screaming and holding his balls and ass together. Kacy quickly redressed her upper half, pulling her sweatshirt back on in a second, rebuckled her belt and jumped up off the bed.

She was about to rush out of the bedroom when she spotted Swann's gun tucked into a holster below his left shoulder. The filthy scumbag was on his knees on the floor with his back to her and his hairy ass up in the air, so, taking advantage of the situation, she lunged forward, reached over his shoulder and grabbed the gun. She plucked it from its holster and then pointed it at the back of her attacker's head.

'Don't fuckin' move!' she yelled at him.

It barely registered with Swann, who was busy inspecting his balls and moaning in agony.

What to do? Kacy thought of all the cop films and cop TV shows she'd seen. *Smack him over the head with the gun*, she told herself. She rearranged her grip on the weapon and did exactly that.

SMACK! Right on the back of Swann's head. The serial rapist yelled out in pain, then took one hand from his groin and placed it on the back of his head where Kacy had hit him. Then he twisted his head around and looked back at her.

'You cunt,' he sneered.

Kacy had had enough. The blow to the head hadn't knocked him out at all; it had only angered him further.

Fuck it. Time to get out of there.

Fifty-Nine

Dante and Peto were soaked through when they finally made it to the Santa Mondega International Hotel. They also looked a little messy on account of the bloodstained police uniforms they were wearing. Neither man could wait to get inside. Dante led the way up the stone steps outside the ten-storey building, shivering violently from the cold rain. Peto followed, trying to squeeze some of the excess moisture out of his heavy dreadlocked hair.

Once through the glass doors at the front they found themselves in the lobby. It came as quite a relief to them both to feel some warm air on their bodies at last. The lobby was clean, dry and civilized, as always. The sight of two bedraggled men dressed as police officers dripping water all over the expensive red Egyptian rug in the middle of the floor brought a tut of disapproval from the girl on the reception desk to their left. She was only young, barely out of her teens, but watching Dante and Peto shake themselves like a couple of hounds who'd been rolling in mud drew a distinctly unamused look from her. Not that either of the two men noticed. They were just relieved to be out of the storm.

The general calming ambience inside the lobby lifted their spirits considerably. The soft lighting, the warm red rug and the beige carpet beneath it, and the brown leather sofas dotted around were extremely comforting sights. There was also some light music playing in the background. Peto recognized it as Andrea Bocelli singing 'Con Te Partiro'. He had taken a distinct liking to classical music and opera in his time away from Hubal, and Bocelli was a particular favourite of his, even when singing pop-opera like Sartori's hit.

Dante didn't even notice the music, however. He just wanted to get to Kacy as quickly as possible. 'She should be on the third floor,' he said to Peto, the urgency in his voice all too evident. 'I'll take the stairs, you catch the elevator. That way we can be sure we don't miss her if she's comin' down.'

'Sure thing.'

Dante rushed off up the beige-carpeted staircase to the right of the elevator, while Peto pressed the button to call the elevator. He watched his friend disappear around the first corner on the stairs and then stood and waited for a good fifteen seconds before the lift eventually arrived on the ground floor. He was enjoying the music so much, that he would have happily waited longer. Bocelli appeared to be dueting with a woman who had the most beautiful, angelic voice Peto could ever recall hearing.

He looked down at his sodden police shirt and tugged at it to try to keep it from sticking to his body. Then, as the polished steel doors to the elevator opened, he stepped forward. *And looked up.*

His path in to the carriage was obstructed by a dark shadow. To his shock a figure loomed out of the lift, dressed all in black and thrusting a shiny silver double-edged sword in his direction. Peto's reactions were quick, but not quick enough for this unexpected assault. The black-clad woman surging out of the elevator was Jessica. With unbelievable speed and accuracy she plunged the sword right into Peto's chest, through his heart and out through the damp blue shirt on his back. Then, using her extraordinary strength, she used the blade to lift the soaking wet monk off the ground. Grinning horribly and looking deep into his stunned eyes, she angled a swift kick of her boot into his stomach and pulled the sword back out. Blood covered all of what had once been bright steel.

Peto slumped to the floor on his knees, dizzy and stunned, blood filling his lungs and spilling up through his throat and into his mouth. His eyes were wide open with the shock of what had just happened to him. He had the Eye of the Moon around his neck so this normally fatal wound had a chance of healing, but it would take a long time. And time was not on his side. Recovering from a wound like this was no thirty-second job.

The only thing keeping him from screaming out in agony at the sheer pain of the blow was shock, which had completely overcome him. He looked up into Jessica's leering eyes as she loomed over him. She could see his blood dripping from her sword and, unable to control her thirst, she lifted the blade to her mouth and ran her tongue along it, licking up as much of the blood as possible with one long stroke of her tongue. It served to quench her thirst a little, but then, like a true professional, she quickly refocused her attentions on the stricken monk kneeling before her.

'So, you're the one. The last of the Hubal monks,' she smiled. It was a smug, self-satisfied smile, a smile that couldn't disguise it's owner's evil nature and hatred of the living. 'Time to say goodbye.'

Then, like a baseball player preparing to take a swing, she lifted her bloodied sword in both hands until it was high above her right shoulder and, almost in the same movement, struck downwards, aiming it at Peto's neck.

Home run.

Peto's head came clean off his shoulders. There was no need for a second swing here. The head landed with a thud three or four feet away, much to the horror of the girl on the reception desk who watched aghast and in silence, open-mouthed. Peto's now headless body slumped forward. The necklace with the Eye of the Moon attached to it fell on to the floor and landed at Jessica's feet. This was what she had been waiting for. Finally, here it was, the precious blue stone she had long coveted, just lying there on the floor at her feet. Oblivious to everything around her she bent and picked it up, raising it in front of her face. Her eyes lit up like fireworks in the darkest night.

'At last,' she hissed.

That, however, was not quite all. When she finally stopped

gazing at the Eye of the Moon, she noticed a golden chalice protruding from a pocket in the dead monk's pants.

Double Jackpot!

From his place behind the bar in the now empty Tapioca, Sanchez finally found the page of *The Book of Death* that he had been looking for. There were three names that stood out. All three were due to die on 1 November. A glance at his watch confirmed that midnight on Halloween had passed. The first day of November was now under way.

The three names read as follows:

Peto Solomon
Dante Vittori
John Doe

Sixty

Heartbreak Hotel on Santa Mondega's South Side was not one of the more pleasant guesthouses. It was home to all manner of lowlife scum. The cops stayed clear of the place – hell, if truth be told, even the vampires steered clear of it. And there was one particular apartment that even the other residents steered clear of.

The apartment at the end of the hall on the second floor had always been creepy. Anvil had never even been within six feet of the door, despite living next to it for almost four years. It became noticeably colder once you walked past apartment Number 23. Apartment Number 24 was hidden from the world by a sturdy, sinister-looking black door. The lighting in the hallway came to an end four feet from the door, and served only to add to the creepiness of the place. The air was visibly dusty on the final approach to that door, even in the dark. The specks of dust didn't seem to want to settle on the ground, and remained always floating in the air, as if recently disturbed. Even if the dust did one day settle on the floor, no chambermaid or janitor in their right mind was going anywhere near door Number 24 with a vacuum cleaner.

Or without one.

Fuck that.

The man who lived there often disappeared for weeks or months at a time. No one ever saw his face, and no one ever tried to see it. He always wore a hood up over his head, be it hot, cold, raining, sunny, or whatever. Everyone in the building knew who he was. No one in the building uttered his name. Not ever. Why would you? This man was not to be talked about. It was him, the man that killed. Killed for a living. Killed for fun. Killed to pass the time. *Killed time, too, probably.*

Earlier in the year his apartment had been empty for more than six months, a joyous six months too. No one knew where he had been, and no one wanted to know. They just didn't want him to come back. *But come back he had.*

Three months ago he had returned unannounced. And it was giving Anvil sleepless nights. Knowing that there was a mass murderer next door was a ticket to the town of Insomnia. How the hell was anyone supposed to sleep when they had a serial killer less than a coffin length away? Well, Anvil now had bags under his eyes big enough to store nuts in for the winter.

It wasn't just knowing that the psycho was back next door that was keeping him up at night, however. It was also the screaming. Oh God, the screaming. Someone was being tortured by the Man every night. The same dull screaming voice every night. Not quite human sounding, but not quite animal, either. Someone had recently remarked to Anvil that it sounded like a wookie, but what it really sounded like was someone without a tongue, screaming as best they could. That would explain why no words were ever shouted out. Just the screams.

And every night it went on for hours at a time. But why was this person or creature screaming? What the hell was being done to them? And why?

The answer lay behind that door. That terrible, horrible door. Somehow, there was never anyone around in the hallway to try to peek past that door on the odd occasion when it was opened. If the hooded man was in the building, everyone was locked inside their apartments.

Until today.

Anvil was one of the braver tenants, as it happened. He was standing at the opposite end of the hallway, at the top of the staircase, ready to run like fuck if anything happened. *Anything.* As far as he knew, the hooded man had gone out for the day. Grocery shopping, maybe? Do hooded men buy groceries? Of course, they must do, *right?* It wasn't something that Anvil had ever thought about before, and now wasn't the time to fret about it either.

There were four heavily armed men dressed in black standing outside the dreaded door Number 24. Their upper bodies were protected by dark body armour that matched their clothes. And all four of them were aiming automatic weapons at the door. These guys were something special. Green Berets? Anvil thought about it for a moment. Nah, they weren't wearing green berets, so probably not. These guys would be called Shadow Company or something cool like that. And the massive guy at the back with the flattop military haircut, he was Shadow Company leader.

Considering that Anvil was a halfwit, his assessment was surprisingly accurate. This *was* Shadow Company. The leader was Bull, and the other three were his blood brothers, Tex, Silvinho and Razor. A fearsome-looking bunch, one of whom stood out due to a large pink mohawk haircut rising from the top of his otherwise shaved head.

There was no mistaking that Bull was the leader of this team of four, and as the leader he was going to do one thing better than the others. Lead. And lead he did. Anvil watched as the three soldiers in front of him stepped aside in unison without even appearing to have been ordered to do so. Then Bull charged forward and kicked door Number 24 clean off its hinges with the sole of the giant black boot on his right foot. The door crashed backwards on to the plain wooden floorboards inside the room, and immediately a foul, rancid, repugnant smell swarmed back out, engulfing the entire floor. Anvil felt himself retching. The soldiers up ahead of him did not react to the smell; they crouched in assault positions, ready to fire on anything making an aggressive move. And there was one thing moving in that apartment. One thing visible through the gap where door Number 24 had been.

Anvil laid eyes on it for less than a second. It was without doubt the most gruesome sight he'd ever seen. A body was hanging upside down from the ceiling. A human body, only with barely any skin on it. Its arms were hanging down, almost touching the floor. Although Anvil didn't know it yet, this unfortunate creature was a vampire named Kione. He had been kept alive and tortured mercilessly every night for the last eighteen years.

Anvil turned his head away, trying his best not to vomit. *Look somewhere else, anywhere else*, he whispered to himself. Then he focused his gaze back down the staircase, and did the one thing he'd always been afraid of doing. *The one thing he'd always vowed never to do.*

He stared deep into the eyes of the hooded man, who was walking up the stairs towards him.

Sixty-One

Kacy was shaking like a leaf. Holding a gun made her nervous at the best of times, and the thought that she might have to fire it made her even more terrified. Where the hell was Dante? *He must be close by. Can't be far,* she thought. She was right, too. Whatever predicament they were in was always best dealt with together. On their own they were vulnerable, but his courage and headstrong tenacity paired with her sensible thinking made them a perfect combination to deal with any problems that they might face when they were together. As a unit, they made a formidable team.

She had left Swann behind in a bloodied mess and with his pants round his ankles in the second bedroom of the suite. Now, as she crept along the corridor of Floor Three, she was gripped by paranoia and a terrible feeling of anxiety. Being on her own was freaking her out. Any decisions would have to be made on her own, without running them past anyone, and when the decisions involved simple choices like turning left or right, but had enormous consequences, like life or death, they were decisions she didn't want to make. Someone was going to jump out of one of the apartment doors, or appear around one of the corners ahead of her or, worse still, behind her. With an irrational logic brought on by the distress and apprehension she felt, she decided not to use the elevator simply because the thought of watching the doors open only to find herself confronted by a vampire or a corrupt cop gave her the shits. The best thing to do would be to head for the stairs that led down to the lobby. *Act casual, like nothing's wrong,* she told herself.

Then, between one second and the next, all was right with her world again. Dante appeared at the opposite end of the corridor. He had obviously just bounded up the stairs because he looked a little out of breath, and he was soaked to the skin. Moreover, for reasons unknown to Kacy he was dressed in a police uniform, with a rain-sodden blue shirt that appeared to be heavily stained with blood. It wasn't something that particularly worried her. It would just signify that he had no doubt managed to get himself into one of his legendary, ridiculous, scrapes which, somehow, he always seemed to come out of unscathed.

A huge smile lit up her face, one she couldn't control. The mere sight of Dante grinning back at her erased all of her fears in an instant. He might not have been the toughest guy in the world, and certainly not the smartest, but he was *her* guy. Always there for her in a crisis. Willing to do whatever it took, no matter how daring or stupid, in order to protect her, the woman he loved. And that was just one of the many reasons why she loved him.

'Oh God, are you a sight for sore eyes,' she called down the hallway to him. He was a good thirty yards away, but that distance could be covered in a matter of seconds. Lowering the pistol to her side she began to walk towards him. She felt a little weaker than she had done only seconds earlier, simply because the adrenalin brought on by Swann's fearful attack was now subsiding. Everything was going to be okay. Dante began jogging towards her with a big smile on his face. 'C'mon, let's get you the fuck outta here,' he yelled.

Kacy tucked the gun into the back of her jeans and opened her arms wide. 'Come and get me, honey!' she beamed. Dante began to run a little faster, ready for an over-the-top embrace like the kind one sees enacted on a beach in a cheesy movie.

Then, BAM! Just as he passed a side corridor a figure dressed in a leopard-skin catsuit flew out from it and slammed him into the opposite wall. It was Roxanne Valdez, and she was in full-on bloodsucking mode. To Kacy, everything seemed to move in slow motion as she looked on aghast as the events unfolded. She watched Dante's expression change from one of joy to one of surprise and utter horror. Valdez had hit him with the speed of an express train. His head was slammed into the wall of the hallway with such force that it was a wonder he hadn't been knocked cold straight away. The vampire-agent's strength was clearly phenomenal, and the fact that she had taken him completely by surprise meant that Dante's attempts to fight her off were futile.

Kacy stared in stunned bewilderment as Valdez opened her mouth wide, revealing a set of fangs which she sank deep into the side of Dante's neck. A horrible crunching sound followed, and Kacy saw fresh blood spurt from her lover's wound. His whole body was pressed up against the wall so that he could muster little of his strength or leverage from his arms to fight back. Worse, by the time Valdez had pulled her head back to allow his blood to trickle down her throat he looked incapable fighting any more. The blood slowly drained from his face, and his knees began to buckle as he stared blankly down the hallway at Kacy with an almost apologetic look.

Kacy finally screamed. 'DANTE!' It felt as if she had been watching this action unfold for an age before her mouth had allowed her to make her inevitable despairing cry.

The scream drew the attention of the blood-crazed Valdez, who released her grip on her latest victim and turned her evil glare on Kacy. Dante's battered and bloodied body slid towards the floor, leaving a thick stain of blood on the wall as he collapsed on the carpet, like an unwanted rag doll.

Valdez took a step towards Kacy and eyed what she probably classed as vampire's dessert. Streaks of Dante's blood were dripping down from her mouth onto her leopard-skin catsuit. Kacy froze, and for a second the two females eyeballed each other. Then the vampire made her move, charging at the wide-eyed innocent before her.

The movement finally brought Kacy to her senses. Reacting instinctively, she pulled the pistol back out from the waistband of her jeans. She fumbled for a solid grip on it as, with trembling hands, she pointed it in the direction of the onrushing bloodsucker. Then for reasons even she herself didn't know, she closed her eyes, looked away and fired blindly.

BANG!

For a few seconds a deafening silence followed the echo of the report. Then Kacy, wincing like someone expecting a custard pie in the face, opened one eye, then the other. Lying on the carpet less than a yard in front of here was a bloodied, smoking mess of a corpse, the remains of Special Agent Roxanne Valdez.

Dante was still in a heap on the floor up against the wall fifteen yards down the hallway. He was looking at Kacy with puppy-dog eyes, but his head was resting on the floor in a pool of blood. The pool was getting bigger and spreading slowly across the carpet. There was blood dribbling from his mouth, but the main cause of the ever-expanding pool was pumping out from the gaping wound in his neck.

In spite of the numbness that she felt, Kacy's mind was racing. She dropped Swann's gun on the floor by the now burning remains of Valdez and ran over to Dante with all the strength her legs could muster in their current turned-to-jelly state. Kneeling, she placed one hand over the hole in his neck to try to stem the flow of blood. Then she used her other hand to lift his head and turn it to face her.

'Baby, don't leave me,' she blurted out. Just saying those words was enough to bring on the tears that had been inevitable from the moment he fell. For the next two minutes she knelt beside him, cradling his head and begging him not to go. Not to leave her all alone in a world full of hatred, spite and evil. But Dante could not respond. His voice had already gone by the time she had got to him. All he could do was stare helplessly back up at her, hoping she could read in his eyes that he was sorry for messing things up right at the end. He had fallen at the final hurdle, after he had made it through the whole ordeal of being undercover in a coven of vampires for the last three nights.

Kacy sobbed as she watched his eyes roll back in his head, signalling that his fight for life was over, but she continued to stroke his hair and wipe the blood away from his face. If he was on his way to the next life, she wanted him to look his best, and create a good impression. Desolate as she felt, as she smartened him up she began remembering all the fun times they had shared. She thought back to some of the dumbass things he had done since she'd met him. Turning up at her door one day with a truckload of *Captain Hook* DVDs, grinning like he'd won the lottery. Embarrassing her by calling Professor Cromwell a cunt. Stealing a yellow Cadillac to impress her when they already had half the city trying to kill them. Dragging her to safety in the middle of a shootout in the Tapioca during last year's eclipse, when he'd been dressed as the Terminator. Most of all, she remembered the way he had proposed to her less than a week earlier. He was the best thing in her life, ever.

Dante had been dead for a good minute before she was distracted. 'You fuckin' bitch!' called a voice from the end of the hallway. It was Agent Swann, and he was bending down to pick up his pistol from the floor where she had dropped it.

'Now you're really gonna be sorry.'

Sixty-Two

As the hooded man walked up another step towards him, Anvil found himself staring down at his shoes in the hope that this would make him invisible. No sense in engaging in a staring contest with the Bourbon Kid. Why rile the fellow up? It wasn't as if this guy needed an excuse to kill anyone. If the rumours about him were true, he'd kill Anvil just for looking at him funny. Unless, of course, he'd recently undergone some sort of epiphany and had decided to give up killing. Either way, someone, at least one person, was about to be blown away. Of that Anvil was sure.

As the Kid stepped past him, his robe brushing lightly against him, Anvil managed to sidle down a step on the staircase, enough to get just a little out of the way of the action that was no doubt about to unfold.

Bull and his men turned just in time to see the hooded figure step up onto the landing they were on. He was no more than twenty feet away, and as soon as he saw them spin round with their weapons aimed in his direction he reached inside his dark robe for a weapon. With uncanny speed he pulled out one of his semi-automatic handguns (a 9mm Beretta, no less), and aimed it down the hallway in the direction of Bull and his three comrades. He managed to get off one shot.

The Shadow Company boys were no slouches. Bull, in particular, hadn't come this far only to blow his best opportunity of revenge. He unloaded on sight, his heavy automatic rifle blasting off at his enemy, peppering him in the chest with a barrage of rounds in the space of a few seconds.

Anvil had just enough time to see that the Kid's solitary

shot had missed Bull and his men. Instead, it flew with lethal accuracy through the open door of Apartment 24 and lodged itself dead centre in the forehead of the wretched creature hanging from the ceiling. Kione had been tortured so mercilessly for so long that he would no doubt have been greatly relieved to be so swiftly put out of his misery. Hell would be a walk in the park compared to the suffering inflicted upon him for the last eighteen years. And Hell was where he was headed. The pitiful remnant of a being was finally dead.

Once Bull and his men opened fire, Anvil was smart enough to duck down on the stairs and cover his ears. The three other members of Shadow Company had instantly followed their commander's lead and also opened fire, blasting their target mercilessly. Crouched on the stairs, Anvil watched the hooded figure stagger backwards, each step back only adding to the certainty that he was about to fall at any second. In fact, Anvil thought, if the soldiers would only stop firing their target would slump to the ground much sooner, rather than being jerked upright by each new bullet that slammed into him. Eventually, though, he did fall, and the firing ceased. He'd been shot at least thirty times. There was a great deal of smoke drifting up from the muzzles of the soldiers' guns, and a great deal of blood from the wounds on Anvil's former next-door neighbour.

The silence after the gunfire was wasted on Anvil, who couldn't hear anything beyond the ringing in his ears (despite having clamped his hands over them) from the deafening barrage of gunfire.

Bull gestured to one of his men to approach the lifeless corpse lying in front of them near the head of the staircase. 'Check him,' he ordered.

The big unshaven one with the horrific scar across his face (Razor, had Anvil known any of their names) did as he was told, placing his fingers on their victim's neck to check for a pulse. He looked back up at Bull after a few seconds and shook his head. 'Yeah, he's dead,' he said.

Bull breathed a sigh of relief. At last. After all these years, he had finally gained the revenge he had craved. 'Hold him up,' he snarled, pulling a machete from a sheath on his left trouser leg. 'I want his head.'

Razor, who, like all of them, was incredibly strong, lifted the corpse up as best he could. He managed to get the body up on its knees, then took a handful of the cloth of the hood and used it to hold the head up so that his boss could get a clean swing.

In a manner not unlike Jessica's recent execution of Peto, Bull swung his blade. A second later his colleague was holding nothing more than an empty hood as the head it had concealed dropped from the corpse's shoulders and rolled across the floor, coming to a stop when it hit the wall by Bull's feet. It was caked in blood and the back of it appeared to have been blown off, possibly from a shot that had gone in through one of the eye sockets.

Bull picked the head up by its hair and held it up before him. 'Not so fuckin' tough now, are ya, huh? Told you I'd get you, you sonofabitch.' He tossed the head back to the pink-haired soldier standing behind him in the hallway.

'Pack that thing away in some ice and let's get the fuck out of here.'

Sixty-Three

Kacy needed one hell of a good reason to drag herself away from Dante's dead body after so short a time. Special Agent Swann pointing a gun at her provided just that reason. He was staggering and looked more than a little unsteady on his feet, no doubt because he had suffered considerable blood loss from the wounds Kacy had recently inflicted upon him.

His military training and incredibly high threshold of pain meant that he could put the injury to the back of his mind and carry on the pursuit of the young woman whom he both lusted after and wished to kill. He had done a quick bandaging job on his ass and crotch, using the hand towels in the suite's bathroom. The crude dressings had stemmed most of the bleeding, and this, coupled with the adrenalin released in him by his fury at Kacy, was keeping him going. Mentally, he shut out the pain, and as a result the wound was already becoming little more than a minor irritation to him. So as Kacy fled towards the far end of the hallway, aiming to disappear around the corner to the flight of stairs leading down to the lobby, he had recovered enough of his wits to squeeze off two shots. The first whistled past her ear and embedded itself in the wall ahead. The second was more hurried due to his erratic running as he chased after her. It hit the ceiling and ricocheted off into one of the side walls. Cursing foully, he holstered the pistol and ran on, limping.

As Kacy hurtled down the stairs she could hear him chasing after her, shouting vile names at her as he did his utmost to close on her. She was not exactly moving at her own best speed, either. Her eyes were so full of tears that she was almost blinded, and her nose was blocked as a consequence. Her heart was pounding like a drum, and deep down she was wondering whether it was really worth fleeing at all. Dante was dead. She had nothing left. If she did escape, what the hell was she going to do? She had nowhere to go, and no one to go anywhere with.

Yet something was making her legs keep moving down those stairs. Maybe it was the thought that Dante's death would all be for nothing if she didn't get away. He would have wanted her to escape. And of course, although she kind of wanted to die because it felt like she had nothing left to live for, she didn't actually want to be mauled and raped by Swann first. If he managed to shoot her in the head and end it all painlessly without her knowing a thing about it, then fine, but the likelihood was that there would be some serious unpleasantness and suffering to go through before she finally joined Dante in the afterworld. So run, and run quickly, was what she did.

When she finally reached the bottom of the staircase and entered the lobby she found a widespread panic under way. To the right of the stairs a headless body lay on the floor outside the elevator. Normally this would have been enough to send Kacy into some kind of fit, but right now it barely registered as a mild shock. There was some nasty shit going down right now, and the decapitated corpse was obviously just another part of it. People in the lobby were screaming, and there appeared to be the beginnings of a mass exodus going on. The only problem was that no one seemed to be going in any particular direction. In all, there were about twenty shrieking individuals – guests and staff – running around like headless chickens. Whoever had beheaded the corpse seemed to be long gone. Maybe he or she had headed out of the front doors? Which might explain why the screaming masses weren't all piling out that way . . .

The sound of Swann bounding around the last corner on the stairs, less than half a floor behind her, ensured that she made her decision quickly. *Out into the street. Go, girl!*

Once she was out through those doors she wished she had found another way to go. It was teeming down with rain outside and the wind was blowing up a gale. Her attempt to run down the steps at the front of the hotel was greatly hampered by the wind howling through the streets. It was so strong that her forward progress was dramatically slowed. It felt as if the wind was working against her, pushing her back towards the hotel. And right back into the arms of Special Agent Swann, who suddenly burst through the doors behind her. As Kacy struggled to get off the bottom step and onto the sidewalk he lurched forward and caught hold of her, his giant hands reaching round her, each conveniently grabbing one of her breasts.

Rather than spin her round to face him, he took the opportunity to squeeze her tits hard through her already very wet T-shirt as he charged into her from behind, his upper body and groin forcibly pushing her towards a yellow cab parked directly outside the hotel entrance. He slammed her violently into the side of the cab, her face pressed right up against the rear passenger window on the driver's side.

There were no passersby out in the thunderstorm, so there was no one to come to her aid. Besides, people had more important things to worry about than Swann and his intentions, whatever they might be, towards Kacy. Only the cabdriver took any notice. The electric window in his door buzzed and slid down. 'Hey, buddy . . . ' he began.

Swann momentarily released his grip on Kacy's right breast and pulled his gun from the holster beneath his shoulder.

BANG!

The shot struck the unsuspecting cabbie in the face. Having watched the hapless man's brains fly out through the back of his head and splatter all over the inside of the front windscreen, Swann calmly tucked the gun back in its shoulder holster. Then he returned to his unpleasant assault on Kacy, who by now was too weak and too exhausted to fight him off. She was merely a weeping mess pressed up against the side of the cab, unable to create any leverage to fight back with.

Swann's hands moved down from her breasts towards her crotch. His upper body was still pressed hard against her back, pinning her to the cab door as he began to tug at her jeans.

The rain was holding Kacy prisoner every bit as much as Swann's lecherous grip. Her clothes were heavy with water and her sodden hair was in her face. The only consolation was that the utterly gross amount of saliva dripping from her attacker's mouth and on to the back of her neck was being washed away as quickly as it was being produced.

As she felt her jeans being forced down a few inches she dimly heard a loud crash, much like the sound of a window being broken. In the midst of the rain that was coming down in sheets she saw something reflected in the cab window against which her face was being pressed. Several huge shards of glass landed on the pavement behind Agent Swann.

And something else.

A dark blur. The size of a man.

Sixty-Four

Beth stared up at the moon as it appeared through a break in the heavy rain clouds. It seemed to occupy exactly the same place in the sky as it had all those years earlier. The night she had been attacked by Kione was still as fresh in her memory now as it had been then. Standing at the end of the pier, she almost wished that the loathsome vampire would jump out and attack her again, simply because it might bring the return of her saviour that night, JD.

Since her release from prison eight years earlier she had waited at the end of the pier on each subsequent Halloween night for JD to return. Every year she stayed until the witching hour was over, and every year she returned home alone and disappointed. Nevertheless, it was still the best hour of every year. There was a twisted pleasure to be had in convincing herself that he would return as he had promised, and as the crazy – and now deceased – Mystic Lady had predicted.

The dark grey clouds seemed to be circling the blue moon, as though to hide it from her. And as the end of the Halloween witching hour approached once again, as it did so quickly every year, she gazed out across the waves. The storm was slowly subsiding. The clouds had been blown to the city centre, having passed over the harbour area from the ocean whence they had come. The chaos of the previous few hours had left a trail of devastation in its wake. The promenade was covered in rubbish that had been blown around from overturned garbage cans and shattered flowerpots. But at least the rain had slowed to a light drizzle, and the howling wind was now nothing more than a gentle breeze that blew Beth's ankle-length blue skirt a little way up her calves. The hooded sweatshirt that Bertram Cromwell had given her was soaked through, yet she felt no chill. The rainwater that was making the clothing on her upper body cling to her was actually quite warm, even comforting, and with a thin mist floating above the waves she felt as if she were in her own giant outdoor steam room.

The build-up to Halloween excited her more than it did any of the local kids. Unfortunately, once she was on the pier it was always a sad letdown as the initial heart-pounding excitement of convincing herself that JD would come gradually faded with the stars. She also invariably found her thoughts returning to the moment when she had killed her stepmother. These images, however, were no more than flashes through her mind. It was JD's warm, smiling face and calm assurance that filled her thoughts for most of the time. There was always one final rush of excitement and sadness in the last few minutes as she prayed that he would make a late appearance. During those minutes she never allowed herself to look back down the pier. Instead, she would face out to sea, convincing herself that he was sneaking up from behind to surprise her just as the moon vanished. Yet every year was disappointing, and this one was no different. She watched as the clouds began to cover the moon, and the horizon hinted at the early glow of the dawn that would eventually follow.

She had hoped that the silver cross and neck chain that the Professor had given her would have brought her some luck this year. If the cross was meant to ward off evil then it seemed to have succeeded, but it hadn't brought back JD. She unclasped the chain and took it off, staring out to sea one last time. Then, as the tears began to stream down her cheeks, she threw the silver chain and cross as far as she could into the waves.

If JD had still been alive, he would have come back for her. She had to believe he was dead, because anything else would mean that he hadn't cared about her as much she cared for him. So now, without the silver cross with its curious blue stone to ward off evil spirits, she secretly hoped that something evil would come, to end her time on earth and send her off to meet JD in the afterlife, where they could spend eternity together.

She wiped away the tears staining her wind-reddened cheeks and turned back towards the city. The walk down the pier was a long one that she never wanted to end. But end it did, and soon she was back on the promenade and walking home again.

Sixty-Five

'HEY, SHITHEAD!' a voice growled loudly above the noise of the wind and rain.

Kacy felt Swann jerk against her and his grip on her slacken, his body no longer pressed so tightly up against her back. Then she felt the toe end of a boot kicking her in the butt. It was evident that the meat of the boot, and the full force of the kick had caught Swann between the legs from behind. Right in the plums. Right where she had recently wounded him with the broken light bulb. She heard him groan in pain and then fall to his knees behind her as his grip on her fell away. Whatever the cause of Swann's discomfiture, Kacy needed no second invitation, and she instantly took the opportunity to jump away out of his reach.

Standing behind Swann and readying himself for a second kick to his nuts was a fearsome-looking vampire. Fearsome to most people, perhaps, but to Kacy he had a certain lovable vulnerability, too. It was Dante, still recognizable even though he now appeared to be a fully fledged creature of the night. As Swann tried to steady himself against the taxi cab, Dante once more swung his right boot into the unfortunate agent's already sliced and swollen balls. Swann was wearing jeans with boxer shorts underneath, but they weren't made of iron, and as a consequence he suffered as if he had been wearing nothing at all. Instinctively he placed both hands down to his groin to cup the rapidly swelling and bleeding area between his legs, doing his best not to throw up. Then he watched in horror as a hand reached through a small gap under his right shoulder between his arm and his chest. The hand pulled Swann's pistol from its holster.

'*Shit!*' was the last word he managed to utter, but it was lost amid the rain and wind. The same was not true of the gunshot that followed a second later, which was loud enough to be heard by anyone within a mile of the hotel.

Kacy looked away just a little too late. As a consequence, she saw Swann's brains fly out through the front of his head and splatter all over the back door of the cab. Then his body slumped forward and hit the door before slowly sliding down into the gutter. The rain washed the blood from his head away as quickly as it poured out from the gaping wound.

The dark-eyed figure of the vampire that Dante had become looked down at the body, unable to hide his disgust at what he realized the agent had been planning to do to the woman he loved.

For Kacy, the sight of her lover standing over the sodden corpse of the man who had planned to rape and kill her was overwhelming. She found herself unable to conceal the elation she felt. All the horror of last few minutes was suddenly washing away faster than Special Agent Swann's blood.

'Baby, I love you!' she squealed, reaching over to grab hold of her returning hero. To her dismay, Dante jumped back.

'Stay away,' he hissed in a horrid voice. 'I ain't human any more. Don't come near me. I'll fuckin' kill ya, I know it.'

'What?' Kacy cried, reaching out an arm in a desperate attempt at least to touch him. He backed away again.

'I'm serious. Stay back. I've got an incredible urge to bite you. Not kiddin', I'm thirsty for blood. Just stay here. Peto has that Eye of the Moon thing. I'll get that from him an' I think it'll turn me back to normal. Then you can hug me all you like. Till then, just hold it in.'

'Is Peto *here?*' asked Kacy.

'Yeah. In the hotel. He took the lift, while I ran up the stairs to find ya.'

'Was he wearing a cop outfit like yours?'

'Yeah. You seen him?'

Kacy nodded sadly. 'Everything apart from his head.'

'Say again?'

'He was in the lobby, but his head was . . . was missing. There was blood everywhere. People are freakin' out.'

'Shit!' Dante turned and ran up the steps, through the doors and on into the hotel lobby. Immediately he saw for himself what Kacy had described. Peto's lifeless body was bleeding all over the carpet from the ghastly stump where his head had once joined his neck. The blue stone and its silver chain were gone, too, and so was the Holy Grail. The only person still in sight was the girl behind the reception desk, who seemed to have gone into shock and was just sitting, staring vacantly at the dead body on the carpet. Dante, forgetting that he was now a full-blown vampire, turned towards her and hissed, *'Where's the blue stone gone?'*

The woman woke from her hypnotized state and turned her head slightly to look at Dante, who was staring right back at her across the lobby with a pair of large razor-sharp fangs on show and a bucket load of blood over him. It wasn't really what she needed to see at that particular moment and she promptly fainted, smacking her head hard on the wall behind her as she fell.

The tired, dishevelled and haggard figure of Kacy arrived in the lobby behind Dante.

'C'mon, baby, let's get outta here!' she pleaded.

Dante turned to face her. In spite of the fangs, the pale veiny face and dark-ringed eyes, and the soaked-through shirt covered in blood, he somehow managed to look completely helpless. The realization had dawned on him that whoever had killed Peto had made off with the Eye of the Moon, and would by now be long gone. *He was fucked.* A vampire for all eternity, most likely. And right now Kacy was looking like his first meal. There's nothing a vampire craves more for a feast than an attractive member of the opposite sex, so to Dante, Kacy was pretty much Christmas dinner.

'Honey, get away from me,' he hissed at her urgently. 'Get as far away from me as you can. I'm gettin' urges to kill you. Drink your blood. Don't make me do it. Get the fuck outta here!'

Kacy's face fell and she looked ready to cry again. 'What?' she gulped. Never in all their time together had Dante not wanted her. This wasn't a feeling she was used to, or wanted to get used to.

'I fuckin' mean it,' Dante scowled. 'Get as far away from me as you can.' He stopped, then added, 'I'm sorry.' With that he began to choke up himself, realizing what he was asking of her. He didn't want to be apart from her any more than she from him, but he had to send her away. It was the only thing he could do. Her best interests were more important than his own desire to drink her blood. And at the moment, while he still had a little control over that urge, which was growing fast, he had to get rid of her. 'I love you Kacy, an' I always will, but get the fuck out. Get away from me. We can't be together. I'll kill you, or worse still, turn you into a fuckin' vampire like me. And trust me, this ain't a nice feeling.'

Kacy stepped towards him. He could see the tears now streaming down her cheeks, brought on by the pain of hearing him rebuke her. It only made him feel worse.

'Dante, baby, haven't you learnt anything?' she asked with pleading eyes.

'Whadda ya mean?' he replied, his voice beginning to crack, revealing the pain he was trying to hide.

'I mean,' said Kacy, forcing a smile, '*bite me*, you moron.'

Dante froze. Was she really asking him to make her a member of the undead like him? Did she really love him enough to let him kill her and commit her to an eternal hell?

'You . . . you sure, Kace? I mean . . . '

'Shut up,' Kacy sniffed, her tears flowing faster than ever. 'Just shut up, will ya? You had me at *"Hey, shithead!"*.'

As soon as she said it she knew she had broken through to him. His eyes betrayed him, and Kacy was sure she saw a tear appear for just a second. It disappeared with one blink, but she'd seen it. He still wanted her, and he couldn't hide it no matter how hard he tried.

'I love you Kace,' he said.

'I know. Now come on and get me before I change my mind.'

Dante walked over and put his arms around her, looking down into her eyes.

'Mind if I kiss you first?'

'You'd better.'

A few minutes later they were both creatures of the night, destined to spend their eternal undead lives hunting for the precious blue stone known as the Eye of the Moon.

Sixty-Six

Rameses Gaius sat contentedly at the desk in his oval office. Everything seemed to have gone according to plan. All he needed to do now was wait for his two new High Priests to return with the merchandise he longed for.

At just after midnight the first one arrived. There was a knock at his door. Not an overly loud knock, in fact, a fairly gentle one by most standards, but perfectly audible. 'Come in,' he called out.

The door swung inwards, opened by a hired mercenary who had been standing guard outside. He was one of the many uniformed police officers, members of the Filthy Pigs clan, who had deserted De La Cruz and Co. in their hour of need. Gaius was a far greater leader, and all the undead were honoured to be allowed to serve him.

The guard held back the door into Gaius's office and the slender figure of his new High Priestess and only daughter, Jessica, dressed in her traditional black outfit, marched past him and into the room. She was holding a package wrapped in thick brown cloth under her right arm. The door was closed behind her by the guard, who remained outside, and once she heard it click shut she lowered her head in acknowledgement of Gaius.

'Father, I have the Eye of the Moon and the Holy Grail,' she said, raising her head back up to look him in the face. 'And the head of the monk who possessed them.'

She pulled the brown cloth package out from under her arm and, no longer able to hide her huge vampire grin, threw it over to Gaius. He caught it with both hands as he was getting up from his seat and placed it down on the desk in front of him. He picked at one of the corners of the cloth and then slowly and carefully unwrapped it. Inside was the deformed and already somewhat shrivelled head of Peto, the last of the Hubal Monks. Gaius ran his hand through the bloodied dreadlocks on Peto's head.

'So, he was hiding in with the Dreads. They should be punished for not sniffing him out. If there's any of them still alive after all of today's killing, make sure they die before I have to see any of them again.'

'It'll be my pleasure,' Jessica smiled. She reached both arms up and behind her head and unclasped a silver necklace she was wearing around her neck. Hanging from its finely worked chain was the Eye of the Moon. She saw her father's face light up as she placed it on the desk in front of him. Then she reached her right hand down into her cleavage (of which plenty was on show in the V of her low-cut black karate top) and pulled out a gleaming golden cup. *The Holy Grail*. She waved it under his nose, grinning at him as she did so. 'Now, what have you got for me?' she asked. 'Any news of the two bastards who shot me up during the eclipse?'

'Both will be dead, my dear. I am just waiting for the final confirmation now.'

'Really? How did the Bourbon Kid die?'

'Your new partner, Bull, took him down.' He pointed at the door. 'That will be him now.' Two knocks on the door followed. 'Enter,' Gaius called out.

The door opened once again and Bull walked in, followed by his three Shadow Company comrades. He was carrying a brown cloth-wrapped package under his arm, much as Jessica had done. Without a word he tossed it over to Gaius. The newly reinstated Dark Lord caught it, set it down and began to unwrap with much greater haste than he had the package Jessica had brought. This was the one he wanted most, unable to hide his eagerness to set eyes upon it.

The blood-stiffened brown cloth fell to the floor and Gaius kicked it aside. Another severed head had been wrapped inside the cloth, but now it was resting in the large hands of Rameses Gaius. He held it up in front of him as Jessica, Bull and his three henchmen looked on, waiting for his reaction.

'So,' he said, taking a deep, contented breath. 'The head of the Bourbon Kid, the son of Taos. Doesn't look so *bad* now, does he?'

The others laughed politely as Gaius stared into the one remaining eye in the bloodied mess of the head in his hands. The thick dark hair, matted with drying, thickly spattered blood, covered much of the upper part of the face, sticking to the forehead. Gaius brushed the hair aside and smiled a contented smile as he looked at the dead face of the Kid. After a few seconds he looked back up at Bull and his henchmen, barely able to contain his delight.

'Thank you, Bull. Your position as High Priest is assured. We shall celebrate our victory with a party this coming evening.'

'Thank you, sir,' said Bull, bowing his head as a mark of respect.

From behind him Jessica called out to Bull in her sexiest voice. 'Hey, soldier, whatcha got planned for the next half hour?'

Bull looked the alluring figure of Jessica up and down. 'Well, me an' the guys were gonna go shower. Get all this blood off, y'know?'

'You know what?' said Jessica, looking across at the Bull's three companions. 'I could use a shower too. Mind if I join you guys?'

There was an immediate and boisterous chorus of approving noises from the four soldiers, and they quickly began to head for the door.

While Jessica and the soldiers had been flirting, Rameses Gaius had taken the opportunity to remove his useless green eye and replace it with the much more aesthetically pleasing blue stone, the Eye of the Moon. As soon as it found its rightful home in his eye socket it began to glow a little in the centre. Gaius felt complete again.

From behind his desk he smiled contentedly as he watched his only daughter turn on the charm with the Shadow Company guys. Bull, in particular, seemed particularly taken with her, just as he had hoped. He nodded approvingly as the Shadow Company leader took Jessica by the hand and barked an order at one of his men. 'Razor, open the door. Ladies first.'

Razor did as instructed and opened the door, allowing Jessica to walk out through it, wiggling her hips for the four soldiers' benefit. As they began to file out after her, Gaius shouted after them.

'One thing I gotta know,' he called, looking back down at the head of the Bourbon Kid on his desk. 'Why has he got the word "*CUNT*" tattooed across his forehead?'

Sixty-Seven

The night sky was still overcast, and the rain continued to fall in occasional drizzle, but the sea was tranquil, making a gently soothing sound as its small waves rippled up against the promenade. The carnage of yet another Halloween filled with bloodshed and death was over. Beth strolled along the deserted pathway gazing up at the sky as she went. This long walk home was such a gut-wrenching disappointment each year, and to make matters worse her feet were beginning to hurt. Her shoes had been soaked through in the storm, and her feet were now throbbing slightly where they had chafed against the damp leather.

She looked up to see if there were any stars visible in the night sky. The clouds were beginning to part and the blue moon was beginning to shine through once more. The faint light touched her face, as if that were the only part of the earth to feel the moon's rays.

Where are you, JD? Whatever happened to you on that long-ago night? It was a question she had asked herself a million times over the years. *I'd give anything to see you again, even just for five minutes. Just to know what happened to you. Wherever you are, I hope your soul is at peace.*

As the clouds departed and the moon shone down fully upon her she heard a noise come from behind. It was the sound of a shoe scuffing on the ground. It was followed almost immediately by the sound of a voice.

'Your mother too, huh?'

Beth's heart skipped a beat. She turned around to see a dark figure standing on the promenade in the moonlight, just a few feet in front of her. He wore a black leather jacket, with a black T-shirt underneath and a pair of scruffy blue jeans. His face had the look of a kind and passionate soul, and showed a smile that could melt a girl's heart.

Scarcely daring to breathe, Beth approached and stared deep into the eyes of this man, and saw within them the face of the boy she once knew.

'Jack?' she blurted out. *'Jack Daniels?'*

'I'm sorry I'm late.'

'Where have you been?'

'I got lost along the way.' His eyes searched hers, and he allowed himself a genuine smile for the first time in a very long while. 'Plus I been waitin' for you to work out my name. So, you ready for that date now, or what?'

Beth was beaming a wide smile back at him when she suddenly remembered the terrible scar across the right side of her face, inflicted on her by her stepmother eighteen years earlier. Instinctively, she put her hand up to cover it, but as she did so she realized that to do so was pointless. He'd probably already noticed it. In fact, he must have done.

'I've got this scar,' she mumbled, looking down at her aching feet, feeling shamed and embarrassed by her disfigurement.

JD reached forward with one hand and lifted her chin up. She waited nervously for his reaction, not daring to look at his face in case it revealed disappointment. His reaction was to lean in and kiss her softly on the lips. She pressed her lips warmly back against his. The feeling was every bit as wonderful as the first kiss they had shared all those years before. When eventually he pulled away again she looked him in the eyes and smiled back at him. And then, with five words, he laid all her fears to rest.

'Babe, we've all got scars.'

Sixty-Eight

Sanchez, having closed up for the night, was reflecting on another shitty day. True, he'd survived another visit from the Bourbon Kid, but Jessica had gone from him again, maybe for good this time. As he sat on a stool on the customer's side of the bar in the Tapioca, flicking through the pages of *The Book of Death*, he couldn't help but feel a little down.

No doubt over the next few days the local kids would once again be running around the streets with toy guns, pretending to be the Bourbon Kid or one of the local cops. The thought of kids idolizing known murderers and corrupt policemen really bugged him. When would *he* ever get to be a hero? Probably never, and yet the scummy community of Santa Mondega would be nothing without him providing a reasonably safe place for people where people could drink and socialize. His hard work, day in and day out, was simply taken for granted. Maybe he should go on a killing spree of his own, and at least earn some notoriety?

Sipping on a glass of warm beer, he tried to console himself with the belief that eventually his time would come. One day, someone like Jessica would appreciate the kindness that lay deep in his heart.* Sanchez hid his good points well, and women, in particular, seemed oblivious to what a great guy he was. He pictured Jessica's beautiful face in his mind once more, and decided it would be best to finish his beer and then head off to bed.

To depress him further, *The Book of Death* hadn't provided him with any of the answers he was looking for.

* Very, very deep indeed.

There was nothing in it about Jessica or the Eye of the Moon or the Bourbon Kid, just a list of names of dead people. Flicking through it one last time, he eventually stopped at a blank page near the end. He stared sightlessly at the yellowing parchment and pondered what to do with his life from here on. No Jessica to look after, fewer customers to serve. Was it all really worth the effort?

As he sat luxuriating in his self-pity, his cell phone rang. It managed only two rings before he pulled it from the pocket of his sweatpants and answered it.

'Yo. Sanchez here.'

'Hey Sanchez, it's Rick. Rick from the Olé Au Lait.'

'Hey, man. Bit late for a social call, ain't it?'

'Got news for you, Sanchez. That Jessica woman you were askin' me 'bout the other day? I got the info you were wantin'.'

Sanchez sat up straighter on his stool. 'Yeah? You really found out who put the missing-person ad in the paper?'

'Not exactly, buddy, but she came in here earlier with some big guy. They looked like a couple. I got his name, if you're interested?'

'Hold on, I gotta get a pen.' Sanchez put his beer and the cell phone down on the bar beside *The Book of Death*, which was still open at the page he'd turned to. There was a black ballpoint just on a shelf of glasses at the back of the bar. He reached over the counter at full stretch and picked it up between the tips of two fingers. Then, sitting back on his stool, he scribbled across one of the blank pages of *The Book of Death* to see if the pen was in working order. He was relieved to find that it was. He picked up the phone and said ''Kay. Go on,'

'The guy's name is Rameses Gaius. Big fuckin' dude he is too, man.'

'Rameses Gaius?' Sanchez thought hard. It wasn't a name he recognized, but some quick research on the Internet might throw up something on him. First things first, though. Wedging the phone under his ample chin, he used the ballpoint to write the name down on the blank page of the book in front of him to make sure he didn't forget it. 'Thanks, Rick. Anythin' else I oughta know?'

'Yeah. That woman, Jessica? Her last name is Xavier, apparently.'

In all the time that Sanchez had known Jessica he had never managed to find out her last name, so again with an Internet search in mind he wrote her full name beneath that of Rameses Gaius in *The Book of Death.*

Rameses Gaius

Jessica Xavier

'Thanks again, Rick. Guess I owe you that bottle of liquor?'

'Damn straight you do, Sanchez,' Rick replied sharply.

'What'll it be, then?'

'Jack Daniel's. I'll come by an' pick it up tomorrow.'

'Okay. Let me write that down so's I don't forget,' said Sanchez. He scribbled the 'J' down on the page beneath the names of Rameses Gaius and Jessica Xavier. Then he had a thought. Jack Daniel's was expensive stuff; maybe a compromise could be reached?

'Rick? You sure you wouldn't prefer a bottle of Jim Beam?'

THE END (maybe . . .)